T0278585

E. LATIMER

The Afterdark

tundra

Text copyright © 2025 by E. Latimer
Cover art copyright © 2025 by Michelle Kwon

Tundra Books, an imprint of Tundra Book Group,
a division of Penguin Random House of Canada Limited

All rights reserved. The use of any part of this publication reproduced, transmitted in any form or by any means, electronic, mechanical, photocopying, recording, or otherwise, or stored in a retrieval system, without the prior written consent of the publisher—or, in case of photocopying or other reprographic copying, a license from the Canadian Copyright Licensing Agency—is an infringement of the copyright law.

Please note that no part of this book may be used or reproduced in any manner for the purpose of training artificial intelligence technologies or systems.

Publisher's note: This book is a work of fiction. Names, characters, places and incidents either are the product of the author's imagination or are used fictitiously, and any resemblance to actual persons living or dead, events, or locales is entirely coincidental.

Library and Archives Canada Cataloguing in Publication

Title: The afterdark / Erin Latimer.
Names: Latimer, E. (Erin), 1987- author.
Identifiers: Canadiana (print) 20240357124 | Canadiana (ebook) 20240357124 |
ISBN 9781774882245 (hardcover) | ISBN 9781774882252 (EPUB)
Subjects: LCGFT: Gothic fiction. | LCGFT: Novels.
Classification: LCC PS8623.A783 A69 2025 | DDC jC813/.6—dc23

Published simultaneously in the United States of America by
Tundra Books of Northern New York, an imprint of Tundra Book Group,
a division of Penguin Random House of Canada Limited

Library of Congress Control Number: 2024936366

Edited by Peter Phillips and Lynne Missen
Cover designed by Matthew Flute
Text designed by Matthew Flute
Typeset by Terra Page
The text was set in Nimbus.

Printed in Canada

www.penguinrandomhouse.ca

1 2 3 4 5   29 28 27 26 25

tundra

Penguin
Random House
TUNDRA BOOKS

For all the girls & forest cryptids
— E.L.

CHAPTER ONE

Evie

THERE'S A SINGLE SOLAR LAMP at the end of the dock, casting watery shadows over the black surface of the lake. The water is cold despite the mid-August warmth, and when I dip my feet in, goosebumps run up both my arms.

It should be relaxing—trailing the lens of my camera over the water, watching the lights from the cabin behind me flicker over the surface. But pounding bass slips out from cracked windows, laughter spilling out with it. The sound of someone screaming rises sharply and then tapers off.

The party is going full swing without me.

Behind me, the dock creaks and sways, and I stiffen, lowering my camera. I know who it is without turning.

"Come on, don't be like that."

"*Leave*, Ada." I don't move.

"What, like you actually cared about Adam?" Her voice is flat, but I can tell she's amused. "You were going to get married?"

I push myself up and turn around. My twin stands at the end of the dock, hands on her hips. Her dress, dark green and overly tight, is twisted around, like she yanked it up while running after me. Her bleached-blond hair is disheveled from rolling around in bed with him.

I don't care about him. I was bored. We kissed. It wasn't anything deeper.

What bothers me is *her*. "Why do you do this?"

She thrives on this. I can see it, the way her eyes glitter as she steps closer, the cruel smile etched across her face.

For the first time I notice the bottle in her hand, the way she sways on her feet. It's not just the movement of the dock.

"Because it's *fun*."

The way she says it, dripping with mockery, makes something start up deep in the pit of my stomach . . . a buzz of dark excitement. It wants me to unsheathe my claws. Charge across the dock and seize her by the throat.

I can picture it: Shoving her over the side, the muscles in my arms flexing as I grit my teeth and force her head under. Watching while she thrashes. Until she goes limp.

The thought is clear in my mind—it would be *so* easy—but I shove it firmly away. I'm used to wrestling with the impulses.

The thing inside me wants Ada's blood. Has always wanted it.

I think about killing her. I *dream* about it.

But she isn't worth violence. I have to deal with her for another two weeks, and then she's gone. Shipping off to boarding school.

When I go to shove past her, she steps into my path. "Stop being such a baby."

Anger blooms in the pit of my stomach. Poisonous and fanged. I rip my arm away. "Stop."

I can't do this. If I engage, I don't know what I'll do. "Just leave me alone." I try to push past her again, and she grabs my shoulder, nails digging into my skin.

"I want to talk."

I twist in her grip, and my hand catches on her necklace. It gives way with a sharp tug, and my palm stings as the necklace clatters on the dock.

The cross glimmers on the boards at our feet, and Ada's expression turns ugly. I know her. I know the bottle will come up before it does, clenched in one fist, beer dripping amber trails down her arm. I can *sense* it.

I duck, and there's a hissing *whoosh* above my head.

What would it have been this time? Sixteen stitches? A story about how I'd tripped on the dock?

There are only so many excuses Dad can make for her.

I can't help myself. I turn on her, teeth bared in a smile. "You keep trying, but you're so *bad* at this."

Ada lets out a scream of frustration, swinging a second time, bottle wobbling in her hand. She's drunker than I'd realized, and when I step out of the way, her momentum takes her past me. She staggers, high heel catching on the boards. The bottle shatters on the dock as she lets out a startled grunt. There's a nasty crack—her ankle or the shoe?—and then she pitches forward, arms pinwheeling.

What happens next is so fast it's difficult to see.

Ada hits the edge of the dock with a terrible thud, boards shaking under my feet. I get a brief impression—a flash of white-blond hair and pale limbs, one red stiletto jutting in the air, and then she crashes through the surface of the water and disappears.

She doesn't scream when she goes under. She doesn't thrash.

For a second, I stand there, stunned. Realizing I've just seen her hit the edge of the dock so hard it shuddered under my feet.

I rush to the edge, heart drumming furiously against my rib cage.

With my back to the solar lamp, it takes a minute for my eyes to adjust, to spot the dark shape in the water. It looks like driftwood at first, a log floating below the surface. And then I see pale hair, like bleached seaweed under the weak light.

She's on her back, suspended in the glassy darkness. I blink, trying to clear my vision as the water around her goes even blacker. Leaning forward, the camera strap drags on the back of my neck, and the light behind me shifts.

Blood. It's Ada's blood, billowing around her, turning the lake crimson. She struck her face on the dock as she went down.

There are no tides in the lake, no currents to push her. But she drifts closer. Close enough that I can see the wound on her forehead, an ugly gash just below her hairline.

Blood thunders in my ears as I tug the strap of my camera up and over my head, setting it gently on the dock. Then I stretch out, leaning so far that cold lake water soaks into my sleeves, the chill leeching into my bones. It makes my left arm ache, the scars throbbing.

I don't move, willing her closer.

I can't swim.

Of course, I could call someone. But deep down, I know it's too late. They won't get here in time. Even running back to the house won't save her.

It's eerie, the way she stays close to the surface, eyes wide and staring as she bleeds into the lake. I'm half expecting one pale hand to shoot out and grab my throat. A siren pulling me under, drowning me.

But she doesn't move.

Looking at her, I can see only myself. A warped, bleeding reflection in the black water below. When she blinks, I blink. When her lips twitch, mine do too.

I'm watching myself drown.

I should move, but numbness spreads through me. Weighs me down. Should I be panicking?

And then Ada *coughs* and the noise is terrible: a rattling, gurgling sound that makes me realize water is lapping over her mouth and nose. She's slipped deeper under the surface.

One arm twitches in the water, the movement so jerky it takes me a second to realize she's trying to *swim*.

Her face is pale and blank, mouth open and gasping as she claws her way back up. She resurfaces once. Twice.

After the third time, Ada slides under almost gracefully, gray eyes fixed on my face as the water closes over her. I wait for her to come back up. To break the surface gasping and sputtering curses at me.

But the water is still—an unbroken pane of glass. It stretches out flat and dark, disappearing into mist on the opposite bank.

And I don't know how, but I can *feel* it. The absence of her. An emptiness that rings in my ears and makes my core feel strangely light.

Ada is gone.

I'm alone again, hanging over the edge of the dock, the faint noises of the party washing over me. A chill runs through me as I stare down at the placid waters. This time, it's only my own face reflected back at me.

CHAPTER TWO

Evie

I TELL MY MOTHER. Somehow, I make myself say the words.

Ada is dead.

My mother, Supreme Court Judge Mariam Laurent, stares at me with the same slate-gray eyes I've inherited.

There's silence between us, heavy enough to steal the air from the room. It goes on long enough that I think she might turn and go. Leave me dripping dirty lake water onto her white sofa, staring straight ahead at her teakwood dining hutch, at the delicate bone china and silverware trapped behind the glass. There's no artwork on the walls, no childhood drawings or framed photos—they're bare and white.

Her office is separate from the cabin. Far enough that the music is muted to a distant, thumping bass line. She doesn't care what we do as long as we don't disturb her work.

I slide my hand into my pocket, wrapping my fingers around the cool metal of Ada's necklace, the sharpened end of the cross pressing into my hand. It fits perfectly into the dull red scar in my palm.

I almost left the necklace, the broken chain snaking over the wet boards, the cross glittering under the yellow light.

But something made me pick it up.

She'd sharpened the end. I'd realized a few months back in the most painful way.

I don't remember the perceived insult, only what had followed. That bright, sharp stab of pain through my hand, the warmth of blood pooling in my palm.

It's *so* Ada, to take something beautiful and turn it into a weapon. Something to draw blood.

There's a teacup on the table next to my mother, steam fanning up from inside. Even in the face of my announcement, she's careful to slide a bookmark into the heavy lawbook in her lap.

When she finally speaks, her voice is even.

"Where?"

"The lake." My tone matches hers. Cold. Monotone.

Neither of us bothers to hide the flat affect in our voice. To fake emotion. There's no point.

"She fell off the dock."

It's not a lie. Not exactly.

She looks at me for a long moment, and I know she's trying to see past my blank expression. Looking for the truth.

Finally, she says, "Did anyone see?"

I shake my head, and she rises slowly. Says the last words she'll say to me for almost two weeks.

"Keep your mouth shut."

I stay in my room after that. Read. Listen to music. I take shelter, while people come and go. The police. The coroner. One hundred sympathetic friends and neighbors.

Students who barely spoke to me keep texting. Ada's friends, sent home from the party, all of them asking what happened.

I leave them on read. None of them knew the *real* Ada.

Mom keeps everyone away. Sometimes, I press my ear to the gap in my door, listening to her cool, wintery voice as she fixes everything. She tells the police I was there. That I tried to fish Ada out, but neither of us can swim. That I came in after she fell, panicked and dripping lake water on her carpet.

She makes phone calls. I hear her arrange the memorial in that same matter-of-fact tone. Pick out a coffin. Order roses.

She even phones someone about dry-cleaning the couch . . .

I don't know why that makes me laugh.

It was only the first call I couldn't listen to. The one that made me turn up the music in my headphones until it hurt.

I imagine how that conversation went. How she delivered the news to Dad in that flat voice. How he must have crumpled, sobbing over the phone.

He might be the only one who truly cares Ada is dead.

Days crawl by, and I keep myself shut away. Sleeping during the day, lying awake at night, trying to block out the noise my brain plays on repeat: that rattling, wet gasp she made before she went under for the final time.

I watch the news obsessively, waiting for something, anything, to point to me.

It never does.

Reporters show up, and the words *tragic accident* are passed around. Mom tells them in glacial tones that I'm not ready to speak. That I'm *grieving*.

The idea is almost comical.

Even now, it's a relief just *thinking* the words: *Ada is dead.* Like I can breathe for the first time in years.

Mom deals with everything. Sweeps everything under the rug. But she never knocks. Never speaks to me, or asks if I'm alright.

I don't think she'd care if we'd both drowned that night.

I think she'd prefer it.

Two weeks into my self-imposed exile, the calls taper off. The house is quiet again. The constant trickle of vans and SUVs parked across the street vanishes.

It's in this sudden silence that I realize my dreams have changed.

I've dreamed about the same clearing in the woods nearly every night.

A huge tree in the center, so dark it's almost black, its trunk as thick and tall as a house. Heavy branches dropping down to brush the tops of roots that come bursting out of the soil.

In the dream, I drag Ada's body to the tree. I bury her between thick, pulsing roots. Like an offering. Then I lie down on top of her grave and stare up at the arcing branches.

Now, there's no Ada. There's only me beneath the tree, laying between the roots.

Sunday morning, my mother looms in the doorway and tells me to pack.

I don't ask where I'm going. I can guess.

If I take Ada's place, she gets rid of us both.

That afternoon, we load my luggage into the airport shuttle. We don't speak, and I realize she can hardly look at me.

No wonder she wants me gone.

Hours later, I step out of the sleek black town car that's delivered me to the front gate of Northcroft's campus. I tilt my head to take in the surrounding forest.

The trees are like nothing I've ever seen. Nothing like my hometown's skinny fir trees. These ones stretch impossibly high, moss-draped and vibrant green, even in the pale evening light. Their branches tangle at the top, huge trunks leaning crookedly against one another.

I knew Hemlock Woods was an old-growth forest, but it hadn't sunk in just what that meant. How colossal the trees would be.

The nearest one is so wide across, the trunk looks more like a wall—a living, lichen-covered tower, its twisted bark pitted with knots.

A chill drops down my spine as I imagine how deep it goes. How easy it would be to lose yourself in the verdant darkness.

Something blooms in my stomach—a familiar dark excitement. It makes me want to drop my luggage and plunge straight into the forest. Leave everything behind to run wild in the woods.

The feeling is so strong it's almost physical. A tugging at my guts that makes me step toward the forest.

It's new. This impulse from the dark thing in my core that *isn't* violence.

Before I can examine this, I'm forced to jump out of the way as the driver, a man with a red-tinged face, dumps my luggage out so hurriedly that one of the wheely bags clips my leg.

He rushes around to the driver's side, head jerking up to take one last look at the forest. Then the town car pulls out so quickly the wheels slide, flinging gravel up behind them.

Slowly, I collect my bags and turn toward the gate.

Will Dad come out to get me? Does the principal do stuff like that? He must know I'm coming, at least. Mom called to chew him out when he didn't show up to the memorial.

I can't blame him for that.

I didn't want to be there either. Didn't want to see her again, not even dead.

It had taken me a moment to get over the uncanny valley feeling as I'd looked at that still, frozen face. They'd done their best to fix the dent in her forehead. Painted her to look alive. After I'd adjusted, I'd felt almost . . . contemptuous.

This was the girl who'd tortured me all my life? Who'd left so many scars? The one who'd loomed so giant in my nightmares?

In death, she just seemed . . . small.

I thought I'd feel something by now. Guilt, maybe, as the realization sets in. Because I'm here in her stead. Stepping straight into her place.

But as I stand in front of the massive stone walls, I just feel cold. The wind bites at my exposed skin, dragging tendrils of hair across my face like a mourning veil.

I don't even know where I am. An island off the West Coast of Canada, is what I've gathered from Dad, though he never seemed keen to get into specifics. He and Ada had fought about

12

it constantly. It was all she'd wanted, and he'd been determined to keep her from it.

Conflict of interest, he'd said. But that wasn't it. Deep down, he was scared of her. Even if he didn't know it.

I was always good at hiding the impulses. Never letting them control me. But Ada . . . Ada never seemed to be able to rein it in.

It got worse over the years.

Mom was always in her office and Dad was always at his school. After we hit a certain age and the nannies stopped coming, there was no one but me to witness Ada become more and more monstrous.

There's a booklet clutched in my hand. Something I didn't realize I was still holding. Dad had dozens in his office at home. Glossy blue pamphlets full of Northcroft information. I don't know why I brought it.

My fingers have creased it, wrinkling the happy faces of half a dozen diverse young people and the words *You're a Norther now!*

Beyond the gate, the campus lawn unfolds, a stretch of wide green grass. On the other side are the steps leading up to Northcroft's main hall. The stone staircase splits into two halves, curling up to meet one another in an open platform at the top. Just before the arched double doors, a pair of ugly stone lions rear up, snarling mouths tilted toward narrow windows.

The building is a massive, sprawling thing, with east and west wings reaching out on either side. Behind the west wing, soaring up taller than some of the trees even, is the bell tower. It's featured on all the pamphlets. According to Dad, it's one of the original buildings, making it more than three hundred years old.

Up close, the bell tower is impressively Gothic. Dark, conical spheres stretching up into the sky.

I'd seen pictures over the years, but nothing prepared me for seeing Northcroft up close. Thick sand-colored stone walls stand tall in a long line, and towers loom from all four corners, the decorative battlements ending in black stone points.

I'm still just standing there, outside the gate.

Unwrapping my fingers from my camera strap creates an ache in my knuckles, and I grasp the camera in both hands, snapping a shot of the front gate. I catch the burnt-orange rays of the setting sun streaming through the iron scrollwork.

Sunlight glares off the silver shield of the school's logo, which shows an open book in the foreground set against the black silhouette of a tree, its roots stretching out below, branches overhead. Beneath, in elegant gold script, is the phrase VERITAS ANTE OMNIA—TRUTH BEFORE ALL.

It's intimately familiar. Practically a family crest. I remember Dad showing me old family photos, faded black-and-white shots of his great-grandfather standing by the sign.

Stopping just in front of the gate, I level my camera at a giant oak growing so close to the wall that it reaches over top, and then pause. Ivy clings to the trunk, but it's curled and dead on one side, some kind of slimy black coating between the leaves. Like the tree is starting to rot.

I snap a series of photos before turning back toward the entrance.

Going through the gate feels like passing through some kind of reverse portal, from wild forest to manicured grass. And even though the walls aren't quite tall enough to block out the largest trees, the way the buildings form a square, hemming themselves in, makes it feel like I'm stepping into a stronghold.

The last great bastion of civilization in the middle of the untamed woods.

My camera is warm in my hands as I crouch down to angle for the top of the wall, catching the way the sunlight brightens the ivy.

Once inside, I stop again, intent on capturing one of the more striking buildings at the other end of the lawn, a massive rotunda done in gray-green stone, with a circle of pillars supporting a domed roof.

Stepping closer, I catch sight of movement on the steps. Someone is sitting at the end of one of the twin staircases, leaning a shoulder against the rails.

He's watching me, a lit cigarette dangling from his fingers.

I'm almost certain smoking is banned on campus, like everywhere else, but this boy doesn't seem to care. There's an air of James Dean suavity about him that I'm sure has taken years of practice.

As I get closer, I can see he's wearing expensive slacks, and his school blazer is draped carelessly over one shoulder. His fair hair is styled to look as though he's slept on it. He has beach-bronzed skin and heavy, hooded eyes, and his brows are dark and sharp at the corners.

The sight of him is strange, and it takes me a moment to realize why. He's the only one around.

I'd expected the lawns to be filled with newly returned students, eager to soak up the last bit of warmth. Lingering under trees, coats spread out on the grass.

But the grounds of Northcroft are silent. Empty. There is only this boy, with his narrow, glittering stare.

They'd told me during registration there would be a student ambassador. One of the other twelfth-graders.

I'd just assumed it would be a girl.

He smiles as I walk toward the stairs. It's a charming grin, mischievous even. But his eyes—wide and dark and gorgeous—are flat.

The sight makes unease prickle at my core. Recognition. A warning from that predatory darkness inside me.

I've spent my life studying people, the way an epidemiologist studies disease. What their body language says. Every tilt of the head and shift of the brow. Every twitch of the mouth.

It was necessary, to survive someone like Ada.

The boy's smile stays in place as I approach, and he tilts his head, scanning me. His expression hides the barest hint of contempt, though he probably doesn't realize it. A flare of the nostrils, the slightest tightening at one side of his mouth.

His posture is relaxed, shifting languidly as he leans back, lifting the cigarette to his lips.

People always say things like *birds of a feather* and *like calls to like* in such offhanded ways. Like it's just a fact. But even as I recognize something in him, even as that strange cold thing inside me roars up inside my chest, I know I want nothing to do with this boy.

There's a moment where he tips his head back to blow smoke into the air and then looks back down at me, and I know he's about to say something. Something to put me off-balance or intrigue me. To draw me in.

When he realizes he can't, will he know my secret? That we're the same, he and I?

For a moment, I think about what would happen if I crossed the space between us and seized a fistful of those tousled blond waves. If I gripped his hair tightly and slammed his head sideways into the stone railing. What sound would that make? What expression would replace his charming smile?

It takes me a second to realize I've stepped toward him, that I've got one fist clenched at my side.

I let out a breath, alarmed at how strong the impulse had been.

That was new too.

I slide one hand into my pocket, gripping Ada's necklace. The metal point bites into my fingers, grounding me.

The impulses scare me. I watched Ada give in to them more and more, until she seemed almost feral. Less human than she should have been.

There's a noise on the steps above us, the scrape of a boot on stone, and the boy and I both look up. There's a girl at the top of the opposite staircase. She doesn't look at me as she moves toward us, glaring down at the boy instead.

My stomach tightens. I *recognize* her. The full, strawberry lips and wide green eyes. The pale, freckled skin and cascades of copper-colored hair. Holland Morgan. Ada's friend through all of ninth grade. Of course, that isn't the real reason I know her face as intimately as I do.

I used to watch *The Wizards* obsessively. Every Saturday morning, there she was, Holland Morgan on my TV screen, fighting evil and flubbing spells in the most comical way possible.

It was my favorite show for all of seventh and eighth grade. It was *everyone's* favorite show. *The Wizards* had been hugely popular.

And I'd had a massive crush on the actress. Ada knew that, so it wasn't the least bit surprising when my twin jumped on Holland the second she enrolled at our private school. Ada had relished my jealousy.

Of course, her leverage had disappeared when Holland's parents pulled her out to film the *Wizards* relaunch. She'd never been back.

It made sense she'd ended up at Northcroft. Hidden away. Elite.

I shouldn't stare, but I can't help it. She looks like some avenging queen as she descends, wind pushing waves of long hair back from her face, the black pashmina she wears swirling out behind her. She must be cold, with only a sheer blue dress underneath, bare legs, and red ankle boots. But if she is, she doesn't show it.

She looks at me, and I know she must remember me from high school. I'm about to hear the always popular, ever-dreaded question: *You're Ada's sister, aren't you?*

Does she know her friend is dead? Has she heard?

Maybe she was expecting Ada, and now here I am instead.

But no, that's ridiculous. The administration would have told her who she was meeting. Especially considering all the paperwork I did to take Ada's spot.

Then Holland directs her stare to the boy on the bottom of the stairs. "I don't remember *you* being appointed student ambassador, Aukley."

Her tone is playful, but there's something in her face, a hardening around the eyes that doesn't match her smile.

The boy, Aukley, lets out a stream of smoke in her direction, like he's some kind of blazer-wearing dragon crouched there on the steps. But I notice the way he looks at her, the flicker of hunger in his eyes. "Hey, go easy on me, Bad Half. We were just saying hello."

Funny, since we haven't said a word out loud to one another.

My gaze is drawn back to Holland Morgan. Before I can think about what I'm doing, my camera is in my hands. She's in my viewfinder, towering over me on the stairs, eyes flashing, red hair streaming in the wind.

She's center stage, and the planes and angles of her face, the fire of freckles across pale skin, and those eyes . . . that bright green. She's perfect for the camera.

There's a flash and a whir, and I'm so used to the sound that for a moment I don't understand why she turns and looks at me the way she does. I stare at her, breathless. Knowing the picture I've taken is going to turn out perfectly. The scene clicked together so well. Like a still from one of her episodes.

And then I see the faint tug at the edge of her mouth, the furrowing of copper brows, and my stomach sinks. People don't like to be photographed without permission . . . celebrities especially. That was a rule at school when she was there.

Don't take pictures of Holland Morgan or ask for autographs. That's not why she's here.

I know this. I know better.

Slowly, I lower the camera and press my lips together tightly, waiting for her to tell me to delete it. I'm probably no better than some pushy paparazzo to her now. The thought makes me feel a little ill.

Instead, we're all jolted into stillness by a brassy, echoing note from somewhere overhead.

It takes me a second to figure it out.

It's a church bell. And not the usual clamor, the sound of multiple bells in quick succession, but a series of slow, drawn-out notes, each one echoing into the next.

There's something eerie about the measured, one-tone sound.

"That's the curfew bell," Holland says. "When you hear it, you have ten minutes until the sun sets."

Her gaze flicks briefly toward the walls, to the forest beyond, before she turns to the doorway. I trail after her without a word, knowing I shouldn't let myself talk to her.

She was Ada's best friend. Nothing good can come of this.

I shouldn't let myself become involved or invested in Holland Morgan in any way.

I'm here to keep quiet. To stick to the shadows and corners of this place. To stay away from people.

Because that darkness coiled in my core is always there. Always waiting.

So I follow Holland, my childhood hero and crush, and I keep my eyes on her back and my mouth firmly shut. Because I can't start conversations, or make friends, or fall in love.

I won't let myself.

CHAPTER THREE

Evie

HOLLAND INTRODUCES HERSELF as we make our way up the split staircase and into a wide, echoing hall. She says it so casually, *I'm Holland.* Like I don't already know her name. Like *everyone* doesn't know it.

I'd forgotten what it was like, seeing her up close.

It's not just the copper waves of her hair or her sharp side profile—it's the way she holds herself. How she walks. Every movement is precise yet graceful.

It's the way she'd always moved on the show, and one of the first things I'd noticed in person. I don't know why I'd anticipated something different, like maybe the graceful way she held herself was part of Felicity, her character.

But it was never an act. It's just *her.*

It feels like ninth grade all over again. Like I'm fifteen years old and desperate to stay cool. Lurking in hallways and corners, forcing myself not to stare.

Except this time, Ada isn't here to step between us. To smile that vicious smile as she slips an arm around Holland's shoulders. To torture me.

She's six feet under. Sealed inside an expensive wooden box.

Ada is never coming back.

Holland talks as we go, pointing out the structure of the vaulted ceilings high overhead. When she glances over, I shift my attention quickly to the ceiling, nodding thoughtfully, like I've been examining the wooden beams this entire time.

I'm almost certain she caught me staring, but she continues the tour, pointing out statues that appear along the walkway.

"That's Ezekiel Blackwood." Holland tosses her hair back over her shoulder, lifting her brows at one of the statues. "One of the founders. Dude was like five foot nothing. And a real bigot." She shrugs. "We tried to get them to remove the old founder statues, but they wouldn't."

We walk on for a moment more, and I hope my face doesn't look as hot as it feels. I know all about Ezekial Blackwood. When I slide Holland another sideways look, there's the tiniest smirk at one corner of her mouth. Her gaze cuts away to the left and down, dark lashes shadowing pale cheeks.

I'm not one to blush, generally, but I bring my camera up to shield my face, tilting the lens to get a shot of the stained-glass windows along the hall, the forest warped and multicolored behind the glass.

How much did Ada say about us?

Does Holland know I'm descended from one of the founders?

The walkway ends in a series of wide hallways and staircases and Holland glances down at her watch, brows furrowed. "This way."

She seems more hurried now, and my heart sinks.

What if she noticed me staring? I'm not great at hiding it sometimes, particularly not if I'm flustered.

For the most part, I can get by socially, but sometimes I slip. It's like I've got the same song as everyone else, and I know all the notes, but occasionally I'll hit the wrong key. Say something too bluntly, or stare too long without blinking, and I'll catch that *look*. Like they're wondering what's wrong with me.

Or maybe Holland is remembering something Ada told her, and now I'm proving her right.

The thought makes me cling to my camera, feeling a little sick. I pause, staring through the viewfinder, trying to find my center again.

I'm trailing my lens over a set of tall, narrow windows when Holland finally speaks.

"So . . . ," she says, and then stops. "There are uniforms for you in the dorm. But, um, I'm hoping they'll be okay. They were . . ." She pulls up short, clearly unsure, and my stomach sinks.

I say it for her. "They were for Ada."

"Yeah."

There's silence for a beat. Then she says, haltingly, "I heard a couple days ago. I'm—I wanted to say how sorry I am."

Immediately, I want to know how much she knows.

I've read through the articles. They were all the same. PRETTY WHITE GIRL FALLS OFF DOCK, DROWNS IN TERRIBLE ACCIDENT.

They also loved the twin angle, but so far, no one seems to know I was there. That I watched it happen.

Those rattling gasps play in my ears, and I clench my teeth so hard it makes my jaw ache.

23

Holland falters again, and I realize I've left the silence for too long. "Thanks," I say hurriedly. "I—I know you were friends."

Holland flinches. Then her expression goes carefully smooth. "We were, yeah."

Interesting. It makes me realize I don't know how Ada and Holland left off. After Holland left to film the *Wizards* relaunch, Ada had complained that Holland had been *so obsessed* with her. To fuck with me, I'd assumed . . .

Holland clears her throat. "Oh, and I meant to say. About Aukley . . ."

"The boy on the steps." I'm utterly relieved to be on a new subject.

"Yes, him." She says it quietly, glancing back over her shoulder. "Stay clear."

"Why?"

I know why. But it would be good to hear someone say it.

Holland purses her lips, gaze fixed on the top of the winding staircase we're ascending. For a moment I'm sure she's going to brush past the question. Then she says, "He's run into trouble with girls. He even used to be a Gravesman until he got kicked out for it."

It takes me a second to put it together. Crown and Grave. Northcroft's secret society.

I'd run more than one Internet search over the years, come up empty. A mention on some forum, the name on a chat room transcript from years ago. And then . . . nothing. Just the name of the society, and the implication it operates out of Northcroft.

"He gets away with it because of his family."

Holland looks grave, and alarm shudders through me.

I pause at a tiny stone alcove at the top of the stairs, pointing my camera out the narrow window's diamond-shaped latticework. The glimpse of sky beyond is tinted orange, dotted by curling wisps of clouds.

I should warn Holland. Tell her Aukley goes *so* far beyond trouble. That the girls of this school need to find a way to protect themselves.

But I can't tell her how I know. That I recognize what he is because we're the same.

So instead I say, "He called you Bad Half."

Holland snorts. "He thinks it's funny. Because he's a *child.*"

Neither of us says anything for a moment, our footsteps echoing off the high ceiling. All I can do is shield myself with my camera.

Bad Half, the pilot for what was supposed to be the triumphant relaunch of *The Wizards*, had been an embarrassing flop.

Holland had just hit sixteen, and the producers wanted to try something new. Something dangerous.

In the pilot, Felicity—now older and attending wizard high school—runs afoul of a curse that pulls out her evil side. An evil side that apparently likes to wear leather and throw out thinly veiled innuendos between bouts of black magic.

It was the timing of the relaunch that had been its undoing. Somehow not soon enough, and entirely *too* soon. There wasn't enough nostalgia to make it work, and the audience, now made up of older teens, had been less than impressed with the uninspired writing and terrible special effects.

Season two had been immediately and unceremoniously canceled. Even a die-hard fan like me had seen that *Bad Half* had been . . . well, *bad.* But it was also the moment where I fell for

Holland Morgan so completely, so *intensely*, that it hurt. A real, visceral ache, somewhere deep in my gut.

Eventually, the hallway takes us out onto a covered stone walkway, a series of arched windows revealing a stretch of green lawn wound through with walkways shaded by clusters of oaks. It's beautiful, but the click of my camera is followed by a shuffle behind me, and Holland is at my elbow suddenly. The scent of something faintly citrus surrounds her, shampoo or soap maybe, and she clears her throat, glancing down at her watch.

"We should get going."

Right. The bell that rang earlier. "Curfew's at sundown?"

"Yes." She's moving faster down the walkway now. I have to jog to catch up.

The sun is going down now, sure. I can see the orange glow over the top of the tree line outside the windows. But we still have time. "Are they really that strict about—" I stop, letting out a breath as we turn the corner.

The covered walkway ends in a huge entranceway done in white stone, and Holland makes her way across it, leading me toward the staircase on the other side. We're clearly entering another building here. A stark contrast to the bleak splendor of Blackwood Hall.

It's lit by clusters of gold-stemmed lamps, tall, delicate things that seem to bloom golden orbs of light at the ends of their stems.

They're hazy in the lens of my camera, almost ethereal. Like fairy lights.

"Welcome to Stowe House. We just call it the girls' dorms," Holland says, and it's the tension in her voice that draws my gaze back to her.

She's standing several steps up, which makes her tower over me, one hand on the rail. There's a restlessness in her limbs I hadn't noticed before. Fingers drumming on the banister, one foot tapping an impatient rhythm on the stairs.

"The girls' dorms are up there." She waves at the upper floors. "The common room is back in Blackwood Hall. You'll see it later."

Carefully, I let my camera rest on the end of its strap, scanning her face. "I guess curfew is really strict?"

"You get expelled if they catch you out after." Holland turns and moves up the staircase again. I hurry across the foyer after her, even though I realize the ceiling has elaborate stone carvings of giant flowers all along the outer edges. My fingers itch to grasp my camera.

It's not like it matters if I get expelled. It might even be better, but Holland hasn't done anything wrong. She doesn't deserve to get in trouble.

It shouldn't matter, but it does.

I want her to like me.

CHAPTER FOUR

Holland

SHE KEEPS GLANCING AT ME when she thinks I'm not looking.

I keep my attention trained straight ahead, my eye on the time. Checking my watch. Hoping my blush isn't too obvious.

Even with the time constraint and rushing down the halls, my gaze keeps straying back to her. Little pangs of shock go through my chest every time.

She looks *so much* like Ada.

Seeing her on the steps, it all came flooding back. I'd thought I was prepared. I knew in advance she was coming.

Laurent. The label on the file had made my breath stick in my throat. I'd had a ridiculous thought—*but then, she's not really dead*—before I'd realized the name on the file was *Evie*.

It unsettled me, my own reaction. A jolt of panic, mixed with something else. Longing, maybe? Anger, certainly.

The confused tangle of emotions has only grown worse. Evie

is identical to her twin. Their features the same. *Exactly* the same. It's almost eerie.

I steal another look while she's taking pictures.

She has the same pale skin and dark brows. The same intense, gray-eyed stare. The same narrow, fox-like features and upturned nose with a splash of freckles. Her hair is cut shorter than Ada's, and wavy, just above her shoulders. But I could be looking at Ada, if I didn't know better.

Six days. That's how long ago I heard. Since I got an email from an old school acquaintance telling me how sorry she was. She was digging for information, as if I've spoken to anyone from that school. As if I'd want to remind myself.

The news had filled me with a strange, burning anger. Anger that I'd never get to see her again.

There are still so many things I'd say. So many things I've thought about, lying awake at night, staring at the canopy above me, rage smoldering in my chest.

I need to know if Evie is the same. If she's a stand-in. If I can say those things to her instead.

So I'd swapped out the room assignment. Made sure we were in the same suite.

There isn't a lot I remember about Evie Laurent. I'd never bothered to speak to her. Ada had told me about middle school, how her twin had spread nasty rumors and turned the entire class on her.

Ada was good at that, twisting things around on you. Making you seem like the bad guy.

But I'm starting to realize how different Evie is.

Ada had been bubbly. Outgoing and talkative. Drawing in a crowd at every opportunity. She was never still, always flitting from one cluster of people to the next, presiding over the hallway like she was Queen of High School and she had to speak to every subject. She was . . . vibrant.

In contrast, there's something cool and calculating about Evie. The way she examines her surroundings. The way she pauses before she speaks, as if she's weighing every word. There's something cautious about her. Almost watchful.

I drag my gaze away and check my watch again, chest tightening. *Five minutes.*

Picking up the pace, I feel my phone vibrate in my pocket. I don't have to check to know it's Beth. Probably freaking out that I'm not there yet.

Ironic, since it's her fault I was late to get Evie.

She'd found out who our new roommate was just before I'd walked out the door. It's been a while since I've seen her that furious. She'd accused me of rigging things. Manipulating Mia from the office, because Mia is "infatuated" with me.

She's right. But I'd never admit that.

I glance down at my watch and quicken my pace. *Three minutes.*

We're halfway up the stairs, and I glance over my shoulder, half expecting one of the Gravesmen to be waiting, tapping his watch, brows raised. Or the vice principal patrolling the dorm.

We're pushing it.

I want to tell Evie to hurry. And then the door above us opens and Beth is in the hall, her face anxious, Leta crowding up behind her.

One minute.

CHAPTER FIVE

Evie

THE SECOND MY FOOT hits the bottom step, one of the doors flies open on the second floor.

There are two girls looking down over the stone balcony. The first is blond, with brows so pale they almost blend into the rest of her face. The other is petite and brown-skinned, with long black hair and blunt-cut bangs. She's standing at the top of the stairs, thumbs hooked into the pockets of her jeans as she grins down at Holland.

"Finally!" she says. "Hurry it up, Morgan."

Holland seems to relax a little, because she turns and smiles at me. "Evie, meet Leta. She's the mastermind behind the welcome party. And this is Beth."

The pale girl only tilts her head at me, the barest movement. She has a full, down-turned mouth, and her serious, blue-eyed gaze tracks me as I make my way up the staircase.

And then there's that heavy, one-tone tolling.

The curfew bell.

It feels just overhead, close enough to reverberate through the building. Which must mean we're in the west wing now.

When I look up, Holland is hurrying back down the steps, hand outstretched, like she means to grab my arm and haul me up the stairs.

"Final warning bell." She raises her voice above the sound. "Everyone inside."

I don't protest when she takes one of my bags and passes it up to Leta, who winks at me before turning to wheel it into the room. The girls are retreating toward the open door, like the bell simply cannot be disobeyed.

Northcroft is secretive, I knew that. The admissions process is proof. Only a third of those who apply get in. And no one knows how they choose. It's like the entire school is one giant secret society.

I expected elite clubs and strict class deadlines. A large course load, but this . . . the curfew, the bell . . .

Leta and Beth usher us in. I follow close behind Holland, nearly running into her as she pauses in the doorway. She turns, eyes glittering, expression unreadable. "You're not supposed to be here."

For a moment, I just stare at her, startled, before I realize she's not talking to me.

When I turn, my stomach sinks.

It's the same boy. Aukley. He's standing at the bottom of the staircase grinning up at us. There are two blond boys flanking him. They look like a set, standing there. School Boy Kens. Smooth beige skin, plastic smiles, sharp-collared white shirts under school sweater vests. All artfully tousled hair and shiny shoes.

I don't have to ask Holland to know—Gravesmen.

It's clear in the way they hold themselves. Unhurried. Arrogant. Like the rules don't apply. They're not worried about curfew, or that they're standing in the girls' dorm.

Their smiles are knowing as they glance at one another and then at me, and I don't need to have studied a single minute of body language to figure this out.

I'm fresh meat.

Aukley watches me just like before, with that cold, direct stare.

When I lock gazes with him, his smile stretches wider, and the dark thing inside me stirs. Abruptly, the peal of the bell from overhead stops. He speaks into the silence, his voice low and velvety.

"You never told me your name, new girl."

There's something in me that wants to drop my hat in the ring. I know he's picturing himself the wolf in the fold, a predator with his sights on some dumb, helpless lamb.

It's infuriating, and for a moment, I think about baring my teeth. Showing him what I really am.

I want to tell him his mask isn't nearly as good as he thinks. He needs more practice.

Blink more. Match his eyes to his lips. Emote.

He's handsome, but his face in motion is a badly assembled jigsaw puzzle. All the pieces fit, but the picture doesn't quite match up. He'll skate by on his looks for a while, sure, but eventually other people will figure him out.

But I don't say that. Instead, I follow Holland through the doorway.

I fix one last look on Aukley, still lingering at the bottom of the stairs. Then I turn away, shutting the door on him without a word.

Let him think I'm a lamb.

There are no gauzy curtains, no strings of decorative fairy lights or messy collages. The room is massive, more like a hotel suite than a dorm, with a sitting room and a second identical suite leading off from it.

The girls' dorm seems more modern than the rest of the school, but it still echoes the same grandeur. The stone overlay on the far wall looks cut from delicate river rock, and there's a wide fireplace in the center, with two narrow windows on either side, showing off a breathtaking view of the forest.

There are a pair of twin-size beds against the other wall. They're done in dark cherrywood that arches up, forming a miniature canopy edged with burgundy privacy curtains.

As I walk inside, my footsteps are muffled by a thick Persian rug over the hardwood; the room smells faintly of pine.

Leta and Beth are crowded by a table in the center of the sitting room, which is full of food, and the murmur of conversation mixes with the crackle of the fire in the hearth.

They both turn, gazes flickering back and forth, first to me and then to Holland. Expectant and waiting.

There are plates of brownies and cookies, bowls of kettle corn and trail mix, and decorative goblets of punch. On the edge of the table, someone has draped a hand-drawn banner, and WELCOME

EVELYN is spelled out in huge, glittering letters. As a crowning touch, there's a pink balloon tied to each of the overstuffed armchairs beside the fire.

"This is Evie," Holland says, and the dark-haired girl, Leta, scoops one of the goblets up and presses it into my hand.

"Hope you like the banner. My extensive arts and crafts education from Northcroft really paid off."

"It's brilliant. Thanks." Up close, Leta's face is interesting. She has wide, dark eyes, accented with smudged, coal-colored liner and thick black brows. Her face is a striking combination of masculine and feminine, with a slender jaw and a notched chin. When she smiles, I get a flash of too-sharp canines.

With that, she launches into what feels like a hundred questions. Where I'm from. Which classes I'm taking. How my trip over was. I do my best to answer, but my attention is drawn back to Holland. When I catch her eye, she smiles, and I feel a surge of relief I wasn't expecting. Her posture is relaxed now, and she leans against the wall beside the door. Her blond friend, Beth, has pulled her aside and is saying something to her.

Beth's mouth is turned down even more severely as she stares across the room toward the windows. Her side profile is sharp, her shoulders stiff.

From here, I spot something I hadn't noticed—a tiny freckle-like mark on her temple, so dark it's almost black.

A birthmark, maybe.

Beth's voice is low, but Holland responds at regular volume.

"We're not doing anything wrong. It's not like we're having a wild party with Gorski just down the hall." She grins at me. "Dorm monitor."

"Also vice principal," Leta grumbles. "And notorious fun-hater."

"Shutters are about to go down," Beth cuts in.

"Shutters," I say, "is that a curfew thing?"

At the mention of curfew, Holland cuts a quick look at Beth. It's a subtle movement, but there's tension to her brow. Meanwhile, Beth drops her gaze to the goblet of punch in her hand, her face closed off.

A second later, Holland's expression is smooth again. "It's the blackout blinds. They're on an automatic timer."

When Holland speaks, the other two girls inch closer, and even I find myself leaning forward.

It brings memories back. Students clustered around Holland and Ada. Ada relishing the attention. Because she was like that too—able to draw people in with a smile or a look. She had a magnetic quality to her, something she carefully cultivated and used to her full advantage.

"Yeah, it's weird and mysterious." Leta lifts her punch goblet in a toast. "Welcome to Northcroft. First class is Weird and Mysterious 101."

Beth doesn't laugh. Instead, her head snaps up, blue eyes narrow. "The *rules* aren't a joke. You're in the room before the blinds come down. And then you don't touch them, not ever."

The laughter trails off and there's a stretch of silence, during which Leta clears her throat and rolls her eyes to the ceiling.

"It's okay, Beth, we know." Holland touches her arm, and Beth seems to relax a little. But I catch the look she casts toward the window, the way her face pales.

Eventually, the conversation turns to Crown and Grave.

"No one knows what's in their clubhouse," Leta is saying. "My money is on piles of empty beer cans and a kiddy pool filled with Jell-O."

We've gravitated to various seats now, with me on the floor, leaning against one of the armchairs. Leta settles down next to me, balancing a bowl of trail mix on one leg, her arm draped over the base of the chair as she picks chocolates out of the mix.

Holland is sprawled on the other chair, long legs clad in pajama shorts. She lifts a brow. "Why the Jell-O?"

"That's what secret societies do." Leta grins. "They do creepy rituals and humiliate one another. Like weird team building."

"Right. I guess when you've seen your bro roll around naked in a pool of Jell-O, it really bonds you," Holland says.

Their suggestions for what could be in the clubhouse continue, becoming increasingly ridiculous. Occasionally, I steal a look in Holland's direction, peering at her over the rim of my goblet. She gestures widely when she speaks, her face animated.

It's hard to look away, but my attention is finally caught when I realize the sun has set farther, casting long shadows through the room. The forest outside is all jagged silhouettes now, and that dark curiosity blooms in my chest again.

"The forest is pretty old, isn't it?"

There's a second of silence, and I feel myself flush. I'd forgotten the natural rhythm of conversation again. Interrupted.

But . . . no one is looking at me. Both Holland and Leta are looking at Beth, whose mouth has flattened into a pinched line. Abruptly, she stands, pushing blond hair over her shoulder, marching to the snack table without looking at us.

Leta turns back to me. "It's the oldest forest in the Pacific Northwest."

"It's kind of crazy how big it is," I say.

"Yeah, it goes for miles." Holland's face is serious. "And it's full of animals. You *never* go in after dark, rule number one."

I'm watching their faces carefully. Beth in particular.

She's on the other side of the table now, tidying up the snacks, holding an empty bowl in one hand. She glances sideways at the window and fumbles the bowl, dropping it onto the table with a sharp crack.

Holland stands abruptly, startling me. When she makes her way over to Beth and touches her shoulder, Beth jumps.

"Come on." Holland's voice is gentle, like she's trying to quiet a wild animal. "Come sit down."

I watch as Holland leads her back to our circle, only visibly relaxing once Beth sits down beside her.

Their dynamic is strange.

When Beth looks up, she notices me staring, and contempt twists her mouth before she drops her gaze.

An answering fury flickers to life in my core. The darkness unfurling inside me.

I think about lunging. Grabbing her by the throat before she can react. Shoving her into the wall so hard it knocks the breath out of her.

I imagine how her face would look, how her blue eyes would go round. Contempt replaced by fear.

The thought feels stronger than usual, and I stamp it down, disturbed. I tell myself what I always do. That I'm not like Ada.

More importantly, I don't *really* want to do any of that. The thoughts aren't real.

Everyone has that little voice in their head telling them to jump when they climb too high, or wrench their steering wheel to the left and drive into traffic.

The French even have a name for it.

L'appel du vide. The call of the void.

Some strange human response to perceived danger.

Only, my thoughts have never been about flinging myself out over an endless drop or driving my car off a bridge.

And if it's never me who ends up at the bottom of the lake in these scenarios, if the danger isn't the *other* person, does that make *me* the void?

Again, the darkness stirs at my center, as if in answer. I push a hand into my sweater pocket and close my fist around the cool metal cross.

"Sure, the 'don't go into the woods at night' rule makes it sound real spooky," Leta says acerbically, "but this island is small enough that you could walk across in a day. There's nothing mysterious about it. It's just . . . Northcroft tradition. Another way of proving how elite they are. How *secretive*."

All through this little speech, I can't look away from Beth. Her lips press together hard, and her eyes are shuttered. Under her thin red sweater, her shoulders bow inward.

She's strange. There's something in me that wants to study her. Pick her apart and see what lies underneath. It's tempting to push the subject, prod at her, like looking for a sore tooth. Is it the thought of breaking the rules? Or something about the forest outside these walls?

Holland clears her throat. "Anyway, Crown and Grave are always patrolling the corridors for people breaking curfew."

Leta has produced a pen from somewhere, flicking it back and forth through her fingers. I notice for the first time that her fingertips are stained with black ink. "Yeah, and don't we all feel safer because of it." Her tone is heavily laden with sarcasm. "Glorified hall monitors."

"Not true. Some have been presidents," Holland says, and Leta rolls her eyes.

"Okay, like two."

"Last three in a row," Holland says pointedly. "And you *know* they run this school."

"There's nothing about them online," I say.

Holland holds up her phone. "The outside is on an 'information diet' about Northcroft. We don't post specifics, usually. Everything is filtered. Oh, and no phones on campus except for weekends. They stay in the dorm."

"It's *filtered*? What does that mean?"

"Means you can't put in certain keywords." Leta smirks at me over the rim of her goblet. "You think that's weird? Just wait. They're even weirder about Crown and Grave. Because they *don't exist*. Seriously, no one even knows who the leader is. Dude is just called *the Rook*, and he literally shows up at ceremonies in a mask. They say he's got body doubles, like some kind of medieval king."

I think about the boys in the hallway, staring up at us with those flat, predatory gazes. "They make sure people don't go into the forest?"

Holland shifts, glancing over at Beth again. "They enforce curfew."

It's becoming obvious how much she skirts around any mention of the forest. And how Beth reacts every time.

Something inside me stirs. This time it's a subtler sensation. Something other than anger breaking through the numbness. The slumbering creature inside me cracks an eye open, just a sliver.

There's something here. Something they aren't saying.

I have a million questions, but before I can ask even one, the deep, ringing gong of the bell starts again.

CHAPTER SIX

Evie

A MECHANICAL WHIRRING BEGINS, loud enough to be heard over the sound of the bell. Beth jumps, and Leta shouts over the noise, "Shutters are coming down. Look."

I watch with interest as the shutters begin their slow descent over the windows. They're made from thick canvas, the material a solid black, dark enough to block out the light. The noise they make, a shuddering creaking and groaning, has me wondering exactly how old these things are. In fact, the blind on the right window seems to have reacted to the timer a moment later than the one on the left, which is already halfway down.

The deeper parts of the forest are full of shadows as the evening light fades, and I watch as it slowly disappears behind the shade, cutting off the hulking trees an inch at a time, throwing the room into shadow.

The other girls aren't nearly as riveted. Holland is up, padding around the room, turning all the lamps on. Leta is refilling her goblet, her gaze darting back to Beth, who half watches the blinds while she picks at the plate of food on her lap.

The first blind touches down on the windowsill with a heavy clunk, and then a sharp click follows.

A strict curfew *and* locking blinds.

The blind on the right window is struggling. It's only halfway down when there comes a horrible, metallic screech.

As I watch, the shutter slows, jerking down another inch. Then another. The gears at the top make terrible grinding sounds.

And then . . . it stops.

I'm sure this isn't supposed to happen.

The shade is halfway down, the forest beyond clear through the glass. The stark outlines of the trees seem to blur and warp in the light from the setting sun, and the orange lamps from inside reflect on the pane.

There's a sharp cry, and Beth shoots up from the floor, flipping her plate over. Celery sticks and baby carrots roll across the rug.

"No." She's at the window so fast, stretching desperately for the end of the thick, black shade, that it takes me a moment to process.

It's too high for her by a foot. "This can't happen. Holland, *help* me."

Holland stands by the table, one hand hovering above the trail mix, lips parted in shock. "But—we're not supposed to touch—"

"*Holland.*"

Holland jerks, face reddening, and then rushes forward. She's nearly a head taller than Beth, and she manages to jump up and catch the thick canvas between her fingers.

The shade unrolls another inch, mechanisms grinding and shrieking. Then it jerks to a stop. Holland's slender body shakes with the effort.

I think about going over there, but I don't know if I can reach the shade—Holland is taller than me. Besides, it's becoming apparent that something is very wrong with Beth.

She's crouched behind Holland, hands pressed to her mouth. When she turns from the window, I catch the look on her face. The mark on her temple stands out like an inkblot on her pale skin, but it's her eyes that make me stay where I am. They're huge, whites shining in the dim light.

It reminds me of the night my cat, Bella, cornered a raccoon against the fence. The wide, white eyes, the hunted expression just before it lunged . . . it took over twenty stitches to put Bella back together.

Beth is muttering now, frantic noises muffled by her fingers. It sounds like *No. No. No.* The sheer terror in her voice makes the back of my neck prickle. It's the way her gaze keeps jerking back to the window—like she's expecting to see something out there—that makes me look out at the forest beyond the glass.

The sky is darkening, but the fading light is still enough to illuminate the tops of massive trees just beyond the wall, reaching branches painted in a wash of black and gold. Shadows stretch between the stark shapes of the boughs, and there's a thin white fog collecting between the trees.

There are hushed voices behind me, as Leta tries to reassure Beth. Beth's still panicking, muttering frantically. But it's all background noise now, nothing but a distant echo.

Something about the forest draws me forward. I step closer, unable to look away, watching as the fog curls from one dark shape to the next, washing out the tree trunks in a gentle haze.

The way it moves, like a living tide rippling over the trees . . .

And then, a *flicker*. Like a burst of static in the thin mist. It's so fast I almost don't catch it, and then it happens again.

The fog . . . *stutters*, like a TV flipping from one empty channel to the next. It's still the same blank, white fog. Still the same nothing. But something happened. A burst of movement. A transition.

My pulse hammers in my throat, and the dark thing coiled in the pit of my stomach twitches. The urge to move forward takes over, presses my hands to the window.

What is that? I want to *see* . . . I want—

There's a horrible crunch from somewhere above the window, like bones breaking, and the blind comes crashing down, slamming into the sill. Holland jumps back, hands in the air, fingers splayed.

There's a beat of silence after this. Leta seems frozen to her spot on the floor, holding so tightly to the stem of her punch glass that her fingertips have gone pale. There's half a bowl of trail mix tipped over on the carpet in front of her.

We're all staring at Beth, not sure what she might do next. She's still looking up at the blind, shivering, arms clasped around herself like she feels a chill emanating from the window no one else does.

"Well, it's down," Leta finally says, her voice tentative, "so, that's good."

Holland murmurs something in reply, but I'm not listening. All I can think about is that flash of static. I'm not sure what I just saw.

After a moment, Beth turns, retreating to the empty bed on the far side of the room. There's a rattle and rasp as she draws the privacy curtain and vanishes behind it, leaving us staring after her.

With the shade down, there's nothing but blank, dark space there.

I glance at the bed, at the curtain pulled tight across the frame and the silence behind it. The memory of that strange flicker in the mist comes back and replays over and over in my mind.

What the hell is in the forest?

We retreat to the curtained-off beds after that.

Leta helps me drag my luggage into the adjoining suite—identical to the first, minus the sitting room—and I pitch one suitcase onto the mattress and turn back to her. She's stronger than I pegged her for, muscles standing out on her slender arms as she hefts my other suitcase onto the bed.

"Hey, thanks."

She gives me a crooked grin before striding back to her side of the room and rifling through her drawers. She jingles when she moves, each wrist covered in leather cords and beaded bracelets, a series of necklace chains and pendants draping her front.

My side of the bedroom is neat and tidy. Not yet lived in.

Leta's side, by contrast, has a bookshelf stuffed haphazardly full of paperbacks. Her bed is unmade and covered with a scattering of notebooks and papers. Her nightstand is the same, with the addition of a thick leather journal and a half-full mug of tea.

I don't bother unpacking anything but pajamas and a toothbrush, but if Leta thinks it strange, she doesn't say anything.

There's a bathroom off the bedroom, but she doesn't bother to use it, just turns her back and yanks her shirt up. I turn away hastily and then retreat to my own bed, sinking down on the mattress.

I'm still buzzing from the drama with the stuck shutter, and it takes me a minute to catch my breath. Then I yank the bed curtain forward a few inches and use the privacy to steal a quick look at my phone. The screen is blank.

Nothing from Dad.

I text him a quick *We need to talk* and then scroll back up to the last text, reading it over, stomach sinking.

You promised.

There's a dull ache in my left arm, as if in response, and I rub at it absently.

Three months ago, on my eighteenth birthday. I'd wanted to go on a hike, just the two of us.

He'd make a trip back from the island especially for our birthdays. Ada would always have school friends over, or ask for increasingly expensive presents, but Dad and I would do a "Dad and daughter date." We'd sit in a greasy pizza parlor and eat too many slices of pepperoni, or he'd surprise me with a picnic on the beach.

I'd insisted on it being just him and me. We'd had enough joint birthdays as kids, and Ada had always ruined them. She couldn't stand not being the center of attention.

As if to prove this point, Ada had crashed my birthday hike.

Which was how I'd ended up dangling from a rocky ledge overhanging the ravine, pain spiking through my left arm as Ada shrieked above me. *Oh my god, she slipped. Oh my god.*

I should probably be dead. But I'd felt her coming just before she pushed me. I'd twisted around, arms shooting out as I fell, crashing into a rock on the way down.

I'd *heard* my arm break, a sharp snap of bone. Hot adrenaline had surged through me. With it had come an almost impossible strength, and I'd snatched at a root jutting out from the soil. Kept myself dangling by one arm while Dad figured out a way to get me up.

By the time he'd managed, pulling me over the lip of the ravine by my jacket, Ada was leaning against the nearest tree, staring down at her phone.

Something must have finally clicked for him.

It was easier to make excuses when we were young. When she'd held me under in the pool, she'd *just been playing.* Pushing me down the stairs and into the window on the landing? *An accident.*

But he'd seen it this time.

I remember his expression so clearly. The horror and resignation.

After that, he'd given in. Ada was going to Northcroft for twelfth grade.

Funny, looking back. I'd been so relieved.

Shaking myself, I read the text again. The little circles underneath telling me he's left me on read.

Well, he can't hide from me anymore.

I imagine knocking at his office tomorrow. What will his face look like when he answers and finds me standing on his doorstep?

At least when I pull up the local news site, there are no headlines about her this time. No news articles about the tragic, hard-partying teenager who fell into the lake.

"There's earplugs in the nightstand."

"Hmm?" I jerk upright, shoving my phone into my pocket. Turning, I see Leta in a loose-fitting gray tee that goes down just past her thighs.

"You'll need them. You might hear the animals in the woods," she says.

The single remaining light from the room's lamp is a dull, orange glow. It stretches shadows over the space, illuminating one side of her face.

"Animals?"

"Wolves. Cougars. Foxes. Honestly, it's the foxes that get you. I don't know if you've ever heard one, but they sound like women screaming." Leta shudders, sinking down onto the edge of her bed. "It's an old-growth forest, so we get animals you don't see anywhere else. They're way out there, though, so we don't have to worry."

I copy her, laying back in bed. The mattress is hotel-bed firm, the pillow soft down, but my mind is racing.

What I saw out there had nothing to do with animals. But I can't even begin to grasp what it might be. What had caused that odd flicker, so fast I'd almost missed it?

And Beth's reaction to my questions about the woods had been anything but normal.

There's the faint rasp of the privacy curtain, but Leta tugs hers only halfway across and props herself up on one elbow. I can see her face better now as my eyes adjust, and I realize she's staring at me, head tilted. Like I'm a puzzle, and she's found a piece missing. My thoughts derail, my pulse picking up.

"What?" It comes out sharp, but Leta seems unfazed.

"Just . . . you rolled in pretty late." When I only stare at her, she explains. "Close to curfew, I mean. I thought Beth was gonna shit herself." She grins. "Most of the students came yesterday or early this morning."

"Yeah." I stare at her through the darkness. For one wild, reckless moment, I think about blurting it out.

I watched my sister drown, and my mom isn't sure if I killed her and doesn't want to ask. So now I'm my father's problem. He's the principal, by the way.

But even that last bit is too much. Part of myself I don't want to share.

A few years back, I'd stubbornly insisted on taking Mom's last name, not wanting to be referred to as "the Blackwood Twins."

It feels less silly now, lending me anonymity.

So instead, I say, "My enrollment was a bit last minute."

Leta's brows shoot up. "Oh, shit. Of course it was. I'm an idiot."

So she knows about Ada. Holland told her. "It's okay. Honestly, I'm just happy to be out of the house." When Leta looks vaguely startled, I add, "Mom and I never got along, even before it happened." I say it with a smile, a wry twist of my mouth. A partial truth. Enough of an explanation to satisfy but not invite further prying.

Leta grimaces. "I get it. I didn't go home for summer. I stayed and binged every episode of *The Wizards*, just so I could make fun of Holland more accurately." She raises her voice on the last sentence, and Holland's aggrieved reply comes from next door. "I swear to god. Don't make me come over there and beat you."

We both laugh, and Leta calls back, "In, like, a sexual way?" I hear Holland's exasperated groan.

"We have to get up early." Beth's voice. Quieter, clearly not meant for Leta and me. "You've got dorm duties—"

Leta makes a rude sound and raises her voice again. "You're not her mom. You can't send her to bed."

There's a low murmur after that—Beth again—and then silence.

I sneak a look at the doorway, sure to keep my voice low. "So, is she liable to shank me at some point for talking to Holland?"

Leta snorts, her expression knowing. "Picked up on that, did you? I've been roommates with Holland for the exact same amount of time, but she told me I don't *know* Holland. No one knows her like *she* does." Leta rolls her eyes to the ceiling.

I can picture that. Beth sulking as more and more people find out Holland Morgan is at Northcroft. People falling into her orbit while Beth convinces herself she's the actress's only true friend. Jealously guarding the other girl.

The dark looks she was shooting me are starting to make sense.

I'm about to reply when something stops me. A faraway sound, quiet at first, and then louder. It's coming from outside, I think. A distant, howling scream.

Leta goes still and we lie there, quiet. Listening.

She says it's nothing—just a fox shrieking in the night.

But it doesn't sound like that. There's a kind of fury in the inhuman, multivoiced wail, an inflection I've never heard from an animal. Again, I think of the flicker I saw, the burst of static in the mist.

Every hair on my body stands up as the noise comes again. My skin is crawling.

It's an eerie cry. Maybe an animal being hunted. A deer brought down by wolves.

I can feel the darkness responding. It makes my blood hum in false anticipation. Some small part of me wants to be out there. Hurtling through the trees, bare feet on the forest floor, heart beating hard in my ears.

Maybe it's animals that force us inside at night.

A pack of wolves, deep in the forest. Maybe that's the reason for the curfew. They're trying to protect their students from predators.

It makes me think about Aukley. His flat black stare. The menace in his expression.

It seems like Northcroft has wolves both inside the walls and out.

For the first time, I wonder if maybe I do belong here.

CHAPTER SEVEN

Holland

THE COMMON ROOM AT NORTHCROFT is on the third floor of Blackwood Hall, which means it's about a million years old.

It has creaky floors and this god-awful, puke-colored damask wallpaper. When I got here a year ago, Beth and I used to lie on the carpet in front of the fireplace, trying to pick out shapes. She'd point out clouds and ships and roses, but I'd only ever see the same thing: the face of a sleek Chinese dragon repeated again and again, all curling whiskers and razor-like fangs.

When I stand in the center of the room, in just the right spot, the massive chandelier sends slivers of multicolored light dancing over my skin, tiny rainbows scattering around the room as the morning sun pours in. I know it's just white light passing through the crystals, splitting the spectrum into different colors, but it's more fun to pretend it's some small bit of unexpected fairy magic.

There are ashes from last night's fire coating the bottom of the fireplace, so I sigh and leave my little fantasy world to weave around the overstuffed couches and grab the metal dustpan and wire brush beside the hearth.

The principal glommed onto me the moment I set foot at Northcroft, overeager and cloying. He'd offered me one of the biggest rooms, as well as the position of "dorm mother," handing it out like it was some kind of enormous privilege. And yet . . . right now I'm up to my elbows in ash, like a redheaded Cinderella. Lucky me.

I sigh again, swiping at a patch of ash on the sleeve of my sweater. It's Northcroft blue and black, with a crest on the left breast—TRUTH BEFORE ALL.

I know that's not quite the right translation. In Latin, it's closer to "knowledge." But I can't help but feel it's ironic on me right now.

I should tell Evie about me and Ada. Withholding is just another form of lying. But . . . I don't want it to be over so soon.

I've known her for one day, and I catch myself wanting to impress her. I liked the way she looked at me on the steps yesterday, like I was the most fascinating creature she'd ever seen.

I don't know if she's a fan of the show, or if she's seen me in tabloids. Or if she just remembers me from high school . . .

Whatever it is, I want her to look at me like that again.

My weakness has always been a thirst for attention, though I'd drop dead before I'd admit *that* out loud. And not just attention like tabloid articles, or interviews. But the *real* kind, from individual people.

Admiration, praise, worship. I'll take it all. Inject it straight into my veins.

For some reason, there'd been something extra special about having Ada's undivided focus. Like it was higher octane, pure and uncut. Lighting me up from the inside.

Evie, I'm learning, feels dangerously similar. My thoughts loop in circles, always returning to her.

After working for all of five minutes, I lean back against the mantle and let out a breath, staring up at the gold-framed pictures on the walls, all dull-green landscapes and pastoral scenes. There are two windows opposite the fireplace and the shutters are up, curled tight at the top like wide black scrolls. It reminds me of last night.

I can't help thinking about the way Evie stared at the window, even after the shutters had finally come down. The intensity of her expression.

The questions she'd kept asking had me on edge. An uncomfortable reminder of last year.

There's a soft throat-clearing behind me.

Beth stands in the doorway, as if summoned by the thought. She pulls her school blazer on, buttoning the front. When she raises a pale brow, I turn back to the fireplace, lips pressed in a tight line.

"You were gone when I woke up."

Her footsteps are muffled by the thick rug as she moves beside me, reaching out to fidget with the fire poker. I study her in my peripheral, noting the dark circles under her eyes. She's paler than usual, which is saying something.

"I couldn't sleep. Didn't want to wake you."

I want to ask about her reaction to the stuck shutter. About her nightmares. She always gets them, but they've been especially bad the last couple of nights. It seems to make her progressively more anxious each night as curfew approaches. And if the noises start, I'll find her in my bed, her body shuddering beneath the covers.

I don't push her, though, too afraid it might send her toppling over the edge. That it might bring back that almost catatonic silence from last year.

I still remember my first day here, how different she was. I'd been on the steps of Blackwood Hall, watching students go by. Everyone eyeing me but never daring to approach. Beth had been different. She'd zoned in on me immediately, smile wide and warm.

Past-Beth had been bubbly and happy, which was surprising when I'd learned she'd lost her best friend the year before.

And then, slowly, things had changed. *She'd* changed.

She'd become obsessed. Preoccupied with the forest that had swallowed her friend.

Beth had gone looking for clues, spending more and more time out there. Until one day she went in and didn't come back.

She was gone for twenty-four hours.

As if sensing my thoughts, Beth sets the poker back in the stand and slides me a sideways look. "You two seem to get along well."

She's smiling, but I've known Beth long enough to tell she's forcing it.

That's one of the ways she's changed. She'd never hung onto me so hard before. Had never been jealous or possessive.

I'm intimately familiar with that *look* she gets now. The hardening of her jaw, the way her eyes grow flinty. I see it to varying degrees. It's there, just barely, when we're in the dining hall and classmates drift past the table to say hello. It's ever-present at each fresh wave of new students, at each group that shuffles past us on the quad or in the halls, all of them sneaking nervous, wide-eyed glances at me.

And once, and only once, have I seen it come out in all its glory.

The principal reassured me when I enrolled that my privacy was of the utmost import. Everyone is briefed on my attendance and told in no uncertain terms that I'm here as a student. But once, at the beginning of last year, a new student had stopped at our table in the middle of breakfast and pulled out a camera.

I'd never seen Beth move the way she did that day, darting up to slap the girl's camera out of her hand. Sending it crashing to the stone floor.

I know it makes me a terrible person, but there's something in me that secretly anticipates that look. There's something satisfying about having a person like you *that much*.

"She's nice," I say lightly.

Beth hesitates. I can tell she's about to broach the subject. The one I don't want to talk about.

I stalk over to the couch and fluff the pillows more aggressively than I need to. "I don't know, but everything with the shutter last night . . . she probably thinks this whole place is bizarre."

Not to mention Aukley harassing her at the door, and the Gravesmen standing at the bottom of the stairs with their silent, meaningful gazes. Like they own the school. Like they know all its secrets.

Turning back, I find Beth scowling at me, though she quickly composes herself.

"Are you okay?" She grabs my hand, and I don't resist, letting her pull me down onto the couch beside her. "Talk to me. This can't be easy." She looks at the empty doorway. "It's only been two weeks since Ada died, and now this."

"Beth . . ." *I don't want to talk about this.*

"Just . . . don't forget what she did." Beth frowns. "People forget about the negative stuff after someone dies. But we know better. And Evie"—she pauses, waving a hand at the doorway— "is an exact copy."

"She's a twin, Beth. Not a doppelgänger." I try to give her a wry smile, but my stomach is churning. "Can we stop talking about this? I'll be careful." Anything to end this conversation.

Beth shifts, smoothing her palms over the fabric of her slacks. My heart sinks because she's got that face on. *The look.* And this time, its intensity is directed at me.

"Will you, though?"

"What's that supposed to mean?"

"I saw the way you looked at her." When I open my mouth to protest, she pushes on. "I know how you felt about Ada. It must be like seeing her all over again."

My head whips toward the doorway, heart galloping in my chest. "God, Beth, keep your voice down."

"It's early. No one is awake yet." Beth looks unperturbed by my panic. "I'm just saying, I know why. But falling for your dead ex's twin is a recipe for *years* of therapy. I don't want you to go through that." Her face is grave. "I know how hard it was for you, what she did."

"She wasn't an ex." I can't help it—I dart another look toward the door. "Can this conversation be over? I promise to be careful, guard my heart, whatever Hollywood bullshit sounds best. I'm not planning on dating anyone for the rest of my natural life anyway. Not after Gianna."

Beth's mouth quirks into a smile. "I *did* warn you about her."

"And I will never hear the end of it." I grumble and poke her in the arm, but it's good-natured. I'm relieved to be off the subject of Ada. "But you were right. She turned out to be a nut."

Beth laughs, and there's a hint of meanness there. "Oh my god, her *face* when all the photos of you fell out of the textbook."

"I still can't believe she made a collage." I groan, slumping back on the couch.

"She's probably sleeping with a papier-mâché statue of you as we speak."

"Oh my god, shut up."

Beth shrieks as I lean over and poke her in the armpit, falling sideways into the couch cushions, laughing and swatting my hand away.

Then we both go quiet and she peers up at me, yellow hair splayed out on the pillows beneath her head. "Gianna wasn't even that bad. Stephanie Boland spread all those rumors. And don't forget about Stacey."

I grimace at her and she shrugs.

Stacey Hornshaw had broken up with her girlfriend halfway through the year and proceeded to flirt with me outrageously. We'd made out behind the library exactly once. The week after, every gossip rag and celebrity website had somehow acquired blurry pictures of us.

The school had launched an investigation, finding said photographs under the ex's bunk. She'd denied it, even as she was hauled into the office and expelled.

Stacey dropped out a few weeks later, claiming online harassment.

I'd kept to myself after that. Stuck with Leta and Beth.

Easier to avoid drama that way.

I get to my feet slowly, dusting my shirt off like our conversation wrinkled it. Then I busy myself straightening cushions on the couches and armchairs. I can feel Beth's eyes tracking me.

When I turn, Evie is standing in the doorway. She's still wearing her camera, hair hanging in damp waves around her face, the ends brushing the green cardigan she's wearing over her uniform.

The kilt and blouse fit her perfectly, which makes me wonder how it felt, putting on her dead twin's clothing.

"Leta said you'd be here."

Even with her black waves tamed by water, she's like some woodland creature who's wandered into the room, with her upturned nose and storm-gray eyes, her cheeks still flushed from the heat of the shower. There's a line of prose that floated through my head when I first saw her yesterday, silhouetted against the forest. Some scrap left behind from English class.

And way into the trees I see, a nymph with hair as black as coal . . .

The rest alludes me, but I know it ends with the narrator, the Greek hero Actaeon, discovering too late that the nymph is Artemis. She turns him into a stag for spying on her and he gets ripped apart by his own hunting dogs. A moral lesson about being lured in by the beauty of the wilderness.

Thankfully, she doesn't catch me staring, too busy looking around the common room. One hand drifts up, fingers wrapping around her camera. I wonder if she knows she's doing that.

"Need any help?"

"You and Holland can do the windows." Beth crouches by the hearth, brushing the corners of the fireplace with the whisk, like I've missed something, even though I know I haven't. "It's stuffy in here."

Evie waits for me to move to the first window, where I drag the latch to one side and push the pane outward a crack. She does the same on the other side.

Hands on the sill, I pause. From this high up, I can see the woods stretch out beyond the wall. The forest is bright with daylight, mossy trunks vibrant green in the light filtering through the branches. Fresh sprouts of supple ferns, soft and cloudlike, carpet the forest floor, and massive, thick-trunked trees stand like lichen-covered sentinels among wisps of new growth.

Whatever was making that noise last night is out there, curled in its burrow or den. Or maybe it's dead, guts strewn across the forest floor.

Not for the first time, I'm thankful for how high the walls are.

I almost say this to Evie, but Beth is scraping at the stones of the fireplace behind me, and I think about the way her entire body shook last night. How she buried her face in my shoulder, shivering so hard I thought she might break apart.

I keep my mouth shut.

From my spot at the window, I catch Evie's profile reflected back at me. She's examining the tree line with the intensity of someone deep in thought, and for a second, I get to study her without looking away. All I can think is *Ada*, and my heart stutters painfully in my chest. I force myself to look away. Gather myself.

When I turn back, she starts, like I've caught her staring.

I'm sure to linger there a moment, tilting my face toward her, letting my lashes slip shut as I draw in fresh morning air. I can feel her eyes on me, and I can't help smiling. Her stare is like sunlight warming my skin.

When I open my eyes, Evie glances away again, blinking, fixing her gaze on the window. She says nothing, just leans her elbows against the sill but she's so obvious.

It sends a flush of excitement through me, but I make sure to keep my expression perfectly neutral.

"Do you think there are wolves out there?"

As soon as she says it, my stomach drops. I see Beth stiffen out of the corner of my eye. "Probably. That's why we stay out of there."

"I'd like to see one." She watches my face when she says it.

"That's how people die in the woods." Beth's voice is flat, but it trembles slightly, and her fists are clenched at her sides. "With idiotic ideas like that."

I tense and glance over at Evie, alarmed. She isn't looking at Beth, though, attention still fixed on the forest.

"Have people really died out there?"

This conversation is hurtling out of control, and I grasp for something to change the subject. "I don't think—"

"Of course they do." Beth's voice is sharp. "My best friend died out there."

I clear my throat, panic prickling my insides.

"What happened?" Evie looks shockingly unperturbed.

I clear my throat, and give Beth a quick look. "It was two years ago, after curfew. Nobody knows why she went out."

Evie takes a breath, like she's trying to collect her thoughts. "The principal . . . can't he—"

"What, Blackwood?" Beth's voice is scornful. She settles on the hearth, arms crossed over her chest. "He's barely around anymore. And even before that, he did nothing but send *thoughts and prayers*. For all the good it did Amanda."

Evie grimaces, fingers tightening on the strap of her camera. She's not used to Beth yet, to her peaks and valleys. Quiet and withdrawn one moment and sharp the next.

"Let's go to breakfast." I keep my voice even, trying to smooth out the jagged edges of the conversation. There's a growing tension in the set of Evie's shoulders. It makes me nervous, because I'm beginning to realize how vital it is that they at least tolerate one another.

Beth is just going to have to adjust, whether she likes it or not.

Thankfully, when Beth turns to me, her smile is tight, but it's there. "Right. Let's grab coffee."

"Leta's probably already had two." I grin at Evie. "Typical writer."

The air is cooler out in the hallway, the carpet muffling our footsteps.

"Leta's a writer?" Evie says. "She didn't say."

"How very Leta of her." I'm hardly surprised. Leta doesn't withhold information so much as forget to communicate it at all.

There's always been a detached quality to her, as if she's halfway into some other world—one that simply doesn't include you. It isn't malicious, but it gives her a certain aloofness.

"What does she write?"

"Horror." Leta stands at the end of the hallway, hands in the pockets of her oversize black cardigan. This morning, her long hair is in a neat fishtail braid, and she's got a pen tucked behind one ear.

As we make our way down the stairs, Evie asks questions about writing and Leta answers. And I lead the way through the hallways and corridors, trying to pretend I'm not jealous of the attention Evie is giving her.

Blackwood Hall in the early hours reminds me of the silence of the forest. Sometimes, if you listen hard enough, you can hear stirring. The muffled scrape of furniture or footsteps as breakfast is prepared in the dining hall. But for the most part it's completely quiet, the stone walls soaking up every scrap of sound.

We make our way past portraits and statues, ignoring the scowls of dead Northcroft founders along the walls. Down a series of sprawling hallways that take us to the back of the building, to the dining hall. Here, the hallway expands, turning to towering vaulted ceilings, Gothic arches over stained-glass windows.

The stone floors echo our footsteps back at us as we enter the dining hall, and Evie stares around wide-eyed, pulling her camera up. She snaps a picture of the arched ceiling with its rows of circular chandeliers.

I remember my reaction to the dining room the first time I saw it. Gaping at the rows of tall windows, the way they flood the enormous room with light, creating a golden glow in the rich wooden interior.

"Is it digital?"

"What?" She turns back to me, camera held to her chest like a shield.

"Your camera, I mean."

"Yeah." She ducks her head, running one thumb along the edge of the camera. "I like being able to look at the pictures right away."

"You'll have to show me some of your pictures sometime," I tell her, and Evie smiles at me. It's a small smile, tentative. But at the same time, her gray eyes seem to drink in my face. Again, I feel that same heady sensation.

I'm beginning to think it might be addictive, having her focus on me that way.

Someone appears in the center aisle before us, between the rows of tables. A tall, slender figure in an eye-catching periwinkle duster jacket, dark hair sticking up in riotous curls.

Ewan Stowe.

When she sees him, Evie's eyes widen, and I know she's putting two and two together.

Chadwick Stowe is one of the highest-grossing actors of the last century, and his son looks almost exactly like him.

He's fresher-faced, of course. Younger. And his eyes are a soft doe-brown instead of blue, but he has the same high cheekbones and sharp jaw. He even sports a lighter version of his father's famous beard, which makes him look a little like a washed-up rock star.

There's always a crowd behind him, and the buzz of noise echoes through the dining hall, as Stowe is flanked on all sides by whispering students. He's always been a media darling, the press all waiting to see what he does next. Crashing his car, public drinking, making out with a costar . . .

As one gossip columnist put it: *always up to some kind of heathenry, but never without style.*

I'd been so jealous reading that. It's the kind of quote you put on the back of your biography.

"Holland Morgan, I've been *waiting.*"

The hall is starting to fill now, newly arrived students wandering around looking a little dumbstruck, returning Northcroft veterans settling in at tables. Laughter and chatter ring off the rafters overhead.

The growing crowd seems to encourage Stowe to get louder, drawing people's attention. "How I've missed you. Too long apart, my dove."

He's been gone only for the summer, so he has exactly zero reason to make a scene, but that's Stowe for you. His fan club crowds closer, faces rapt, and Beth glares around at them.

"Good morning, Ewan Stowe." I match his playful tone. He's been a flirt since day one, acting like we're best friends even though I hadn't seen him in years.

Stowe pauses, swaying on his feet. There's a loose-boned, lolling quality to the way he stands, head tipping to the side as he stares at me.

His eyes are huge and dark, accented by smudged black liner. "Lovely to see you again."

"Yes, it's been ages." I can't help it. My tone goes a little dry.

I'd heard from reputable sources that Stowe had been at rehab over the summer. One of those fancy resort types where the food is "farm-fresh organic" and they have yoga classes.

If that was the case, they should have spent more time on the recovery part and less on downward-dogging, because he's definitely had a few drinks this morning.

It's technically not allowed on campus. But of course, Stowe is famous. And a member of Crown and Grave. He's practically untouchable.

I think about the catching up I did before I'd arrived last year. Reading gossip magazines and trashy websites. Gleaning little pieces of truth out of the bullshit.

The implications are that alcohol is the least of Stowe's proclivities.

"Summer's over, Morgan." Stowe reaches out and pulls me in. The fur collar on his coat brushes my cheek, and his breath touches my neck. He smells like cinnamon.

Then he speaks. Low. Near my left ear. "Back into the fray we go, eh?"

Stowe pulls away, leaving me shaking my head as he glides past us, that ridiculous coat drifting behind him. His fan club follows, darting curious looks at me as they go.

"Did he just quote *Wizards* at you?" Evie stares after him.

I roll my eyes. "He's always doing stuff like that."

"He's a super fan." Leta's smile is teasing. "Plus, they go way back."

"We worked together on a show like six years ago." I shrug. "So we kinda knew one another before Northcroft."

"Oh yeah. *Supersonics*, right?" As soon as she says it, Evie flushes bright red and looks away.

A thrill goes through me, and I bite back a grin. *Supersonics* was a huge flop. Canceled after season one. Which means either

Evie has a thing for obscure kids shows, or she's a Holland Morgan fan.

The idea makes me almost giddy, and I suck in a breath to keep myself from laughing out loud in sheer delight. "That's the one. So yeah, I guess we know one another pretty well. Or . . . we did."

"He just wants attention." Beth's expression is sour as she watches Stowe lope away, moving to the far corner of the room where the Crown and Grave members sit. "He zoned in on her the moment she showed up. It's gross."

Leta makes a rude noise in her throat. "Extremely hot, famous movie star with a crush on you? Yeah, super gross."

"Right, he's a real catch." Beth smirks at Evie. "He had some kind of nervous breakdown last year. He was gone for a month. Not to mention, everyone knows he went to rehab this summer." She glances across the hall, to where Stowe is holding court with his followers. "Though it clearly didn't stick."

"Beth, come on." I keep my voice low, looping my arm through hers, tugging her away so we can line up at the breakfast bar. I relax only when we're surrounded by the sound of clinking cutlery, waiting for scrambled eggs and fruit.

When Beth gets started on something, it's hard to stop her, and I can't have Ewan Stowe overhear her ranting.

Behind me, Evie brushes my elbow, and I turn to find her idly examining the buffet, a plate pressed into the front of her sweater, the waves of her dark hair falling over her face.

"Holland, hey." Someone crowds up behind me, and I drag my attention away. Mia Green is blond-haired and intense, with a pale freckled face that lights up as she talks to me.

By now I'm used to people acting like they know me. Like the character they know from TV is actually real.

"They were talking about *The Wizards* on this new murder podcast I'm listening to. Oh, nothing to do with the murder, of course." She's practically vibrating as she speaks. "Just that it was the host's favorite show. And they're investigating how many people go missing in the Pacific Northwest. It's so crazy . . ."

I let her ramble for a few minutes, nodding and smiling, and she looks positively thrilled. Mia Green is a huge *Wizards* fan. She also volunteers at the secretary's office, which made it easy to get my hands on Evie's file.

Beth, still with her arm in mine, tugs me forward. "Come on, they've got the fruit mix you like." She ignores Mia completely, steering me away. On the way past, I snatch a croissant, and Beth purses her lips at me.

"You shouldn't humor Mia," she whispers. "You'll give her false hope. Like you're going to be best friends or something."

I want to say being nice isn't the same thing as *humoring* someone, but there's no sense in arguing, so I shrug. "We'd better eat quick. Class is in ten."

As we make our way to the back of the dining hall, we pass the Crown and Grave table. Ewan Stowe sits up a little taller, lowering his book.

As we go past, he catches my eye and winks.

CHAPTER EIGHT

Holland

HOMEROOM TURNS OUT TO BE ENGLISH THIS YEAR, which is in one of the old, creaky-floored classrooms on the second floor of Blackwood Hall.

The boards groan beneath us as we stream into the dusty hallways. I always picture the floors just giving up one day, plunging us down into the cavernous ceiling of the dining hall.

The room is undeniably beautiful, though. Our classroom has an entire wall of windows facing the forest. The glass reaches up to the ceiling, its top tapered like a church gable, intricate carvings etched across the surface.

We pause inside the classroom door, and I draw Evie's attention back to me with a gentle touch of her elbow, nodding to the first two empty rows.

Ewan Stowe sits near the center. He's kicked back in one of the seats at the end, feet propped on the wooden desk, reading a tattered paperback.

Since Beth has advanced math after check-in, we find a spot near the end of the row and settle in. It's still early, the classroom slowly filling, students muttering under their breath and shuffling toward their seats with coffee mugs in hand. No sign of Mrs. McAllister yet.

Evie stares at the windows, wide-eyed, while Leta talks her ear off.

"This is one of the original buildings, so this classroom is over three hundred years old. Did you tour other schools before you came? I was torn between Beachgrove and here."

Behind us, someone clears their throat pointedly.

Aukley lounges there, the sleeves of his school blazer rolled up to his elbows, a number of thick silver watches lining both arms. He also sports a slender, diamond-studded tie clip.

Aukley, always the diplomat, once told me the clip was *worth more than your summer home and your real house put together.*

It's ridiculous, but it's a typical Gravesman move, skirting around the dress code in a way specifically meant to show how much money he has.

He's got a coffee mug in one hand and a handful of crumpled papers in the other. "Beachgrove. What would even be the *point*?" He smirks at Leta. "I suppose if Daddy has no other options . . ."

Leta bristles, and I lean sideways, nudging her shoulder. She presses her lips together, dark eyes narrow, but then relaxes back into her seat.

"Ignore him." Beth darts a worried look at Leta, and then, when Evie seems puzzled, adds, "Aukley's one of those 'True Northmen' idiots."

"True Northmen?" Evie looks at Aukley, and then glances away quickly when he grins back at her.

I give him a cool smile. "Yeah, all their *unbroken line* garbage. They're a bunch of snobs, calling themselves True Northmen because they've all gone here for generations."

"It's a point of pride for some of the old families," Beth says. "Half these buildings are named after them."

The Gravesmen file in, taking over the front rows. They settle around Ewan Stowe, who doesn't look up from his book.

You can always tell the Gravesmen right off, even if you don't know their names. It's not just the way they stride around Northcroft, like they know their family donated a wing, but that they all wear the uniform a certain way.

An unspoken dress code. School blazers with sewn-on elbow patches. Black leather boots. The girls wear the kilts, never the dress pants. And all of them are decked out and glittering— expensive watches and jewelry, shiny silver belt buckles.

I watch as they trickle in.

There's Jason Cooper, of Cooper House, with his too-young face and blond hair. And Elijah Archer, youngest person ever featured on the *Forbes* list. Apparently, it caused quite a stir when he'd been tapped. The first Black Gravesman. It was the same year two girls had been picked; reportedly, some of the old guard had balked.

With Elijah is Patricia Harper, who always wears a Northcroft cardigan over her collared shirt. She looks like she stepped out of a Banana Republic catalog, with her delicate features and smooth blond hair.

Natalie Kim trails behind them, dark hair swinging halfway down her back. She's clearly rolled the top of her kilt, revealing long, tanned legs, and she's wearing enough jewelry that she jingles with every step. Behind her, Daniel Prince hurries in, his tie slightly askew. He's wearing all the same expensive accessories, but amusingly, his hands and arms are covered in smudges of charcoal, and he has several art books tucked under one arm.

I watch as he catches up with Natalie and says something, too low for me to hear. She nods before turning away.

It's interesting, the way they interact. Speaking in whispers and code, exchanging meaningful looks.

When Beth had come back so changed, the Gravesmen had looked at her like that. I'd been certain they *knew* something. They knew what happened out there.

It makes me resent them. If they knew, why hadn't they stopped her? Why hadn't they *said* something?

Muldoon shuffles in next. With his crooked, twice-broken nose and close-shorn head, he looks more like a hired goon than someone in the three percent. Behind him comes Steven Blackwood, of Blackwood Hall fame. Tall. Gangly. Sporting the Double Windsor tie knot and shiny, slicked-back hair. He looks like he's perpetually waiting for the call to say he's inherited his father's firm.

The latter two skip the back row and settle in on either side of Aukley instead—some rich frat boy version of Jasper and Horace.

Alliances are still fractured after Aukley was kicked out.

When I glance around, I'm not the only one watching. It's hard to blame people. The Gravesmen are like colorful preening birds, attracting attention the second they enter the room.

They also effectively run the school.

Someone calls for attention, voice echoing across the classroom. It's Mrs. McAllister, the English teacher, who does the orientation this year.

"Still no sign of Blackwood," Beth whispers.

I lean over to Evie, clarifying, "He always stays the summer, but he's been shut in his office for two weeks now. No idea why."

Evie hesitates, but before she can reply, we're being told to pair off for the first project, and the classroom bursts to life, echoing with a dozen different conversations.

When I glance sideways, I meet Evie's eyes and find myself flushing.

CHAPTER NINE

Evie

WHEN THE ENGLISH TEACHER instructs us to pair off, my gaze is immediately drawn to Holland.

Beth has already left for math, which seems like the perfect opportunity.

Several people are already darting sideways looks at Holland, and across the classroom, Ewan Stowe pushes himself up from his desk, eyes fixed on her.

I lean over hurriedly and nudge Holland and she nods. Stowe sinks back down with a wry smile, and several of the other students look crestfallen.

When we'd first walked in, I'd noticed people staring. Holland draws attention like a flame does oxygen. Eyes tracking our progress across the classroom, heads turning. She doesn't seem to notice.

I can hardly blame them. Every time she shifts beside me, my gaze is drawn back to her like a magnet.

Though . . . Holland isn't the only thing distracting me. I keep finding myself drawn back to windows. To the forest waiting outside.

I can *feel* that strange, electric surge every time I focus on it, lighting me up from the inside. It's the same way I felt hearing the howling in the woods last night. Strangely *alive*.

It makes me shift in my seat, antsy.

Mrs. McAllister is facing the whiteboard, and Holland leans over to whisper. "Oh, by the way, the autumn dance is end of October." She touches my wrist, just the barest brush.

It feels like a shock, and heat blooms in my chest.

I can't do this. Can't fixate on Holland Morgan like I did in ninth grade. It feels dangerous.

She's still talking.

"The mainland trip happens once a week. You should come. Pick something out. It's fairy-tale themed." She grins and touches her hair. "I'm going as a wolf-hunting Red Riding Hood. I've got a red cape and a black dress with a slit up the side so I can strap a fake axe to my leg."

Good god. Now all I can do is picture her in this getup. My face feels warm, and I clear my throat. "You can go as anything from a fairy tale?"

Leta leans across Holland to whisper, "I'm going as a dragon. I've got a pocket in the tail so I can smuggle stuff in." She gives Holland a sideways look. "Bet they crack down 'cause of Parker."

"Who's Parker?" I whisper back.

"Sara Parker," Holland answers. "Someone dared her to go out after curfew during the Founders Day party. Got herself expelled. She was very drunk."

"Yeah, and the Founders Day thing is a *luncheon*." Leta snorts, and then there's a sharp throat-clearing from the front. Mrs. McAllister is writing the assignment out on the board.

Holland and I end up writing a short story, heads bent together, scribbling in our notebooks. I suggest writing about the forest, but Holland's expression closes off, the same way it does every time I mention the woods.

"I don't think that's a good idea."

"You know everyone here is super weird about it, right?"

"It's just . . . dangerous."

"Why dangerous?"

Holland glances around, dropping her voice. "It just is. We don't have to talk about it, okay?"

It only makes me want to talk about it more. Only makes me more curious.

I want to go out into the woods right now, weave my way through the giant trunks. Go in deeper until it gets dark.

I have a spare after class, and as we exit with the flood of students, Holland falls into step with me. "What's your timetable? You have a spare too?"

"Yeah. I think I'm going in." I'm already heading for the front gate. My pulse races in my throat, the monstrous thing inside me stirring.

I dreamed last night. The same dream as always. Only this time there was no Ada. It was just me and the tree, its massive black branches stretching out overhead.

"Wait, seriously?" Holland's expression is worried. "You're really going in?"

"Why not?" She's following me, and it gives me a ripple of excitement. Holland Morgan trailing behind *me*. "I have an hour, right?"

She's quiet for a moment. Then she lets out a breath. "Let me come with you at least. And you're not going to want to walk. Here."

She beckons me to follow, and we move around the side of Blackwood Hall. There's a wide metal rack there, housing a dozen bikes, and she pulls a navy blue one from the stand. There's a black wicker basket attached to the handlebars, the Northcroft crest stamped on the front.

"We can take them?"

"Bike share program." Holland settles on the seat, one foot on the peddle. I pick the bike next to hers, identical except for a faint layer of rust on the chain. "Trust me, you don't want to walk. Campus is too big."

It's been years since I rode a bike, but I settle onto the seat and push off, gravel popping under my tires. Holland follows behind me.

Then my pocket buzzes and I jam on the brakes, setting my feet back on the ground. Pulling my phone out, I see Holland's eyes widen.

"You're supposed to leave that in the dorm."

"Shit. Right." I'm already full of annoyance, which peaks when I see the message from my mother.

Talk some sense into your father. I'm ignoring his calls.

"Uh, I gotta . . . call my mom." I glance down at the timetable. "Crap. That's going to cut into our time."

Holland leans in to peer at the paper, her arm brushing mine. "Damn, you have way more spares than me. Okay, here." She traces a finger over a blank space on the timetable. "I've got bio there, but I have a spare after. Meet me at the gate?"

I brighten. "Yeah, that's perfect."

She gives me a mock stern look. "Don't go in without me."

"Cross my heart."

We split up and I turn right at the fork in the path, which takes me around the building. I checked out the shiny Northcroft map yesterday—the offices are around the back.

I pass the boys' dorms. While Stowe House is made of smooth gray rock on the outside, the walls of this building are weathered with age and the architecture looks different, with its Gothic arches and high, narrow windows.

The map calls it Cooper House, and I remember one of the Gravesmen Holland pointed out: a slender blond boy with a baby face.

Strange, to live in a building named after you. It would make me feel exposed, like I might walk in and find all my innermost thoughts painted on the walls.

The path takes me past the back of the girls' dorms, past the bell tower, and I squeeze the brakes to slow down, gaze drawn up by the dark stone structure, the jagged peaks and scowling gargoyles. The bell inside isn't visible, but I imagine it as a heavy lead thing, weathered and cracked with age.

There are more bikes here, leaned up against the railing, and I leave mine with them.

The office building has to be just as old as Blackwood Hall, with ivy coating the front so heavily that barely any brick peeks through. Inside, it smells faintly of mildew, and floorboards groan under my feet as I make my way past the first office. The door is open a crack, and the bronze sign plate reads VICE PRINCIPAL. Beyond that, the hall divides in two, and there's a spiral staircase on the left side.

Another bronze plaque declares that this leads to the bell tower, and I stare up at the narrow wooden staircase vanishing into the floor above.

I expected the bell to be automated, but this place is hundreds of years old.

I have the sudden image of Dad running up the stairs in his tweed jacket, yanking hard on the rope as the bell rings ponderously overhead.

Ridiculous. Dad hired people to fix the sink and chop firewood. He could hardly be convinced to blister his hands ringing an old lead bell.

Finally, the hallway ends, opening into a wide reception area. It's decorated with a red and gray rug and an assortment of draping vines in colorful pots. As I enter, a girl looks up from the desk at the center.

She's blond-haired and delicate-featured. And familiar. The eleventh-grader Holland talked to earlier. Mia, I think.

The girl smiles politely. "Can I help you?"

"I think so." My gaze wanders over her shoulder. There's a door just behind her, and the metal plate spells out PRINCIPAL BLACKWOOD.

"I wanted to speak to the principal." I keep my expression smooth, trying not to let on how weird it feels to call him that.

Or how nervous I am.

No phone call. Not so much as a fucking text since she died. And now here I am at his door. An ugly reminder of what he is. *Coward. Runaway. Deadbeat.*

Mia gives me an apologetic smile. "He's not available right now. But the vice principal is in." When she gets a blank look in response, she says brightly, "She's down that way."

She gestures back the way I came.

I step closer, leaning my elbows on the surface of the desk. Over the lip of the desk, I can make out the mess. Pens and papers scattered. A file drawer sagging open beside her foot.

"Mia, right?"

Mia looks startled. It's a more genuine expression than her customer service smile. "Yes, how . . . ?"

"You were talking to my roommate this morning. Holland? About a podcast, I think." Leaning over the top of the desk, I can see the door of Dad's office is open a crack.

"Holland Morgan?" Mia's face lights up. "You're her roommate?"

"Yup." Beyond the crack in the door, something stirs.

He's in there.

"Oh my *god*. You're so lucky," she stammers, suddenly bright red. "I applied to be in dorm B last year, but I couldn't get a spot. And yeah, the podcast I was telling her about is 'PNW Murders.' Me and my friend are obsessed."

She says this all in the same breath, practically vibrating in her chair.

True crime. Of course.

I can't let myself listen to that kind of thing. It gives me too many ideas.

Over her left shoulder, the crack in the door goes suddenly dark.

He turned the light out.

That *fucker*.

"It's part of why I volunteer." Mia looks down the hall. "The actual secretary is basically never here, so I get to listen on her computer. I love true crime. Even though, like, obviously the idea of murder keeps me awake at night."

"Me too." I stare at the black slice in the door. The message couldn't be clearer.

He wants me gone.

"It's not as good as 'PNW Murders,' but I started this other new one called 'Crime Spree.'" Mia is still talking. "We were actually thinking about starting our own, you know?"

I drop my gaze to her face, blinking. It takes me too long to realize she means a *podcast*, and she's not debating starting her own killing spree.

Idiot. I tame my expression into blankness. Thankfully Mia isn't watching; she's glancing down the hall again.

She seems almost jumpy, though the enormous coffee mug and the shadows under her eyes might explain that. "Like, an investigation podcast, you know? Maybe investigating Crown and Grave, because the Rook is totally a serial killer. Why else would you wear a mask all the time?"

There's something disturbing about the raw eagerness in her face.

"Right." I lean away, like it might be contagious. If I stay too long, that bright, hectic look on her face might transfer to mine.

Something beside Mia's left elbow catches my eye. A banker's notebook, spread open to the middle, hastily scribbled notes across its surface. It looks like a schedule of some kind. Even though it's upside down, I can make out:

8 p.m.—in office.

9 p.m.—noise?

11 p.m.—out.

". . . he keeps saying we need to pick a theme—"

The click of heels on hardwood makes Mia jerk like she's been stung. She turns, sweeping one arm across the desk, knocking the notebook into the drawer. She slams it shut just as Gorski strides in.

She needn't have worried, because the vice principal zeroes in on me with laser-like intensity.

"Evelyn, perfect timing. Do you have a moment?"

I have several moments. But there's a large part of me that wants to rush out of here. Mainly because Gorski's smile is fixed in place, her eyes hard.

She looks uncomfortably severe.

It reminds me of Mom, which I'm unprepared to deal with.

"I was hoping to see"—I pull myself up short before saying *my father*—"the principal."

"Come this way." Gorksi waves me forward, and I follow her reluctantly down the hallway to the first office I'd passed. It's sparsely furnished, and she settles in behind a wide oak desk. The surface is spotless, entirely clear of books and papers.

"Evelyn . . ."

"Evie." I sink into the chair across from her.

Gorski looks briefly annoyed before smoothing her expression into neutrality. "Excuse me. Evie . . . look, this isn't easy."

A beat, and she looks at me expectantly. When I don't say anything, she lets out a breath and nudges her glasses up. "When your mother called about enrollment, I agreed, assuming your father would approve it." Her lips thin. "I've been notified in no uncertain terms that this isn't the case. You'll forgive me for being blunt, Ms. Laurent, but your father seems eager to see you gone."

My stomach clenches. Suspicions confirmed.

"Your mother, however, is refusing his request to send you home. You can imagine what a difficult spot this puts me in."

I stare at her, my mouth dry. There's no way to respond to this, and the longer I'm silent, the more annoyed she looks. Like we're in a play and I'm the idiot missing all my lines.

"The third option"—the vice principal lowers her voice and smiles tightly—"is that you simply drop out."

A second of silence follows this blunt statement. We stare at one another.

"You can't be serious."

The woman's face twitches almost imperceptibly. She tilts her head, pale brows rising above her glasses. "It's not the best solution, but surely your father—"

"I know why he doesn't want me here." The anger is building now, tangling with the darkness in my core, conjuring images of slamming Gorski's head into the polished surface of her own desk. I shove the thought away, forcing my voice to stay calm. "I remind him of my dead twin."

Gorski flinches. It's one of those things people don't expect you to say out loud. She folds her hands on the desk and then unfolds them, like she doesn't know what to do with herself.

"Evelyn—"

"No."

She hesitates. "No . . . ?"

"I'm not leaving."

The office is silent as Gorski stares at me, nostrils flaring like she smells something unpleasant. "It isn't just you, you know."

"What?"

"It was already bad before . . ." She clears her throat. "Before it happened. I haven't seen him in . . . a month? He emails me." She taps the phone on her desk with one French-tipped nail. "He'd become withdrawn. The last two weeks have been especially bad, of course."

"I don't care." It comes out sharp, and she raises a brow. I hate the way she's staring at me. Like she's trying to decide how damaged I am.

"You know, Evelyn, we all work through grief differently—"

This conversation is over.

I stand, pushing my chair back. The vice principal stares at me, startled. "Ev—"

"Tell him if he wants me gone, he can say it to my face."

CHAPTER TEN

Evie

THAT AFTERNOON, I MAKE MY WAY BACK to the dorm to grab my jacket and find a folded square of paper on my pillow, my name printed neatly across the front. The note inside is short.

See you at the gate.

Leave your phone!

There's no signature, but it must be from Holland. Sliding the note into my pocket, I abandon my phone in the desk drawer before making my way to the front gate.

I'm there before her, and I pause below the tilted tree, with its shriveled black ivy. Leaning my bike against the gate, I stare up at the wall where it droops overtop.

Yesterday, half its trunk had been coated in the strange, inky rot. Now, it's entirely covered.

It doesn't make sense.

I scan the rest of the wall. Maybe it's a different tree. Or . . .

I'd missed seeing the other side. It can't possibly have rotted that much overnight.

Pulling my camera up, I snap a picture of the blackened tree, silhouetted against the forest beyond.

The rest of the trees seem untouched. The towering giants are as green as ever, coated in shaggy moss and sprouting ferns. Aside from the rotting tree, the woods here are beautiful. Lush and deep and filled with velvet shadows.

Just the sight of it makes my insides buzz. I want to drop my book bag and plunge in. Shed my human skin and run through the woods like a wild animal.

And then, suddenly, there's a figure coming out of the forest, emerging from the trees. The school uniform, with its dark blue blazer and tie, is a strange contrast to the wilderness. I stiffen.

When he gets closer, I can make out the fine-boned features. The shock of blond hair.

Jack Aukley pauses at the gate, eyeing me. "Going into the woods, new girl?"

Something warns me not to interact. But my gaze drifts over the jagged shapes of the trees behind him and I find myself saying, "Same as you, I guess."

Aukley's smile grows wider. "Hardly surprising."

I don't know what that means, so I fold my arms over my chest and wait. He steps closer, and the back of my neck prickles. "You know what's out there."

"Animals."

Aukley pauses, brows creased as he scans my face. "Come on, Laurent. We both know that's bullshit."

It feels like he's baiting me, talking nonsense to throw me off. "Tell me what *you* think is out there."

He just grins in reply, and now I'm sure he's taunting me. Playing games.

The darkness roars through me like a train through a tunnel.

It would be easy to reach out and grab his throat. Dig my fingers into the hollow between his collarbones.

I move toward him, heat burning in my chest. And then Holland suddenly looms in front of me and I jerk back, blood thundering in my ears.

Shit. What was I about to do?

Holland grimaces at Aukley. She's got her book bag slung over one shoulder, bike propped against her hip, and she's very noticeably placed herself between us. "Don't you have somewhere to be?"

He gives her a sharp smile and then winks at me before turning to slink away. Back toward the school. I watch him go, eyes narrowed.

"What was that about?"

I start, turning to find Holland holding the gate open.

It takes me a second to reply, to make sure the words come out normal. Not laced with cold rage or some underlying threat. "Nothing. He was just . . . being friendly."

Holland looks critical, but she just shrugs, and we move past the gate and into the trees, shoes crunching over dead leaves on the forest floor.

Holland leads us down a narrow dirt path. It gets cooler as we go in, the air fresh and biting, and I pull my jacket tight around me.

"Alright, spill. What did he say?"

I keep my voice flat. "He was being weird. Kept talking about the forest, implying there's something out there."

"Of course he did." Holland's voice is sharp in the relative quiet. Up ahead, there's the distant trickling of water. "He's talking shit. Ignore him."

I force myself to stay composed, but I'm struggling. I want to turn and seize her by the shoulders. *She's* the one acting weird about the forest. She didn't even want me to come out here.

We walk in silence for a few seconds. The sound of running water gets louder as we come around an outcrop of trees. There's a narrow stream beside the path, clear water trickling over mossy rocks.

"So, Beth . . ."

Holland lets out a sigh, like she knows what I'm asking before I've said it. "She's in therapy. She's working on things."

"Well . . . that's good." I try to keep the scorn out of my voice. Whatever therapy Beth is getting, it isn't working.

"Look, I can't say too much. It's not my story. But there's a reason she acts this way. Something happened last year."

"With the forest," I say. "And curfew."

Holland bites her lip and nods. "She didn't make it in one night. Leta and I were freaking out but we didn't want to rat on her. It was awful."

My eyes go wide. "She was in the forest after curfew?" When Holland nods, I can focus only on one thing. "*Why?* Why the hell would she do that?"

Holland shakes her head, staring down at the path. "She says she got lost."

Silence for a moment. I clear my throat. "But . . . ?"

"I think she was trying to figure out what happened. With Amanda." Her expression is closed off now. She's clearly done talking.

I press my lips together hard, forcing the questions down.

We're passing a huge, hollow-trunked cedar tree now, the top blackened by some past fire. Lightning, if I had to guess.

There's only the sound of us moving through the forest and the faint rustle of wind through heavy branches above us. It's darker the deeper we go, the trees growing closer together, massive trunks and dense foliage blocking out the midafternoon sun.

There's something strange here. A low, constant hum in the branches overhead. It's likely just wind, but the noise sets my heart fluttering. Goosebumps erupt over my skin. The sound makes me feel . . . heightened.

Or maybe it's just the fresh air waking me up.

Holland finally breaks the silence. "Maybe we should go back." She sounds nervous, glancing up at the treetops. "We've gone pretty far."

We have. And there's something pulling me deeper. I'm not sure I can ignore it . . . or that I want to. "Just a little farther. It's so peaceful."

I catch the sideways look she gives me. Like she knows whatever's drawing me forward has nothing to do with peace.

We move around a bend in the path and I stop suddenly. There's a wide stretch of crimson in front of us, the path blanketed in red-speckled leaves.

"Red hemlock." Holland pauses beside me, hands on her hips as she surveys the scene. "It's really rare. Only grows here on the island."

Taking a breath, I pick my way through the leaves, reluctant to let them brush my skin. "They're beautiful, but I'm guessing poisonous."

"Yeah. Just . . . don't eat them." Holland laughs, but she copies me, navigating the field of hemlock carefully.

There's something itching at the back of my mind as we move through the hemlock, a strange feeling . . . almost recognition. Like I've been here before.

I haven't, of course.

We stray off the path to avoid the hemlock, and there's a flash of white against the plants up ahead. My breath catches in my throat, and I dart sideways to grab her arm, tugging her back. Holland lets out a startled squeak and we're suddenly close. I get a whiff of citrus, and her hair tickles my shoulder.

All I can do is point wordlessly.

Bleached white bones stick up from the earth. A skeletal form curled on the ground, tangled through with red ivy and vines. Colors bright against old bones.

It has a slender, delicate skull and a long muzzle.

I creep closer, curiosity drawing me forward like a hook in my gut.

Holland follows, her voice shaky. "What is it?"

"I don't know." We speak in hushed voices, like we might disturb this dead thing. "It's small. Probably a fox or a badger."

Slowly, I edge around to the other side and stop as the face comes into view.

The skull's mouth is open, revealing pointed canines on the top and bottom jaw. They're delicate, only a little longer than my thumbnail, but they're followed by a row of similarly sharp teeth all the way to the back of the jaw.

More startling still are the clusters of pointed red leaves crawling over its face, bursting up from the empty eye sockets.

"A fox." I let out a breath. "Judging by the teeth."

Maybe one of its family is the source of the horrible screams from last night.

We're silent for a moment, standing close enough that I can feel the warmth of Holland's arm through my jacket as the wind tangles my hair around my face. It lifts the scent of pine around us and whistles faintly through the trees.

Then another, louder noise breaks the silence.

A low, brassy gong somewhere in the distance.

It's so unexpected that Holland gasps and stumbles back a step. Her hand is on my sleeve now, and she pulls me with her.

"Is that the bell? I thought it only rang for curfew."

It takes her a second, but she collects herself and turns toward the distant ringing. Back the way we came.

"And for emergencies. Come on, we better go." She starts back down the path, moving quickly, and I hurry to catch up. "The muster point is the front gate."

It takes only a minute—we're moving at such a clip. Up ahead, the stone wall appears through the trees, and I catch flashes of the front gate as we hurry closer.

"What does it mean?" I have to raise my voice over the ponderous tones of the bell.

"I don't know." Holland commits to another burst of speed, heading for the gate. "Whatever it is, it's nothing good."

The muster point is to the left of the front gate, right under the dead tree.

It seems like a bad sign, meeting under its crooked, rotting trunk, and I find myself glancing up at the curling branches every few seconds until Leta and Beth join us.

Leta's face is flushed. "What's happening? Does anyone know?"

I shake my head. Before we can say anything, Mrs. McAllister hurries over. The English teacher's short hair is disheveled, and she brushes strands of silver-gray away from her face.

"Holland, do you mind doing a head count? Hey—*Gorski.*" Mrs. McAllister practically lunges at the vice principal as she walks past, and the two of them step aside and begin a low, hurried conversation.

Holland is already cupping her hands around her mouth, calling over the noise. "Twelfth-grade students, over here."

The sight of her at the gates, her bright hair stirring in the wind, seems to catch the attention of the crowd. It transfixes me, even, pulling me away from the sight of the dying tree. The students drift toward her as she begins her count.

The other grades are sectioning off now, and there are more of us than I thought. With the entire school out like this we fill most of the front lawn. At least three hundred.

It seems to take forever, but eventually the buzz of confusion dies down as head counts are checked and double-checked.

Meanwhile, Gorski is joined by other teachers, who cluster at the front gate. The vice principal's face is flinty, her mouth a tight line as she hands a sheet of paper to Mr. Allen, the PE teacher. Mr. Allen is short and wide. Built like a brick. He's an ex-football player whose volume always seems to be set at a ten. When he glances at the note, he goes pale. "It might not be real. Some kind of joke . . ."

"Some joke," Gorski snaps, and then flinches, glancing around at the students.

"I saw her in the office this morning." Ms. Trembley, the art teacher, has also gone pale. One skinny hand hovers near her mouth like she might feel sick. "She seemed fine."

Mia.

They have to be talking about Mia.

My stomach sinks. She'd been bubbly and overly talkative, but nothing had seemed out of the ordinary, besides Dad being in his office and refusing to see me. "Let's not panic yet." Gorski drops her voice, leaning toward Mrs. McAllister. Whatever she says makes the English teacher shake her head vigorously, expression dark.

Holland finishes the count and her face is grim. She doesn't have to tell us we're missing Mia—the buzz of gossip has already started.

When did you last see her?

I can't even remember.

She was at breakfast.

When Holland returns to our small group, I think about telling her I saw Mia this morning, but I can't bring that attention down on myself. I can't be the last person to have seen her.

Besides, as soon as Holland rejoins us, she's zeroing in on Beth, who's gone so pale she looks like she might pass out. The blond girl keeps darting wide-eyed looks at the forest. Holland loops an arm around her waist and tugs her gently around so she's facing away.

A flare of anger goes through me. I press my thumb hard into the scar on my palm, letting the dull pain pull me out of my own head.

Gorski strides away from the group, still clutching the paper, pausing next to a group of Gravesmen. They speak in low, hurried voices before the Gravesmen break away. Surprisingly, they're heading for the forest, and I watch them vanish between the trees, my pulse picking up. Does that mean the note said she'd be there?

Holland looks faintly startled when Gorski joins her. The vice principal gives her a tight smile and turns to the waiting audience.

"We are concerned about Mia Green. If you know where she is, please seek out one of your teachers and tell them immediately. This is of the utmost urgency."

She pauses, clears her throat, and nods briskly. "Thank you." The second she steps away, the students practically erupt, everyone talking at once.

"What does *that* mean?"

Beth's pale brow is furrowed, watching the vice principal as she heads back to the teachers.

"It means she went into the forest."

Aukley stands behind us, hands in his pockets. He's still wearing that cold smirk.

The sight of him makes the darkness in my core flare. A warning that raises the hair at the back of my neck.

"Why would she do that?" Holland's expression is guarded, and she glances over at Beth—she's scowling at Aukley, two spots of color appearing high on her cheeks.

"She thought she was *investigating*." His voice is loaded with scorn.

He's a dick, but he's not wrong. Mia had been obsessively focused on murder podcasts. Talking about investigating the Rook . . .

But why would investigating Crown and Grave take her into the forest?

"And we all know what happens in the woods. Or . . . some of us do." He focuses on Beth with a sneer.

A pause, and then Beth tugs herself out of Holland's grip and marches away.

"You are such a *dick*, Aukley." Holland glares at him.

He's watching Beth walk away, expression flat. "She knows."

"Knows *what*?" Holland keeps looking at him and then back over her shoulder, like she's torn between drilling him for information and going after Beth.

"She knows what got Mia," Aukley says.

"Nothing *got* her." Leta scoffs. "You're not special. You don't know anything the rest of us don't."

"Crown and Grave knows everything about this place. I was with them for years," Aukley says.

"Yeah," Leta says coolly. "And now you're not."

I'm not listening anymore; I'm concentrating on what he's just said.

She knows what got Mia.

All I can think about are those blood-chilling screams. The way the dark thing inside me reared up at the noise. Like whatever it was, it was calling to me.

The flicker of movement in the fog, just before the shades slammed down. That odd, low hum in the trees . . .

I find my gaze straying toward the forest again, but there's a gentle touch on my shoulder, pulling me out of my thoughts.

"You're not thinking of going in again, are you?" Holland's face is concerned.

I hesitate, and Aukley laughs.

"Of course she is. She wants to know what's out there."

Leta glowers at him. "You're so full of shit."

Aukley ignores her. Focusing on Holland. "Ask your friend what she thinks of the foxes out there, the way they scream."

Holland flinches, her face pale. She glances back at Beth again. Beth, who's on the edge of the campus now, her eyes fixed on the front gate, thin shoulders hunched. Even from here I can tell she's trembling.

"Shit." Holland turns and jabs a finger at Aukley. "Just . . . shut up." Then she wheels around and jogs toward Beth.

Annoyed, I turn to find Aukley grinning at me. When he steps closer, I tense, but Leta slips an arm through mine and tugs me away, scowling at him.

The teachers by the gate are breaking away from their huddle now, and Aukley backs away from us with a pointed "See you in class, Laurent" before vanishing into the crowd.

We make our way slowly back to the dorms, with Holland up ahead, shepherding Beth forward. Beth focuses on the ground as Holland leans in, saying something too low for me to hear.

I find myself navigating the crowd with Leta, her arm still hooked through mine. She's gone quiet now.

"You okay?"

She gives me a tight smile, gaze trailing Holland and Beth. "I'm hoping this won't be a repeat of last year." When I wait, she continues, "Beth went off the deep end."

"What happened?" I try not to sound too eager.

Leta's expression sours. "Her friend committed suicide in the woods, and it was like . . . she blamed the actual forest, you know?"

"Is that why she went out after curfew?"

Leta hesitates. "I mean, she says she got lost, but she also refuses to talk about it. Which I kind of get. People at this school are gossipy bitches." She glances at the crowd flowing around us. "Did you know there was a girl who left last year? Jessica Thorn. You wouldn't believe the shit they made up. Like she drowned herself. Or Aukley followed her into the woods and killed her. So dumb."

"Why would they say that?" It feels like my pulse is beating in my throat. When I glance sideways, I find Aukley and Muldoon keeping pace with us on the other side of the lawn, hands in their pockets, heads bent in conversation.

"She lodged a sexual harassment complaint against him, and Crown and Grave kicked him out. She left after that. Cleared out her dorm and disappeared. Then the rumor mill went to work."

We're passing the final stretch of the lawn, heading around the wide stone steps of Blackwood Hall.

"It's bullshit." Leta's voice is firm, gaze fixed on the dorms in front of us.

Yet, as we walk toward the school, both of us glance back at the high stone walls of Northcroft and the shadowy forest beyond.

CHAPTER ELEVEN

Holland

CLASSES ARE CANCELED for the rest of the day. We get the news in science, and Mr. Hansley looks relieved to be dismissing us. His face is flushed as he scrubs the whiteboard off hurriedly before exiting with the rest of us.

The dorms buzz with gossip, and the twelfth-grade students end up camping out together in the afternoon, scattered about the wide oak common room. Evie, Leta, Beth, and I form one end of a straggling semicircle in front of the fireplace.

Evie is focused on the window, and Leta has her notebook balanced on her knees, but she's not writing, staring at the fireplace with glassy eyes instead. To my left, Beth worries at the tassels of the rug, running her fingers over the fine strands. She's gone quiet, her face pale. It reminds me uncomfortably of the first day she came back from the forest. How she seemed like a shell of herself.

I keep thinking about Aukley's words.

Ask your friend what she thinks about the foxes out there, the way they scream.

He couldn't possibly know the way she reacts. How she climbs into my bed the second they start. How hard she trembles.

And I know she didn't tell him.

He knows something. *Crown and Grave* know something.

Leaning toward her, I elbow Beth gently, relieved when it draws her gaze back. "Hey, come back, okay? Don't drift off on me."

She gives me a weak smile, but there's something terribly haunted behind her eyes. She'll be sleeping in my bed again tonight.

On the other side of me, Leta shifts. "Sun's going down soon." To my surprise, Evie leans over and nudges her, and Leta smiles and touches her knee.

There's some kind of communication going on there, and I feel a stab of jealousy.

They seem suddenly close.

Of course, I've been sticking close to Beth, so it makes sense they'd gravitate toward one another.

Still, Evie doesn't seem totally focused on Leta. She stares out into the distance, or . . . I realize a moment later, out the window. At the forest. There's a strange expression on her face. Bright and hard. Eyes shining.

It makes my stomach drop.

Something in her posture, the way she leans toward the window, reminds me so strongly of Beth that it makes me turn to look at her.

Beth is staring out the window too, but her face is drained of blood, her eyes wide and shadowed. She looks haunted.

It's like seeing a before and after.

I bite the inside of my cheek, stomach churning. At what point does Evie's interest turn to obsession too?

I remember the mutinous look she gave me when I told her we should turn back. She'd wanted to go in deeper.

Like something was drawing her in.

I feel strangely helpless, thinking about Evie sliding into that familiar obsession. This is the forest that took my best friend and hollowed her out before handing her back to me.

This place destroyed Beth. What if it does the same to Evie?

There's a stir from across the room. A few people have crowded up to the window.

"They're searching the woods." Aukley pulls the velvet curtain back.

Most of the students in the room make their way over, pressing up against one another, trying to see through the steadily fogging glass. I push through and peer out, breath catching in my throat.

The trees stretch for miles out past the walls, growing darker near the center. The sun is just beginning to sink down, turning the clouds rust-red, the tree line casting a jagged, sawtooth silhouette.

In the center of the forest, spots of yellow light appear—small enough to be fireflies, bobbing and flickering through gaps in the foliage.

They're out in the deep woods, searching for Mia.

The lights are erratic, scattered for miles. But I count at least fifteen, which means every single Northcroft teacher is out searching the woods right now.

Beth's voice is thin and wavering. "It's almost curfew."

I grip the window frame, leaning to peer through the glass. Like I can see through the thick greenery and find her myself.

The low murmur of conversation starts eventually, and a few of us wander back to our various corners.

I spot a group of people moving across the lawn just past the library. The lamps along the walkway shine down on Patricia Harper and Daniel Prince, heads bowed as they speak to one another. Behind them, Elijah Archer passes Natalie Kim a flashlight, and she turns toward the forest, light shining off her long dark hair.

The Gravesmen are out there too, searching the grounds for Mia.

The only exceptions are Aukley's cronies. I notice with disgust that they're lounging on either side of him while he watches out the window. Occasionally, they'll look at one another, brows raised, and there's something in their expressions that makes my stomach sink.

I'm more certain than ever that Aukley wasn't lying. They know something.

I peer over at Beth.

She's still sitting by the fireplace, posture stiff. Her eyes are fixed on the hearth, and I know it's to keep from looking toward the window.

An hour passes. The shadows along the walls stretch long, throwing half the room into darkness. I can't help staring at the dragons in the wallpaper. Their coiled bodies and horned faces. Mouths gaping, razor-sharp teeth bared.

Another five minutes pass. Then ten.

My gaze strays to the window.

Ten minutes until curfew.

I'm only half listening to the conversations around me, so I hear it before the others do. A distant, static chopping, fading in and out.

Gradually, it grows sharper, and I push myself up and drift over to the window. Behind me, Leta's voice trails off.

As the noise gets louder, the room goes quiet.

It's the whirr of a helicopter. I know the sound before I spot the white and red chopper hovering over the tops of the trees. The buzz of conversation surges again as everyone rushes back to the window.

"Are they getting her out?"

"Maybe they called it in to search."

To my left, Beth is silent and tense. I know she must be thinking the same thing. I don't remember a helicopter coming for Amanda.

"Maybe they found her." Leta's face is pale. "Maybe she's okay."

Nobody answers. Another minute goes by, and the helicopter stays in one spot, just . . . hovering. Which must mean it isn't searching—it's found her.

Evie pushes closer to the window, her elbows on the frame.

The waiting is almost unbearable. The backs of my eyes prickle, like tears are threatening, but I force myself not to blink.

Outside, the helicopter slowly ascends. There's something attached to a thick strap hanging from the base. A bright red stretcher.

Only . . . even from here, it's obvious it's not actually a stretcher. There's no opening anywhere.

It's unquestionably a body bag.

CHAPTER TWELVE

Evie

CLASSES RESUME LIKE NORMAL over the next few days. On the surface, it's as if nothing has happened. But there's an undercurrent of unease, made sharper by the Longfellow poem we're studying in English—"this is the forest primeval." I can't stop thinking about the woods.

The hunt for Mia, seeing those lights bobbing in the dark forest, seems to have tripped something in my brain.

I keep dreaming about walking through the forest, slinking deeper into the shadows between the trunks.

I daydream about the forest through math, fumbling simple equations. And then through art class, where Ms. Trembley is trying to get us to draw still life. In the dining hall, while Holland and Leta chatter about plans for the autumn dance. In the evening, while I'm supposed to be catching up on homework.

Friday morning in the computer lab, we're supposed to be building websites. Instead, I look up the history of Hemlock Woods.

It's a gold mine.

I read about the company that attempted to log the forest. Accounts of rusted-out machinery. Strange accidents. Dead loggers.

Apparently, they got only a few miles in before refusing to go farther. Someone on Reddit says his dad was one of the crew. That he "came back different." Refused to talk about it.

It's fascinating. And frustrating. There's nothing that mentions the wild, howling screams. The flicker I saw in the mist.

Thinking of Holland's warning about filters, I experiment by typing up a post on social media, and find my way blocked by a red error box. *Certain keywords have been blocked.*

What. *Forest? Trees?*

Maybe you can't post about Hemlock Woods. It makes the back of my neck prickle. There's definitely something weird about that.

"What kind of website are you building?"

I go still, a whiff of citrus drifting over me as Holland leans down, her long hair tickling my shoulder.

Silence, as she takes in what I'm looking at. Then she lets out a breath. "Beth was looking at all the same sites, before she went out there."

I swivel in the chair and stare up at her. She's frowning, brow creased.

"Holland . . ."

She sinks down into the chair beside me, darting a look over her shoulder. "Just drop it. Don't go in there."

She can't possibly be telling me to stay out of the woods altogether. "I won't go in after dark."

Holland hesitates. "Look, you have no idea what it was like after she went in. She was . . . catatonic. It's the only word I can think of. Whatever happened, it was bad."

"You really don't know?" I find myself inching toward her. "She didn't say?"

Holland shakes her head. "She didn't talk for nearly a week after. And whenever the noises in the woods start up, she has a breakdown."

She looks like she's going to say something else, but the teacher is coming around, checking each student's progress, and Holland slips away, back to her own computer.

I minimize the webpage, but despite Holland's grim warnings, I can't seem to stop thinking about it.

I think about Mia too. The way she talked about investigating.

I try to remember exactly what she talked about, but mostly what comes back to me is her nervous energy. The way she kept looking down the hall. How she'd reacted when Gorski came in, sweeping the notebook into the bottom drawer.

I keep thinking about that notebook. The scribbled rows of columns. Like she'd been tracking something.

Her words echo in my head. *Like, an investigation podcast . . .*

Maybe that's what she'd been doing when she died. Investigating.

It's the notebook that finally drives me back to my father's office.

I have to know what was in it. If whatever it was drove her into the forest. Or . . . got her killed somehow.

Slipping out when class is over is easy, especially because Holland is hovering beside Beth again, her hand on the small of

Beth's back. She's been babying her since Mia's body was discovered, constantly by her side.

I make my way down the hall, past the bell tower entrance, pausing at Gorski's office. The door is open a crack, and light falls in a shaft onto the hardwood. It's empty. She's probably running around the school trying to do damage control.

At the end of the hall, Mia's desk is also vacant.

Moving fast, I dart around the side and try the bottom drawer. At first it sticks, and I yank harder, praying it isn't locked. Another tug, and the drawer gives a shrieking protest, shuddering open a few inches.

Yes. There it is, a tattered spiral-bound notebook. I snatch it up before pawing through the drawer again. A few loose papers, a pencil that rattles noisily across the bottom. Nothing else.

I keep picturing Mia at this desk . . . her over-bright smile, her eager expression.

Darting a look down the hall, I quickly page through the notebook.

Mia's notes are done in loopy blue pen. A log of some kind. Times and dates noted in the margins.

Most of them say things like *in his office,* or *gone for lunch: 1 p.m.*

I press my lips together tightly, stomach plunging. Mia was tracking my father right before she died.

There's a note scribbled in the margin, heavily underlined: *Out at time of Parker?* I don't know what it means and I flip past it. Then I pause, heart beating hard.

In one corner, there's a scribble of red pen, like she'd jotted it down in a rush.

Called me Evie today. Dementia?

It takes me a minute to recover from that, paging past with trembling fingers.

There's nothing interesting for the next few pages. The same times and actions noted. He takes meetings. He eats lunch. He talks to Gorski.

Then, a few pages in, it begins to change.

Hasn't left office.

Hasn't left.

Skipped lunch.

There are a few notes on Gorski's comings and goings— apparently, she'd attempted to see him and been turned away— and a couple of scribbles to indicate food being dropped off. But that seems to be it. Just the same notes over and over.

Hasn't left office.

Won't talk to anyone.

After that, I find a note that says Aukley had come to see him—that makes me pause. Apparently, he'd been having disciplinary meetings.

So Jack Aukley gets himself in trouble. Big surprise.

Toward the back of the book, I pause, smoothing the pages out. They're more hastily scribbled than usual, and one side is slightly crumpled. But it's dated just last week, and Mia had underlined the words at the top.

Gone into forest?

My heart picks up. Skimming through the rest, the pattern repeats again and again.

Gone into forest.

Gone into forest.

Gone into forest.

The notes seem to unravel from there, the writing getting progressively sloppier until the sprawling script is barely legible. But it's all the same thing.

Gone into forest every day.

Why so obsessed with the forest?

What's out there? Note: Research Hemlock Woods.

It goes on for pages like that, questions scribbled in the margins. Messy notes from Mia's research.

There are the dates Northcroft was built, records about the red hemlock and its poisonous leaves. When I hit the section of notes on the logging company, I get chills.

It's eerily similar to my own research.

In any case, none of it tells me anything except, ironically, that Mia tracking my father's obsession with the forest had resulted in the development of her own. And the forest may have ruined Beth, according to Holland, but it had killed Mia.

What the fuck is out there?

When I turn to face the desk, I catch sight of light flickering beneath my father's door.

My chest tightens.

I didn't come here to confront my father. I came to find answers about Mia. But the door is right there, and suddenly it's all I can think about.

He shouldn't be able to go on pretending the outside world doesn't exist. That *I* don't exist.

I hesitate, slipping Mia's notebook into my bag before moving closer. Something on the carpet catches my eye, a smear of dark mud at the edge of the door. Or . . . it looks like mud until I inch closer and catch the oily black hue under the light.

Stranger still, the door looks wrong. It's not ajar, I realize . . . it's *broken*. The frame is cracked, and a good chunk of the wood is splintered away.

Creeping closer, I can make out splinters on the carpet.

It's like someone kicked the door in. I reach out to rap my knuckles on the edge. "It's Evie. I'm coming in, okay?"

There's no reply, but I'm already pushing my way through the broken door, stepping into the office.

I stop, stunned.

Years ago, Dad sent pictures of his office. It was the epitome of snooty boarding school, full of oak paneling and shelves of thick leather books. Every corner polished and neatly arranged.

It's unrecognizable now. The interior is dim, the curtains pulled over the windows. In the light from the desk lamp, the shelves look like they've been torn apart—books tipped over and spilling off the sides, lying in piles on the floor. There's another smear of black oil marking the ornate rug in front of the fireplace.

Behind the desk, there's a circular mirror on the wall, golden script on the bottom spelling out LOOKIN' GOOD!

Seeing it makes a strange, heavy sadness bloom in my chest. It's amazing he still has it.

I'd made it when I was seven. Grace, one of our first nannies, had helped me stick glittering plastic gems around the edges, tracing the words in her elegant cursive script.

I remember it so well. Mom had had some kind of break, I think. She'd been anxious for months. Fighting with Dad. Plagued by panic attacks.

Dad had decided she needed to get away, and had taken her to the island for spring break.

That week, Grace stayed with us. She'd looked pale and worried, even to my seven-year-old mind, but she'd sat us down and made crafts with us, helping me put together the frame for Dad. And another for Mom's office.

I'd never given it to Mom.

They came back . . . strange. Dad was sad and withdrawn. But it was like Mom had gone cold. Quiet and blank-faced.

There were no more fights after that. In fact, she barely spoke.

Stepping closer, I notice a thin spiderweb of cracks in the center of the mirror, reflecting my pale face in strange, disorienting fragments.

I inch forward, pulse thundering in my ears. "Dad?"

There's no reply. On the other side of the desk, light seeps in through the curtains, and I pause, watching the shadows of branches fall across the floor.

My heart sinks. The light under the door must have been shifting shadows, that's all.

As the light moves, the glitter of broken glass on the desk catches my eye, and I step closer. The desk is just as chaotic as the rest of the room, file folders and papers strewn across the surface. There's a picture frame on its side—I step around the books on the floor and lift the frame up, careful to avoid the glass.

My breath catches. I haven't seen this picture in years.

It's Ada and me, no more than four years old. We're wearing identical flowered dresses, our dark hair done in braids. Mom sits at the center and we're posed on either side, backed by the Christmas tree.

The memory of that Christmas is strangely foggy. Blurred

and grainy, like an old home movie that doesn't quite hold up over time.

It doesn't match reality.

The way Ada and I are reaching over Mom's shoulders—like we'd insisted on holding hands for the picture, both of us smiling brightly—it simply doesn't line up with the Ada I know. The true version of my dead twin.

The real Ada is the one who spread rumors about me through middle school. The one who gave herself a black eye so she could tell our parents I'd hit her. The one who'd tortured me every way she could think of.

I find myself pressing my thumb hard into the scar on my palm, biting the inside of my cheek.

And then I look harder at the picture, and it makes even less sense. There's no sign of my actual mother there. The woman in the photo looks like her, sure, but she's smiling. Her eyes are warm and sparkling, arms wrapped around us.

My mother is the woman who talked to the nannies about "the twins," instead of addressing us. *Make sure the twins are in bed when I get back* and *have the twins ready for seven.*

She's the one who pretended we weren't there, to the point I used to step directly into her path, just so she'd look at me.

This is like looking at a different person.

I put the frame down so quickly it overbalances, toppling onto the desk with a muffled thud. The cardboard backing slides out and I curse under my breath.

Picking the frame up, I go to put the picture back and pause. There's a second slip of glossy paper beneath the backing. When I slide it out, it takes me a minute to figure out what I'm looking at.

It's old and faded, slightly creased. But unmistakably, an ultrasound. There's a single white silhouette in the center and I can make out the side profile. Nose, lips, chin. Underneath, in elegant looping handwriting, is IT'S A GIRL!

It's my mother's handwriting, but I spend a few seconds staring at the heart over the letter *i* and the smiley-face doodle at the end of the sentence.

When has Mom ever doodled a heart in her life?

It takes another few seconds for the strangeness of this to sink in.

It's a girl. *One* girl.

What the hell?

I end up turning the ultrasound this way and that, like there will be a secret, hidden twin revealed if I angle it a certain way.

This doesn't make sense.

There are all kinds of things going through my head now. A secret older sister. A miscarriage we were never told about . . . but when I turn the photo over, it reveals the date. It's definitely me or Ada. Maybe the other twin is behind?

But . . . *it's a girl.*

A shuffle from behind. I jerk around, dropping the photo.

There's a tall, slender shadow peeling away from the side of the bookcase. The sight sends shock rippling through me, and I stumble back, striking my hip on the desk.

My father is almost unrecognizable.

Shrunken is the first word that comes to mind. He's always been tall and thin, but this is another level. His shoulders are bowed, lost in his overlarge suit. His face is sallow and thin, and there are bruise-like circles under his eyes.

"Dad?"

When I meet his eyes, they're wide and glassy, so dark they're almost black. Shock hits me like ice water, spreading through my chest. *Not Dad*, something inside me insists.

"You." His voice is a hoarse whisper.

My gaze drops down to his feet. His shoes are caked in dirt, and he's leaving wide, muddy tracks on the carpet.

His expression contorts into something almost like pain, and he croaks out, "Ada?"

I snap upright. For a second, we just stare at one another. Slowly, I shake my head, heart drumming against my rib cage.

He blinks, tilts his head to one side, movements jerky and stiff.

Inside, the darkness bursts to life, setting my insides ablaze, my skin erupting with goosebumps. It's a lizard-brain reaction. My self-preservation instincts telling me to run.

But this is my *father*.

"Dad, it's me. It's Evie." Maybe this is why he won't see anyone. Is he having some kind of mental break?

He recoils suddenly, expression shuttering. "You need to leave."

"What? You can't—"

"Get *out*." He lunges, face twisted in rage, and I shriek, lurching back, out the doorway. Grasping the doorknob with shaking hands, I slam it shut. There's a solid thud and a splintering crunch as the door hits the broken frame.

I find myself standing on the other side, my entire body trembling.

There's nothing coming from my father's office. The only sound is my ragged breathing and the furious drumming of my own heartbeat in my ears.

I don't know what that was. *Who* that was.

From beyond the broken door comes a sudden soft thumping of footsteps. He's pacing.

I back away slowly, keeping an eye on the door.

The sliver of light at the bottom wavers every time he stalks past.

Unease follows me, even as I move down the hall and out onto the steps, the sunlit quad stretching out in front of me.

It looks like the most normal day outside. Students grouped under the oaks at the center, biking or walking along the pathways.

But as I duck into the covered walkway and make my way toward Blackwood Hall, all I can think about is my father's gaunt face. The flat, black gaze he'd turned on me. Like he didn't recognize me.

It occurs to me, as I pass through the wide hallway inside, that there's something very wrong with this place, and whatever it is, it seems to have dug its claws into my father.

CHAPTER THIRTEEN

Holland

THE CLASSROOM IS ONLY HALF FULL when Beth and I arrive, settling in at the back. Low chatter and the scrape of chairs against wooden floorboards echo around us.

Almost as soon as we sit, Beth sucks in a breath. I spot it a second later. Someone has left a handful of wildflowers on Mia's old desk, their colorful purple petals a bright contrast to the scratched surface.

It's beautiful, a memorial of sorts. But beside me, Beth is already squirming in her seat, eyes welling with tears.

When I reach over and place a hand on her arm, she gives me a watery smile.

A wave of frustration goes through me. I don't know how to comfort someone who won't talk to me. How can I be there for her if she won't explain what happened?

And, more than that, how can I keep it from happening again?

When my attention isn't on Beth, it's on Evie lately. Watching her as she watches the forest.

I notice how she stares into space at dinner, or tracks the shutters as they go down at night. Like she's determined to keep her eyes on the forest until the last second.

In fact, she's staring now, apparently only half listening as Leta talks to her. She's nodding along, gaze fixed on the window.

It's a horrible reminder of how Beth behaved. Like seeing it play out all over again.

What if Evie is next? What if the forest destroys her like it destroyed Beth, and I can't stop it because I don't know what's going on?

Stomach roiling, I turn to Beth. She frowns at me. Like she can already tell what's coming. "I know I've asked before, but with Mia—"

"Holland, don't."

Her voice is reproachful, and the tone sets my teeth on edge. How can she climb into my bed at night, expect me to comfort her while she spirals, and then get mad at me for this?

"I can't help you if you don't tell me."

"I'm not going to talk about this." Her expression is closed off. She turns to face forward, like the conversation is over.

Our argument has caught Evie and Leta's attention. They're both leaning forward and Leta raises a brow at me just as another wave of students comes in, their chatter and laughter drowning out anything she might say.

We watch as the Gravesmen filter in. They attract even more attention than usual, since the tap is coming up. Three full weeks, all with the tantalizing promise of a chance at membership.

Muldoon and Cooper shuffle in last, the latter holding up his English textbook, making a rude gesture behind it at one of the girls, which is followed by muffled laughter.

They settle at the back and it doesn't take them long to spot the flowers on Mia's desk. Muldoon and Cooper exchange a look, and Cooper snorts, shaking his head.

I don't know what it means, but there's so much *knowing* in their expressions. It lights a slow-burning fire in my stomach.

Simmering rage. And with it, something starts to take shape in my mind.

A thought. An idea fueled by anger and desperation.

It's a little crazy, but it might be the only way to find out what's in the forest. To keep Evie from throwing herself headlong into the jaws of whatever got Beth.

I have to get into the club.

Mrs. McAllister clears her throat pointedly, which yanks me out of my speculations. She's reaching for the English textbook just as Stowe strides in.

It feels almost like fate. Like my thoughts summoned him. His appearance makes the final piece click into place, and I know suddenly, without a doubt . . . *he's it.* My ticket into Crown and Grave.

He's unhurried, despite being obviously late. Wearing a black, military-style jacket with brass buttons and a high collar. His curls are wild and there's a purple bruise blooming under one eye. Somehow it only serves to increase his air of disheveled rock-star-dom.

He slouches his way through the desks, hardly seeming to notice the stares or the way Mrs. McAllister watches him, hands on her hips. He passes several empty spots, then meets my eyes with his black-lined gaze as he sinks into the seat beside me.

Stowe grins and I can't help staring at his lips. At the thing that is most definitely a joint dangling from the side of his mouth. It's amazing how ballsy he is.

"Mr. Stowe." Mrs. McAllister's voice is sharp, her face full of disbelief. "Do you mind?"

He tears his gaze away from me. "Hmm?"

"Do you *mind*?" She jabs a finger at him. "We do not bring cigarettes into the classroom."

"It's not a cigarette."

There's a general, astonished murmur from the rest of the class and a few low snickers.

"Put it away," she says.

For a second, he only stares at her, and I think he's about to get kicked out. Then he sighs and plucks the joint out of his mouth, tucking it into his pocket, spreading his hands with a flourish. Like he's done a magic trick. "Gone."

Mrs. McAllister narrows her eyes, and the two of them stare at one another.

From the back, someone lets out a low, musical whistle. The gunslinger standoff song from every cowboy movie.

More snickering, and Mrs. McAllister finally shakes her head, letting out a long-suffering sigh before turning back to the whiteboard.

"I'm going to pretend I didn't see that, Mr. Stowe. Not because you deserve leniency, but because it is too early for your bullshit."

Laughter greets this, and then settles as Mrs. McAllister begins scribbling on the board, the marker squeaking.

Beside me, Stowe turns in his seat, shooting me a wide grin. I shake my head and return the smile, brows raised. Like I can't believe he's so bold. *Wow, such a rebel.*

Class goes by in a blur. I'm distracted by Stowe's presence in my periphery, the new plan taking shape in my head.

A few minutes before the bell rings, I lean back in my chair and pull out my notebook, scribbling a few quick lines, pretending I don't notice him watching.

"Replying to fan mail, sugar?"

Stowe's voice is suddenly right in my ear and I jerk upright. He's practically leaning over my shoulder.

I press the notebook to my chest, blinking up at him. He definitely saw the first few lines. "Uh. My dad. And no, he's not a fan."

He's still grinning. "Not nearly as fun."

I wrinkle my nose at him. "You know, most people consider reading over a shoulder kinda rude?" It's half flirty, and Stowe grins and leans in even closer.

"Politeness doesn't get you anywhere, does it?" He winks.

It's another line from *The Wizards.*

"You been rewatching old episodes or something?"

His grin only grows wider. "I admit to nothing."

I'm thinking of my next reply when I catch sight of Evie just beyond Stowe. Her gaze is fixed on him with startling intensity, gray eyes narrow. It's unexpected and it makes excitement bloom in my stomach.

I'm used to seeing that look on Beth. But this is Evie, and it feels strangely thrilling.

Stowe leans back against my desk, drawing my attention again. He's still staring at my notebook. "I will say, though, my father is a colossal prick, so I spent most of my childhood raised by television."

The forthrightness catches me off guard. Ewan Stowe has always been a huge flirt, but this is new.

I regroup quickly. It's the perfect segue.

"I get that." I press my lips together hard, smiling. "Welcome to the 'I hate my dad' club. We meet on Tuesdays."

It's an interpretation of the truth. In my experience, you have to care about something to really hate it.

It seems to work, though, because Stowe's charming grin flickers, replaced by a real, genuine smile. It makes his face even more handsome. I slide the letter back into my pocket, feeling a swell of triumph.

There are a few things I've put together by now. How Stowe has a penchant for redheads. That he's dated several, and the last one is in rehab now. That he drinks almost nonstop and clearly has a drug problem . . .

But there was one thing I was taking a gamble on. One thing that was only ever rumors. And now I know it's true.

Ewan Stowe seems to have a deep and profound hatred for his father.

This is going to be almost too easy.

CHAPTER FOURTEEN

Evie

SATURDAY MORNING, I'M UP BEFORE DAWN. Throwing on a pair of sweatpants to combat the chill, I pace the common room, my shadow rippling tall and thin over the wallpaper in the soft orange of the lamps.

The last couple mornings I've come in early to take pictures of the sun rising over the forest. But I'm too distracted right now.

Mom's latest text message has me fuming.

I'd messaged her about Dad. His weird behavior. The way he'd called me Ada. He's clearly having some kind of break with reality.

I'd almost asked about the ultrasound. Had typed and deleted what felt like a hundred questions.

And then I'd chickened out and said nothing.

Mom hadn't replied until the morning anyway, and then only with *Tell him to keep it together. He'll be fine.*

I read it again, in her voice, flat and emotionless, then jam my phone back into my pocket.

He's not fine. Nothing about this place is fine.

Missing students. Curfews. Mutant hemlock. Mia's notebook, still in my book bag back at the dorm, full of strange, cryptic notes.

There's something seriously fucking wrong with this place.

Still, I'm surprised Mom answered at all. She finally got what she wanted: all of us gone.

She'd been trying for the last few months.

The fighting had started again right after our birthday. After the hiking "incident," there'd been heated discussions in the kitchen. Whispered arguments in the hallways. I'd come around the corner one morning and heard Mom hiss, *Take her with you*, and Dad reply, bizarrely, *We don't know which one*.

I don't know what it meant, but Mom had laughed—a cold, sharp sound—and stomped away. Dad had gone back to the school after that. Washed his hands of all of us.

She must be thrilled now. Husband *and* both twins gone.

No more knockdown, drag-out fights. No more screaming.

I can imagine her wandering around the empty house, savoring the silence.

A sudden metallic rattling makes me jerk around, heart in my throat. But it's only the shutters beginning their slow upward crawl. I watch, fixated on the forest as it's revealed an inch at a time, the shapes of treetops silhouetted against the murky orange of predawn.

It draws me forward. I find myself almost pressed against the window, elbows on the sill. It's only then I notice the note there. The small, folded square with Holland's writing on it.

Inside, it says only *This afternoon. Don't go in without me.*

It makes me blush. So she knows I've been here the last couple mornings.

Don't go in without me.

Out the window, the heart of the forest is black. I can't make out individual trunks or branches except along the closest row. I pull up my camera, capturing the fire-blackened top of the lightning-struck tree. It's flanked on either side by a crooked pine and a wide arbutus.

Frowning, I trail my lens over them. There's something off. The spaces between them are different. Wider.

Maybe it's the angle. I must have been at the other window yesterday.

Still, something about that intrigues me. I want to go out into the woods and see them up close.

That afternoon, I meet Holland by the front doors, moving down Blackwood Hall's double staircase. At the bottom, our debate on biking versus walking is interrupted as Beth rushes after us.

I wait impatiently while they talk in low tones, too quiet for me to hear what's being said. It sounds tense, though.

After a second, I creep closer and overhear the end of Holland's sentence, in exasperated tones: "if you won't *tell* me." Then she glances back at me, brows furrowed. Beth leans around her to glare at me.

"Go in alone."

I stare at her.

When Holland starts to turn, Beth grabs her wrist. "Just wait."

Holland tears out of her grip. "Let's go, Evie."

As we move for the forest, Beth shouts after us. "Don't drag her down with you."

Anger stabs at my chest and I start to turn, but Holland lets out a low, annoyed growl and reaches for my hand, yanking me forward. I let her, feeling a surge of dark excitement at the firm grip she has on me.

At last, we're past the stone wall, plunging into the cool spaces between massive tree trunks. I'm in the lead this time, somehow confident I know where I'm going.

On the path, I know we're both thinking about the fox skeleton. There's something intriguing about it. Something haunting.

I want to take pictures.

There's a faint mist hanging between the trees, blurring the forest around us as we move deeper.

It reminds me of the dream. Of the huge, hulking black tree.

Walking deeper feels right, like I'm following a path I've taken before. The farther we go, the more I feel that tugging in my gut. Something tangible drawing me forward.

I'm not sure I could stop if I wanted to.

Holland trails behind me, silent. Her brow is furrowed, like she's thinking about the fight she had with Beth.

I don't ask.

Pulling up my camera, I take a few shots of the branches overhead and then shift to the fog hanging over the forest floor. I pause. There's something strange about the nearest tree. Its crooked trunk is coated with moss, gnarled roots nearly as thick as my wrist. There are black streaks along the knotted wood, oozing down in thick, oily tracks.

I inch closer, throat tight, and snap a picture. Behind my lens, the strange oil slick shimmers.

"Gross, what is that?" Holland crowds up behind me.

"I don't know. It looks rotten. Like the tree by the gate, you know?" I frown at it. "I don't remember seeing it last time."

"Maybe it's new."

I nod, but unease creeps through me. There's too much of the strange black slick. It doesn't look like something that just started.

We walk on, coming to the red hemlock spread out over the mossy ground. It's beautiful, but if anything, it confuses me.

"Is there . . . less?"

"What?"

I nod at the hemlock, the clumps of red leaves scattered over the roots of the trees. "I could have sworn there was more last time."

Holland frowns, glancing around. "Maybe we're walking at a different angle."

It would make sense. Only . . . we both know there's only one path, and we haven't left it.

We go deeper into the woods. Another few feet should take us to the fox skeleton. But as we move down the trail, there's no sign of it.

We press on, until we pass the huge, hollowed-out form of the lightning-struck tree, with its ragged black top.

We've passed it.

I pause, turning to sweep the forest floor again, frowning. There's nothing there. The fox skeleton is gone.

Predators. Something must have dragged it away.

Though . . . why would anything want *just* bones? There hadn't been any meat left on the skeleton.

We wander forward, Holland still watching the trees while I hunt for any sign of bleached white bones.

Nothing. Just more towering forest.

At last, we come to the crest of a gentle hill, and the feeling in the pit of my stomach intensifies so quickly my breath catches. I barrel over the top of the slope and then stumble to a halt, breathing hard.

There. A clearing in the middle of the trees. Just looking at it, the feeling in my stomach eases off.

This is it.

It's at least twenty feet across, the ground covered in a blanket of crimson hemlock. There's a tangle of branches turning to mulch on one side, and ferns and hemlock leaves are sprouting from the mossy surface of a wide, fallen trunk.

In the center, a huge black walnut tree grows out of the thickest batch of hemlock. Its dark, oily bark is a startling contrast to the brilliant red leaves. Its heavy roots are so thick, its boughs draping down so dramatically, that it looks as though it's growing in reverse. Like you could look at it from either direction and not be able to tell crown from roots.

It's so familiar it sends a shockwave through me. I take a step back.

It's the tree from my dreams.

I'd buried Ada's body between those roots over and over. I'd laid down at its base, staring up at those same heavy branches.

This isn't possible.

Unless . . . maybe I'm remembering wrong. Maybe Dad *did* take me to this island.

How else would my subconscious know about it?

128

My camera is in my hands before I can even think about it—like if I can document it, I can prove to myself I'm not crazy. That I really do dream about this place.

Holland walks into the clearing, pressing her palm to the trunk experimentally.

It sends a prickle of warning through me but I stamp it out, concentrating on her. The way the wind stirs her hair around her face. She pulls back, expression twisting with disgust. "Gross, it's sticky."

I step closer, fascinated by the glistening black that coats the surface of the tree. It almost looks like tar, or ink . . .

"Don't touch it." Holland rubs her hand on her pants, grimacing.

I hunker close to the roots, focusing on the black goo that coats the surface, taking a series of close-ups before stepping back to gaze up into the wide spread of branches.

It makes something electric go through me, like the pulling in my guts has transformed into something else. Something that feels *good* . . . alive and vibrant.

Looking at it, I know I'm not imagining things. This is what was calling me. The tree drew me into the forest.

Now I just have to find out why.

CHAPTER FIFTEEN

Holland

THE MORE EVIE FOCUSES on the clearing, taking picture after picture, the more unease grows inside me. It's the intensity in her expression.

Warning bells go off in the back of my mind—she's sliding into this obsession with open arms.

But maybe it doesn't have to be this way. Maybe *I* want to be that obsession.

I don't know if it's selfishness that drives me, the need to have her look at *me* that way. Or if it's about distracting her. Either way, I don't think about it when I step in front of the camera.

She glances up, startled, and I flash her a coy smile. Wordlessly, I tilt my head to one side and touch my chin, giving her my best photo shoot smile.

To my relief, Evie laughs.

"I never thought I'd get a photo shoot with Holland Morgan."

Her tone is teasing, and it makes me flush to the tips of my ears. I pretend I'm not. Like I'm completely cool and unflustered. A reflex from so many photo shoots for *The Wizards*.

I put on a show for Evie, like I'm at a promo shoot, like I'm in front of a studio. The whole time, all I can do is focus on her face. On the way she looks at me.

I can *feel* myself slipping. Sliding into my own obsession.

I should turn and bolt into the woods. Run, before she rips my heart out. Before she destroys me like Ada did.

At the very least, I should tell her what Ada and I really were.

If I tell her, this is over.

I almost say it. Almost open my mouth and end everything.

And then she looks at me with those cool gray eyes and says, "You're perfect," and my resolve shatters.

You're perfect.

She means the position. The photos. But I can't stop myself from flushing.

I keep catching her glancing sideways at me as she angles the camera, and I wonder if she's just setting up the shot or . . . it's more than that.

"This is a good one." She's down on one knee on the forest floor, lens tilted up at me. "Wait a sec."

Evie darts forward. I go still as she stretches up and takes a handful of my hair. Her fingers brush the back of my neck, and I repress a shiver as she pulls my hair gently over my shoulder, stepping back to survey me.

"Amazing."

I know she's looking at me like a photographer. I'm the one behind the lens, that's all.

Still, my skin is covered in goosebumps. There's something in Evie's face when she looks up at me. For a moment, I can pretend something other than a photo shoot has brought Evie to her knees before me.

The thought is so foolish it makes my face warm with silent embarrassment.

Light streams through the branches overhead, playing across Evie's face as she shifts from one position to another, lining up shots from different angles. The oversize green cardigan falls off one slender shoulder as she leans sideways.

The wind rustles the branches. It stirs the waves of her hair, dragging dark strands across her face.

This immersed in the shoot, she doesn't seem to realize she's let her guard down. That I can see naked emotion on her face. The furious concentration as she lines up a shot just right, her frown as she glances at the viewfinder and doesn't like it. The way her face lights up when she does.

Watching her feels like observing something intimate.

She straightens, glancing down at her camera. Whatever she sees on the screen makes her cheeks color.

My pulse quickens. "What?"

CHAPTER SIXTEEN

Evie

WHEN I SWIPE THROUGH THE PICTURES, there's one that catches my eye.

It's a close-up. Holland under the tree, the late-afternoon sunlight filtering through the branches, crowning her copper hair in glittering light.

It's her pose that makes my breath catch. It's undirected, natural, like I caught her in a moment she wasn't expecting.

In the picture, one arm is crossed over her stomach, almost self-consciously, and she has her thumb pressed against her lower lip. Her eyes, heavy lidded and a little dreamy, are fixed on the camera.

All of my photographs get a title, and this one pops into my head immediately.

Bedroom Eyes.

My pulse quickens, but when she asks what it is, I keep my voice casual. "Just . . . your expression . . ."

It's hungry. I don't say it, just turn to look at her. Holland's eyes are wide as she stares down at the picture. She looks remarkably composed, but when she reaches up to wind a strand of hair around her finger, I catch sight of how red the tip of her ear is.

It could be the cold.

I hope it isn't.

Holland clears her throat. "You're a good photographer."

"It's not just that." I find myself fidgeting, rolling the button of my cardigan between finger and thumb. "What were you thinking when I took this? Do you remember?"

It's bold, but I dare myself to look into her eyes, and Holland does the same. Her ears might be red, but when she leans toward me, her gaze is intense, like she's drinking in the sight of me. A pang goes through my chest.

"You really want to know?"

"I—yes."

I'm trying to stay calm. Hoping she'll say . . . I'm not sure what I hope she'll say.

"I was looking at you," she says slowly. "And I was wondering . . . what it would be like to kiss you."

My lips part. For a moment, nothing comes out.

The silence is a second too long. Holland's gaze darts away, and I let out a breath. "I think you could find out."

God. I'm an idiot. I can feel my face going hot. There's no way—

She moves so suddenly it startles me. Reaching out, sliding a hand around the back of my neck.

Then she's kissing me. And it's somehow both fierce and soft. *God, her lips are so soft.* She tastes like strawberries, and she smells *so damn good*—like shampoo and clean laundry—and I'm half falling, back pressed into the tree. Our bodies are flush against one another, a million little points of contact sending an electric shiver through me.

Holland kisses me until I'm dizzy and breathless. And I kiss her back, and all I want is more of this. More of her.

There's something deliciously feral about kissing Holland in the middle of the woods, my back pressed into the rough bark of the tree, her hands in my hair.

And then, somewhere out in the trees, there's the heavy sound of a branch breaking.

Holland jerks back, leaving me off-balance.

We both go silent, listening.

My heart pounds hard, ears ringing in the silence. Every part of my body is still tingling. It feels like whiplash, going from pleasure to fear. Like being doused in cold water.

The woods are silent now.

A second later, I realize how much the light has faded. The sun is halfway behind the tree line. There's a strange, burnt-orange quality to the forest now, the spaces between the trees filled with shadow.

How long have we been out here?

We went in the afternoon. How is the sun already setting?

The trees seem impossibly tall, blocking out the last vestiges of fading light. In the dim surroundings, the fallen tree, with its tangle of branches, looks like some primeval creature with too many limbs. A hulking shape near the edge of the woods.

The back of my neck prickles.

The shadows between the trees seem strange, too deep. Like there's something there.

Overhead, the wind picks up, hissing through the branches. Only . . . there's no wind on my face. Nothing stirs my hair.

And the sound is almost like whispering . . . like distant voices I can't quite make out.

And then . . . *there*. There it is again, that strange low hum.

It starts somewhere overhead and spreads, like it's jumping from one treetop to the next. It seems to cancel out the other noises. There's no buzz of insects. No birdsong.

Another crackling, this time somewhere to my left. We both jump, and I peer at the edges of the forest.

There's nothing, but I feel electric. Alive.

The thing inside me urges me to hurtle headfirst into the underbrush. Go deeper into the darkness.

When Holland speaks, her voice trembles.

"We should go. We went too far."

I can't remember how far we walked. Or how long we've been under this tree. Holland glances back toward the school, brow creased.

There's no sign of the towering walls.

I inch closer, my arm pressing against hers. She's shivering all over now.

Another sound, a thin crackling near us, and we both wheel around. Moving in front of Holland, I scan the underbrush. My heart is hammering so hard I have to strain to hear anything.

The darkness at my core flickers. A strange, muted excitement.

Some part of me wants a fight.

I don't know why I do it—there's nothing there—but I raise my camera and take a picture of the shadowed tree line.

"We should go." Holland tilts her wrist, and her watch lights up, the screen casting a blue glow onto her face. "I'm not sure what time—*shit*."

She looks so horrified it freezes the breath in my chest. "What—?"

A distant, brassy clanging interrupts me.

The fucking warning bell. Curfew.

Shit.

"Go. *Run*." Holland wrenches me around, shoving me forward. I stumble, and then we're both flat-out sprinting through the trees.

My bag bumps on my hip. The light from Holland's watch makes crazy arcs on the ground. We nearly trip over roots and rocks in the path. Holland wipes out, but she's up again in an instant. Launching to her feet with a curt, "*Go.*"

We could both be expelled. I know that.

Still, part of me thrills at this.

The first night, I'd pictured it—hurtling through the darkened forest, feet kicking up dirt, heart singing in my chest.

The wind slaps at my face and tugs my hair back. I'm running headlong into it, towering trees flying by. The *thing* inside me swells, filling my body with fierce, burning delight.

In that moment, a sudden, strange thought occurs.

The forest wants me here. I belong.

We're through the gates now. Across the lawn. Holland, with her long legs, is a pace or two ahead of me. But I'm gaining fast, watching her red hair stream behind her, the way her slender body moves in full flight. Tipped forward, ever pushing to go *faster, faster, faster.*

And then we're at the front steps of Stowe House, our feet pounding on the stones. At the top, Holland tries to wrench the door open, struggling with the heavy iron handle. I twist around, breathing hard, peering back toward the forest.

The trees are crooked, towering giants in the fading light, branches silhouetted by the orange wash of the setting sun. From the top of the step, I can see the forest stretching out beyond the wall for miles—a rolling hill of distant treetops, completely blocking the ocean on the other side.

There's something inviting about the velvet darkness. The green-tinged shadows stretch out to blend with creeping fog. For a moment, it seems like something within is stirring. I squint, pulse picking up. Something takes shape through the mist . . . a long, thin shape slinking close to the ground.

What *is* that?

"Evie. *Evie!*"

Holland says my name with the sharpness of someone repeating themselves. She grabs my sleeve, and we stagger through the door and into the foyer just as a long, echoing tone comes from somewhere above.

We've made it. But just barely.

And what the hell did I see back there?

"Up to the rooms." She speaks loudly over the sonorous tone, her voice brittle, about to break. "*Now.*"

We find Leta sitting by the fireplace, laptop perched on her knees, pen tapping against her lower lip. She seems too distracted by her writing to notice our disheveled state, and Holland doesn't say anything about our close call, so I follow suit. Thankfully Beth is in the shower, so we don't have to field awkward questions.

I sink down beside Leta. Already, the bright insides of Northcroft are making me rethink what we heard out there. And what I saw—the shadow slinking along the ground.

A fox, maybe.

Calmer now, I start to flip through my photos, which prompts both girls to lean in on either side of me. Holland is close enough that I catch the sweet scent of her skin and clothes.

The thing inside me roars to life in response. I want to turn and grab her, press my mouth to hers.

"You guys did a full photo shoot, huh?" Leta says.

"We were just goofing around." Holland sounds slightly embarrassed. "Then it . . . evolved."

"Meaning it turned into a full-on *Vogue* shoot," I say, and she grins.

Flicking through the photos, I pause on the last one. The picture I'd snapped back in the clearing.

It's just a blanket of fog and the dim silhouettes of tree trunks.

But something near the center catches my eye: a smudgy, charcoal shape against the fog. It seems like part of a trunk at first, until I look more closely. The shape doesn't look right. It's almost . . . hunched.

A shadow, maybe . . . but from what?

I can almost make out the fuzzy shape of a head and shoulder. Like someone crouching behind the tree, half out of sight.

My chest tightens. The shadow at the edge of the forest could have been a fox. But this . . .

"Too dark, I guess."

I start, finding Leta staring over my shoulder. "Uh, yeah. I guess."

I wonder if I'm seeing things. Am I overly paranoid? And then Holland leans in, shoulder brushing mine. She taps one fingernail on the viewing screen, right over the shadow.

"Is that part of the tree?"

"I don't know. It almost looks . . ." I hesitate, and she fills the thought in.

"Like some creeper crawling around the forest floor?"

She laughs, but the hairs on the back of my neck prickle.

There's a shuffle and a thump, and I look up to find Beth in the bathroom doorframe, a towel wrapped around her, blond hair hanging in wet strings around her face. She glares at us.

"So not only did you go in, you were still there when it got dark? Holland, seriously . . ."

Holland shrugs. "It was fine."

Beth stomps over. I expect her to demand to see the photo, but she stops just short of us and very deliberately doesn't look down at it.

She looks . . . bad. Her face has gone pale, two blotches of red high on her cheeks. "You can't keep dragging her in with you."

Heat surges through me. I want to vault off the couch. Drive the heel of my hand into her nose. Send her head snapping back.

Instead, I sit very still and turn the camera around. Hold it up so she can see the picture. Beth's gaze drops down instinctively.

She reacts like she's been stung, jerking back with a yelp, one hand clapped to her chest.

Leta and Holland both stare at her, stunned, but I can feel the triumph on my face.

Beth turns on me, eyes wide. "What the fuck is *wrong* with you?"

Holland shoots up off the couch. "*Beth—*"

She doesn't get to finish because Beth whirls around and stomps away, vanishing behind her privacy curtain.

There's silence for a moment and Leta glances over at me, brows raised. Obviously, she thinks Beth overreacted, but she says only, "Looks like part of the tree to me. Like it's casting a weird shadow."

"Yeah, probably." Holland shrugs. "It's just a shadow." There's a tremor in her voice, though, and she keeps glancing at the photo.

I know she remembers the noises in the woods. The way it felt like something was there.

I can't help thinking about Aukley's words . . . that *something* out there got Mia.

After a second, Holland stalks over to Beth's bed, vanishing behind the privacy screen. Low murmurs of conversation drift from behind the curtain, and I clench my teeth, trying to ignore it.

Even with irritation pulsing through me, I can't look away from the picture.

It triggers something in my brain, some indistinct feeling of *wrongness*.

It makes me think of the way the forest felt. Familiar, yet changed. Like things had somehow shifted.

The hemlock. The fox skeleton.

I stare at the dark spaces between the tree trunks, undeniably empty. And then at the figure hunched at the base of the tree.

I know a shadow when I see one, and this isn't it.

CHAPTER SEVENTEEN

Evie

THE NEXT DAY, I set out to get answers.

I try the notebook first. Holland is in class, so Leta and I retreat to the forest, poring over its pages. We talk about the podcasts and try to figure out which days Mia was tracking. Why she was tracking anything at all. Why she went missing.

When Leta has to leave for class, I resort to more obvious means.

It's not until he's halfway across the front lawn that Jack Aukley realizes I'm following him. *Embarrassing.*

Just before the front steps, he whirls around, pulling headphones out of his ears. I'm trailing a few feet behind him, kicking my feet in the wet grass.

I give him my most sharklike smile. To my intense pleasure, he looks off-balance for a second, then shoves his headphones into his pocket, giving me his classic smirk.

"Can I help you, darling?"

"Depends if you're all talk or not." I want answers. About Mia. About the forest.

Aukley is either stupid or brave because he edges closer, hands in his pockets. "You know, I was just listening to one of my favorite podcasts, 'PNW Murders'? Sort of surprised your sister hasn't shown up yet."

The thing inside me flares to life, rage blooming in my chest. Part of me wants to hit him, despite the fact that we're in the middle of the front lawn with people crossing back and forth around us. There's the crunch of bicycle tires on gravel paths and murmured conversations as people head for class.

So he knows my sister is dead. How she died. Not hard information to find if you know where to look.

It doesn't mean he *knows* anything. "What were you talking about earlier? What *got* Mia?"

"There's only one way to find out."

"What's that supposed to mean?"

He steps closer, his smile flirtatious. "I could be convinced to share. If the price is right."

I want to seize him by the front of his shirt and drag him into the woods. Find the most remote, desolate spot and indulge my baser instincts.

I can imagine the kind of savage joy it would bring me, wrapping my hands around his throat.

"Just say you know nothing and go." I turn. There's a shuffle, and the back of my neck prickles. I whirl around just as Aukley seizes my shirtsleeve. "I'll tell you, you just have to—"

I snap my arm up. Knock his hand away. Twist sideways and drive my arm up, the heel of my hand connecting with his nose.

A crack and a cry of pain. Aukley collapses to one knee, blood gushing between his fingers.

I freeze, startled, pulse thundering in my ears. I didn't even get the chance to stop myself. I didn't *try*.

Shit.

There are distant, muffled noises. A cluster of passing students stop on one of the bike paths, their shapes a vague blur on my periphery.

My mouth tastes metallic. I bit my tongue.

To my shock, Aukley lifts his head, smiling through the blood. It's terrible—a wide joker grin. "There's so much you don't know, Laurent."

The sight drives me forward. I shove him, hard, and he overbalances, catching himself on his hands. He's still grinning.

I want to hit him again. Drive my fist into his face until that smile disappears.

Three steps and I'm on him, fists clenching the fabric of his jacket. I'm going to rip the answers right out of him.

"You don't know *shit*."

Aukley laughs. The sound garbled through the blood leaking into his mouth. "I know your girl was dating your sister. How's that for information?"

I hit him again. His head snaps back, sending an arc of crimson droplets into the grass. Behind me, there's a buzz of excitement. A crowd gathering.

Somewhere in the back of my mind, a voice tells me to stop.

But it's too faint, buried beneath layers of pure, red-tinted rage. "You're fucking lying."

He coughs, shaking his head. "That nutcase screamed it at me. Told me to lay off Holland because her ex just died."

Beth. He means Beth told him.

It shouldn't line up, but it does. Some of the whispered conversations between Beth and Holland are coming back to me now.

The way Holland had looked at me on the front steps when I'd first arrived. The intensity of her gaze, like there was no one else in the world.

Had she been looking at me and seeing my twin?

Ada's face swims in my memory now, pale and warped under the black water, eyes shining with malice.

It makes the rage broil even hotter. Aukley smiles at me. "Hit me again. I know you have it in you."

I'm going to drill the toe of my boot into his ribs until he screams. Drag him up by the hair. Drive my fist into his face, again and again.

"Evie, no!"

I jerk to a stop. It's like a hook in my gut, that voice. The scent of citrus hits me first and then a cool hand slides over my wrist.

Holland stares down at me, red lips parted, eyes round with horror. Something inside me dies a little at her expression, as I realize what I've done. The side of me she's just seen.

But there's another part that doesn't care. That's still raging. I look at her and picture Ada now. In my imagination, it's Ada and Holland under that tree.

Maybe she pictured that too. Maybe she looked at me and pretended.

I jerk out of her grip and she blinks, startled.

"You should have told me you were dating Ada."

The way her face goes white tells me everything I need to know.

Students cluster on the lawn in a wide semicircle, whispers buzzing around us.

I push through the crowd, ignoring Holland as she calls after me, stalking across the lawn toward the front gate. Toward the cool darkness of the forest.

CHAPTER EIGHTEEN
Evie

HOLLAND MUST KNOW it was Beth who told Aukley, because she refuses to talk to her for the next three days. Meanwhile, I won't talk to either of them, though Holland desperately tries to apologize.

I sit on the other side of the classroom. Eat separately in the dining hall.

On the second day, Leta slides onto the bench beside me at breakfast. She doesn't seem to need to know what's happened, and we're mostly silent. But this time, it's me that hooks my arm through hers as we walk to homeroom together.

In the evenings, avoiding Holland becomes difficult. She tries to make eye contact in the common room, or catch me alone in our rooms. She keeps saying my name in that tone, like she's desperate to talk. Several times she leaves notes on my pillow and I toss them away, unread. I can't even look at her without thinking of Ada.

I want to throw up. So instead, I focus on the forest.

Every morning, I'm in the common room just after the shutters go up, taking pictures of the forest.

I can't stop thinking about it.

I keep staring out the window, questioning myself. *Do* the trees look different? Is the tree line changing, or am I just looking for anything to grasp on to?

And the photo I took in the clearing, that strange shadow. I'm second-guessing myself. Maybe it *is* just a shadow. Maybe it's the way I shot the picture.

I can't let it go. It seeps into every thought, every waking moment.

For the next three mornings, I wake at sunrise and take pictures of the tree line. Always from the same spot. Always the same trees. I memorize them: the tall, craggily pine on the far left, the blackened cedar in the center. The spreading limbs of the arbutus that line up just right with the front gate. They become intimately familiar.

Each day I use my spare in the afternoon to trek into the forest. Make my way into the clearing. Track the patterns of red hemlock on the forest floor.

I document every detail, from the rotted, black roots of certain trees to the way the moss sits on the boulders by the stream.

Holland almost follows me in a few times.

She's never subtle. I see her out of the corner of my eye, the flame of her red hair catching my attention. Each time, she lingers by the edge of the tree line like she's determined to watch over me.

There's a part of me that gets a sick enjoyment out of Holland Morgan following me, desperate for my attention.

But I refuse to give in. Not after what she did.

It would have been different if she told me.

I never would have kissed her. Never would have let myself fall for her.

That third afternoon I head straight for the forest as usual. But this time I exit the gate and find her standing in the middle of the forest path. My heart stops in my chest.

She speaks fast, like she's afraid I'll interrupt. "Evie, just wait."

I almost stop, shaken by the pleading in her voice. But I'm afraid if I look at her, I'll see Ada. I'll picture them together.

"Go away, Holland." There's no bite to my voice. I can feel myself shaking and hate myself for it.

"You can't keep doing this."

I almost pause, and then she adds, "It's not safe out here," and I scowl and loop my way around her, dodging her outstretched hand.

"Don't go in alone, at least."

I don't reply. I don't turn. I just keep walking until the forest swallows me.

That night, I find myself awake in the darkness, staring up at the canopy.

It feels like I've barely slept. All I can do is think about the forest. Even I can admit it's too much, the way I keep repeating the same questions, circling back again and again.

What did I see before the blinds closed? What was in that picture? What happened to Beth, and Mia, and my father?

I roll over, restless and annoyed. My camera is there on the mattress, waiting. And I know I shouldn't feed the obsession, but I flick through the pictures again, finding the photo of the clearing.

Looking at the hunched shadow makes my chest tight.

I've looked at this photograph for hours. Far too long to be objective. So I flip to the tree line shots instead. There are five, and when I scan through them fast enough, it makes my breath catch.

The first photo and the last look different.

It should be easy to reason this away. Say I took them from different angles.

But I know that's not true. I've been careful to stand in the same spot every morning, aim at the same group of trees.

I go through them again, heart clenching in my chest.

I'm sure of it now.

The arbutus is gone from behind the gate. In its place is a towering spruce, twisted branches stripped bare by some past storm.

I shut the camera off and lie in the dark, mind reeling.

I was right. The forest is . . . shifting.

There's something deeply unsettling about that, and as I stare up at the canopy with wide, unblinking eyes, I know I won't be sleeping for a long time.

I spend the next afternoon trekking into the forest.

I don't know what I'm looking for.

Some sign of what I saw the other night. A flicker of static. An unnatural shadow at the edges of the trees. Anything.

Instead, it's peaceful. Just the sound of birds, mixed with the distant trickle of the stream and the crunch of my boots on the path.

The trail winds upward, taking me past massive, bent-trunked trees, through patches grown over with ferns and rivers of draping moss.

For the last few minutes, the beast inside me has been sleeping. Which is why it's so noticeable when the back of my neck suddenly prickles.

Something cracks in the underbrush, but I force myself to keep walking.

Aukley. It has to be him, looking for revenge.

I walk a few more feet without turning, and then duck behind a wide-trunked tree, holding my breath.

For a few seconds, only silence follows, and I think I'm hearing things. That it was just a squirrel or a rabbit. I'm being paranoid.

And then the noise starts again. It's clearer this time, the quiet tread of someone on the trail behind me.

They get closer, and I wait for Aukley's tall silhouette to slink into view, my entire body tense. Coiled to spring.

A shuffle on the path. A flash of black as he steps into view. I hurtle forward, eager. I want a *fight.* I yank him around, slam him back into the tree.

He lets out a startled sound, and then I'm staring him right in the face.

And . . . it's not Aukley.

CHAPTER NINETEEN
Holland

THE SECOND I ROUND THE TREE, something grabs my shoulders. I find myself slammed hard into the trunk, letting out a startled squeak. A hand wraps around my throat and I go still.

I'm breathing hard, staring straight into Evie's face. Her expression is cold fury all over, gray eyes like flint.

"Holland?" The cold expression vanishes, replaced by shock. For a moment, we're both frozen.

It makes me realize what it looks like. What it *is*.

I'm stalking her. Lurking in the trees like some predator.

Evie is driving me to obsession. It's Ada all over again.

When she fixes me with that glittering stare, adrenaline courses through me, lighting my insides on fire. Her knee is between my legs. Her hip digging into my stomach. She doesn't pull away, though her grip on my throat loosens and I draw in a sharp breath.

Evie's dark lashes flutter, gaze dipping down in a way that makes my cheeks flush. "Why are you following me?"

"You can't keep going in alone." I can't hide the tremor in my voice. "I won't let you."

She stares at me for a second and I can't help it—my gaze drops down to her mouth. I want her to kiss me. I want it so badly it makes my chest ache.

"You're not going to *let* me?" Her voice is low, dangerous. Something in me responds to that tone, sending a delicious shiver down my spine.

"You can't stop me from following you."

Evie leans forward, grip tightening on my throat the tiniest bit. It makes my breath catch. I feel my lips part, and then she leans in, leg thrust between my thighs, pressing my body into the tree.

"I'm still mad at you," she says, and then she kisses me.

CHAPTER TWENTY
Evie

SHE'S A LIAR.

She dated my sister.

She followed me into the woods.

There are so many reasons I should turn and walk away from Holland Morgan.

Instead, I kiss her. My fingertips bite into her jaw, my other hand tangles in her hair. I press her hard against the trunk of the tree.

The monster in my chest is raging. It wants violence. It wants to be satiated. It wants . . . *her*.

I turn, grasping her by the wrist, dragging her toward the clearing. She lets out a shaky breath but she doesn't protest.

And then we're sprawled over the roots of the great black tree, tangled in one another. This time, it's different. This time I pull her hair, and she bites my neck hard enough to sting.

It's fierce and desperate, and maybe a little angry.

I never want it to be over.

Holland grasps my hips and rolls over, pushing me into the roots of the tree, maneuvering so she's astride my hips. She leans down to kiss me with bruising force, and I arch beneath her, a groan tearing from my throat. I can feel the way she smiles against my lips. It makes my stomach clench.

We're both breathing hard now, hands exploring.

Holland dips her head and kisses down my neck, igniting a fire everywhere her mouth touches. Shivering, I trace my hands down her arms, over her sides and hips. She's soft. So soft.

Holland reaches under my shirt, inching up slowly, asking soundless permission until I grasp both hands and draw them over my skin. *Touch me.*

I let out a sigh when she does; she's sliding lower, trailing kisses down my stomach. Then she's grasping at the band of my pants, and I'm fumbling at the buttons.

A moment later, I'm lying back against the roots of the tree, staring up at the spread of branches above me while I come unraveled under her touch. Under the heat of her breath. The way her mouth moves against me.

Time trickles away, slipping like sand through glass. I don't know how long it's been before I shift under her and something pokes me in the back so sharply I jerk upright.

"Evie?" Holland pulls back. "What's the matter?" Her voice is concerned, but I'm too focused on the thing half buried in the dirt beneath me.

Inching away, I glare down at the gnarled roots. There are objects tangled there . . . bleached white bits of rock, some of them the size of my fist.

No. I look again. *Not rock. Bone.*

I scramble up so fast it makes me dizzy, yanking my pants up as my heart beats hard in my ears. The fox skeleton is the first thing that comes to mind. Maybe whatever killed it stashes its prize here.

What hunts foxes?

Casting around, I find a thin, cracked-off splinter of wood and use it to scrape around the roots, revealing more dirty white bones. Behind me, Holland lets out a shaky breath and I know she's seen them.

Some are thin and frail like chicken bones. Others are thicker, about the size of my wrist.

It makes the hairs on the back of my neck stand on end, and I glance over my shoulder at her. We exchange a silent look, and I know we're both thinking about that terrible screeching.

Holland follows when I move to the other side of the tree. Digging under the roots reveals a long, white-gray bone the size of my forearm. This feels off to me, and I back up a step before something catches my eye.

There's something snagged on one of the thick roots, almost buried underneath. A flash of red.

It's the bright, unnatural color that draws me. I drop to a crouch and a chill goes down my spine.

Holland spots it at the same time, staggering back a step. "Is that . . . ?"

I can only nod.

A shoe.

Unmistakably, there's a woman's flat beneath the root, poking out to show the dirty leather tip. No surprise Holland and I didn't see it before—it's buried so far beneath the root it looks like it's growing there in the dirt.

Stomach twisting, I reach down and tug at the shoe.

It takes a minute; it's so wedged in, like the tree is trying to cling to its prize.

Then it comes free, so abruptly I nearly overbalance. Letting out a shaky breath, I crouch back down and lay the newly freed object on the ground.

Definitely a woman's shoe.

About my size, maybe a little smaller. A red Mary Jane flat, the toe covered with oily black earth, the strap frayed almost in half.

Mouth dry, I pick my camera up to snap a picture. Always my first reaction.

It occurs to me that I probably shouldn't have touched it, if it's from where they found her.

"Evie, I think we should go . . ."

"Just a sec." I zoom in, getting a close-up of the oily substance crusted on the toe. It's the same thing that stained the roots of the tree and the carpet in Dad's office.

When I lean in, a strange, sweet scent wafts up.

It's definitely the oily stuff. It smells sickly sweet, like honey or sap.

When I glance around, the ground is flat, packed earth, coated in leaves and pine needles. There's no sign of the black oil.

I should head straight for the school. To Gorski's office. Tell her what we found.

But first, I hunker down, scraping at the earth. It reveals only more packed brown soil. Puzzled, I dig deeper, brushing away pine needles and moss. I dig under the roots in first one spot and then another.

There's nothing.

"Evie."

I keep digging until there's dirt wedged under my fingernails. It doesn't make sense.

"*Evie.* There's nothing there."

I pause, staring down at the disturbed soil, all of it the same shade of dark brown. She's right. There's no black oil. So where did the shoe come from?

This time it's Holland who grabs my hand, leading me away from the tree, back toward the school. But I can't help looking back. Until the dark branches of the walnut tree vanish behind the rest of the forest.

CHAPTER TWENTY-ONE

Evie

BY THE TIME WE GET BACK, Gorski's office is closed and locked.

Walking from the wilderness into the somber structure of Stowe House makes us realize we're covered in dirt, and we spend a couple minutes picking sticks and leaves out of one another's hair before we go in.

Thankfully Leta gives us only a cursory wave from the couch, where she's scribbling in a notebook, and Beth peeks out from her privacy curtain to shoot me a murderous glare before yanking it back into place.

Holland whispers that she's going to try calling Gorski, slipping into the bathroom. She's keeping our discovery a secret from Beth.

I sink down onto the edge of my bed and pull my camera up.

I keep looking at the picture of the shoe. At the smears of oily black. The battered toe. The frayed strap.

It doesn't make sense.

If it had been Mia's shoe, it would be covered in mud, sure. But it's been only a few days . . . why would the strap be frayed? How did it get tangled in roots?

Maybe this isn't even Mia's shoe. Maybe it's old.

But where did it come from, then?

And the bones scattered around the tree. I'd assumed they were animal bones, but I'd found them near the shoe . . .

After the shutters go down, I lie awake and stare at the canopy above me, mind going in circles.

It takes forever to fall asleep. When I finally do, I dream about Ada. I dream about the lake.

I'm leaning over the dock, staring down at my twin's face through the murky water. This time, her hair is short and dark, strands floating around her face. Her eyes are open wide, fixed on me.

I watch myself drown.

And then one pale arm shoots up, cold water spraying my face. A hand wraps around my throat. Drags me under.

The lake closes over my head, dark and cold, filling my ears with the rush of waves lapping on the shore.

Gradually the noise changes—blends and warps, becomes frantic scratching from somewhere in the distance.

I jolt awake.

Relief floods me—*Ada is dead, I'm not at the lake*—then dissolves just as fast.

Noises come from just beyond our wall. A distant shuffling scrape. A pause. More scraping.

"Evie?" Leta's voice is a low whisper in the darkness. "Is that you?"

"No." I slide out from under the covers, and she follows suit, both of us creeping into the next room.

Holland and Beth are already sitting up in bed. Holland's bleary and confused, her hair sleep-tossed. But Beth is sitting bolt upright, eyes wide and fixed on the door.

When she sees us, she waves at Leta. "Call Gorski."

Leta's eyes widen, and she nods, vanishing back into our room.

I creep toward the door. There's no need to press my ear to it—the noises are clear. Shuffling footsteps. Someone walking up and down the hallway.

It goes on for a few seconds, then stops. Then goes again.

Someone on the other side of the door is *pacing*, sporadic and halting. Like they're frantic. Or angry.

It makes me think of the clash with Aukley. Swinging at him. The ugly *crunch* his nose made. Blood trailing down onto his teeth.

Maybe it's him.

I move forward, pressing one hand to the door. Behind me, Beth whispers sharply, "Don't open it!"

I shoot her an annoyed look, and then say loudly, "We can hear you. You need to leave."

The footsteps stop. Whoever it is, they're on the other side of the door. We're essentially face-to-face.

Silence. All of us strain to hear.

There's another shuffle. At first, I think they're leaving. Then a heavy thump and the door shakes under my palm. I jump back. Behind me, someone shrieks.

Another thump, harder this time. The frame rattles.

They're trying to break in.

Another thud and a splintering crack as the doorframe begins to split. I turn, lunging across the room, planting my hip into the nearest piece of heavy furniture. Beth's dresser. "Holland!"

She catches on immediately, moving to the other side. The dresser's legs grate against the floor as we shove it forward, slamming it into the door.

Another crash. Another horrible splintering. There's a dark sliver appearing beside the doorframe. Through it, I see a flicker of movement. A flash of a single, shining eye—wide, and entirely black.

Impossible.

My breath catches in my throat.

Another thud, and I jerk back.

"Leave us alone!" It comes out in a scream and the crashing blows cut off abruptly, leaving sudden, startling silence.

And then the footsteps start. Faster, fading rapidly. Like . . . they're running away.

There's another long moment where we all listen, barely moving. Then Leta lets out a breath.

"We have to tell Gorksi." Beth's voice wobbles.

Holland and I exchange a look. We were going to Gorski anyway. Now we have even more reason.

Outside, the hallway is cold and empty. We're still for a moment, unsure. Then a loud rattling breaks the silence, making us all jump, and we watch as the shutters roll slowly up the windows down the length of the hallway.

"*Fuck* me." Leta lets out a shaky laugh.

The morning light slides under the blinds as we slowly file

out. It makes me wonder if that's why that thing left. The sun rising scared it off.

Holland is first out, and she jerks to a stop, making a strangled noise in her throat.

"What's . . . ," Beth says, and then she stops. We can all see it.

The stone floor is covered in footprints, oily black marks that show the distinct outline of bare feet. There's a trail in front of our door, overlapping again and again.

There are black smudges all over the door too, staining the white surface.

I snap a quick picture before we make our way through the hallway and down the empty staircase.

At six in the morning, the hallways are empty. We hurry outside and around the back of Stowe House, heading for the ivy-coated office building without a word. In fact, no one says anything until we're inside, and we find Gorski's office empty.

"She probably isn't up yet," Beth says. "Let's try Blackwood."

My heart jolts in my chest. "I'm not sure that's a good idea."

Beth doesn't reply, already marching past Mia's messy desk toward my father's door.

She goes to knock and then seems to notice the door is broken, reaching to push it open. Dread gathers in my chest, and then a sharp voice says, "Get away from there."

Gorski stands in the doorway, her face pale, a cup of coffee in one hand.

She blinks, like her own vehemence has startled her, and clears her throat. "He's asked not to be disturbed." She sets her mug down on Mia's desk.

This close, it's obvious how exhausted she is. There are dark circles under her eyes, and her hair is falling out of its usual tight bun. "What can I do for you?"

Beth tells her what happened. When Gorski looks unconvinced, I pull out my camera, showing her the picture.

Gorski snorts. "Crown and Grave. The tap is coming up."

Leta gives her a look of disbelief. "They broke the *door*."

Gorski shakes her head, sighing. "Not the first time those buffoons have caused property damage. I'll talk to them."

Beth's face is going a deep shade of red. "Look at the door. What if—?"

Gorski clears her throat loudly. "I have it under control." She leans forward, eyes narrowing. "You're looking unwell, Beth. Do you need another session? I'm happy to talk."

Beth flinches. Shakes her head.

What the hell was that?

The vice principal lets out an exasperated sigh, already turning back to her office, clearly finished with the subject.

Holland and I exchange a look, and Holland raises her brows, clearly waiting for me to say something.

I trail after Gorski, and she pauses. "Ms. Laurent, is there something else?"

"Yeah." I pull up the photo I took yesterday. "It's about the shoe we found."

"Yes, I got your voice message." Gorski pauses inside the door to her office, frowning at the photo. It could be my imagination, but her face seems a shade paler. "Ms. Laurent, I'm not sure why you felt the need to poke around where the unfortunate girl was found, but please refrain from sharing that with anyone."

Where she was found. So I was right. It *is* her shoe.

She shakes her head. "I think you should delete it."

I glare at her in disbelief. "What if it's evidence?"

"It's evidence you have a sick fascination." Gorski returns my scowl. "Delete it, please."

When I glance at Holland, she just shakes her head, and I know what she's saying.

There's no point fighting.

And I have backups. I hit the delete button, and Gorski seems satisfied, giving me a sharp nod. "I don't know when young people got so macabre, but it was just as bad last year when Ms. Thorn ran away. She was a troubled young woman with very little reliability."

"The shoe—"

"Enough." Gorski's tone is final. "In fact, I'll ask you to stay out of the forest going forward."

Then she walks into her office and slams the door shut.

We're dismissed.

CHAPTER TWENTY-TWO

Holland

HEADING FOR GYM THAT AFTERNOON, I find myself still thinking about Gorski's reaction. The way she'd flipped straight to angry disapproval.

And forcing Evie to delete the picture . . .

That couldn't be right. Even if Mia had been attacked by animals, wouldn't you want to send that picture to someone? And shouldn't someone go get the shoe?

What we found in the woods makes it utterly clear that the forest isn't safe. And Evie is more intrigued than ever.

It's time to put my plan into motion.

The gym is one of the newest buildings, and my sneakers squeak on the still-shiny floor, footsteps echoing off the high ceilings. There's a plaque right inside the door, like they don't want you to leave the building without knowing it was donated by the Fisher family.

I make a face at it before walking in.

Ewan Stowe isn't hard to find. There's a series of mats laid out in the center for martial arts, and inexplicably, Stowe is lying in the middle, hands tucked behind his head. He's staring fixedly up at the ceiling.

For a moment I hesitate, and then force myself forward.

He's going to tap me for Crown and Grave.

I can do this. For Evie.

He doesn't move when I approach. "Is there a reason famous actor Ewan Stowe is lying in the middle of the mats?" I put on my most playful tone. "Other people might like to use them."

Stowe doesn't look at me, but his lips quirk in the hint of a smile. "Holland, I'm having a pity party and you're invited. Come have a drink."

He produces something from his jacket pocket—a flat metallic container.

Unbelievable. He's got a flask out in the middle of the gym.

When I glance back, a few students are filing in, but there's no sign of Mr. Allen.

"I'm good. Thanks."

Stowe sets the flask down and shuts his eyes. "Suit yourself."

Ewan Stowe might as well have absolute immunity here. And he seems to know that.

There's no way they'll kick him out, not when their school can claim to have produced yet another star. Even if he's having a drunken breakdown in the middle of gym class.

Disgust dissolves some of the nerves gnawing at my stomach. Lying there, Stowe doesn't seem famous and untouchable. Just kind of . . . pathetic.

"And why are we having a pity party?"

Stowe lifts the flask again. "My father called this morning. He had lots of opinions about who I should tap for Crown and Grave. Of course, I'm putting it off, so we had a *lovely* little conversation about what a failure I am."

Who he's going to tap. A flicker of excitement goes through me.

It makes sense that Chadwick Stowe would want some say in the tap process. He's heavily involved in politics.

Interesting that he has his sights set so far ahead. Influencing future politicians.

This could work for me. I just have to play it right.

"You know," I say slowly, "I met your father once. He came to visit you on set. Only, he didn't. He talked to the director the entire time. Never even looked at you. I remember thinking . . . this guy *sucks*."

For a second, Stowe only stares at me. It's a calculated risk, and my stomach sinks.

If I offended him . . .

Then he tips his head back and laughs.

At the edges of the gym, other students creep closer, all of them watching. Pretending they're not.

"You're clearly very astute." He pushes his sleeves up and tilts his head to stare at me. "Because yes. Yes, he does."

"Like I said, join the club." I sit down and fold my legs underneath me, elbows on my knees.

"Are there snacks?" Stowe grins.

"Of course," I say glibly, "but only during circle time where we share our dramatic backstories." Pausing, I examine his face, testing the waters. "You know, went out for milk and never came back.

168

Cheated on Mom with the mailman. Is such an abusive narcissist you can't even go back for reading break."

I pull myself up short, very deliberately breaking eye contact with him, leaving a too-heavy silence between us before clearing my throat.

Like I've said too much and I'm recovering myself.

Stowe is staring at me intently now. Thankfully, years of acting have taught me how to blush. It's impossible to fake without thinking of certain things . . . which means it's completely authentic.

It just has more to do with Evie than Ewan Stowe.

That's why I'm doing this. Who all of this is for.

"Anyway. It's a good time all around."

It's incredibly bold, given that I don't know if Stowe can see through me.

Or even if he can't, if it will affect him.

On the mat, Stowe sits up straight. His smile falters, and there's a flicker of something in his face. Almost like . . . anger. Then his smile is back, casual. Careless. But his hands give him away—his fingers are tight on the flask, knuckles white.

I'm the cat who ate the canary, so smug I could preen.

But I force my expression into something resembling "closed off" as Stowe inches closer.

Even if the brief change in his demeanor hadn't told me I've won, his body language practically shouts it.

I had a theory about Stowe, purely based on his history. Things anyone can look up on his Wikipedia page. Now I'm sure I'm right.

Ewan Stowe likes to *rescue* people.

He's just about primed for me to swoop in.

Stowe is leaning in, saying something about the autumn dance. But I'm only half listening, because more people have filed into the gym now.

Evie.

She hangs back, looking around with faint curiosity. She somehow makes even the gym uniform look good, the shorts showing off her long, toned legs.

I don't realize I've said her name out loud until Stowe says, "Oh yeah? Going with the new girl?"

"I . . . yeah." It's not really confirmed. In fact, I'm not sure if Evie wants anything to do with me despite what happened in the woods the other night. She walks in without so much as looking at me, and my stomach clenches.

I remember what she said before she dragged me to the clearing.

I'm still mad at you.

I pull my gaze away. Of course she's still mad. It was ridiculous to think she'd be over this right away.

I should give her time, take a step back and let her cool off.

But I can't seem to stop staring. All I want to do is march over there and grab her face. Kiss her hard. It feels like there's a magnet in my core, drawing my attention back to her.

This time, I find her staring at Stowe, eyes narrow and glittering.

Something in my chest expands.

Mr. Allen arrives a second later, shouting at us to pair off. Beside me, Stowe shifts. He's about to say something, but when I glance up, Evie is marching toward us, gray eyes fixed on me, her expression set in a way that makes my stomach flutter.

I go still as she stops in front of me, reaching out to grab my wrist. It feels so much like the prelude to that moment under the tree that my face flushes hot.

"Pair up with me."

It's not even a question, but I find myself nodding. Mr. Allen tells us to spread out over the mats.

I recognize the setup from last year, and my pulse goes into overdrive. We're practicing judo holds. Which means Evie and I are about to get very close.

I want her to touch me. I crave it, even. But the hard, glittering look on her face makes me pause. "I'm sorry, Evie. How many times do you want me to say it?"

"More times, I guess." She doesn't look away from my face as I back toward the corner of the mat.

"I almost told you so many times."

"But you didn't."

She's circling now, looking for openings. I fall back, forcing her to adjust her tactics. Something shifts in her expression and she drops closer to the ground. The way she moves is almost too fluid. Predatory. It sends a shiver through me.

"I don't blame you for falling for her. That's not the part I'm mad about."

My pulse picks up, but I keep an eye on her feet. "I don't understand."

"Ada was good at playing people." She's watching as I move around her. "If she wanted something, she got it. I'm mad because you lied."

I feint to the left and she matches me perfectly. Adrenaline surges, lighting me from the inside. "I never actually lied." It's a stupid thing to say, since I just *withheld*, but it comes out before I can stop it.

Evie laughs, a short, sharp sound. Then she pushes back her sleeve. For a moment I think she's gearing up, getting ready to come after me. Instead, she turns her arm, revealing the long, red line of a scar. It's wide, as thick as my pinkie.

"Ada did that three months ago. On my birthday. There's more, but this one was especially nasty. Bone came right through the skin."

I draw back, dismayed, and she lunges.

Timing is everything, and I realize I've screwed up about the same moment she snatches my wrist and hooks a leg around the back of my calves. I hit the mat hard on my back.

And then she's on top of me, pulling my arm over in a shoulder-hold, pinning me.

Ada was good at playing people.

I think maybe she wasn't the only one, but I don't dare say it out loud.

We're inches apart. Her breath smells like peppermint, gray eyes wide, fixed on my face with the kind of intensity that makes it difficult to breathe.

Neither of us moves, or speaks. Until Evie breathes out, "It's no good, the two of us. You should leave me alone."

My chest constricts, anger blooming in the pit of my stomach. "I can't. I *won't*."

Silence, and she leans harder into the hold. It strains my arm, but I meet her gaze squarely, grimacing up at her.

"Tap out."

"No." I grind my teeth.

"Tap out, Holland." Her tone is full of warning.

My eyes are watering now, but I shake my head. "No."

"*Fuck*." Evie leans back, easing off my arm, and I let out a breath of relief. She pushes to her feet and glares down at me. "I'm still mad at you," she says, and then she reaches down and offers me her hand. "Come on."

CHAPTER TWENTY-THREE

Holland

EVERY SATURDAY MORNING, around ten, Ewan Stowe takes a coffee into the common room and reads by the fire. Since his weekend schedule is so predictable, I use it to my advantage, sliding into the other armchair by the fire at exactly nine fifty.

The common room is full, but thankfully no one approaches.

Eventually, there's a polite throat-clearing, and I look up to find Stowe settling into the chair across from me.

"So, you and Evie." It's the first thing he says, and his teasing smile makes my cheeks instantly hot.

"Yeah," I say, and then don't really know what else to add. I'm not sure I want to talk about this here, where people are obviously trying to eavesdrop.

Sure enough, whatever Stowe is about to say is interrupted by someone coughing pointedly from across the room.

It's the kind of cough with something sandwiched in between. Usually an insult.

A few of the Gravesmen at the long table at the back of the room are snickering. A lot of them seem to be watching the exchange. Some with amusement. A few with what seems like something on the edge of contempt.

Maybe our nighttime visitor *was* a Gravesman.

The class clown, Cooper, does it again, hand to his mouth.

This time I make it out when he slips the word *lesbians* between his fake hacking.

"You should get a lozenge for that cough, Cooper," Stowe says dryly. "Would be a shame if you choked to death."

Laughter greets this. A few of the Gravesmen hoot and slap Cooper on the back.

"Shut it, Coop." Elijah Archer punches Cooper in the arm with enough vigor that Cooper winces.

"Ignore them." Stowe pushes himself out of his chair and crosses the space between us, settling onto the arm of my chair. "Homework, darlin'?"

I start fumbling with the letter in my lap before shoving it into my pocket. "Uh. Just . . . a letter from my dad."

Judging by the glimmer of interest in his expression, he managed to catch a glimpse before I'd hidden it.

I don't even have to pretend to blush—my cheeks heat up automatically.

Up close, I notice his eyes aren't just brown. His pupils are haloed by amber, a kaleidoscope pattern that turns them hazel the longer I look.

Stowe tilts his head, brows creasing as he examines me.

Now is the perfect time. I know he has to tap someone, and for some reason, he's putting it off.

All I have to do is lay some groundwork . . .

Before I can start, there's a shuffle from the doorway, and the conversation around us drops off.

There's a tall figure in a black suit, his white mask stark in the firelight. His voice from beneath the mask is low. Slightly muffled.

"May I have the room, please? I'll just be a moment."

The Rook's voice is mild, but everyone moves like he's shouted, the table vacating in record time.

Curiosity prickles through me. If the Rook is here in his mask, he's making some kind of statement. I'm just not sure who it's meant for.

I stay seated, watching as the Rook moves toward us. He's weirdly graceful as he walks over and settles into the armchair across from us.

He regards me silently for a moment, like he's assessing me. I give him a wide-eyed look in response, and then flinch back against Stowe, making sure it's noticeable.

"Miss Morgan," the Rook says, "that includes you."

I don't even look at him, my attention fixed on Stowe. I know my little show has worked when his expression goes dark and he gets to his feet, moving between me and the Rook. They're almost the same height.

Stowe's posture is casual, hands in his pockets, but he fixes the Rook with a withering stare. "Stay, Holland. He's all bark and no bite."

I have to repress a grin as I glance at the Rook. He only shrugs. "If you want her present for this, that's your choice."

176

"Uh-oh." Stowe settles back onto the arm of my chair, putting a hand on his chin, widening his eyes. "Am I in trouble?"

"Your audacity never fails to astonish." The Rook stares at him, eyes hard through the mask.

So many times, I've tried to picture a face. Put the low, muted voice to a name. I can never put my finger on it, though.

"I don't know what you mean." Stowe smirks.

"I think you do." The Rook reaches into the pocket of his black slacks and fishes something out.

There, in the center of his palm, is a small plastic troll doll with bright pink hair.

"You don't like my candidate?" Stowe's expression is full of innocence. "I thought he had chutzpah."

"Your note was amusing, I'll admit," the Rook says flatly. "But my patience is running thin. I've given you two perfectly reasonable choices."

Stowe plucks the troll doll out of the Rook's hand. "Is it that he's . . . naked? We *did* have a talk about that, but he's a free spirit, ultimately—"

"*Ewan Stowe*, listen to me." The Rook's voice drops lower. It's a tone approaching dangerous, and I find myself clutching the armrest. Stowe presses his lips shut, going still.

"You will choose a suitable candidate. No more jokes from you." The Rook leans down, the white mask inches from Stowe's face.

To his credit, Ewan Stowe doesn't flinch, staring boldly into the black eyeholes. "I thought you liked my jokes. Are you not entertained?"

"Of course I am." I find myself frozen as the Rook reaches out to grip Stowe's chin, tilting his face up. Stowe's dark lashes flicker as the Rook strokes his thumb over the line of his jaw.

"The only reason you are still here at all is because you entertain me."

For the first time, Stowe's careless facade seems to slip. He flinches and then stills again. His jaw is tight as he says through his teeth, "Not in front of her."

The mask tips to one side. I find myself frozen under his glittering stare. "You wanted her to stay. I wouldn't want to be *rude*."

The Rook turns back, sliding his hand up until his fingers grip Stowe's jaw just under the ear. Stowe flinches again and sucks in a breath. He doesn't pull away, though, and my face burns as I realize how glassy his eyes look.

It's not *fear* I'm seeing on Ewan Stowe's face.

Thankfully, the Rook releases him a second later, straightening. His voice is curt again. "One week, Stowe. Pick before the autumn dance, or I pick for you. It's not hard."

Stowe lets out a bark of laughter and shuts his eyes, head dropping against the back of the chair as the Rook strides away.

There's silence after he leaves—just the snap of the fire, a shifting log sending up a shower of sparks. I finally stand, moving so quickly my head spins.

Stowe's eyes snap open. "Wait, Holland."

I know what he's going to say. He's going to beg me not to tell anyone. That it wasn't what it looked like.

Instead, he says, "Stay?"

Slowly, I turn and sink down into the armchair opposite him, waiting for him to speak.

"I'm sorry," he says. "For the PDA."

Public affection, with the *Rook* of all people. Though I'm not sure I'd call it affection. Tension, maybe. Aggression, even.

I hesitate. "Are you and him . . . ?"

The question hangs in the air between us, and Stowe shrugs. Then he leans back, draping his arms over the armrests, one ankle crossed over his knee. He looks completely relaxed again. Coolly indifferent. "We don't call it anything, if that's what you're wondering. You don't *date* the Rook." He snorts. "We have dalliances, I guess? If that's a word we use these days."

I crack a smile. "It's really not."

"Well, I'm bringing it back." He looks relaxed enough, but his hands are restless, flipping idly through the pages of his paperback. "And no, before you ask, I don't know who he is. And if I did, I would be tarred and feathered and run out of town."

"I have . . . so many questions."

"If he takes his mask off during said dalliances? The answer is no."

"Oh my god." I can't help laughing, and Stowe's grin is wicked.

"Believe me, it makes it better."

"You must have guesses." Now I'm leaning in, curiosity piqued. "He must have freckles? Birthmarks?"

Stowe throws his head back, his laughter startling me. Then he reaches forward and whacks my knee gently with the book. "No more questions out of you, Holland Morgan."

"Oh, come *on*," I protest. "This is *way* too good."

Stowe groans, leaning back in his chair. In the pause, my mind is already racing. This seems like a natural lead-in, somehow. When I lean forward, he cracks an eye open.

"No more questions about the Rook naked."

"I promise." I tilt my head, considering, and Stowe takes the bait, sitting up to frown at me.

"What?"

"Why the troll doll?"

His expression sobers. "He says I have to pick one. Prove my loyalty and all that shit. But I hate both choices."

"Why? Who is it?"

"Legacy members. All the brains and charisma of a sack of hammers." He rotates sideways in the armchair, stretching out to drape his arm across the armrests between us, his fingers brushing my elbow. Then he stretches his legs out so far his feet are propped on the hearth.

I have the thought then that Stowe is like the pick-up sticks of people. Too many sharp angles. Too many long, skinny limbs. There's an impossible amount of him.

Grouchy, I nudge his intruding limb out of my space. "Yeah, I still don't get what you're mad about. *You're* a legacy member."

"I know. It's obnoxious." He fishes into one of his sleeves, bringing out a paper-wrapped sucker. He noisily unwraps it before sticking it into his mouth.

"Besides, you think I had a choice? Have you ever seen someone turn the Gravesmen down?"

The thought never occurred to me, mostly because, *why* would you turn it down? Because you didn't want the influence over the school? The future political connections?

The idea that this rich, entitled prick is *complaining* about being in one of the most elite secret societies in North America is too much. Annoyed, I lean forward and punch him in the shoulder before I can stop myself.

It's not hard, but it's enough to make my fingers ache—I made a fist all wrong, with my thumb inside—and Stowe's mouth falls open in surprise. His sucker drops out onto his front, where it sticks to the fur on his jacket.

"Ow, what the hell, Morgan?" He rubs his shoulder. "None of the gossip magazines warned me you were so violent."

"Funny," I say, and then snap my mouth shut because I'm a little shocked at what I just did.

"See? You clearly have some fight in you." Stowe grins at me, like punching him is the most amusing thing I could have possibly done, and then fishes into his sleeve again, pulling out his flask. It makes me wonder if the sleeve of his coat has a Mary Poppins quality to it and he's going to keep pulling out one thing after the next until he gets to the standing lamp with the tassels.

He tips the flask back and drinks, and I pull a face at him.

"Your Tootsie Pop is on your jacket."

"Oh." He glances down and plucks it off, thrusting it in my direction. "Want a lick?"

"I . . . do not." I press my lips together, fighting back a smile, trying to hang onto my annoyance. It's hard, though, especially when Stowe sticks the furry sucker back into his mouth.

"Oh, ew. Really?"

He shrugs and then says around it, "I have to invite someone to the Secret Wankers Club. He's instructed me to pick either Hernshaw or Desmond."

Hernshaw or Desmond. Both burly, blond, white boys. Square jaws and blue eyes.

"Oh, right."

"Right." Stowe's expression is knowing, as if I've said something more. "Those future-Republican, sweater-vest-wearing baboons." He pulls the sucker out with a pointed *thwop* and says acidly, "What if I get them mixed up when I tap one? *Embarrassing.*"

"I don't get it." When he lifts a brow, I press on. "You're kind of all the same brand. Influential parents. Lots of connections. What's to complain about?"

He leans forward. "You think I get taken seriously here? That I'm making decisions and influencing people?"

I stay silent, my heart racing.

"I'm a joke to these people." His voice is laced with bitterness. "I'm a joke to *him*. Just another resource—and an exceptional lay, I might add. Which, by the way, is just another conquest to him." When he sees my horrified look, he shrugs. "I'm attracted to power. Daddy issues and all that." He lifts the flask in the air, like he's toasting. "Thanks, Chadwick, you flaming asshole."

Guilt twists my stomach. When I meet Stowe's eyes, I get the sense he's waiting for me to say something.

I clench my fists at my sides. Picture Evie's face.

"I'm sorry. I . . . feel like I should have had your back when the Rook was coming at you like that. But . . . I dunno, the way he talks." I shift, sucking in a breath. Stowe leans forward, eyes fixed on my face. "It reminds me of my dad. And I've never been able to . . ." I let my words trail off, and sag back in the chair.

Stowe is watching me so intensely it makes me sweat.

182

He can't see through me. He can't know I'm lying.

I let out a breath and clear my throat, like I've embarrassed myself. "Anyway, what will you do when you have to tap someone?"

"I won't do it." He shrugs. "Even though it's just as bad."

The wheels in my head are turning. I'm trying to figure out how to word things. "Why just as bad?"

I want him to say it out loud. Walk himself to the conclusion.

"He gives me two choices." Stowe ticks them off on his fingers. "Jerk-off one, or jerk-off two. I hate them both. Naturally, I don't choose, which means I don't have a man in the club. The Rook retains all his power."

A pause. A breath. Stowe's brow furrows.

I press on, triumph swelling at his transfixed expression. "Or you pick one of the jerk-offs . . ."

"Who is, of course, his man," Stowe says. "Rinse, repeat. Every year, every tap." His expression is dark. "This is how it works."

"And everyone just follows the system? Picks what he chooses or doesn't pick at all?"

"I guess so."

This should work. I think about every story I've ever heard. Speeding tickets. Sneaking into abandoned buildings. Nights in the drunk tank.

Ewan Stowe has never met an authority he doesn't want to rebel against.

"So . . . the system is rigged. You can't win." It's such a delicate game I'm playing, and when Stowe looks at me, brow furrowed, my heart skips a beat. I think I've revealed my hand.

But he shakes his head, gaze distant. "Yeah."

I clear my throat softly, and his attention shifts back to me. "Like I said, my dad is like that. Good at manipulation."

My face is flushed. This is such a gamble. "When you two are alone . . . he's not . . . he isn't violent, is he?"

Stowe jerks upright and blinks at me. Slowly, he shakes his head. "Your dad . . . ?"

It's almost laughable, the idea that my dad would bother to hit me. He doesn't even talk to me. Still, I take care to avoid the question—I just shrug and drop my gaze.

A beat, and then Stowe says softly, "I'm sorry, Holland."

We're both quiet for a moment, and I shift my attention to the fire, guilt pulsing through me with each heartbeat.

I force myself to think of Evie. Picture the forest swallowing her whole like it did Mia.

I need to know how to save her.

I need Crown and Grave.

I let my gaze go distant and bite my lip. I can feel him staring, searching my face. Maybe thinking about how he can save me.

"Has anyone ever done it before?" I clear my throat. "Like, tapped someone they weren't supposed to?"

He doesn't answer right away, and then he says slowly, "Not yet." My face is perfectly neutral, but my stomach is churning. This conversation is going exactly the way I'd hoped.

There are two things that drive Ewan Stowe: saving people and a constant need to rebel. Against his father. Against the system. Against authority.

All I have to do is feed that.

"Are you . . . you're going to do it?"

"I could," Stowe says. "That would really piss him off."

"That's really cool." I watch his face carefully. "Tapping a non-legacy for the first time. It's like . . . I dunno, breaking down walls. Showing everyone Crown and Grave are progressive."

Stowe tilts his head, brown eyes locking on mine. There's a glittering light there, almost like mischief. "Sure. And it would be hard to take that back, wouldn't it?"

"That's . . . sort of genius."

It is. It's my genius.

But he has to think it's his.

"The Rook will be pissed, won't he?" I hesitate. "He won't expect anyone to go against him."

Stowe leans toward me, a smile spreading across his face. "There's a first time for everything, isn't there?"

CHAPTER TWENTY-FOUR

Holland

THE FIRST OF OCTOBER means a weeklong reading break, and I spend it only half interested in my work. I leave notes on Evie's pillow twice. Apologizing. Begging her to talk to me.

They go unanswered, but she can't shake me that easily. I'm determined to keep her safe. Watching to make sure she doesn't go into the forest alone.

She's been spending a lot of time with Leta. There's a small part of me that seethes with jealousy at this. But I tell myself it's better. It's good she isn't going in by herself.

When the students come back by the boatload Monday morning, it fills homeroom with noisy chatter and the scrape of desk chairs.

After check-in, I use my spare to bike down to the duck pond. I'm only away from Evie because I spotted her in the library studying with Leta. There won't be a chance for her to slip away until later. By then I'll be waiting at the gate for her.

When I get to the pond, the sun is starting to spill out from behind the clouds, and the water is a deep black color. Usually, the shore is full of students, gathering beneath the trees or feeding the ducks, a few blankets spread out on the dock in spite of the chill.

Today, there are only a handful of eleventh-graders under one of the draping willows, the murmur of conversation drifting out across the water.

I lean my bike against the trunk of a thick maple and lay out my jacket. I'm trying to get comfortable when a commotion across the pond draws my attention.

Just behind the stooping form of the willow, a group of black-clad figures approaches.

My stomach sinks as the group under the tree shrieks in surprise, the noise quickly turning to shouts of laughter. A crowd is forming on the back lawn as students stop to watch the first tap of the week.

The cloaked figures pull one of the students up, moving around him, the low hum of chanting echoing over the pond.

There's a ripple of surprise from the watchers as the Rook appears.

The way he moves is so confident—a tall figure in a stark white mask, his strides long, pushing up his sleeves as he moves toward the group. Up close, he was intimidating enough, but now he's in his element, surrounded by the low thrum of chanting, making his dramatic entrance for a rapt audience.

His voice booms out. "Jeremy Henderson. You have been chosen."

The name makes some of the heaviness in my stomach dissolve. Not one of Stowe's required taps, then.

I watch as the wraiths circle Jeremy. And then the Rook turns, and the black-robed figures flank him as he strides away.

As soon as they're gone, the group celebrates, a tangle of cheerful noise echoing over the water. There's an ache in my chest as I sit back against the tree.

Every time a new tap happens, I'm going to be scared it'll be one of Stowe's choices. That he'll cave to the Rook before I can stop it from happening.

I force myself to look away, to lose myself in the assigned reading for the next half hour, the sun warming my shoulders.

"Morgan."

I start, then realize Stowe is standing next to me. He's wearing a pair of tinted aviators and a silky black poet shirt that shows off far too much of his chest. His hair is full bed head this morning, and I frown up at him, trying to figure out if his rumpled look is "rock star chic" or he's just extra hungover.

The press would love to see him like this. Bringing the *artistic bad boy* thing to all new levels.

"Hey," I falter, and then start again. "How was reading break?"

Stowe grunts, sinking down beside me on the grass. It's got to be wet, but he doesn't seem to notice. "Saw my dad. The bastard isn't inducive to reading."

I wait for him to add more. When he doesn't, I clear my throat. "You see the tap?"

"What, that disgusting little display?" He leans against the tree, flicking a hand toward the pond. "The Rook does like his dramatics."

"You tapping soon?" My stomach sinks and then lifts when Stowe shakes his head.

"I'm still stubbornly holding out." He pulls his aviators off, regarding me with sparkling brown eyes.

"You're braver than I am." I force a grin, like I'm in on the joke and not longing to scream at him. *Pick me, goddamnit.* "I'm looking forward to seeing the look on his face. Or, at least, what you can actually see of his face."

Stowe laughs. He inches closer, stretching his long legs in front of him. "I'm planning to pick *just* before the deadline—too late for him to do anything. And really publicly, so he can't take it back."

I can hardly sit still. I want to ask who he's going to pick, if he even knows yet. It's a horrible thought, but he might pick someone random, just to spite the Rook.

It needs to be his idea, though. I can't force this. "English project is due Friday. You got yours finished?"

Stowe lifts a brow. He wasn't expecting me to change the subject. He *wants* me to ask.

It's a small triumph, but a triumph nevertheless.

"I guess I should start, shouldn't I?"

I give him an incredulous look. "*Tell* me you're joking."

Stowe laughs, leaning forward to pull his notes out of his book bag. The movement makes his ridiculous silk shirt slide down a few inches, revealing a dark spot of color above his collarbone.

It's a bruise—a mottled chain of purple and black spreading up his neck like charcoal smudges. Without thinking, I shift forward, gripping his collar. The questions die on my lips.

Stowe grins down at me. "Morgan, what—?"

"Your neck." Tugging his collar back, a pang of shock goes through me. The bruises vanish farther down his shoulder, but there's a thick, raised scar there, the pale skin turning twisted and red in a patch as wide as my thumb.

"What happened?" I reach for the scar before I can think about what I'm doing, and find my wrist caught in his grip. Stowe's face is inches from mine. His smile is gone.

"Don't. Please . . ." He eases back, releasing my wrist a second later. Then Stowe shakes his shirt back into place and clears his throat, rubbing the back of his neck. There's a deep crease between his brows.

"I . . . maybe we can study later."

Before I can say anything, he climbs to his feet and lopes away, heading down the embankment for the pond. For one strange, slow second, I think he's going to continue down the bank and walk straight into the dark water, disappearing beneath the surface.

But of course, he doesn't. He sits down at the edge.

Shit. I shouldn't have said anything. *Certainly* shouldn't have reached for his bruise like some idiot girl in a romance novel. What was I *thinking*?

All the rumors are coming back now. Stories that went around the Hollywood circles. Stowe's expression when I asked him how reading break went.

That bastard isn't inducive to reading.

His father did that. The famous Chadwick Stowe made those bruises.

No wonder he doesn't want me to see them . . . the press would have a field day with that.

190

And of course, it makes the guilt of what I'm about to do one hundred times worse, but . . . it's such perfect timing.

I'm still sitting under the tree, caught in my uncertainty. Slipping my hand into my pocket, I brush the note, folded into a tight square. The third letter, this one written in my father's heavy, slashing handwriting.

I've been undecided on this one, wondering if it's too much. But again, I force myself to picture Evie.

I need to bond with Ewan Stowe. Get him to trust me fast.

It's just another role . . . the damsel in distress.

Stowe is already hooked. I'd seen his face when he'd noticed the last letter, the fascination. I've set everything in motion.

That steels my resolve. I walk down the embankment toward the pond, wet grass spraying flecks of water up onto my pant legs.

The crunch of sand makes Stowe's shoulders stiffen as I approach, but he doesn't say anything as I sit down. The shore is rocky and uneven, the dampness soaking into my backside.

A handful of seconds pass and neither of us says anything. He doesn't look at me, just stares out at the flat black surface of the pond.

He doesn't ask me to go away either.

I sigh, easing back to reach into my pocket. The paper crackles as I unfold it, and my heart crashes in my chest.

This could be an incredibly brilliant move or it could ruin everything. But I have to take the gamble.

Now he does look over, brows raised, like he can't help his curiosity.

I let out a breath. "I have something to show you."

191

When I hold out the letter, he stares at it, blinking. After a second, he takes it, smoothing it on his knee.

I don't look at him while he reads. Heat burns my cheeks, and I stare stubbornly out at the pond. There's no noise between us, only the distant sound of students walking from one class to the next, and the chatter of birdsong overhead.

It takes an agonizing amount of time. It seems like hours of staring out at the pond while Ewan Stowe reads the letter.

Finally, he sits up straight and sets the letter between us, carefully, almost reverently. Then he looks at me, brow creased. "Is this what I think it is?"

"A list of extremely detailed facts about you and a completely unsubtle insinuation I should sleep with you because my career is threatening to stagnate? Yes."

To my surprise, Ewan Stowe inches closer until our shoulders are touching. "That may be the most fucked-up thing I've ever seen."

God. He has no idea.

"Yeah. I wanted to tell him off." My face is hot. The blush coloring my cheeks is very real.

While the premise may be a lie, the letter is full of ugly truths. My agent isn't getting the phone calls she should be. The roles are hardly pouring in. "He's hard to say no to." I shiver, looking out over the water. I can sense Stowe's eyes on me, and at last he says softly, "I'm sorry."

"Yeah. Me too."

We're both staring out at the pond now, at the flat surface, so dark it reflects the sky like a fathomless black mirror. I wish it would swallow my guilt so that all I have left is resolve.

I glance over at Stowe, at the letter on the sand between us.

It's never been hard to forge my father's writing. I've done it dozens of times for school. Permission slips went unsigned otherwise. Unless it made him money, he didn't notice it.

Writing it, it had felt almost too much, especially the parts where I'd insinuated violence. Threatened myself, basically.

But now it seems perfect, like I couldn't have written it better.

It's strangely peaceful, sitting in silence, even with my own guilty conscience. And then Stowe finally says, in a low voice, "You ever wish you could be someone else? You know, someone braver?"

I don't look away from the mirror surface of the pond, but my pulse picks up. "I dunno, I just want . . . power. Whatever form that takes. As long as it's enough to . . . I don't know . . ."

"Face him," Stowe says softly. When I glance over, his gaze is distant, and I think he's talking about himself more than me.

It almost startles me, this piece of honesty. It makes me feel worse about the lies. But I know in that moment that Ewan Stowe is completely and totally mine.

CHAPTER TWENTY-FIVE

Holland

THE TAPS CONTINUE INTO THE WEEK.

In one instance, the art classroom is plunged into darkness, and by the time Ms. Trembley recovers enough to get the lights back on, the words *You are chosen, Theodore Barkley* are painted on a banner draped from the ceiling.

A second, later in the week, is equally dramatic, with Harold Sanders being appointed as chosen in the middle of dinner. There's a riotous blare of horns over the loudspeakers as he walks into the dining hall like an entering king.

The Rook is there for each one, standing stoic in that blank white mask.

Some of the teachers seem entertained by it. Others mildly annoyed as classes are interrupted and schedules thrown off. But no one protests.

A week passes, and then two. As the end of October approaches, I find myself counting off the remaining days.

Stowe hasn't picked anyone and time is almost up.

It isn't until the afternoon of the autumn dance that I force myself to put it aside and concentrate on my costume. I'm a wolf-hunting Red Riding Hood, and Evie is my wolf.

I'd been startled when she'd suggested it, and utterly relieved. She'd never answered any of my notes, or seemed ready to talk about it. But for now, she seems content to put aside her anger.

We do one another's makeup at my desk, propping Leta's vanity mirror beside my laptop.

Leaning over her to finish her eyeliner, I catch the scent of her shampoo and it sets my stomach fluttering.

I shift my red cloak out of the way, ignoring the plastic axe strapped to my thigh even as it pokes me in the leg.

"You're the perfect wolf-hunter." Evie grins at me in the mirror. She's already slipped the dental caps over her canines, giving her werewolf fangs. It makes her smile sharp. Predatory. A shiver goes through me before I turn my attention back to the headband in her hair.

"Hold still," I tell her, but I catch sight of her watching me and can't help grinning. She's adorable in her wolf-ears headband, the tip of her nose painted black.

"Truly the scariest werewolf I've ever seen."

"You two are so cute." Leta walks in, sweeping her cloak over her shoulders. "It makes me sick. How do I look?"

She's wearing a green cloak with a tail underneath and a pair of scaley green ears.

"Ready to breathe fire," I tell her.

"We're going to be late." Beth is seated on the bed behind us. She's already in her swan princess costume—a white dress with puffy sleeves and a delicate golden crown. She's been sullen for the last hour.

She'd been furious when she'd realized that not only were Evie and I back on speaking terms, but we were going to the dance together. It had become pretty obvious during last week's trip to the mainland when we'd bought what was essentially a couples' costume.

She's already tried to pull me aside once, no doubt to give me another lecture about not falling for Evie.

Too late for that.

It's hard to stop myself from staring at Evie in the mirror.

"Alright, we're ready." I touch her headband one final time and then we head for the stairs, joining a crowd of colorful fairy-tale characters going the same way.

We make our way to the gym, which the art class has decorated to look like a fairy-tale forest, with cardboard trees and a blue foil waterfall. The soft buzz of conversation echoes off the ceiling. The shutters have been pulled down and decorated with lights and tree branches. The curfew bell hasn't gone yet, but the shutters will stay down for the afternoon, making the room dim enough for clusters of pillar candles on every table to cast a warm orange glow. There's a buffet dinner on one side, and students line up with plates.

The autumn dance is an all-nighter. The one opportunity in a year to stay up past curfew.

Thumping music starts, the sound booth manned by a student in a tall, pointed wizard's hat.

Beneath the stage, a series of ice chests are set up, full to the brim with glass bottles of soda. Leta winks at me, flashing the silver flask she's smuggled in in her dragon tail.

The dancing starts off slow, with only a few groups on the floor, most of us hanging around the sides. And then a few minutes in, a song with heavy bass comes on and Leta squeals. Grabbing me and Evie by the hand, she drags us onto the dance floor, dragon wings fluttering.

"It's my favorite. We *have* to dance!"

We join the scattering of students, and once we're out there, the crowd holding up the walls slowly trickles onto the floor. Only the chaperones remain, Mr. Allen leaning against one of the benches and chatting to Ms. Trembley, both of them mostly ignoring the party.

People crowd around us, dressed in every fairy-tale costume imaginable. There are matching prince and princess outfits, pirates and knights, and even one boy in a giant Humpty-Dumpty costume who bumps into everyone as he makes his way through the dance floor, laughter rising in his wake.

When Stowe pops out of the crowd, I can't help laughing at his costume—a green tunic and matching leggings.

I lean in, raising my voice. "Are you Peter Pan?"

He only grins and nods, shaking his shoulders to the beat, until Daniel Prince and Elijah Archer join him. They're both dressed in woodsmen costumes, plaid shirts and suspenders with plastic axes. Patricia Harper trails after them, dressed in a peach-colored dress and huge fake pearls. There's a plastic crown woven into her blond hair, and I snort, watching her and Beth eyeball one another across the circle.

Prince drapes an arm across Stowe's shoulders, thrusting a red Solo cup into his hand. Stowe grins at him.

"You got drinks?" Prince jabs an ink-stained finger at us. "I'm the official drink getter. Gotta make sure you all got drinks."

"Getter of drinks," Elijah Archer crows, and Patricia Harper groans and rolls her eyes.

Beth hangs back during all of this, arms crossed over her chest. Her expression is flat. Like a dark cloud hanging forebodingly over the party.

I try to ignore it, watching Stowe as Prince plies him with a second drink. Then Evie reaches out and grabs my hand, and I laugh as she spins me around.

When a new song starts, Stowe leans in. "Can I steal you for a second?"

I nod, a little out of breath, and Stowe beckons me to follow him toward the stage.

"What are you doing?" I glance back, uneasy at the narrow look Evie is shooting us. "Stowe, what—?"

"Up here." He leads us up the stairs and onto the stage. We move past a few students perched on the edge, and he stops.

"Why?" I can feel my face flushing. People on the dance floor are turning toward us, expectant.

Stowe sways on the spot, searching my face. A jolt of annoyance goes through me. Did he drag me up here because he's drunk? If he wants to dance, it doesn't have to be onstage.

He gives me a charming smile, one hand on my waist, leaning close to say over the music, "I know you came with Evie. You seem to really like her."

That's an understatement, but I only nod, heart racing. *What's he about to say?*

"I respect that, but I think you know I carried a torch for you when we were nine."

It's almost funny, but his face is so earnest that I nod again, lips pressed together hard.

"Before I do this, I want you to know that torch never died."

I open my mouth and then stop. He's shaking his head.

"You don't owe me an answer. If you're with Evie, that's okay. It's just . . . something I wanted you to know before this happens."

I'm almost dizzy now. Before *what* happens?

Stowe grins. "This is how we get what we want." Before I can ask, he draws back, turning to the dance floor.

Overhead, the music cuts out and the lights flicker. There's a thunderclap from the speakers and the crowd on the dance floor stills.

Even in the dim light, I catch sight of them—four cloaked figures in masks making their way up to the stage. My insides buzz as they approach and I make out their outfits.

Flowing, multicolored cloaks, glass beads glittering under the stage lights, giving the impression of flashing scales. They're dressed as fairy-tale sprites.

A dramatic, rolling symphony comes on over the speakers and there's a ripple of surprise from the crowd as fog creeps out onto the stage, spreading rapidly around us. Stowe turns to me, dipping low in a bow before holding out a hand. I take it, and he leads me to center stage, under the heat of a single spotlight.

The robed figures flow up the stairs. One of them throws an arm out and smoke rises in a vaporous purple cloud as a deep voice comes over the speaker.

"Holland Morgan, you have been chosen."

The sound cuts off abruptly and the sprites whirl past me. Close up, I recognize the costumes from the play Northcroft put on last year. Stowe recruited his drama student entourage for this. That explains the fog and the lights.

On the surface, though, it looks like the final tap has been given the most fanfare. The biggest reveal.

The Rook is going to be pissed.

The last sprite pauses, pressing a cream-colored envelope into my hand before vanishing down the stairs. I'm practically vibrating as I take it, smoothing my fingers over the wax seal.

The Gravesmen's seal, an elaborate golden crown draped over a gravestone.

Again, Stowe takes my hand, and we bow together, like we've just come to the last act in a play. The buzz from the audience turns to applause, slow at first, and then louder. A few people cheer.

"We're breaking down barriers today, ladies and gentlemen." Stowe's voice carries over it all and the cheers only get louder. "Let's burn down capitalism. Let's murder classism. Crown and Grave welcomes their first-*ever* non-legacy tap: *Holland Morgan!*"

There's movement near the back of the crowd. Again, I peer through the glare of stage lights. There's a cluster of costumed figures at the back. One stands tallest at the center, the light reflecting off the sharp angles of his white mask.

I lose track of time as the evening goes on. As people crowd around me, yelling congratulations over the music.

Leta keeps tipping her flask over my cup, until I'm elated and a little dizzy, warmth spreading through my stomach.

It's Evie who surprises me. She's three drinks in before it starts to affect her, and even then, it's not like she gets sloppy. It's more like . . . she comes alive. Her eyes glitter with a frenetic energy, and when she bares her teeth at me in that sharp smile, heat rushes through my core.

She pulls me in closer, pressing her hips to mine as we dance. She seems different suddenly. Almost feral.

When the song ends we break apart, and Beth waves at me to rescue her from an overeager eleventh-grader. I pull her between Leta and me and then look around for Evie.

A shout goes up from the stage.

Stowe stands on the stairs and I groan as he thrusts his hips in the most ridiculous fashion possible. I push my way through the crowd, determined to get him down before he breaks his neck.

But before I can get to the stairs, he reaches down and pulls Evie up beside him. I stop dead as she ascends. Even drunk, she's graceful.

Evie lifts her hands above her head as she dances. The spotlight frames her against the wall, sending up a warped, wolf-eared shadow. The crowd is growing at the base of the stairs, cheering them on.

And then Evie throws her head back and *howls.*

A shiver goes through me. I'm drawn forward almost without thought. Unable to tear my gaze away.

Someone catches my arm, tugging me back. Beth's face is flushed, her brows drawn in a scowl. "Holland, don't."

Her voice is faint under the music and I shake my head, irritated, pulling out of her grip.

I'm at the bottom of the stairs now, and when Evie looks down and sees me, her smile is glittering. Savage and beautiful.

There's something wild about her right now. That feral light in her eyes sends a tremor through my body.

She moves down the steps until she stands a head taller, and we're nearly face-to-face. Reaching out, she grabs my jaw, fingers sliding under my chin, tilting my face toward hers.

Heat blazes in my chest.

She gives me time to pull away. When I don't, she presses her lips hard against mine. The crowd roars. Some enterprising partygoer takes up her call, howling long and loud at the ceiling until he's joined by others, until there are a dozen different voices howling along—coyote yips and raucous laughter over a thumping bass soundtrack.

All of that is background. All that matters is Evie, her lips on mine, her fingers spread along my jaw. She kisses like she might devour me, and my only thought is, *I'd let her.*

CHAPTER TWENTY-SIX

Evie

WE BREAK APART, and there are costumed students around us. Pressing forward. I ignore the drunken jeering. The staring. But then Beth is there, appearing out of the crowd in her white princess dress. With her blond hair haloed by the stage lights, she looks like some pissed-off heavenly angel.

She doesn't look at me, grabbing Holland's arm, voice raised over the music. "Can I talk to you?"

Holland looks irritated, but she allows Beth to drag her to the side and whisper into her ear, her face stony.

I don't think I've met anyone who acts more like a jealous girlfriend.

Stowe dances beside me. He tries to pull me in, but even with the liquor warming my insides, I'm too annoyed.

Stumbling up the narrow stairs and across the stage, I push past groups of inebriated partygoers. As I enter the storage room behind the curtain, the music is muted to a dull throb. It's dim back here, smelling of dust and mildew. Stacks of crates piled along the back wall cast hulking shadows.

Leaning against the shelves, I wait for my anger to settle.

I shouldn't let Beth get to me.

Holland kissed *me*, not her.

The night has been a blur, but it's been a blur consisting of Holland. Of red hair and lips and green, green eyes.

The *want* seizes me all over again. I picture how she looked on the dance floor, graceful and slender in that black dress, bright eyes burning up at me, the waves of her hair spilling over her shoulders.

And then Beth had to fucking ruin it, like she always does.

Someone is going to have to put her in her place.

Pushing off the rack, I'm turning for the door when I hear it. Someone calling my name in a low, singsong voice.

"Evelyn! Where are you?"

The noise echoes in the vast space backstage. They come into view one at a time, appearing in the doorway.

The liquor makes the room swim as they approach. The way they move is slow and strange. Unhurried.

Three. All dressed in black, faces hidden behind angular white masks with jutting ears.

The rabbit masks look stark and hollow-eyed in the shadowy room. The sight like some kind of fever dream.

"We have a present for you, Evelyn."

The voice is low and familiar. *Jack Aukley.* He steps forward, holding something toward me—a glass jar, half full of red powder. The vibrant color is immediately identifiable: red hemlock.

"Fuck off."

It spills out of me, the only appropriate response to his so-called gift. He's insane.

He laughs, and it echoes around the room as he advances. I jerk back as he grabs my arm, yanking me sideways, slamming my back into the metal shelf. And then I'm on my knees gasping for air.

A shuffle from above, and there's a heavy, choking hand over my mouth and nose.

I thrash and kick, bruising myself on the cement floor, desperate for air.

Through the haze of panic, I keep waiting for that familiar darkness to stir. To rise up and take over. *Save me.*

It's the first time I can remember welcoming it. Begging for it.

But there's nothing.

The hand comes away and I gasp, frantic to gulp in air. Someone seizes my jaw, wrenching my face up. My mouth is suddenly full of bitter-tasting powder. I cough and gasp, and the hand smashes over my mouth, driving my lips painfully into my teeth.

The rabbit masks loom over me, blurring in and out. One of them, I can't tell who anymore, says, "That's enough."

And then the pressure over my mouth is gone and I'm clutching at my throat, dragging in deep, rasping breaths, gagging at the rising acid.

"What if she throws it up?"

The reply is distant, echoing. "She won't."

He's right.

I know I should. I urge myself to roll over and shove my finger down my throat. Get the hemlock out of my system.

But I can't move.

Rabbit Mask leans in close. I can make out a pair of cold blue eyes through the mask. The glitter of diamonds on his tie clip.

And then my vision blurs and fades around the edges. The mask warps and dissolves into black.

I'm fading. And then the darkness sharpens. Lightens. Turns to green.

I'm dead. I must be dead. But . . .

No.

I'm in the woods. I'm wrapped in roots.

I don't know how I got here.

They weigh down my arms and legs, curling around my back in a heavy embrace. I'm drawn down, the forest floor embracing me, surrounding me with the rich scent of earth.

And then the soil closes over my head and I'm gone.

CHAPTER TWENTY-SEVEN
Holland

BETH RAISES HER VOICE over the music, even though she's practically speaking in my ear. "Are you even listening to me?"

I'm not. I'm too busy scanning the crowd for Evie.

I see the Rook instead, standing at the back of the auditorium. Almost like he's waiting for something.

Is he looking at me?

"*Holland.*" Beth's voice is sharp, and I turn back to her. She's glaring at me, her plastic crown tilted to one side, blond hair escaping in strands around her face. She looks like a disheveled Disney princess.

"Yeah, I get it," I snap. "Kissing in public is bad."

"People filmed," she hisses. "Do you know where that footage is going to end up? Do you know how many tabloids would pay to get their hands on it?"

"I don't care." I sound defensive, even to my own ears. "Let them."

Beth's eyes are wide. "Don't you remember what happened with Stacey? The pictures in the magazines? You got *lucky*. Can you imagine if they'd caught what you guys did after? It would have been career-ending!"

"*Beth*." I can feel my ears burning.

"Morgan."

The voice jerks me around and I find the Rook staring at me again. When we make eye contact, I ignore Beth's protests, moving away without a word.

I'll deal with her later.

I weave my way through the crowd and the white mask swivels as I approach. "Ms. Morgan." The Rook's voice is made hollow by his mask. "Lovely to see you."

"Rook." I give him a nod, keeping my tone formal. "You wanted to speak with me?"

"I might." His head tilts, and now his tone is laced with amusement. "Let's go somewhere private."

When I turn back to the crowd, people are openly staring. "Of course."

We move through the doorway and into the foyer. There, the Rook slips a key out of his pocket and unlocks one of the side doors.

Only . . . when he slides it open, I'm left staring in surprise. It's not a door that leads anywhere—it's . . . an elevator, the old-fashioned kind with a metal gate on the front.

The Rook chuckles, pulling the gate back with a metallic shriek before he steps inside. After a second, I follow, heart beating hard. Stepping inside feels like a gamble, especially when the floor lurches beneath my feet.

On the wall over the door, there's a brass half-dial, the arrow pointing to the *L* at the bottom. The Rook presses a button on the brass plate by the door and the elevator shakes violently, dropping so fast my stomach swoops.

I catch myself against the wall. "My god, is this thing safe?"

He stares at me, eyes shadowed by the mask. "Cable hasn't snapped yet."

"Hardly reassuring."

Another low chuckle. Then the elevator jerks to a stop and a terrific screech echoes out as he pulls the door open.

We step out into a wide, echoing space.

A basement, made bright by old-fashioned, electric hurricane lamps.

Bookshelves line the walls, stocked with thick, golden-spined texts, and there is a series of framed photographs beside them. When the Rook sees me looking, he smiles. "Crown and Grave alumni."

They're startlingly familiar faces. Politicians and businessmen. Influential. Powerful.

I know if I asked any one of these people, they'd deny belonging to Crown and Grave.

A huge brick fireplace looms at the back, with a pair of red wingback chairs in front. The whole thing looks straight out of a movie about secret societies, and I find myself holding back laughter.

A chill radiates from the stone floor as we walk in, and a fire sparks and sputters in the grate, flickering yellow behind the glass.

I take a breath and turn to the Rook. He's looking at me, waiting.

"I'm sure you're not happy with us," I say.

His head tilts. I'd wager he's raising a brow at me. "What makes you think that?"

Silence hangs between us. Is this some kind of test?

"I'm not a True Northman, but I can promise I'll be just as valuable. More, in the case of people like Aukley. You do know he's running around bragging about knowing *the secrets of the forest*, right?"

The Rook lets out a breath, loud and harsh through the mask, and turns for the fireplace, beckoning me to follow.

I trail after, following suit when he sinks down into one of the armchairs. There's a huge oil painting over the mantel. It shows the scrolling iron of Northcroft's gate, the forest stretching out behind it. Before the gate stand the three founders in old-fashioned suits and bowler hats. Hands resting on canes or tucked into vest pockets. The one in the middle is a full head shorter than the other two, with dark, bushy brows. All three have been painted staring straight ahead, expressions stern.

"That's Blackwood in the middle," the Rook says. "Poor bugger."

I have no idea what that means, so I don't reply, watching as he turns to a low side table between the chairs. There's a gorgeous decanter there, a blown-glass bottle with a delicate carving of a sunken ship in the center. I watch as he fills a pair of shallow crystal glasses.

"Stowe has asked me for a personal favor. A rare occurrence. And . . . I'm not as cold as people would have you think." The Rook passes me one of the glasses. There's nothing remarkable about his hands—long fingers and short nails. White skin. There's nothing to hint at who he might be.

I take the drink with a murmured thanks.

"Of course, he also made it rather impossible to turn you down," he says dryly, "what with the public appeal for a more diverse membership. I had no idea he was so anti-classism."

I keep a straight face. "The crowd certainly seemed to like it. Didn't they?"

He pauses and shakes his head. "Yes, well, Stowe seems to think very highly of you. I do hope you realize that."

There's some warning there, like he's worried I'm taking advantage.

As if he isn't just as bad . . .

"But it's . . . difficult." The Rook sets his glass on the table. "As fond as I am of Ewan Stowe, he is out of his mind ninety percent of the time. He really has *zero* idea what he's asking."

For a moment, we only stare at one another. I don't know what to say to that. What it means.

"There are long-standing traditions every Gravesman must keep," the Rook finally says. "I'm sure you're imagining silly, faux-occult rituals. Naked mud-painting and dick-measuring contests."

I take a sip instead of replying, and the liquid seers my throat. Whiskey.

"And while those things have their place, I'm afraid Crown and Grave's purpose goes deeper. Our secrets are dark. Once you're a Gravesman, it's for life. In fact, each member is prepared from the moment of birth."

"The True Northman." I'd been afraid of that. It makes my plan so much less likely to work.

The Rook inclines his head. "You're smart, Ms. Morgan. I'll give you that. But you weren't prepared for membership."

The anger hits me all at once and I lean forward, fingers digging into the soft leather arms of the chair. "Then *prepare* me. I promise you, whatever secrets you have aren't going to be enough to put me off."

Not with so much on the line. Not with the taste of Evie's lips still on mine.

Silence again. This time, I let it drag out, leaning back in the chair to take a sip of fiery whiskey.

Finally, he speaks. "There's a test every potential Gravesman must pass. It's . . . trying."

"I'll do it." My stomach is churning, though I'm not sure if it's excitement or nerves.

"It's not what you think."

"What does that mean?" I grip the arms of the chair. "Or can't you tell me?"

"I can warn you," the Rook says. There's no joking in his tone now. "I can advise you not to do this."

My heart is racing. I want to shout at him. I want the secrets of this place, no matter how dark they are. It's the only way I can keep Evie safe.

I square my shoulders. "Does it have something to do with the forest?"

"Yes, I suppose that part is obvious." He leans forward, gripping the decanter. To my surprise, he slides the bottle forward and the top comes off, revealing a hollow base. Inside, there's a single red-tinged leaf.

For a moment I stare at it uncomprehendingly. It's six-sectioned and sharp-edged. Vibrant red.

Red hemlock.

I stare at him, aghast. "What's the test? Surviving being *poisoned*?"

"I promise you, it's not." He sounds amused. "It's not deadly in this quantity. Only, as Stowe so eloquently puts it, a *damn good trip*."

There's a beat of silence and he leans back in his chair. "This is how every Graveman begins his induction."

This is it. This is how I save Evie.

"We're doing it now?" I work to keep my voice even. "*Right* now?"

"If you like." The Rook places the decanter lid carefully back onto the table. "It's entirely up to you. Or we can go outside and have another drink. You can tell everyone I'm a huge Holland Morgan groupie and I wanted your autograph."

Again, he's smiling. "Which is true, by the way. I was a big *Wizards* fan, like so many people."

"I . . . thank you." Between being offered the hemlock and having the Rook casually drop that he's a *Wizards* fan, I'm starting to feel like I'm in a bizarre dream.

"Or . . . you can take this, and we can begin the induction ceremony. You have"—he pulls his sleeve back, peering at the face of a thick silver watch—"roughly an hour. That's when everything begins."

I stare down at the leaf. Taking red hemlock could . . . no, *would*, get me expelled if anyone knew.

This part of the ceremony makes sense. By eating it, you're saying you're willing to do anything for the Gravesmen—to risk expulsion, not to mention being poisoned.

"And after I take it?"

"If you pass the test," the Rook says, "then you get an introduction to everything we know." He leans forward suddenly, making me freeze. "And that's the part that might ruin you."

For a beat or two, I stare down at the leaf.

I could walk out, go back to the dorm, and sleep off the hangover. But then I picture Evie's face. Her gray eyes. That sharp smile. Her hands in my hair. Trailing kisses over my throat.

I can do this.

Holding my breath, I reach out and set my empty glass down, plucking up the leaf. It's so small—only half the length of my hand. Even if it was classic hemlock, this amount probably wouldn't kill me.

Plus . . . Stowe has done this. He wouldn't have picked me if he thought something bad would happen.

The thought makes me realize that, in that moment, I *trust* Ewan Stowe. So completely that I'll apparently take his word on something this important.

The revelation makes me want to laugh. I'd never have believed that if someone told me a week ago.

"Consider carefully." The Rook's voice is soft. "That represents a new life. A new world."

I return my gaze to the hemlock, to the delicate, blade-shaped sections along the stem.

"You'll gain access to resources. Hidden knowledge. Power. But there's a cost, Ms. Morgan. You should think about that."

Hidden knowledge. Whatever it is, I need it to save Evie.

"I'll do it."

It's hard to guess at the Rook's expression, but I swear he's smiling as I place the leaf on my tongue. It tastes bitter and grassy. And then it's gone, and it's too late to change my mind. I turn to find him staring at me, my heart beating a fast rhythm against my rib cage.

"Now what? That was hardly enough to . . ." I pause, suddenly sure the lights on either side of the fireplace are too bright. When I look at the Rook, his mask is blurred at the edges, the white surface shifting and moving.

"How . . . ?"

"The hemlock was the first step. A trust exercise, if you will. It's completely harmless in that amount." The Rook's eyes glitter as he reaches over and picks up my empty whiskey glass. "This, however, contains more than enough."

A strangled gasp escapes me, but it sounds distant. I'm not even sure it was me.

"Please don't be alarmed, Ms. Morgan. This is all part of the process. Had you refused the hemlock, you would have found yourself safe in your bed tomorrow morning."

He moves to stand, and when I try to track his movement, my head falls back against the chair, impossibly heavy. My entire body feels like it's weighed down, trapped under heavy layers, like a weighted blanket is pressing down on all my limbs.

"But you didn't."

He's saying something else, but his voice is hollow now. It's a million miles away. And then he's gone.

CHAPTER TWENTY-EIGHT

Evie

PONDEROUS, RINGING TONES. A bell, penetrating the fog, dragging me out of unconsciousness.

My shoulders burn, and pins and needles run through my hands. I struggle to lift my head and the world surges. *Pain.* Oh god. It's white-hot, throbbing at my temples as my eyes slowly focus, surroundings coming into view.

Looming trees . . . the craggy silhouettes of moss-covered giants.

I jerk upright, thrashing, pain running up my arms in ragged bursts, before I register what's going on. There's a thin, plastic cord around my wrists. A zip tie, attached to one of the bars of the gate behind me.

Northcroft's front gate.

Horror washes over me. I'm outside, lashed to the gates, facing the forest like an offering.

Twisting around, I spot the peaks and crests of the school buildings. The round top of the library, the tower of the gym's roof behind the sloping black tiles of Cooper House.

It's coming back in bursts: the looming figures in their stark white rabbit masks. The bitter taste of red hemlock on my tongue. Instinctively, my gaze sweeps over the edge of the forest, drawn to the shadowed spaces between the trees. I'm half expecting to see something move.

There's another long, ponderous tolling from somewhere behind me.

The curfew bell.

I yank at the zip tie again, letting out a strangled gasp as bile rises in my throat.

I have to get out of here. There has to be a way to cut through the tie.

The cross. Ada's necklace.

I strain against the cord, gathering the fabric of my sweater in one hand, pulling the pocket closer.

Grinding my teeth, I manage to slide the tips of my fingers into the pocket. Despite the pain, I feel a measure of triumph, fingers closing around the metal cross. Holding my breath, I drag it upward, nearly losing my grip before I manage to slide it out.

I press the sharp edge into the zip tie. This is going to be difficult without stabbing my palm, but I don't have time to be careful.

As if to confirm this, the jarring tone of the curfew bell comes again, loud enough to make me jump. I jerk my wrists against the cords, eyes watering.

Aukley timed this perfectly.

"That motherfucker . . ."

The words die on my tongue. There's something happening in the distance, a stirring in the tree line. At first, it's just a rustle of branches . . . the tops of trees swaying. And I realize something strange.

The skyline looks . . . wrong.

I've memorized the trees by the gate now—the straggling pine, the tree with the burnt top, and the tall, spreading arbutus.

They're nowhere to be seen, replaced by new, unfamiliar trees.

Uneasy, I crane my neck, trying to spot the familiar skyline. Maybe I'm at a different angle. Maybe I can only see those trees from the common room.

But that doesn't make sense . . .

A thunderous noise jerks me upright as a black cloud bursts out of the forest.

I watch, open-mouthed, shrinking against the gate as the cloud swirls above the trees, so thick it nearly blocks out the setting sun. There's a thunderous sound, a repeated, echoing cry.

Birds.

The flock surges across the sky.

The raucous sound of hundreds of crows echoes in my ears as the birds sweep over me, hovering over the bell tower. Some come to rest on the peaks and towers, lining the ledges and nooks and settling on the shoulders of statues. The rest funnel up and up, forming an impossible shape in the sky . . . a bird tornado.

I can't understand what's making them do this, what made them flee the woods.

Until I turn and see the ripple of shadows in the distance.

It could be nothing—the sun finally setting, the shade stretching in wavering lines across the landscape.

But . . . it doesn't look right.

After a second, I realize it's *moving*, rolling outward like smoke billowing between the trees. An oily black fog, just a shade too dark to be real.

There's a rustling at the bottom of the gate. I recoil in horror as the ground ripples beneath my feet.

Only . . . no. It's a wave of churning insects. Thousands of glittering, hard-backed beetles. Skittering spiders. Never-ending streams of tiny black ants.

It's like every insect in the forest is surging straight toward me in a writhing black wave.

I scramble higher on the gate, clutching the cross pendant tightly. I'm picturing the insect hoard swarming up my legs, but they don't.

Instead, they surge beneath me, through the gate in a steady stream, like they have a destination. Like some kind of hive mind is driving them on.

The school.

They're fleeing the forest and heading straight for the school, just like the birds.

Twisting around, I find the fog creeping closer. It's blacker than before, consuming the landscape, sending the woods into darkness. And then there's movement along the forest edge. I watch, stunned, as hundreds of fawn-colored shapes burst from the trees.

Deer. All of them charging for the school, wide white eyes flashing in the dark.

"Shit!" Panic jolts through me, and I jab frantically at the zip tie, catching my hand, eyes watering at the pain.

Finally, the cross pierces through, but it's slow. Too slow. *Shit.*

All I can do is stab at the plastic again and again, gaze fixed on the deer hurtling out of the woods, driven forward by the incoming darkness. Smaller shapes run along the ground between them, flashes of red and brown. One of them reaches me first, a streak of rusty red slipping past. I make out huge eyes and delicate, pointed ears before it vanishes.

Foxes. Running between the panicking deer.

I turn back, jerking in shock as a huge shape charges past, the prongs of antlers coming so close they nearly scrape my cheek. The deer make a dull thundering sound as they pass me, fleeing shadows eating the landscape like fire.

God. *The shadows.*

Wherever they touch, moss shrivels and turns gray, covering the ground with dust. Trunks twist and creak, borne down by sudden rot, and leaves fall away, leaving the twisted, ash-colored claws of branches behind.

I must be dreaming. I'm still unconscious. Or . . . the hemlock. *None of this is real.*

The zip tie snaps and I jerk forward, heart in my throat. And then I'm running. Running like the deer, feeling their panic as they weave around me. I'm past the front gate now, down the winding path toward Blackwood Hall, the noise of hooves striking the grass thundering in my ears. My wrists are on fire and I'm dizzy, half-blinded by tears.

I barely register the crunch and pop as I run over the surging river of insects. The wide double doors of Blackwood Hall are the only thing I can think about. I'm locked onto them, blocking out everything else, ignoring the strange, chill wind that pushes at my back.

My boots slide on the stairs and I'm down suddenly, scraping my palms on the stones, scrambling up again just as fast. At the top steps, I slam a shoulder into the door like I can batter my way to safety.

I twist at the doorknobs, letting out a strangled growl as my hand slips and smears blood across the brass.

It's locked.

He can't do this. He can't leave me out here.

"*Hey!*" I scream up at the dark, shuttered windows. "I'm out here! Open the doors. *Open the fucking doors.*"

My feet continue to slide on the stairs. I'm leaving behind trails of crushed insects like snail tracks.

Pausing to drag in breath, I hear it . . . a high, keening scream that makes the back of my neck prickle.

Slowly, I turn back to the forest.

The landscape is a washed-out gray canvas. Like everything is lit by the static from a broken television. It's the same strange static burst I saw in the mist on the night I arrived.

This isn't happening. It isn't real.

My back turned toward the forest, I see it when the wave of black shadows finally hits the gate, and I watch in horror as the iron metalwork begins to decay. It happens like a film reel on fast-forward, rust creeping over the top. There's a grating shriek as it sags inward, like some giant invisible hand is bearing down on it.

The wave passes the gate, blackness seeping over the ivy on the wall. Crawling onto the tree just inside, the oak withering and drooping.

Every instinct in me screams *run*.

I bolt down one side of the staircase, running parallel to the wide, blocky front of Blackwood Hall. Overhead, the bird tornado is still churning. The thunderous sound of beating wings almost drowns out the thrum of my blood in my ears.

When I round the corner, I pull up short, shoes sliding on the grass.

There's a woman.

She stands dead center in the narrow pathway between Blackwood Hall and the dorm, staring at me. Her hair is blond and matted with what looks like tar. Her naked body is whip-thin and sickly pale, skin smeared with patches of inky black.

Her eyes are huge and blue in her white face. A familiar face.

"Beth?"

Shock forces the name out before I can stop it. The woman jerks and opens her mouth like she might answer.

Then her lips peel back, revealing a rotten, gap-toothed smile . . . a row of broken, bone-white tombstones set into bleeding gums. A thin line of black sludge trickles out one side of her ruined mouth, creeping slowly down her chin.

I stay where I am, frozen, until she tips her head back and shrieks—a shrill noise made from overlapping sound. The same high, unearthly scream we hear at night.

Not foxes, then.

And not Beth. *Definitely* not Beth.

I'm already wheeling on the spot, turning back for the woods, heart jamming into my throat. And *now* that thing in me finally bursts to life. The darkness surges in my chest, urging me on, screaming at me to *run, run, run.*

I crash through the underbrush, sticks and leaves snapping underfoot. Over the slamming of my pulse, I can hear a terrible rasping behind me.

It's chasing me.

I don't look back, running for what seems like forever, hurtling around trees and patches of tangled brambles, tripping over roots and jutting rocks. I'm going so fast I only catch a glimpse of the dull white patch off to my left, faded bones tangled in red hemlock.

The fox skeleton.

The farther I run into the forest, the more familiar it feels. A sense of déjà vu keeps hitting me, making my head spin. But . . . it can't be.

I haven't been here. I would remember this nightmare version of the forest.

When I finally dare a glance over my shoulder, I can't see the creature, but the shadows between the trees waver menacingly. I put on another burst of panicked speed.

Then something slams into my foot, sending a jolt of pain up my leg. I pitch forward, hitting the ground hard, crashing onto my side with bruising force.

The blow pushes the wind out of my lungs. I wheeze, thrashing weakly in my panic to get up. My efforts earn me a face full of wet earth, and when I finally scramble up, I find my hands coated with oily darkness.

The black ooze on the office carpet. On Mia's shoe . . .

Teeth clenched, I wipe it off on my jeans.

A giant, gnarled root is what tripped me, one of many that stretch out from the enormous tree towering overhead.

I'm in the middle of the clearing now. And at first, I'm sure it's the one that Holland and I took pictures in.

But . . . it's different.

The clearing is hedged with black brambles, thorns nearly as big as my thumb. The center is crawling with red hemlock, blanketed completely.

And looming over it all is the black walnut tree. It's monstrous now, stretching so high that the top branches are lost in the mist. It's taller than the highest peak of Northcroft, yet somehow, I've never seen it out the window. It's never shown up in my photos.

Its trunk is wide enough to drive through, and though the top half of the tree stretches up into the sky, there's a row of thick bottom branches slouching to the ground. A weird tangle of moss-covered arms reaching every which way.

Worst of all, the bark is a slick, toxic-looking black.

At first, I think it's rotting, poisoned by the same fungus killing the oak at Northcroft's gates.

But looking closer at the bulging roots, it seems like the bark itself is leaking inky black.

Instantly, all I can think about is the black tar oozing out the side of the Beth-creature's mouth. I scramble away, circling around the wide trunk like I'm facing off with some kind of hulking animal.

What the hell is wrong with this place?

Halfway around the tree, I stop, incomprehension paralyzing me.

At first, it doesn't make sense. The pale, twisted figure sprawled at the base of the tree can't be real.

A sliver of that strange, static light slips through the bows overhead, highlighting the angles of her pale face.

It takes me a moment to recognize her, with her face absent of all its frenetic energy.

Mia.

She sits with her back against the gnarled trunk, looking for all the world like she's nodded off there. Her arms hang limp at her sides, fingers curled loosely in the dirt.

She's wearing jeans and a white camisole, both stained black in places. Her legs are stretched out in front of her. One foot is bare. On the other, she wears a red Mary Jane flat.

Maybe the strangest thing of all is that her hair has been hacked off to the shoulders, the ends crooked and blunt. It's like she'd tried to give herself a haircut before walking out into the forest.

I have a horrible flash of déjà vu, of Ada under the water, her hair floating around her face, staring up at me while she chokes on dirty lake water.

By contrast, Mia looks almost peaceful.

In spite of this, her pale skin is stained with black and there's a fine layer of dead leaves scattered over her.

She was never airlifted off campus. She's been here, in the middle of the feral woods, curled up asleep under the monster tree.

Although *asleep* is not the right word.

She's definitely dead.

Mia's body is hemmed in by thick black roots. They curl tightly around her arms and waist. There's even a thin root wrapped up the length of her throat, disappearing into the side of her mouth. And they're all leaking the same black substance.

Clamping a hand over my mouth, I stare at Mia again, the way the tree bows over her like an angry child clinging stubbornly to a broken doll . . .

I shouldn't leave her like this.

Gathering myself, I inch forward, reaching out with trembling fingers.

When I brush her arm, she *twitches.*

My heart jams into my throat and I leap forward—*holy shit, she's alive*—but when my hand closes over her arm, I jerk back, startled by how cold she feels. And then I see it in my periphery— one of the *roots* near Mia's left foot shifts.

I'm stuck suddenly, frozen to the spot, breath coming fast and harsh in the silence.

I don't know what I just saw.

And then it happens again—the root wrapped around Mia's middle slithers forward. She slumps down another inch, hair sliding over one shoulder. Mia didn't move . . . the *tree* did.

I'm already backing away, breathing in sharp, ragged gasps, and then a root near my foot twitches, sending a shower of dirt over my shoes.

I'm running again. Plunging through the trees, spiny branches slapping me in the face, scratching my cheeks like bony claws.

I don't even think about where I'm going. Just *away, away, away.*

CHAPTER TWENTY-NINE
Holland

IT TAKES A WHILE to claw my way to consciousness, but even before my vision clears, I know where I am. I can hear the familiar wash of waves against shore.

Hemlock Beach, with its rocky coast and glittering, endless stretch of blue water, is a place for weekends. For Saturday mornings in the early summer. Where Leta plunges recklessly into the freezing Pacific Ocean and Beth and I skip stones over the water.

As my vision clears, the only thing I can see is that mask.

The sharp white lines and hollow eyes.

The Rook. I struggle to sit up and a surge of dizziness knocks me straight back down, the world blurring at the edges.

"Careful. It will take a while to regain the use of your limbs." The mask swivels to something behind me. "Boys?"

There's a scuffle and a boy in a brown-and-white owl costume, mask pushed up on the top of his head, offers me a hand up.

Beside me, a hulking figure in a pirate costume struggles to sit up. When he shoves his hat back, I recognize the panicked face of Jeremy Henderson, the tap before me.

Next to him is a slender, dark-skinned boy in some kind of prince costume, crown crooked on his messy curls. He's already pulled himself up on his knees, swaying slightly.

"Welcome to Hemlock Beach." The Rook sweeps out a hand. "Where nothing is like you remember."

I blink around and discover he's right.

Gone are the gently sloping bluffs covered in underbrush. The stony outcrops and scattered shells have vanished, replaced by a plain of flat, black sand.

Most disturbingly, the ocean has darkened, gone from deep blue to an oily blackness. It ripples listlessly over the shore, leaving a widening stain behind.

Even the tide pools are the same color.

Breathless, I stagger forward and the sand sinks and ripples strangely under my feet. I squeak and grip the owl's hand harder, suddenly afraid it might suck me under like quicksand.

The Rook speaks in the same flat voice. "Strange, isn't it? It's Hemlock Beach, but then again . . . it's not."

He's right.

Looking out over the coast, I suck in a sharp breath. Above the slate-black ocean, the night sky is a strange static gray. It's like a film negative, with the water and sky reversed.

And there's something awful about the shapes of the trees along the shore, like a row of jagged teeth in a snarling mouth. Their vibrant green color has drained away, replaced by ashen trunks and twisted branches, skeleton-bare where there should be leaves. Even the shape of the tree line is different. The trees are . . . bigger. And there's a huge, black-limbed tree stretching above the rest. Something I've never seen before.

There's an unsettling current running through this place. I can feel it in the sand beneath my feet, sense it with every shaky breath. I can't put my finger on the exact sensation, but it's enough to make the hair on my arms stand up.

This place feels alive, like it knows we're here.

"Recruits. On your knees." The Rook's voice booms out, carrying over the sound of the waves.

Beside me, the pirate is already on his hands and knees, looking stunned and shaky. The boy in the prince costume drops down and I follow suit.

The Rook moves to stand beside one of the tide pools. "Ladies and gentlemen, welcome to the Afterdark. Witnessing the forest after sunset is only the first part of your induction. And now, we introduce you to the second. Welcome to your first graduation ceremony."

He pauses and silence hangs heavy in the strange, static air. "The graduation is a time-honored tradition. It signifies giving a piece of yourself to the sacred body of Northcroft and taking a piece with you in exchange. It means knowledge and strength. It means power."

There's a stirring beside me, a low, panicked muttering coming from the pirate. Behind us, a cluster of costumed Gravesmen wait silently while the Rook makes his speech.

"Cooke, approach."

A boy pushes his way forward. He's tall and thin, dressed all in black. He shifts nervously from foot to foot as the others slap his back and pat his shoulders. He stops before the Rook and there's an expectant silence.

This is interrupted a moment later by muffled cursing from the back of the crowd, and someone pushes through, dragging a stumbling figure behind him.

"Found him lurking in the tree line."

The intruder is dragged forward.

Ewan Stowe's eyes are wild. His Peter Pan tunic is stained and torn on one side and his hat is gone. He crashes to his hands and knees, staring wide-eyed at the Rook. "It's happening again."

I don't know what that means, and before I can ask, the Rook strides over.

Even with the mask, it's obvious he's irritated. "Yes, welcome to the consequences of your own actions." He flicks a hand at one of the Gravesmen. "Deacon, if you would? Keep him with the recruits."

Deacon, a heavy-set boy in a red cape, grumbles and stomps forward, putting one thick hand on Stowe's shoulder.

"Keep quiet."

Stowe gives a squawk of protest, staring around with wide, bloodshot eyes. "What the fuck? What the *fuck*?"

"Shut it," Deacon snarls.

Stowe goes quiet, but only because his gaze has fallen on me, and I flinch as he lunges and seizes my arm.

"I didn't know you'd be here. You have to help—"

Before I can say anything, there's a heavy sigh.

"You'll have to forgive our errant member," the Rook says. "Like I said, he's never quite all there. Isn't that right, Stowe?"

The Rook reaches down and grabs Stowe's chin in one gloved

hand, forcing him to look up into his mask. "It's tough when reality is constantly shattering into pieces around you, isn't it?" The Rook gives a derisive laugh.

Stowe goes stiff but says nothing as the Rook turns back to the tide pool.

"Let's begin."

Strangely, the water in the pool is moving, rippling outward. At first, I think one of the Gravesmen kicked a rock in and disturbed the water. But then the ripples grow and spread until the oily water laps at the edges.

My chest tightens.

There's something in the tide pool. Something that emerges an inch at a time, water running in rivulets down the slick surface, the dome of a head, the blank surface of a face and neck, shoulders and arms.

It rises slowly from the black until, at last, something crouches in the center, oily liquid oozing from its gray skin.

Impossible. My heart thunders in my ears as the thing turns to *look* at us.

It has a face, I think. It's tilted up toward us. But it's blank and smooth, without indents to even hint at features. One arm is stretched out, spindly fingers touching the lip of the pool. A strangely human gesture for something so alien.

The hulking boy in the pirate costume staggers back with a strangled moan. Even the silent boy in the prince costume goes completely rigid.

Despite my own panic, I can't help feeling annoyed. According to the Rook, my fellow recruits have been prepared for this. Isn't that what it means if they're True Northmen?

So why are *they* freaking out?

I watch, fascinated, as Henry Cooke approaches the gray-skinned creature.

"Recruits." The Rook's voice is low. "Witness the transfer. The Crown and Grave Society has defeated sickness, age . . . even *death*. We have defeated the grave and seized the power that is our birthright. We are kings of our time."

The intonation is measured, formal, like he's recited these words many times before. But his voice also holds a note of reverence.

"Henry Cooke, do you accept this gift, given freely by the woods? And do you accept its cost, that all men are required to pay?"

"I do," Henry answers gravely, without looking away from the creature in the tide pool. "*Cape coronam.*"

The remaining Gravesmen chorus back, "*Mortem decipere!*" and the noise echoes over the water, making me jump.

Henry moves closer. When he's at the edge of the pool, he pauses, kneeling, and the creature stretches to touch his cheek with thin, spiderlike fingers. Oily black water drips off its limbs and onto the stones in stringy, viscous ropes.

Cold horror clutches my chest. I can't look away.

As soon as it makes contact, something strange begins to happen. Where the creature's finger touches, an inky black spot spreads out over Henry's skin and then dissolves.

At the same time, the creature's face is . . . moving. Its skin ripples like the rings in water, the gray pallor slowly dissolving and revealing the beginning of features.

Nausea grips me as the features sharpen, settling into pale

skin and black arched brows. A second Henry Cooke slowly forming before our eyes.

It feels like a dream, with the Rook presiding over this strange transformation. With Henry patient and smiling and the Gravesmen a silent audience. Paralyzed, I glance over at Stowe, who's breathing heavily, one hand clutched over his mouth. He keeps shaking his head like he doesn't believe what he's seeing.

He's a Gravesman. Why is *he* freaking out?

And then the silence is interrupted as the water in the tide pool ripples again and the creature gives a sudden, violent jerk. It staggers back, water sloshing around its torso.

There's a shout from Henry as he overbalances, landing half in the pool. He tries to scramble up, but the creature shoots an arm out, grasping his shoulder. It's thrashing now, the black water roiling around it.

Horribly, the creature is only half finished, huge black eyes in a pale face, a hollow crater where its nose should be. There's a high-pitched, multitoned whine coming from it as it uses Henry to pull itself up out of the water and Henry fights to scramble away.

The Rook jerks around as Stowe lets out a horrified gasp. "What the fuck is that?"

Behind him, a nervous hum goes through the crowd. Even the Rook only stands there, hands raised, like he's about to say something. Only . . . he doesn't.

Clearly, this has never happened before.

Henry shouts. The creature has managed to grip him around the throat, dragging him down the slick stones of the tide pool. The surface churns as he struggles and chokes on the oily water.

Dismay shoots through me. *It's not trying to haul itself out.*

"Help him!" I'm on my feet now, heart slamming against my rib cage. "Someone *grab* him."

The Rook's mask swivels. He stares at me, eyes blank. My stomach sinks as I whirl around to face the crowd. I'm met by a sea of blank faces. Nobody moves.

He's going to drown in a foot of water.

"Fuck!"

I move without thinking. Behind me, Stowe screams my name, but it takes only seconds to cross the rocky shore. Then I'm at the tide pool, shoes slipping on the slick stones just as the creature pulls Henry under.

"No!" I plunge my hand in, catching his wrist, throwing my weight back as hard as I can. "Let go! Let go—"

"Holland, stop!"

I think it's Stowe again, closer this time, but all I can concentrate on is my hand slipping beneath the surface of the water, how *impossible* it is that this thing has vanished and is pulling Henry under.

How deep is it?

I'm still holding onto Henry's wrist, straining against the impossible weight. The water laps up my arm, cold and slimy, leaving an oily stain behind.

I glance down again, panic spiking as I realize the stain from the water is *moving*, traveling up my arm toward my heart, tingling numbness spreading in its wake.

It feels like something hits me in the pit of my stomach, sending a shock of molten heat flooding through me all the way to my fingertips. A scream tears out of my throat and I jerk back, feet skidding on the rocks. The movement sends me pitching violently backward, straight into Stowe. He wraps his arms around me, and I think in the fog of my panic that he's stronger than he looks. He drags me away from the tide pool, his breathing harsh in my ear.

"Give me your arm." The Rook looms over us, making us both jump. The command is sharp enough that I jerk my arm forward without thinking.

The sight sends a bolt of panic through me.

My palm is solid black. Like I've dipped it in ink. Above that, black splotches run all the way up to my elbow, patterns where the water struck and sunk in.

Behind me, Stowe still has hold of my other arm. I can feel him trembling, and I'm not sure if he's holding on for my sake or his.

The Rook keeps a tight hold on my wrist, rotating it slowly as he examines the front and back of my arm. Then he glances back at the tide pool. It's gone still now, a sheet of black glass.

Henry Cooke is gone.

I feel like I might be sick. Instead, I suck in a breath and pull away from Stowe. Force myself to stand up straight and meet the Rook's eyes. "That was screwed up."

The mask tilts again. The Rook surveys me for a long moment before releasing my wrist. "Welcome to Crown and Grave, Ms. Morgan," he says, and then he turns away from the tide pool and the beach, heading for the forest without looking back.

CHAPTER THIRTY

Evie

THE FOREST IS *UTTERLY* QUIET.

It's not night-quiet, with the faint sound of crickets and the rustle of hunting creatures. It's the kind of silence that belongs to crypts and graveyards . . . the kind that sinks into your bones and settles in your core.

My chest is tight, but I press on, keeping my gaze fixed on Northcroft's bell tower, rising out of the fog.

I pass trees that twist and bend in unnatural patterns, in ways that should be impossible to grow. I skirt around patches of fog that settle in thick pools, like the mist is being drawn to something.

As I get closer to the school, the chilling silence eases. A breeze stirs the tops of the trees, rustling leaves and swaying branches, producing a gentle hum.

It's almost comforting at first . . . wind is normal.

But then . . . the shushing grows louder and morphs back into that strange, low hum. It sends an electric current through my chest, making the back of my neck prickle.

Instinctively, I glance up. The dark, crooked branches overhead are moving erratically. It has to be the wind. Only . . . my hair still hangs limp around my face.

I'm close enough to catch glimpses of the wall through the trees now, and I quicken my pace. From above, the hum grows louder. Changes. Like it's shifting keys. It sounds like whispering now.

A name, drawn out long and repeated over and over in a chorus of rattling branches and scraping leaves.

Evelyn. Evelyn. Evelyn.

I bolt for the tower rising in the distance, just as crashing footfalls start behind me. Terror surges in my chest as I picture the monstrous version of Beth. Her pale, black-streaked face.

Don't look back.

I can't look back, not even when the footsteps get closer. Not even when they're joined by a strange rasping sound like branches dragging over stone.

Adrenaline floods my veins. And then . . . *there*. The wall looms up through the trees.

At the angle I'm approaching, I can see the round top of the observatory and, just behind it, the bell tower.

I'm on the south side. There should be a gate—narrow and rusted, covered with a blanket of ivy. Unless the forest has rotted it away like everything else.

But no, there it is, mercifully still intact.

Skidding to a stop, I waste a precious half-second clawing at the bars until I find the lock. It opens with a shriek, and I stumble through and slam it shut just as something crashes into the other side.

Behind the gate, a figure staggers back, clutching its face. Then it shakes itself and tries again, hurling itself at the bars. I catch a glimpse of it for the first time.

My stomach flips and I press my hand to my mouth, swallowing bile.

It isn't the monster version of Beth; it's worse.

Its face is blank, save for a thin black slash of a mouth. Everything above that is empty—just a smooth surface streaked with black slime. It throws itself into the gate again, limbs overlong and stringy.

It's like a poorly made copy. Something that's formed itself into the closest approximation of a human it can.

Horribly, there are more behind it. My heart seizes in my chest at the sight. I count at least six tall, spindly figures, some swaying on two legs, others crawling on all fours. All of them look grotesque and warped . . . blank-faced and slick with oil, their bodies misshapen.

The one at the gate howls again. Its spiderlike fingers wrap around the bars. Then, abruptly, it falls silent.

I pause, heart beating frantically in my throat.

They're all frozen, facing me, heads tilted. Somehow, I can tell they're staring at me, even without eyes.

Horror roots me to the spot. What the fuck are those things? What do they want?

The whispers in the forest. My name, over and over.

Mia at the base of the walnut tree.

What *is* this place? Tentatively, I take a step toward the gate, half expecting the creature to throw itself against the bars again.

Instead, it stays still, face tilting this way and that like it's able to track my movements.

Can it hear me?

"What do you want?" My voice is almost shocking in the quiet.

The creature cocks its head and my pulse picks up. It definitely heard me.

I take a step toward it, heart thundering in my chest. The sight of it pulls me closer.

I flinch back when the thing moves, reaching one long arm through the gate, movements surprisingly careful. Like it's trying not to scare me.

Its hand is long and five-fingered. Slender. It turns its palm up and I stare in disbelief.

"You want my hand?" The burning need to *know* is taking me over, like something in my gut is tugging me forward.

At my question, the creature inclines its head—an eerily human gesture.

I'm holding my breath now, stretching one hand toward it.

This is so fucking stupid. I'm the first to die in a horror movie. The idiot girl who makes idiot choices and deserves to get murdered.

I'm near enough now, barely brushing the creature's fingers.

It lunges, fingers locking around my wrist. I jerk against its grip. Its skin is cold and wet, but that's not the shocking part.

As soon as it has me, heat flares in my core. Something breaks open inside me and the darkness surges, eager to meet this strange creature.

And I can suddenly *feel* it. It wants something. I can feel its desperation like it's my own.

Horrified, I scramble back, but it tightens its grip. A flood of images crashes into me and I clutch at the gate, frantic, half-blind. Blood thundering in my ears.

Everything is a blur, a jumble of colors and images. Chaotic patterns.

I squeeze my eyes shut.

A tree. The big walnut in the clearing. There's a figure stretched out beneath it, dark hair spread out around her head, her face white and drawn under the static light. Her stomach is bare, and the telltale swell of pregnancy draws my eye a second before I see the man crouching beside her, guiding her hand up toward the tree.

Shock goes through me. He's younger, but I recognize his thin, pale face.

My parents, sitting under the tree. My father drawing my mother's arm up, touching her limp hand to the tree. I suck in a breath as black veins ripple up her arm, appearing on her stomach a moment later. And then her belly *grows*. Rippling out and up in a motion that makes me feel distinctly nauseous.

Then the vision blurs. Changes so fast it leaves me dizzy.

Two small figures stand beneath the outstretched branches. Twin, black-haired toddler girls, holding hands and smiling sweetly. Me and Ada, posing like we did for so many photos.

Only . . . the twin on the left has black eyes.

Black like the forest at night. Black like the stains on the roots of the tree.

Horror crawls up my throat, bursting from me in a high, stran-gled scream. The creature jerks back and I turn and stumble away from the gate.

I run without looking back. Around Blackwood Hall, with its locked doors, and the side of the girls' dorms, all the shutters pulled down tight.

My breathing is ragged, my pulse thundering in my ears.

There. The greenhouse. The glass peaks of the roof rise beyond the girls' dorm. I run as fast as I can.

At last, the glass front looms over me. The greenhouse is blanketed in ivy and the light of the static sky glitters off the walls. I glance around at the still, silent buildings. Their shut-tered windows are blank. Nothing stirs.

And then I see it.

Eyes. White and glittering in the darkness all around me. Hundreds of them. For a second, I can think only about those misshapen creatures.

I can't move, terror seizing my muscles.

And then, slowly, the shapes come into focus, and I realize it's not the mutant creatures. It's *deer*. Hundreds of them, all stand-ing stock-still on the lawn. All of them staring at me with wide, shining eyes. *Holy shit.*

Their stillness scares me.

Normal deer would run away, wouldn't they? But maybe they know I'm not the danger here.

They're taking shelter. Just like I am.

I catch my breath and move slowly over to the greenhouse. The deer move finally, heads swiveling in unison as they track me. The sight sends unease crawling through me, but I force myself to turn away.

The greenhouse doors are locked, but they're made entirely of glass. It takes seconds to snatch up a paving stone and smash through the pane above the handle.

My hand stings, blood pooling between thumb and ring finger. I ignore it, pulling my sleeve over my arm before plunging my hand into the jagged hole, grasping for the lock.

There's a click and then I'm in the humid building. Here, the darkness is interrupted by tiny, circular plant lights. They illuminate a series of tropical flowers along the back table, all bright reds and yellows.

The light also reveals stacks of heavy ceramic pots just inside the door. I drag them over one at a time, the muscles in my arms protesting.

I work until I'm sweating, until my lower back aches fiercely, stacking them against the door until the pile reaches the door handle. Then I collapse in front of it, my back to the barricade, chest heaving.

Above me, the glass ceiling is black, reflecting the tropical plants below. The lamps aren't bright but I still feel exposed, and I hold my breath and dart under one of the long wooden repotting tables. It's still set up with students' work: scattered trowels and bags of soil. I find a set of sharp pruning shears and snatch them up, clutching the handles hard to my chest.

Here, I'm surrounded by the heavy scent of earth, and my

body finally starts to relax. I just have to wait for morning . . . until the sun comes up.

The sky is still dark, which means it'll be hours. Hours I don't want to spend thinking about the way that creature's black-stained skin felt. Or the images that flashed behind my eyes.

The pieces are starting to slide together, and I don't like the picture they're making. Why this place is so familiar. Why it keeps showing up in my dreams. That terrible copy of Beth. Ada and I by the monstrous tree, one of us with night-black eyes.

How that dark thing inside me feels so connected to the forest. And . . . it makes me realize . . . *I was connected to Ada.* I could *feel* her.

That was what had saved me when she pushed me over the cliff. And that night on the dock, I'd ducked *before* she swung the bottle.

And then, when she was in the water, I'd felt it cut off so abruptly. Had known immediately she was dead.

Both of us were connected. Both of us were here.

But only one of us is real.

My chest tightens. It's getting harder to breathe. I try to push the thought down. I can't consider the implications. Not right now. Not here.

So instead, I clutch the wooden handles of the pruning shears so tightly my fingers ache and I think about one thing and one thing only.

When the sun rises, I will walk back up the steps and over the threshold of Blackwood Hall. Back into the real world, the non-nightmare world.

And when I get back, Jack Aukley is going to pay.

CHAPTER THIRTY-ONE

Holland

THE RATTLE OF THE SHUTTERS pulls me out of the fog of sleep. For a moment I just lie there, head throbbing as light crawls up the walls and illuminates my thin privacy curtain.

Groaning, I start to roll over and tug at my comforter. My hand drags over something smooth and silky instead, and a flash of inky black catches my eye. I'm suddenly wholly awake, sitting up so fast my head swims, heart beating a thunderous rhythm in my ears.

There is a series of inky blotches trailing down my arm, just under the elbow. When I flip my hand over, my palm is fully black, like I've dipped it in paint. Panicked, I clap my other hand to my mouth as last night comes flooding back.

The party. That strange version of the beach after dark. The creature in the pool. *Oh my god.*

The thing draped over me isn't my blanket, it turns out. It's a suit jacket. I shove it away, a lump rising in my throat.

Vaguely, I remember someone walking me through the passages last night. I remember tilting my head to look up at the white mask. The blurry form guiding me, delivering me to my door before vanishing. I'd stumbled to bed, telling myself the hemlock is a hallucinogenic.

There's a shuffle from beyond the curtain. I jump, jerking the jacket back over my arm. Beth's voice comes from the other side.

"I'm going to breakfast. You want caffeine, party girl?"

"Uh. I'd love that. As much coffee as you can fit in a cup."

"Alright." A pause, and Beth adds, "Look, we need to talk about last night."

For one panicked moment, I think she's talking about the Afterdark. But then the memories kick in.

She means kissing Evie.

"Later, Beth."

"You can't sweep this under the rug." Beth's voice is tight. She's getting ready for a lecture.

I can't deal with this.

"*Please* don't. Not right now."

A sigh, heavy and long-suffering. It floods me with annoyance, but thankfully she shuffles away. The bump of the door follows and I sag back onto my pillow with a groan.

The room is silent. Nothing stirs from next door. Leta usually sleeps in on weekends, and if Evie is awake, she's keeping to herself.

Evie. Just thinking her name makes something happen in my chest—a sudden, sharp pang of longing. I drag in a breath, startled by the intensity.

Okay, yes, I basically abandoned Evie at the party. She's probably going to be super pissed, but right now, that isn't the most pressing matter. Again, I suck in a breath, pulling my arm out from under the jacket.

This time, I run my fingers down the back of my arm, relieved it feels nothing like the slick, oily skin of the monster.

A distant thump of footsteps, and through the crack in my curtains, I see Evie coming through the front door. The wolf tail and ears are gone, and her hair is a wild mess of curls; her eyes are shadowed and tired in her pale face.

The sight of her wakes something in the pit of my stomach. A dark heat roars to life, driving me up and out of bed, heart beating hard in my ears. I clench my fists, shocked at my own reaction.

Evie stops in the doorway, face flushing red. "Holland." For a moment, I think she feels the same thing. But when she says my name, there's an edge to it.

She's angry.

When I meet her eyes, something unravels inside me. A swell of emotion starts in the pit of my stomach, crashing over me like a wave—an urgent *need* that rocks me with its intensity. My arm *burns* suddenly, and I clench my hand into a fist.

The emotion feels off. It's almost . . . alien.

The Rook's words echo in my head: . . . *giving a piece of yourself and taking a piece with you* . . .

No. That can't be it. I didn't do the ceremony. I never agreed to give the Afterdark anything.

"Holland."

Evie repeats my name, more sharply this time. It jerks my attention back to her. Dread clenches my chest as the feeling spikes again. It makes me want to reach out and grab her, wrap my arms around her and . . . and what?

The feeling is wordless—an urgent, animal need.

"What happened last night?" Evie asks, and the accusatory tone startles me into stillness.

How do I answer that?

I'm a Gravesman. That's one thing I could say. I passed the test and now I'm a member. And there's a terrifying, nighttime version of the forest all around us, and it marked me. And maybe . . . maybe there's a piece inside me right now, sprouting roots. Weaving tendrils through my insides.

When I look up and catch her staring, I realize I'm touching my arm, rubbing my fingers over the sleeve covering the mark. I've been doing it without even noticing.

"Are you hurt?" She steps closer, irritation turning to concern. "What's the matter with your arm?"

I glance down, stomach twisting. You can see the black part of my palm just beyond the tips of my curled fingers. "Nothing." I slide the jacket back over my hand.

Before I can react, she reaches out and snatches my arm. "Let me look."

"Evie, don't." I stumble back, panicked, but it's too late.

"What is this? What happened?"

She grasps my wrist, trailing one finger cautiously over the inky spots. I can't help the shiver that runs over my skin. I know I should pull away, but everything in me screams to step closer.

Something inside me wants her . . . wants me to grab her and pull her close, to press my mouth to hers. To *have* her in every way possible.

Again, I get the creeping sensation that I'm pushing back against something foreign. Something separate from my own feelings.

"You should let go."

Evie stares at me, eyes combing my face. She's frowning now, like she knows something is wrong.

The door crashes open, making us both jump. Beth's voice, high and indignant: "She said let go!"

I'm half turning, about to tell her it's okay, but Beth hurtles through the doorway, paper coffee cup in one hand. She pushes past me and plants her palm in the center of Evie's chest, shoving her steadily back until Evie's shoulders hit the wall. Coffee spills down the side of the cup and over Beth's hand, but she doesn't seem to notice. "Stay away from her."

Leta appears in the opposite doorway, still in her pajamas, dark eyes wide. "Beth, what the fuck?" All I can see is Evie's face, the shutters that go down over her expression. The cold, glittering light in her eyes.

I'm tense all over, expecting Evie to lash out. To bring Beth down like she did Aukley. But Evie only stares at her.

Then, to my shock, she steps past Beth's guard and seizes her chin. Beth makes a startled noise, trying to pull back, but Evie wraps her other hand in Beth's collar, fingers clamping over the base of her jaw, forcing her head to one side.

I'm shocked out of my stupor. "Evie, what—?"

"She's marked too." Evie's voice is low and flat. It freezes me to the spot. Even with Beth facing away from me, I can see how stiff she's gone.

No. That can't be what she means.

A strangled whimper escapes Beth's throat as Evie grips her jaw.

A crushing sense of unreality settles on me. "What's she talking about, Beth?"

Beth's voice is an uneven rasp. "I'm not—" She flinches as Evie reaches up to press a fingertip to her temple, just above her ear.

My heart squeezes in my chest. The black spot. The one I'd been thinking was a mole the entire time . . . so tiny it's hardly noticeable.

Of course. I'm starting to feel incredibly stupid.

Beth went out into the Afterdark. And if she's marked, it means that nightmare creature in the tide pool touched her.

No wonder she was practically comatose the first week. No wonder she came back different.

So many things are starting to click: her anxiety around curfew, the way she reacted to the noises from the forest, the nightmares . . .

She never told me. She never *warned* me.

"Don't lie." Evie's voice is soft and deadly. "I saw that *thing* out there."

I don't know what that means until Beth jerks like she's been stabbed, glancing toward the window.

That *thing* out there. The one that turned into Henry Cooke, dragging him below the surface of the water.

A chill runs through me.

Evie shifts her gaze over Beth's shoulder, looking at me now. "Think about it. The obsession with the shutters. Her fear of the forest . . ." She looks at Beth again. "You were out after curfew."

I sag down onto the bed. "You know about the Afterdark?"

"Had a run-in last night," Evie says shortly. "Courtesy of Aukley. Looks like you got an introduction too."

My head is spinning now. "You . . . Aukley?"

"I guess he wanted to return the favor for the beating I gave him." Evie releases Beth, who stumbles back, hugging herself. She won't meet my eyes. "I stayed in the greenhouse overnight, though I can't say I had much sleep."

There's a moment of loaded silence as we both look at Beth. And then, at last, Leta says, "Okay, what the fuck are you all talking about?"

CHAPTER THIRTY-TWO

Evie

EVERYTHING COMES OUT AFTER THAT.

We end up in an uneven semicircle in front of the cold fireplace. My knee almost touching Holland's. For some reason it's like I can suddenly *feel* her, even without looking over.

It takes a minute to shake it off. Collect myself so I can tell them what happened: waking up in the Afterdark, running from the spindly, no-faced creatures . . . I don't mention the forest whispering my name or the creature communicating. I keep the vision to myself.

It had to be Ada with the black eyes.

Ada is the monster.

Then why do I feel the Afterdark all the time? The thought keeps coming back over and over. I think I've always been able to feel it.

Holland tells us about the so-called graduation ceremony. The creature that dragged the boy to his death. The tide pool that marked her.

When she tells us about the last part, she clutches her arm to her chest, shielding it like it's broken rather than turned a deep, inky black. When Beth reaches for her, Holland draws back.

"What is it?" Leta says. "What's in the tide pool?"

No one answers. We're all thinking about that strange oily substance, the sickly sweet smell, the way it oozes from the roots of the trees.

Holland shakes her head. "I'll ask the Rook now that I'm in."

I want to tell her she can't be *in*.

It doesn't feel right, Holland joining them. They've been protecting this monstrous secret. Keeping it from the students.

After she's done explaining, we go silent. Everyone looks at Beth.

She flinches, dropping her gaze. Reaching up to touch the black dot on her temple. "I knew something in the woods got Amanda. I was stupid, thinking I could go out there and figure out what they were hiding. I saw it . . . set in, and I ran." She swallows hard, face pale. "I ended up on the beach."

The beach. The one in Holland's story, with the terrible creature in the tide pool. The half-formed copy.

A copy like Ada.

It *has* to be Ada.

It makes a horrible kind of sense. The dull, red scar on my palm tingles, and I press my thumb into the spot while memories trickle back slowly.

Days after an argument, I'd find pins stuck into my bedroom carpet. Or she'd help Mom with dinner, and I'd be the only one to end up violently ill.

I'd thought the worst of it was when I found my cat in the forest behind the house, the stringy pink ribbons of her intestines spilled out over the autumn leaves.

Dad said the neighbor's dog did it, but I never believed him. I don't think he did either, because we never got another pet.

She'd set her sights on me after that. Like murdering my cat had been a precursor.

Doesn't it all mean the copy *has to* have been Ada?

But then my mind goes back to her face, blurred under the water as I hung over the dock and watched her drown . . .

I push the thought away.

Beth has gone quiet, eyes on the carpet. She doesn't mention anything about her doppelgänger. For once, I almost feel bad for her. She's had to listen to that thing screaming out in the woods every night, knowing exactly what it is.

"And you just . . . never told anyone?" Leta says.

"Somehow Gorski knew. She cornered me the next morning."

Holland's eyes go wide. "That's what your therapy sessions have been about?"

"She told me it was stress. That none of it happened. I pretended to go along with it . . ." Beth hesitates. "I mean, I've always known it wasn't, but she hinted I might need to be institutionalized if I kept talking about monsters."

Holland's expression is dark. "She threatened you."

My mind is racing. The vice principal knows. And Crown and Grave. Who else?

The answer is obvious . . . the oily, black substance on my father's doorframe, his gaunt face and wild eyes. I'd thought he was having some kind of breakdown, but . . .

He knows. Maybe Mia was onto something. Maybe she uncovered the wrong thing in her podcast research.

He wouldn't have done anything to her—not the man I knew.

But then, I think about the way he loomed over me, screamed at me to get out. Maybe I don't know him anymore. Maybe I haven't for a long time.

My heart squeezes in my chest.

Holland blows out a breath. "I have . . . so many questions. Like, how many people are in on this?"

"Also, why the fuck did the pond eat that one guy?" Leta's voice is strained. "And how can we make sure it doesn't eat me?"

I raise a brow at her. "You may want to skip the graduation ceremony."

"Are you two *joking* right now?" Beth glares at us and then glances up, clearly distracted when Holland stands. "Where are you going?"

"I can't just sit here. I'm going to see him."

The Rook. I stand up too, following her to the door. Something in my chest aches as she walks away. It feels as if there's a line drawing tight between us.

It's ridiculous, but I want to beg her not to go.

"Hey, wait." I reach out and catch her arm. When I make contact, a shock goes through me, a kind of electric current that sends the hairs on my arms standing on end.

Holland jerks and I know she's felt it too. Her eyes are huge, red lips parted in surprise.

"Holland, what is it?" Beth pushes forward, nearly elbowing me out of the way. I resist the urge to punch her in the throat. Holland *does* look shaken.

She backs away, gaze darting down to my hand. I pull back, stomach sinking.

What the hell was that?

"I'd better go" is all she says. "I have questions for the Rook."

"You shouldn't go alone," Beth says. "I'll come."

"No." Holland's voice is sharp, and Beth looks startled.

"It's just . . . I need to go alone. Otherwise, he might not tell me what I need to know."

Before I can say anything, she turns and vanishes out the door.

CHAPTER THIRTY-THREE

Holland

OUT IN THE HALL, I drag in a breath, trying to calm down. I'd snapped at Beth back there, but sometimes she's suffocating.

She's always going on about caring. About keeping me safe. But she'd been out there and never told me. Hadn't *warned* me.

Apparently *keeping me safe* only means controlling my social life.

My temper flares as I remember last night. I'd kissed Evie, and Beth reminded me of Stacey. Implied it could have been worse if they saw *the things we did after.*

Like what Stacey and I did was automatically bad and dirty if it went past kissing.

The thought brings me up short, because how does Beth even know that?

Was she *watching* me that day? Following me around in some misguided attempt to keep me out of trouble?

I breathe in deep and try to wrestle the anger down.

It feels like my emotions are out of control. It makes me think of the way I reacted to Evie. How I could *feel* her. Like something was connecting us. When she'd grabbed my arm, I'd felt my entire body respond.

Unease prickles through me.

I have to get to the Rook and ask him about this thing on my arm—what it means. Why I'm having these extreme reactions.

My thoughts are in such turmoil that I'm halfway around Blackwood Hall before I realize someone's following me.

I whirl around and he nearly crashes into me—a tall, gangly someone with wild black curls and smudged eyeliner.

"Stowe, god!"

He's wearing a bright blue jacket this morning, the silver buckles down the front making him look like some kind of hung-over circus ringleader.

Stowe is breathing heavily. He stops and doubles over, bracing himself with his palms on his knees. "Oh shit, cramp. I was *running*. Why do people *do* that?"

When I look at Stowe, with his smeared eyeliner and his ridiculous outfit, a flare of anger goes through me. This is *his* fault. How could he not know about the Afterdark?

Pressing my lips together, I look around campus. It's still too early for crowds, but we're standing right in the open. There's a handful of students walking past and I can't risk saying the things I want to . . . or yelling them, more likely.

When I turn back, he's staring at me, and I realize how bad he looks. His dark curls are rumpled and bare of product, his eyeliner streaked down one cheek. As he blinks at me, his eyes look glassy, and he sways on the spot.

Seeing him this way should fill me with pity. He's an addict. Instead, I want to reach out and shake him.

"Leave me alone, Stowe." I walk away, heading for the gym, for the elevator that will take me down to Crown and Grave. For answers.

"I . . . I have to know what I saw last night." He's following me again. "That thing in the pool—"

I whirl around, grabbing him by the front of his stupid coat. Stowe lets out a startled grunt as I drag him forward, until we're on the narrow path between Blackwood Hall and the boys' dorms.

The tramp of footsteps comes from the covered walkway above us, and I keep my voice low.

"Are you insane? Don't talk about it in the open." My tone is heated and my arm prickles. "In fact, don't talk at all. You're a disaster." I gesture at his smudged eyeliner and wild hair.

He isn't the one who nearly got pulled into the pool. He isn't the one with a messed-up arm. So why does he look like he's falling apart?

I turn on my heel and Stowe darts forward, grabbing my arm. "Holland. Wait." He's pleading now, voice uneven. "I . . . what I saw out there . . . I don't know what's real."

Laughter bubbles up in my chest and I squeeze my eyes shut. He wants real? I could show him my black-stained arm. *That's* real.

The black streaks on my clothing in the hamper. The scuffs on my hands and knees from falling on the rocks. All of it, real.

It should be terrifying, overwhelming. But all I can seem to access right now is anger—anger at Stowe for being so *stupid*. So oblivious. So pathetic.

For letting me do the test. For not warning me what was out there. No amount of drugs could make me forget the Afterdark. How could he not know?

It makes me want to *punish* him.

When I open my eyes, he's standing in front of me, swaying like he's on a ship at sea. "Tell me I'm not crazy."

"You need to get a handle on your day drinking." My voice is cool but he cringes like I've slapped him. "Rehab clearly didn't do anything."

It's cruel. But that doesn't stop the flood of savage satisfaction washing over me.

He should have known not to tap me.

Somewhere in the back of my mind, a faint alarm goes off. I'm saying too much, going too far. And . . . isn't there something strange about the surge of rage?

But all of that is buried. I'm reckless enough to ignore it, advancing on Stowe.

He backs away like he isn't a foot taller—like he couldn't simply overpower me if he needed to—until he's pressed against the wall, flinching as I jab a finger into his chest.

"How can you not know?" Our faces are inches apart. I'm straining up onto my tiptoes, fury coursing through me. "Is your grasp on reality really so tenuous?" It's all coming out now. Words spilling out on a tide of sheer, boiling rage. "How could you *do* this to me?"

I'm breathing hard, chest heaving. Stowe stares down at me with huge eyes, shining with what might be the start of tears. It makes me even angrier.

I lean in, seizing the lapels of his jacket, drawing him so close our noses nearly brush. "Look at you. You're pathetic."

Stowe drags in a shuddering breath and I realize he's trembling. Cowering away from me, his gaze on his feet, tangled curls spilling over one wide, charcoal-smudged eye.

"Holland." His voice breaks on my name. "Please."

The way he cringes back makes some animal instinct roar up in my gut, like a predator spotting weakness.

I want to grab his jaw and dig my nails in, wrench his chin up to expose his pale, stubble-covered throat.

What would his fangirls think to see him like this? What would the critics say, seeing their rising star brought so low?

"Can't you even look at me?" My voice is hard but quiet. There's a small, vindictive part of me that knows silence is power.

I could draw this out. Make him beg.

It makes something blossom in the pit of my stomach—a strange, dark excitement.

My arm burns suddenly . . . a sharp, searing pain. It makes me glance down at my hands, still wrapped around Stowe's collar. The inky black of my palm makes me suck in a breath. I jerk away, clasping my hands to my chest.

The rage in my chest dies off so fast it leaves me dizzy.

What the hell am I doing?

"I . . . I'm sorry. I don't know—" I shake my head, shoving my sleeve up.

"It was real. Here." And there it is, the ink-black splatter running up the length of my forearm. Proof that last night was horrifyingly real.

Stowe stares at my arm and then back at me. His eyes are wild, but his expression is almost hopeful now. "It was real. It's always *been* real. The forest . . ."

"The Afterdark." The words taste sour in my mouth. "That's what the Rook calls it."

Stowe tips his head back, resting it against the wall, eyes fluttering shut. He lets out a long, trembling breath, almost a whimper.

A beat, and then he opens his eyes. He looks calmer now, almost himself again. "I've been twice, I think. The first time, I thought for sure it was the acid. I swore off it, but it happened again. They told me . . ." He shakes his head, blinking hard. "They told me I still did the drugs. That I forgot." He rubs a hand over his face, expression haunted. "Schizophrenia runs in my family. My mom . . ." His voice trails off.

Horror washes through me, and then a wave of hot shame.

The Rook had been playing with him. Torturing him with uncertainty, because he'd had no idea if it was in his head or not. And I'd just done the same thing.

Now I remember our conversation by the fire. How Crown and Grave never took him seriously. How the Rook used him.

I can barely look him in the face now. "I'm so sorry. I don't know what came over me."

Only, I think I do . . .

My arm prickles again and I stiffen, shoulders hunched. I won't touch it. I can't bear to think I'm connected. That the strange new sensation in the back of my mind—the low thrum of emotion—doesn't belong to me.

"Holland?" His voice is tentative. "Are you alright?"

Alright. I'm not even sure what that is right now.

I let out a sharp burst of laughter and then clap my hand over my mouth, shaking my head. My eyes burn and I squeeze them shut hard.

I can't admit there's something *inside* me, that the Afterdark didn't just mark me . . . it left its poisonous thorns embedded in my flesh.

A shuffle and then, to my shock, Stowe gathers me in his arms, pulling me in against his chest. He's tall enough that my cheek presses into that ridiculous silk coat. He smells like cinnamon and cologne.

At first, I stiffen, afraid the thing inside me will surge up, that I'll lose my temper again. But when I try to pull back, Stowe doesn't let go.

After a second, I give in, letting my head drop against his chest, blinking furiously against the tears crowding my eyes.

"It'll be okay." He pauses, then adds, "I mean, all of this is colossally fucked, but we'll stick together. We'll figure it out, alright?"

When I look up, he blinks at me, waiting. I finally nod, slowly, still not sure everything will be okay. If *okay* is a state I can ever reach again.

But it seems to satisfy him, because he pulls back a little and smiles and it's like the sun breaking through clouds—slow to come, but dazzling when it finally emerges.

"Let's go see the Rook."

CHAPTER THIRTY-FOUR
Holland

SITTING IN FRONT of the wide stone hearth across from the Rook, I steel myself to demand answers. The clubhouse is quiet, only a scattering of Gravesmen present.

"I apologize that the test went the way it did, Ms. Morgan. I hope you know it wasn't meant to. You were simply meant to bear witness to a graduation. Nothing so horrifying as what happened."

I try not to wince as his gaze drops to my arm. "I take it the Afterdark wasn't supposed to do that."

Just saying the word sends a pang of unease through me. My arm tingles, and I clamp my fingers around the armrest.

There's silence as the Rook peers through his mask. It's like he's trying to see through me.

"We've been having problems lately. You may have noticed the rotting tree by our front gate?" When I nod, he presses on. "Some of the Afterdark seems to be . . . leaking. Coming through into our world."

The thought makes my skin crawl.

"Honestly," the Rook says, "I'd anticipated something might happen. Though that was far more . . . severe."

Shock goes through me, and I shift in my seat. He *knew* something might go wrong and sent Henry Cooke into the tide pool anyway.

There's a shuffle beside me as Stowe settles onto the arm of my chair. He slides his hand over mine, squeezing gently. I find myself relaxing into him, though my heart is still hammering in my ears as the Rook continues.

"Usually, we have someone to communicate with. The host, we call him. But he's been cooped up in his office for weeks."

Understanding spreads cold fingers through my chest. "The principal."

"Yes, he *was* the host." The Rook rests a hand on the arm of his chair, fingers tapping out a short rhythm. "But his behavior has become more and more erratic." He grimaces. "The Afterdark insists on a human host. But . . .it goes through them too fast."

He must see something in my face because he explains. "Think of the host like a lit match. Once ignited, he burns bright and fast. Fire is power, a type of energy. But it also consumes quickly. Until there's nothing left."

He glances at the wall above the fireplace, where the painting of the three solemn-faced men hangs. "Blackwood was the first, you know." The Rook's chuckle is dark. "He didn't last long. If you ask me, I think that's why the hall is named after him. Cooper and Stowe felt guilty."

There's a moment of silence as I struggle to take this in. It's Stowe who finally asks, "Okay, what in the blue fuck was in that pool?"

The Rook gives him a dry look. "We call them copies, but they're more like . . . a kind of spore. How the Afterdark tries to spread. Thankfully, the founders made a deal to keep it contained."

"What deal?"

The Rook clears his throat. "The Afterdark wants humans. It craves the feeling of hollowing them out, draining them for nutrients."

Cold horror washes over me. Beside me, Stowe shifts, his expression shell-shocked.

The Rook continues. "We provide it with what it wants. People. Crown and Grave members, of course. In exchange, it stays on the island, and away from the school. And we get to experience a kind of rebirth."

"Rebirth?" The word sends a jolt of unease through me.

"Yes." The Rook's voice is matter-of-fact. "It makes a copy. We're the same person. The same likes and dislikes, the same hopes and dreams. Just . . . a better version. There's no fear or pain. No weakness."

I touch my arm, rubbing over the persistent tingling. "So . . . if the graduation had gone right, Cooke would have been . . . ?"

"Copied." The Rook's voice sounds amused, though it never reaches his eyes. It's only now that I realize how flat they are. How even and cold his voice always is. It sends a pang of disquiet through me.

"And then what?" My voice drops to a whisper.

"The better version emerges, and the old, flawed version stays."

"Stays . . . ?" My voice breaks. I picture Henry Cooke slipping under the oily waters. "Wait, like . . . you die?"

I shift, and Stowe's grip tightens on my hand. He looks pale, gaze fixed on the Rook's mask.

"Of course not." The Rook shakes his head. "Think of it as a transference. Your consciousness simply continues in a different body. A better one."

I must look horrified, because he adds, "It's regrettable you had to see a graduation go wrong. The transferal is usually very peaceful. I should know."

I blink at him, and he nods slowly. Beside me, I feel Stowe stiffen.

"A few of our members go through the graduation early. It helps ease any worries our new recruits may have."

My eyes are huge as I sweep the room, and the Rook chuckles. "You won't be able to tell. We're very authentic."

My chest tightens, and I find myself pressing back in my seat. Stowe's grip on my hand is so tight it aches, but neither of us moves.

My gaze strays toward the entrance. I want to run and not look back.

If the Rook notices our discomfort, he doesn't say anything.

"We've had a handful go wrong." His voice is dry. "Even before last night's unfortunate graduate. When that happens, the kind of double it produces is . . . unstable. Still seeks its original purpose." His eyes fix on mine, darkening. "Replacing the original."

Beth.

My chest tightens. Suddenly her fear of the forest takes an even darker turn. Her double isn't just *out there*—it's *searching* for her.

"There's a few of them, which hopefully you never have to see. They're . . . malformed. It's embarrassing, frankly." The Rook grimaces. "Now, I'm afraid that after we ascend and become our new selves, there's no longer a connection. So I can't say what it wants. You, though . . ." His gaze locks on my arm, burning with intensity. "You touched the pool, the raw substance of the Afterdark. Which is a first for us." He leans forward, eyes shining as he studies my face. "I'll be honest with you. I don't know what that means. Or . . . what you are now."

A shiver goes through me as the Rook continues. "You're connected, I think. Can you feel it?"

I bite the inside of my cheek, remembering the swell of *want* when Evie touched me. The rage that overwhelmed me when I snapped at Stowe. *Can I feel it?* Yes, but not in a way that helps.

There's only one answer he wants to hear, though, so I lie. "If you're asking if I'm connected, the answer is yes."

For half a second, there's only the sound of the fire popping in the hearth and the gentle strains of classical music. It makes me realize the conversations around us have dropped off. The Gravesmen are clearly listening.

The Rook lowers his voice. "What has it told you?"

"Well," I speak slowly, stalling for time. "Its method of communication is uneven . . . abstract."

He leans forward in his chair.

I swallow hard and continue. "It's not words. More like . . . emotions." It's half the truth. "I'm hoping it will get clearer."

"We'll experiment," the Rook says. "Make the connection clearer. Perhaps if you touch the pool again."

Beside me, Stowe makes a noise of protest at the same time I say sharply, "That thing tried to *drown* me."

"Naturally we won't let that happen." He seems unperturbed by my protests. "But you'll likely need to go back in, strengthen the connection. We'll accompany you of course, for protection."

The idea sends goosebumps over my skin.

Going back in. Facing the twisted forest, the dark waters washing up on that pale shore. The thought isn't as terrifying as it should be. In fact, there's a small part of me that's intrigued.

I think about the way my insides reacted to the creature touching me, and the strange sensation flares in my core, a dark excitement that sets my teeth on edge.

Part of me *wants* to go back.

Stowe leans forward, glaring at the Rook. Some of the color has returned to his face now. "How do we know it's safe?"

"It's not," the Rook says. "It won't be until we fix this. But you don't have to worry. We'll help you graduate once this is all over."

Cold panic shoots through me, and I blurt out, "No."

There's a long pause as the Rook regards me through the mask. "No?"

There's a dangerous tone to his voice.

"Just . . . what I mean is, give me time." I draw in a breath. "Seeing if I can grow the connection without risking *drowning* seems reasonable, right?"

A pause, then the Rook nods slowly. "Fine. You want time? November sixteenth, we go in. Founders Day seems appropriate."

Founders Day. It's the date Blackwood, Cooper, and Stowe signed an agreement to fund the school.

It's also less than three weeks away.

I open my mouth to protest, but the Rook interrupts.

"It's dangerous to wait. We need to figure out what it wants. Why it's coming into our world."

Three weeks to figure out how the hell to get out of this. Or, maybe, to pack a bag and take the next ferry off this damn island.

"May I see?"

It takes a moment to realize what he's asking.

When I offer him my hand, he takes it gently. Goosebumps run over my skin as his fingers trace my forearm.

I repress a shiver. When I meet his eyes behind the mask, I'm startled to see how hungry they look. It's strange, because when his gaze dips down, I realize it's not *me* that has his attention— but the mark.

A pointed throat-clearing brings us both back to the present. Stowe is leaning sideways from his perch on the chair, waving an arm in the air. The Rook shoots him a withering look.

"Yes, Ewan. You have a question?"

"Mainly," Stowe says, "that you might want to offer a lady dinner before you feel her up like that."

The Rook looks exasperated, but he releases my arm.

"Yes, thank you, Stowe." He turns back to me. "The Gravesmen's duty is to keep students safe. This may be a way to save the situation."

Meaning, he now has a direct line of communication with the Afterdark.

And that line is me. I sit up straight, giving him my best *People* magazine smile—charming and confident. "I'm sure we'll figure it out. You and me."

He gives me a slow nod, eyes shining behind the mask. He's bought it. He thinks I know what I'm doing, that I have control over the situation.

But there's a small, distracting tingle at the base of my spine. It's a chill that goes down my back and lifts the hair on my neck.

I can feel something settling in the pit of my stomach, like the dark silt stirred at the bottom of a pond finally sinking down.

It doesn't mean it's not there anymore. It's just waiting.

CHAPTER THIRTY-FIVE

Evie

THE FIRST THING I DO when I have a spare second is bang on my father's door. I'm angry and I want answers. I try twice. The first time, there's no answer. The second, the secretary, a short blond lady with a smoker's voice, escorts me out with a lecture.

After that, the foremost thing on my mind is avoiding Holland.

It kills me a little. But I have a growing suspicion about the way the Afterdark flares when I see her. The way she makes me feel scares me: almost out of control, like I'm on the precipice of something.

Thankfully, I'm able to time things right. The only class we have together besides homeroom is biology, so I play hooky with Leta that afternoon. We're careful to avoid the forest, even though I can feel it drawing me in. We settle on a blanket under a wide oak on the quad.

Pulling up my camera, I get a shot of the sunlight filtering between the swaying branches overhead while Leta flips idly through Mia's notebook. She's been listening to the podcasts Mia was a fan of, taking her own notes in the back pages of the book.

I'm only half paying attention as she muses out loud.

An hour passes, and when Leta has to go back for class, I finally give in and walk into the forest.

As soon as I walk in, the scent of pine wraps around me. The hum of wind through the branches becomes clear, and I'm more alive. Sharper.

I feel like I could run a mile, and I tell myself it's *not* because I belong here.

It's utterly quiet the deeper I go, and it's in this quiet that something catches my attention. Not a movement or a sound, but a s*ense* of something. The back of my neck prickles. Slowly, I turn.

The peaks and towers of Northcroft can be seen through the trees, but that's not what draws my attention. There's a flicker of movement. Someone walking through the forest.

I know they can't have seen me, so I stay where I am.

The crunching footsteps come into earshot a moment later. As the shape grows clearer, I can tell it's not Holland just by the way the person moves.

Aukley.

Somehow, I know he's been following me.

I'm moving before I have time to question myself. Not bothering to keep quiet, snapping twigs and kicking up handfuls of dead leaves. Let him see me coming.

Aukley stares as I approach. He doesn't take his hands out of his pockets. But he goes still, trying to assess the kind of mood I'm in. If I'm going to charge up and hit him.

That fucker. He *gave* me to the Afterdark. I should beat him until he's a bloody mess.

Instead, I stop a few feet away. Leaning a shoulder against the nearest tree, I keep my face neutral.

"Most people would be afraid of these woods now." Aukley steps closer.

"How did you know I'd be out here?"

He grins. "You're supposed to be in English. But you're not."

Warning bells go off in my head. "Then what?"

"Biology."

He's paying too much attention to where I am. Where I'm going.

I'm already calculating the distance between us—the seconds it would take to reach him, to put my elbow in his solar plexus. How many breaths, how many blinks for him to cross between us and wrap his hands around my throat. If I'd have time to twist away.

"I know you were the one in the rabbit mask."

Aukley's brows lift. "You're so blunt."

"I don't like games." We're close now, within arm's reach.

"Everything is a game." He looks at my mouth when he says it. "You and me, we're the same. We know that better than anyone."

"Everyone wants something." The back of my neck is prickling, the lizard part of my brain screaming *run, run, run.* But Aukley is not a wolf and I am not his prey. "Even that thing out there wants something. *You* want something."

"Oh?" he says. "Why don't you tell me what I want."

Our faces are inches apart now. My pulse is racing in my ears. It's like being here in the forest is charging every inch of my body, urging me to do something reckless. "The Afterdark is taking people, isn't it? Beth's friend, Amanda. Mia . . ."

Aukley looks down at me, brows creased. Like he's searching my face for something.

I go still as he lifts a hand, wary. Then he reaches out and touches my hair, winding a curl around one finger. He's surprisingly gentle. "I didn't think I liked shoulder-length hair. But it's nice on you."

It's such a bizarre statement that I draw back.

"I think you know what the Afterdark wants," he says.

I stare at him, mind racing.

The dreams I've been having since forever. The urge to go into the forest, to touch the hand of the strange, humanoid creature.

The feeling of *belonging*.

Maybe I wasn't the twin in the ultrasound after all.

There's a feeling rising in me, traveling up from the pit of my stomach. Swelling in my chest. I'm hot and cold, and then hot again—panic, mixed with a heated, frantic kind of energy. I feel like I might explode. I force it down, shifting my attention back to Aukley. I remember what he said when he was trying to get me to hit him.

I know you have it in you.

He didn't mean violence. He meant the Afterdark.

But he's wrong. I'm not the copy.

"How do you know so much about the Afterdark?" I step closer, until his back is pressed against a tree.

"I've been in," Aukley says. "I put the pieces together."

"Liar." I reach out, sliding my hand up the side of his neck. He tenses, and I curl my fingers around a fistful of thick blond hair. Pressed against him, I can feel his pulse race like a trapped rabbit. The next few seconds could hold anything. I imagine slamming my forehead into the ridge of his nose. Jabbing my fist into his throat. "Do you know," I say, "how many pounds of force it takes to snap the human neck?"

He blinks down at me and I tilt my head.

In truth, the answer is about a thousand pounds. *Nearly impossible.* But the message is clear and Aukley swallows under my hand.

"Tell me why the Afterdark is taking girls," I say, and then I press up on my toes and kiss him.

He stays frozen for a second, his body stiff with shock. Then his hands are gripping my hair so hard my scalp stings and he's kissing me back, crushing his lips against mine.

This is nothing like kissing Holland. There's no velvety softness, no heady sensation of give-and-take. This is like war, like battling for dominance.

Aukley pushes me back and turns me around, pressing me against the tree trunk. Our shoes kick up dirt and pine needles. His lips are hot on mine, the kiss fierce and demanding.

He slides one hand up my jaw, fingers digging in behind my ear. The other grips the back of my neck hard enough to hurt.

His tongue is inside my mouth. His body presses into mine, my back shoved so hard into the tree I can feel individual knots and whorls.

Tightening my grip on his hair, I yank his head back from mine. "Tell me."

Aukley's eyes are dark and hot, expression hungry. "I don't know. It only speaks to Blackwood." That's all he says before wrenching my face up again. But it's enough.

It's not until I get back to the dorms that the shock and adrenaline finally seem to wear off. I feel exhausted, like I've just fought a real, physical battle. My limbs tremble and I slump onto my mattress, yanking the privacy curtain across. The rattling *shhhk* noise must be clear enough, because Leta doesn't ask where I've been.

For a long time, I stare at the ceiling, thoughts spinning in circles. Kissing Aukley hadn't been the plan. Something about the forest had possessed me to take that leap—some reckless, wild feeling it inspired in me.

I shouldn't have, I know that. Anyone would tell me that.

But . . . I don't regret it.

It only speaks to Blackwood.

CHAPTER THIRTY-SIX

Holland

I DREAM ABOUT EVIE.

In the dream, we lie tangled together at the base of the towering walnut tree. The thick roots cradle us as we explore one another. She reaches up to catch my face in her hands, drawing me down on top of her. We kiss until we're breathless, until we're forced to pull apart for air. Evie's face is flushed, her lips red as she laughs.

My insides burn as our bodies press together. I want her so bad it hurts. I want to be closer. *I want all of her.*

Something inside me shifts in response. Beneath us, the roots of the tree stir, easing up, sliding over our arms and legs. Evie's eyes grow wide. She jerks in my arms.

My lips move. I tell her it's alright.

We can be closer this way.

The roots pull us down into the soft embrace of the earth, enveloping us. Evie thrashes in my arms, but only for a second.

Then she softens against me, her pale face tilted up to mine. Our lips meet. The roots of the tree pull us under the cool, welcoming earth, closer to the heart of the forest.

This is the way it's supposed to be.

CHAPTER THIRTY-SEVEN

Evie

I DREAM ABOUT RUNNING through the Afterdark.

Darting through the trees, plunging deeper into the dark woods. Behind me comes the patter of droplets on leaves. At first, I think it's raining, and then I glance back.

Moonlight filters through the branches, illuminating a figure moving between the trees.

The corpse of my sister. Her face sagging and gray-skinned, hair hanging down like damp weeds. Her body is bloated and putrid, but still she comes, water sloughing off her sodden dress, hitting ferns and low-hanging branches in fat droplets.

I burst out of the tree line and onto the beach, rocks shifting under my feet. Something splashes up my left ankle. Catches my foot, and sends me sprawling. I land at the edge of a tide pool, scraping my palms and knees, half submerged in oily black water.

When I glance down, I find my reflection in the smooth, mirrorlike surface: my pale, heart-shaped face and dark brows.

Black eyes reflected back at me.

No.

I gasp awake. It feels like surfacing from deep water. Confused and winded, I drag in deep breaths as I lie there blinking at the dark drapes. They're open a crack, and something between them interrupts the darkness—a tall, slender silhouette.

I jam myself back against the headboard, the dream coming back all at once—Ada's corpse between the trees.

Heart thundering, I scrabble for my phone. The light comes on, spilling over the bed, illuminating the intruder.

Holland stands at the side of my bed.

She doesn't move, and I catch a glimpse of long, sleep-tossed red hair. Then I flick the light up to her face and suck in a sharp breath.

Holland's eyes are black.

The light swings wildly as I fall back, striking my shoulder on the wall, fumbling my phone.

By the time I get it back up, Holland is blinking at me in confusion. Footsteps sound and then Leta is there, dark hair coming out of its loose braid. "What's happening?"

"Holland?"

Beth's voice comes from the next room and Holland jerks upright. Like she's coming out of a trance. She's still looking straight at me.

Her eyes are completely normal. Green, as they've always been.

The knot in my chest loosens.

Maybe it was just the light. The dream making me see things.

Her eyes weren't really black.

"I must have been sleepwalking." There's a faint crease between her brows. She looks pale and shaken, even in the dim light from my phone.

"You okay?"

Holland just blinks at me and then Beth is there, hands on Holland's shoulders. "Come on, let's go back to bed."

Holland nods, allowing herself to be led toward the door, only glancing over her shoulder once. I lean over the side of the bed to peer past the curtains, watching them vanish into the next room. The way Holland moves, she looks like she's *still* sleepwalking.

For a second, Leta and I are both silent in the dark. My ears ring in the quiet.

"Wow," Leta says. "What the hell was that?"

I press my lips together hard, trying not to think about black eyes staring down at me in the darkness.

"I have no idea."

Holland avoids me for nearly a week after the sleepwalking incident.

Until Saturday afternoon, when we're supposed to meet on the lawn for a movie. *Fast & Furious*, projected on the side of the gym. I'm slow waking, getting out of the shower just before the movie starts, wrapping a towel around myself as Holland walks into the bathroom without knocking.

She's still in a tank top and pajama shorts, showing off her long legs, her hair loose and wavy around her shoulders.

Her gaze drops down to the towel and she lets out a breath, already reaching for me. It's like she's finally giving in to something, and I shiver as she draws me against her, droplets rolling down my shoulders from my damp hair. As soon as she touches me, I can feel the Afterdark flare.

I shouldn't let her do this. But I can't seem to push her away.

"I'm still wet—"

"I don't care. You smell good."

She kisses me hard, hands roaming over my flushed skin. It's exhilarating, like I'm connecting to something inside her. I feel so close. Her heartbeat is mine. Our breaths in sync.

It makes me think of lying under the tree with her, trailing kisses down over her hips.

She tows me forward, out of the bathroom and into the bedroom. We don't even make it to the bed. She's kissing me hard, backing me into the vanity table, dipping down to my neck. Her teeth graze my throat, making me shiver.

She makes a humming noise against my mouth, pressing closer.

And then she goes still suddenly, hands tightening on my arms.

Startled, I open my eyes to see Holland staring over my shoulder at the vanity mirror, eyes wide, face steadily draining of blood.

Something is wrong.

CHAPTER THIRTY-EIGHT
Holland

THERE'S SOMETHING IN THE MIRROR.

It starts small at first, the slightest crack. I catch sight of it over Evie's shoulder and think vaguely, *I didn't know the mirror was broken.*

And then there's another . . . and another. The mirror is breaking up in a fine spider's web of fragments as I watch, tiny cracks running through the surface.

I rear back and stare at it, unease crawling over my skin.

Black begins to leak from a crack at the top, inky liquid trailing slowly down the center of the mirror. My chest goes tight, breath catching in my throat. Evie is still pressed against me. She must feel me go stiff because she draws back and I can feel her searching my face.

"Holland?"

I can't tear my eyes away from the mirror. The cracks open wider, black, tar-like liquid pouring forth. There's a noise now, so faint I can hardly hear it. Growing in volume—a thin, despairing wail. It gets louder, joined by new voices every second, a chorus of horrible shrieking.

I'm frozen to the spot, heartbeat thunderous in my ears.

It's spreading. The cracks lead up from the mirror, spilling from the frame. Snaking up the walls and ceiling like black veins branching onto white skin.

The Rook's words come back to me suddenly. *Some of the Afterdark seems to be . . . leaking. Coming through into our world.*

Is this in my head or is it real?

A black vein blooms directly above me, cracking open the ceiling, dripping a long trail of poison nearly on top of me.

I realize a second later that I'm screaming, drowning out the noise coming from the mirror.

CHAPTER THIRTY-NINE

Evie

HOLLAND SCREAMS AND STAGGERS away from the vanity.

I don't know what she's seeing.

When I wrench her around, she stares at me with wide, unseeing eyes and my heart clenches.

Her eyes are changing, pupils leaking steadily into the whites, turning them black. I stumble back, hand pressed to my chest.

It's like when Holland stood over me in bed. In daylight, it's even more terrifying and unnatural.

Holland wheels around to face the mirror. She lets out a strangled shriek and lunges, snatching up the nearest item—a bottle of nail polish—slamming it hard into the vanity mirror. There's a crack and the frame splinters and sags, glass showering down around us.

"Holland!" Alarmed, I spring forward, hooking my hands under her armpits, teeth clenched as I drag her back. Something stabs me in the foot, pain lancing up my leg. I ignore it, focusing on the way Holland is thrashing, wrapping my arms around her until hers are pinned to her sides.

"There's nothing there!"

Eventually we collapse, Holland falling half on top of me. She curls her knees to her chest, palms pressed into her eyes. The back of her hand is covered in scrapes and cuts, and blood trickles down her arm. She's not screaming anymore, but I can see a muscle in her jaw ticking.

I don't move out from under her, drawing her closer instead, until she's lying half in my lap.

"Let me see." I touch the back of her hand and she flinches. "Holland."

"They burn." She pushes her hands harder over her face when I wrap my fingers around her wrist. "They burned when I had that nightmare. I didn't know . . ."

I didn't tell her about her eyes. Wasn't sure if I'd imagined them that night. "Let me see."

It takes several seconds of coaxing and gently prying her hands off her face. But when she finally blinks up at me, her eyes are a clear green again. She must see my relief, because her eyes slide shut and she lets out a sigh.

"Oh thank god."

We sit in silence after that, broken glass glittering around us, blood staining the carpet in streaks. I'm not sure if it's mine or Holland's.

She's shaking now, her entire body trembling. When I tighten my arms around her, a surge of guilt goes through me. I don't know how, but I know this is my fault. I know because I felt it, just before she started screaming—the Afterdark flaring inside me.

I did this, and that can only mean one thing.

We can't do this anymore.

CHAPTER FORTY

Holland

OVER THE NEXT WEEK, Evie draws back from me.

It seems like she spends all her time with Leta now, heads bent together as they speak in whispers. It makes an ugly, choking jealousy swell in my chest.

It's hard to blame her for staying away, though. I can't think about what happened without my face burning. What it must have looked like. Screaming at things that weren't there. Smashing the mirror . . .

On top of that, I'm starting to feel the effects of whatever the Afterdark has done. I look in the mirror and hardly recognize myself. The purple bruises of under-eye shadows, the pale, sunken features.

And . . . are my eyes darker?

Is this what I'd look like if the Afterdark made me into a copy? Maybe I wouldn't notice a difference at this point.

I start avoiding mirrors altogether.

But others notice. Stowe especially. He hovers behind me in the halls. Asking if I'm okay. If I can feel the Afterdark. And it's even harder to shake Beth. She keeps demanding to know what's wrong. Telling me I need to talk to her.

So I start dodging both of them.

At night, I see the Afterdark every time I shut my eyes, like the twisted shapes of the black trees are imprinted on my eyelids. It's all I can think about, especially when that strange feeling in my gut keeps growing.

Eventually, I start getting up before anyone is awake and turning in early at night, pulling my privacy curtains shut. I don't speak to anyone.

It feels like I'm completely isolating myself, cutting myself off in case anyone guesses what's going on.

It's starting to make sense, the way Blackwood withdrew. How he locked himself in the office. It makes me wonder how bad it was for him.

Tuesday morning, I arrive to English a few minutes late. Careful to step quietly over the hardwood floors, I slide into the only seat left, which Stowe has draped his sweater over. Across the classroom, I can *sense* her.

I know Evie is there beside Leta. She's leaning forward, elbows on her desk, staring at me over the top of her textbook.

I keep my gaze fixed on my desktop.

At the whiteboard, Mrs. McAllister is scribbling in her looping handwriting, silhouetted in the spill of light from the windows behind her.

289

"We're going to read the next chapter with three questions . . ."

There's silence. Just the rustle of paper and the scuff of shoes on hardwood. The tapping of rain against the windows.

It's a relief to concentrate on the pages, to pretend I'm completely absorbed. Because I can *feel* Evie staring, like a weight at the top of my spine.

It unsettles me, the way I sense her. She triggers the alien thing inside me. Brings it to life.

I take a breath, forcing myself to concentrate. Mrs. McAllister is asking questions about theme. But every time Evie shifts in her seat, it catches my eye.

When she clears her throat softly, a shiver jolts down my spine, and I find myself watching as she bends her head to read, the waves of her dark hair falling over her eye. It bares the back of her neck, and the curve of one shoulder as she props an elbow on the desk.

The thing inside me sends tendrils snaking through my rib cage, chest tightening with longing.

We shouldn't be here. We should be out there.

No. I clench my teeth so hard my jaw aches.

It's getting harder to tell my thoughts from the Afterdark's.

I'm not paying attention to the teacher, and when Stowe nudges me, I look up to find Mrs. McAllister staring at me.

"Sorry, what?"

She gives me a bland look. "You missed homeroom check-in, so I thought you might like to contribute."

Panic makes my stomach clench. I grip the edge of my desk. Off to my left I catch sight of the row of Gravesmen desks, as Daniel Prince and Elijah Archer exchange a heavy look. *They know.*

I want to vault out of my seat and run from the room, but before I can move, something catches my eye—a flutter of movement behind Mrs. McAllister. Beyond the window, the forest is a patchwork of light and shadow, fog drifting between the trees.

It's raining harder now, drops dotting the windowpane. As I watch, it gets even heavier, turning to a steady downpour. Strangely, the droplets are getting darker.

Brown, at first, I think, and then . . . *no*, they're a dirty, slate-gray color, darkening until . . .

Oh god. The water hitting the window is *black*, black like the sludge from the tide pool. It sticks to the glass in oily splotches, slowly blocking the light.

This can't be happening.

Panic coils in my chest and I tear my gaze away, desperate to concentrate on something, *anything* else.

Mrs. McAllister is staring at me. "Holland?"

When she says my name, it comes out slow and warped. Her voice doesn't match the movement of her lips.

Her face is rippling now, as if insects are writhing beneath her skin. I watch, frozen, as oily sludge drips from the corners of her eyes and trails down her cheeks.

The writhing beneath her skin increases until her entire face seems to squirm. There's a thin, gray root wiggling its way out of the corner of her mouth.

"Holland," she says, in her warped, mismatched voice, "*answer the question.*"

A scream rises in my chest and sticks in my throat as the mutated Mrs. McAllister takes a step closer. Her voice is a discordant jumble. "*Will you deliver her?*"

"Who?" My voice breaks. The thing that was Mrs. McAllister smiles, and black sludge oozes from her lips. "*Evelyn.*"

Her form seems to stutter suddenly, like static. Blinking in and out. She's closer each time. Lips still moving, sludge trailing down her pale throat. "*Evelyn. Evelyn. Evelyn.*"

"Stop it." I'm clutching the edges of my desk so hard my knuckles ache. Shaking my head frantically. "Stop."

There's a pointed throat-clearing beside me, jerking me back to the present. Stowe is sitting straight, hand waving in the air.

"Oh, pick me. I know who the main character is."

There's a ripple of laughter, and I blink. Mrs. McAllister is staring at Stowe now. Her face looks utterly normal. She hasn't moved from the desk where she'd been standing.

Her expression shifts from exasperation to mild surprise. "Well, that's an incredibly low bar, but I think this might be the first time you've ever done the reading, Mr. Stowe." She folds her arms over her chest. "Alright, if you'd like to jump in." She gives me a look, clearly annoyed. "Since Holland clearly doesn't want to have this conversation."

I'm still reeling, ears ringing, and I only half take in Stowe's reply.

I keep glancing at Mrs. McAllister. She looks normal now. Her skin is smooth and unblemished. And the forest outside the window looks like . . . a forest.

Strangely enough, there isn't any fog between the trees, though it's still drizzling faintly outside.

It takes a second to set in. To really understand what just happened.

Evie. That's what the Afterdark wants. What it's been trying to tell me.

Stowe is still talking—something about symbolism. While he talks, he stretches a hand beneath the table, giving my knee a reassuring squeeze. But I barely notice, gaze drawn straight to Evie. She's staring at me, dark brows creased. Studying my face.

She's why the Afterdark is malfunctioning. She's what it wants.

Just looking at her, I find my resolve strengthening. It can't have her.

We need to get off this island. Now.

CHAPTER FORTY-ONE

Evie

THAT EVENING LETA AND I settle at a corner table in the dining hall, the quiet murmur of conversation and clink of cutlery drifting around us. It's been the two of us for days now. Holland either doesn't eat, or takes food into the dorm.

I left a note on her pillow yesterday and got no reply. It seems like she's withdrawing completely.

Leta sets Mia's notebook between us while she stirs cream into her coffee. The sight gives me a guilty start and I curl my fingers hard around the strap of my camera. I'd almost forgotten.

While we eat, I flip idly through to the end, pausing when I catch sight of the back cover. There's a shallow, plastic pocket with a scrap of paper inside. "There's something here."

Leta leans over the table, practically tipping out of her seat as I coax the paper out.

It's a sheet from the notebook, torn out and folded in half.

I unfold it and we pore over it together. It's a list of names in Mia's looping handwriting—all girls' names, with dates written beside them.

I scan the list and my gaze snags on the one at the bottom.

Amanda Williams.

I sit up straight, heart stuttering, and exchange a wide-eyed look with Leta.

"Do you think it's . . . ?" Leta stops, hesitating.

Do I think it's a list of all the missing and dead girls from Northcroft? Do I think Mia's own name should be added to the end now?

I press my lips together hard, not wanting to answer.

The list includes other familiar names.

Jessica Thorn

Sara Parker

My gaze snags on the last name, and I flip back to the start of the notebook and stab at the note I'd found earlier. "There."

Out at time of Parker?

Now it makes a terrible kind of sense.

"Sara Parker." Leta presses a hand to her mouth, eyes suddenly distant. "They told us she went home. God, it's like a plot from one of my stories."

She pulls up short, expression guilty, and I reach out and touch her knee. She lets out a breath and frowns down at the list.

For the next hour, we look up names online, reading old articles and records. Comparing notes on obituaries and school newsletters.

There's a pattern emerging, and it sends dread crawling through my insides. We find old newsletters. Condolences. Thoughts and prayers. "She will be missed" and "remembered as a true light." One hundred different ways of saying the same thing.

Some of the research is inconclusive. Some are potential runaways or tragic accidents.

But what it boils down to, in the end, is a list of girls who walked into the woods and never came out.

Mia was investigating it. And tracking my father's movements.

I feel sick to my stomach, and I look away from the notes, swallowing the bile rising in my throat. Mia was right to investigate the missing girls, paranoid or not. Podcasts or not . . . she just couldn't have known the truth.

"She emerges." Leta's voice is light.

When I turn, Beth stops in the walkway between two tables, her expression flat. She's holding a plate of food in each hand.

"I'm not staying." She stares straight at me when she says it. "Holland and I are staying in for dinner, since she's avoiding . . . people."

The darkness roars to life, coursing through my insides. "She's avoiding *you* too."

Beth grimaces. "I have no idea what you're talking about. We're still best friends. I can't help it if you were just a fling, Evie."

The way she spits my name, like it's something vile, sends a wave of fury through me. The Afterdark urges me forward, itching to feel bone break beneath my knuckles.

But then Leta says softly, "Evie."

When I glance up, there are people watching. A group of tenth-graders at the table beside us, staring and whispering.

I school my expression into nothingness.

There's something in Beth's face as she watches me, almost like disappointment. "Oh, did you want to punch me?" she says. "Like you hit Aukley? I bet Holland would *really* want to hang out with you then."

"You're pathetic."

Her eyes narrow to slits. "*Excuse* me?"

"You heard me. You think people don't notice the way you bully everyone she gets close to? It's weird, Beth. The whole thing is creepy."

Beth leans toward me. "You should talk. You think you can slide in and replace your sister."

"You're insane."

"Am I? The only reason she liked you in the first place is because of Ada." Beth smirks. "She cried for *two days* when she heard she was dead. And then you come along and she latches onto you like that bitch has returned from the dead. Even though Ada outed Holland to her parents and ruined her entire fucking life."

I lean back, chest tight.

Ruined her life. I try to remember what Holland said to me back in the forest—something about Ada destroying her.

I'd shut her down, told her I didn't want to hear it.

Something in me shatters at the thought. Memories of Ada's wicked smile hit me. I can't stand picturing it aimed at Holland. The thought of that same malice directed at her . . .

Guilt pulses through me and I turn away, blinking hard. I want to hold my head high and march away. Storm out without a word.

But I can't seem to move. My sinews and muscles have turned to stone. My blood is sluggish and cold.

Beth's voice is a sibilant hiss. Sly. Full of cruel enjoyment. "You two are over. I'm putting in a request to change rooms. Until then, stay away from us."

CHAPTER FORTY-TWO

Holland

I FIND MYSELF PACING THE DORM. All day I've been racking my brain for a way to convince Evie to come with me. We need to get off the island.

Is it best to get the first boat tomorrow, or wait until the last, so no one can follow us?

Normally, I'd have to get a ferry pass from the office, but no one can know we're leaving. And I happen to know Beth has a few squirreled away.

I have maybe fifteen minutes before she comes back with dinner.

I start with her desk, pawing through stacks of paper and binders, looking through the wooden jewelry box she keeps at the back.

Nothing.

I don't hit gold until I yank the dust curtains up on the side of her bed, revealing an old shoebox. The ferry passes are inside, on top, and I snatch them up and shove them into my pocket. I'm about to close the box when a handful of papers catches my eye. Neatly bundled with a pink heart-shaped paper clip.

Curious, I shuffle through and find they're receipts—old, faded ones and newer slips. Movie theaters and coffee shops. All of them from the mainland.

It takes me a while, but I eventually realize what I'm looking at. It's like a record of everywhere we've been together.

My stomach sinks a little.

It's . . . weird. Weirder than I thought, even for Beth.

Morbid curiosity drives me to flip through a pink address book, scanning past scribbled phone numbers and addresses. Notes on people's birthdays. Class schedules and appointments. Test dates.

It all seems normal, until I get to the back and find a list of names and phone numbers. Some of the names are faintly familiar. It takes me a second to figure it out . . . and then my breath catches in my throat.

Tara Sanderson is the one I remember best, because she's an *Us Weekly* reporter. She'd seemed the most excited to run the hit piece last year. And now here she is, her name scribbled in Beth's neat handwriting.

The rest of the names are contacts for gossip magazines and websites, and I know without looking that every single one published gossip pieces about me, that had the photo delivered to their inboxes by the "angry ex."

Feeling faintly nauseous, I shuffle through the rest of the papers. When I get to the bottom, the sick feeling is replaced by anger. There, nestled in one corner, is a series of folded notes. Sure enough, I find my own handwriting inside. Others are Evie's notes, but not ones I've ever seen.

Beth's been taking them.

Footsteps from the corridor jerk me out of my thoughts. I jam everything back in the box and shove it under the bed. Straightening, I brush myself down like I can shake it all off.

Like I can pretend none of this is real and Beth hasn't utterly betrayed me.

That night, I dream about the forest. About walking through the cool insides. Hearing the hush of the wind and the faint melodic birdsong above me.

And then it changes.

The soil cracks, dirt and moss crumbling away. Roots writhe beneath the ground, black and rotten. I stumble over one and the oil slick splatters across my shoes as it reaches for me, winding around my leg. It wants to draw me deep under the earth where it will rot my flesh and dissolve my bones.

I jerk awake.

For a moment I lie there, head spinning, darkness warping in strange patterns around me. I blink the sleep out of my eyes and sit up, sweat sticking my shirt to my back.

The windows are still dark, the shutters down. The Afterdark is out there, separated from us by a single, slender pane of glass. The towering black walnut stretches out toward me.

And then the screaming starts out in the woods.

It makes the Afterdark flicker to life inside me. An answering call surging through my chest, sending an electric buzz through my limbs. It feels shockingly good, almost euphoric.

I know Evie feels it too. I can hear her stirring in the other room. I listen for the faint sound of bedsprings as she shifts.

It drives me up and out of bed. I'm on my feet, moving before I can stop myself.

The room next door is dark, lit by a sliver of light falling from the bathroom door.

I pad over to Evie's bed, heart beating in my throat, feet making soft scuffles on the hardwood. I shouldn't.

I should go back to bed, curl under the covers and jam a pillow over my ear . . . force myself to block out the feral howling.

Because there's something wrong with the way my body is reacting. Something strange about this electric feeling, the heat bubbling in my chest. It makes me want to seek her out, and I find myself across the room, drawing back the curtain on Evie's bed.

It's hard to make her out in the dark, but I see her shift. Hear her gentle intake of breath before she pushes herself up on one elbow . . . a dark silhouette against the wall.

My heart squeezes in my chest and I keep my voice to a whisper. "Evie?"

She says nothing, just draws the covers back. An invitation.

I climb in, crawling across the mattress, and she lies back and pulls me into her. When she wraps her arms around me, her skin is feverish, her mouth hot on my neck.

There are no apologies, no excuses—just the taste of her. The feeling of her teeth grazing my neck. The tickle of her hair on my face.

I didn't have a chance to talk to her today, too distracted by Beth's betrayal. But this is the perfect opportunity.

Now is when I ask her to come with me. Tell her we *need* to leave the island. It's not safe for her.

Before I can speak, the howling from outside gets abruptly louder. Closer.

We both go still, listening.

It comes again, raising the hairs on my arms.

In the two years I've been here, it's never sounded like this.

Footsteps from the next room, and then a muffled thump and a shrill cry. Evie and I are both out of bed, moving for the door even as Leta stirs behind us.

"What's happening?"

We find Beth in the next room, standing in front of the window. To my shock, she's jammed the shutters to one side, ripping them off the track to reveal the dark forest beyond. Her face is white as she turns to us.

"Beth, what—?"

She opens her mouth to speak, but she's interrupted by another terrible scream. She flinches away from the window, swaying on her feet like she's about to pass out.

I'm across the room now. At the window.

As I stare out at the dim stretch of woods, movement catches my eye, something on the slope of the roof leading down from our window. It takes a minute for my eyes to adjust or . . . maybe

I just can't register what I'm seeing at first. Because there's a *person* on the roof, a pale figure illuminated by the dim light from the window. I draw back, a gasp tearing from my throat.

The figure looks up. Light falling on blond hair, matted and smeared with black. Her face is gaunt and pale, eyes huge and glistening black.

Her face is horribly familiar.

Beth.

Only, Beth is behind me, backed against the wall beside her bed. I can hear her strangled whimpers as I watch the thing that isn't her crawl its way up the roof. Pale, spiderlike arms work as it pulls itself up, tile by tile, black eyes fixed on me. I watch, pulse thundering in my ears, as it opens its mouth and *screams.*

It's a shrill, overlapping noise. Like a car collision, the shrieking and tearing of twisting metal. I jump, stumbling into Evie.

"What is it?" Leta's voice behind me is shaky and uneven.

I start as Evie grabs me. "We need to barricade the window."

She's right. I realize it a second later as the thing below increases its speed. It's already halfway up.

It's coming for Beth.

CHAPTER FORTY-THREE

Evie

THE DRESSER. I'M ABOUT TO DART OVER and haul on it, barricade the door—but the thing on the roof is coming too fast, making its way up in jerky, unnatural movements.

It wants Beth.

For a second, I think about grabbing Holland and Leta. Dragging them out the door, slamming it shut behind us.

Give the creature what it wants.

But if I do that, doesn't it make me the bad one? Doesn't it mean *I'm* the monster?

Instead, I wheel around, lunging for the fireplace just as the sound of shattering glass comes from behind me. Leta stumbles away from the window, and I snatch at Holland's sleeve, pulling her with me. Someone screams, as my hand closes around the cool metal of the fire poker.

When I turn, Not-Beth is crawling through the broken window. It's strangely silent now, aside from the noises it makes dragging itself over the frame. Shards of glass tear into its pale, stained skin, and black sludge trickles from the wounds.

Beth jams herself into the wall beside her bed, curled up with her knees to her chest, face buried in her arms. A flicker of disgust goes through me. I want to yell at her to get up and fight.

She can't even *look* at it.

Not-Beth spills from the frame, thudding onto the floor, splattering it with black. It scrambles to its feet just as I swing the poker, pulse thundering in my ears. It doesn't even try to move out of the way, too focused on Beth. The poker connects with the side of its head with a sickening thud, the blow rattling up my arms. The dark thing inside sends a shudder of satisfaction through me.

It feels *good*.

The creature staggers, head snapping back under the blow. When it straightens, there's an ugly dent in its forehead, oozing black. It doesn't so much as glance at me. Still moving for Beth.

I swing around, palms sweaty. "Get her out of here!"

Beth is still crouched, hands over her eyes. Holland and Leta haul her up, dragging her toward the door.

Not-Beth lurches forward with another rasping scream. I swing the poker again, arms aching. Another thud, another bone-vibrating blow.

It sends a dark thrill coursing through me as the creature stumbles back.

Leta and Holland shove the real Beth out the door. Leta follows, but Holland stays, slamming the door shut behind them.

A pang of fear goes through me. I want her on the other side. Safe.

The creature has already turned on her, like it knows she's

standing between it and its prize. I step between them, drawing its insect-like gaze.

It sways on its feet, black sludge trickling down its face. I've hit it twice and it's not going down.

I brandish the poker, inching forward, eyes on the window.

"Evie . . ." Holland's voice is tense and I shake my head. I don't need her attracting its attention.

It lunges at me, and I swing the poker around, catching the end with my other hand, using it to shove the creature back. It screams and claws at the iron rod, bare feet scrabbling on the slick hardwood.

My cheek burns when its jagged nails swipe me, but then it's giving way, staggering back. Holland is beside me now, hands on the iron bar, her face twisted in a determined scowl. Together we force it back until it hits the windowsill, and I snatch at its oil-slick limbs, dragging it over the window frame even as it twists against me.

Another rasping scream and the creature snatches at me, one pale hand snagging in my hair, dragging me forward. There's a sharp, stinging pain in my shoulder and palm.

Holland gives a shout above me. There's an ugly gash on her cheek now, trickling blood down her neck, but she doesn't seem to notice, gripping my arms and dragging me back. The creature twists one more time, scrambling to keep hold of me, and I lash out with bloody fists, striking its face.

I feel its grip slide and then it's gone, tumbling down the slope of the roof with a keening wail. Vanishing abruptly.

Silence follows, broken only by the sound of our ragged breathing. Holland is still holding me tightly, and I can feel blood trickling down my arms. The palm of my hand throbs where glass is embedded in my skin. I ignore all of that, fixated on the lawn just below the roof.

Sure enough, there's a flicker of movement and a pale figure darts forward, streaking across the grass. We're silent, watching the creature vanish into the forest.

Neither of us moves or tries to pull the broken shutter down.

I'm thinking about the way the creature was fixated on Beth to the exclusion of all else. How it didn't go down after I struck it. How it kept coming.

At first, neither of us says anything. And then, after a moment, Holland turns toward me. "We should leave."

I just stare at her, uncomprehending, as she rushes on.

"It's not safe here. We should take the first boat. Just . . . get off the island."

I return my gaze to the window, to the forest beyond the gates. Even now, I can feel the draw of it. The idea of leaving it behind is strangely distressing.

"I can't." The excuses already crowd up in my mind. *I need to figure out why the forest is taking girls. I need to find a way to stop this. I need to shut down this school. I need . . .*

I need the forest.

When I turn, Holland is watching me, and I know she won't believe any of my excuses. So I don't say anything. I just turn and walk away from the window.

CHAPTER FORTY-FOUR

Evie

THE NEXT MORNING, the window is mysteriously repaired.

This time, no one bothers to make excuses. No one pins it on Crown and Grave. I don't know what they tell the other students about the noises from our room—the glass shattering, the horrible shrieking.

Maybe they don't tell them anything. Maybe everyone is too afraid to ask.

Several times that morning, Holland tries to pull me aside. I know what she wants to talk about. She wants to flee the island. Leave the forest behind.

And I don't know if I can. If I *want* to.

So I end up spending most of the day in the forest.

Leta joins me for a couple hours in the late afternoon, bringing a picnic blanket and her notes. It doesn't take long for the investigation into Mia to stall out, though, and we skip rocks in the stream until Leta has to leave for gym.

After a time I get bored, wandering deeper into the trees.

The shadows are growing longer when I step out into the clearing and I pull up short, laughing. I didn't mean to, but I always end up here, don't I?

That low humming starts as I step closer to the walnut tree. Its branches stretch up overhead, blocking out the sun as it sinks past the tops of the trees, orange light glowing through the twisted boughs.

The sun is setting.

I don't know how long I've been out here. The forest has a way of making the hours slip, making the edges of reality fuzzy and malleable.

There's a crackle in the underbrush at the edge of the clearing. And I don't have to turn around to know it's her.

"Saw your picnic back there. You were with Leta, weren't you?"

Holland's voice is low. She sounds . . . different. It sends a flicker of unease through me.

When I turn, she's lingering at the edge of the clearing, face shadowed by the trees.

My chest tightens. The way she's holding herself is new. She's just as poised as usual, but when she moves toward me, it's slow and deliberate. Predatory.

When she steps into the light I pause, shocked. The scratch from last night is worse. A deep, mottled red color. Almost black. And it's not just that. There's something in her face. A shadow I've never seen before.

For the first time, the thought occurs to me that I might lose her, that the Afterdark might devour her a little at a time until the Holland I know is gone.

She stalks closer. "You two are close lately."

"Holland." My tone is a warning, but she doesn't stop.

"You best friends now? Or is it more than that?" Holland stops a few feet away, close enough to reach out and touch. And I want to. I *ache* to.

But the tone of her voice is all wrong. It's . . . ugly. Cruel, almost.

I need to know it's really her . . . that I'm talking to *Holland*. "Are you still with me?"

She steps closer, gaze fixed on my face. My stomach plunges.

"Holland, I need to hear you say it." I make my voice firm and Holland blinks down at me.

"I—I'm still with you." She blinks again, glancing around the clearing. Then she frowns at me. "It's not safe, Evie. But I won't leave without you."

Guilt stabs at my chest. Instinctively, I take a step toward her, reaching out to touch her arm. The second I do, the longing hits me straight in the chest, leaving me breathless.

She's shaking, and I can't pull away now. I can't let her go. I draw her into a tight hug, like I can keep her from falling to pieces with sheer force of will.

"Holland . . ."

She melts against me, tucking her face into the side of my neck. Her skin is so soft. My heart flutters in my chest, but I steel my resolve.

Until she lifts her head and kisses me softly on the lips, pressing her body against mine.

I should pull away.

I should stop this.

Pulling back, I start to say "We shouldn't—" and she shakes her head almost frantically.

"Don't talk."

And then she's kissing me again, hard. Pressing me back into the rough bark of the walnut tree, hands smoothing over my shoulders. Her fingers hook around the straps of my camera, tugging my closer. She trails kisses down my neck, one hand grasping my jaw, the other sliding up to grip my hair. I let out a shaky sigh, and when she moves to kiss me again, I kiss her back.

I should say no, but I don't want to.

We sink down onto the roots of the great black tree, Holland settling over my hips, eyes glossy and bright as they comb over me. Leaning forward, she kisses me again and I arch up to meet her, feeling her hips rock, heat blooming in my stomach.

My eyes slide shut as her mouth moves over my throat. Down onto my collarbone. And then she shifts suddenly, fingers tightening around my wrists.

I open my eyes and shock hits me, freezing the breath in my chest. Holland's hair hangs down around her face, her skin porcelain pale in the orange light. Her pupils are completely blown as she stares down at me, whites entirely gone.

"Holland!" I buck against her and she leans down, fingers biting into my wrists. She bares her teeth in a strange, feral smile.

"*Holland!*" I thrash under her. Her grip is cutting off my blood flow as she presses down even harder. Like she's trying to press me into the roots of the tree. "Holland, you're hurting me."

"*Stay, Evelyn.*" When she speaks, cold shock hits at my core. Her voice is *wrong*—a deeper chorus echoing under her own, an unnerving tangle of voices. "*Stay in the woods with me.*"

She bares down harder, until the pain makes my eyes water.

How is she this strong?

Panic makes me thrash under her and I whip my head up, driving the top of my skull into her face. There's a terrible crunch and a gasp from Holland.

And then she's on the ground, hands clapped over her face, staring up at me with huge green eyes while black tar bleeds down her cheeks.

Holland lets out a strangled whimper and a trail of crimson slips between her fingers and I can't . . .

I can't stand the horrified look on her face. The guilt and terror.

And I can't comfort her while dark bruises spring up on my wrists and that voice echoes in my head.

I can't.

"I can't do this."

I turn and run.

Away from Holland. Out of the woods. Toward the school.

CHAPTER FORTY-FIVE

Evie

I RUN BACK IN A DAZE, not even noticing Leta hurrying up to me until she's practically on top of me. "Evie, hey!" Her face is flushed and she has an armload of books.

I suddenly don't know what to say. That this place has taken over Holland? That we need to get her off the island before it's too late? That it might already *be* too late?

But Leta doesn't give me a chance. "Look at this." She seizes my wrist, dragging me up the stairs to the library. At a table just inside the door, she's set up a wide spread of notes. For some reason, she's laid out multiple yearbooks.

"I've been thinking about the names in Mia's notebook. And the podcasts kept talking about *victim type*. It finally clicked. Here."

She spreads one of the yearbooks flat on the table. "That's Jessica Thorn."

Something about Leta's intensity, the alarm in her voice, snaps me back into the present, and I lean over to stare at the photo.

Jessica Thorn is pretty, with dark features and thick brows. She has a delicate silver hoop through the center of her bottom lip.

Leta pages through another book and points out another picture. "Sara Parker."

Another girl. A round, white face. Dark eyes and shoulder-length hair. Frizzy curls.

"And Amanda Williams."

Leta flips the book around. Amanda smiles at the camera. It's a summer beach picture and the sun creates a halo on the crown of her dark, shoulder-length hair.

Some of the shock from the forest is starting to wear off, the wheels in my brain grinding slowly to life. It feels like something should be clicking here, and I frown, staring down at the names.

Jessica Thorn. Sara Parker. Amanda Williams.

"Found it." Leta wheels around, shoving the book down on top of the other two, arranging them so all three photos are as close as possible. "And one more." She's still moving, paging through yet another book. This time, when she finds the picture, she goes still, smoothing the page down carefully.

I know who it is without looking at the name.

Mia is staring up at the camera in the photo, smiling wide, her long hair in waves around her shoulders.

The longer I look at the photos, the more I see it. The row of pale faces. The wide, brown eyes and dark, shoulder-length hair. And Mia, her own hair hacked off at the shoulders . . .

Leta nods, pushing the book up to sit next to the others. There's four of them now, all staring out of the page with fathomless dark eyes.

It reminds me of Ada just below the surface of the water . . . how it felt like watching myself drown.

"Same hair, same eyes, similar face shape and skin tone." Leta checks them off on her fingers, her face grim. "See? Victim type."

"Except Mia." I tip the yearbook toward me, staring down at her face. Her hair is blond and her eyes are blue. Her brows are plucked thin, and so light they almost blend in with her skin.

Looking at the lineup feels like a *one of these things does not belong* game. "Why her?"

For a moment, we're both quiet, staring down at the yearbook photo. And then Leta says, "What if she stumbled across the secret?" She darts a look around us. There are a few Gravesmen at one of the study tables, but none of them so much as glance up. "She was obsessed with this one about missing people on the West Coast, right? 'PNW Murders.'"

"'PNW Murders,'" I echo. And then it's like something shakes loose in the back of my mind.

Aukley. Talking about his favorite podcast.

Oh my god.

I sit up straight, snatching up Mia's notebook. "I just remembered something."

Laying the notebook flat between us, I flip it open to the back, where a few pages of random podcast notes are scribbled.

There. Her looping handwriting spells out *Comps: "Crime Spree" and "PNW Murders."*

She'd talked about it that day in the office. She and a friend were going to start their own.

It's kind of an obscure podcast, as far as true crime goes. Local, of course, so it's not out of the question that they both could have listened to it. But it's a hell of a coincidence.

When I explain it to Leta, her brows shoot up.

"You think Aukley was the friend she talked about?"

I flip the last page over, scanning the notes again. "It seems like a pretty big coincidence otherwise."

Not to mention, Aukley was the one who dragged me into the Afterdark in the first place. So he's done it before.

"And what . . . they tried to give her shoulder-length hair, like the others?"

It's Leta saying *shoulder-length hair* that finally does it. That slams the pieces together in my mind.

I can hear him in my head now as he reaches out to grasp a strand of my hair between finger and thumb.

I didn't think I liked shoulder-length hair. But it's nice on you.

It was such a strangely specific comment that it stuck in my head.

"Aukley." His name comes out on a breath and I glance toward the door. "He's been following me. And Mia's notebook says he was in the office for disciplinary action."

"And he got kicked out of Crown and Grave because of Jessica Thorn." Leta sits up straighter. "And then . . ."

Her words trail off and I finish the sentence for her. "And then she went missing."

We're both quiet for a moment, until I let out a breath. "How many other girls does he have a connection with?"

Maybe *Aukley* is what all the missing girls have in common.

Maybe he drags the bodies into the Afterdark, or he puts girls in and lets the Afterdark kill them—the way he tried to get it to kill me. It still boils down to the same thing.

Jack Aukley is killing girls.

Leta's voice is hushed now. "Evie. The pictures . . ."

"I know."

She doesn't have to say it. They *look* like me.

It makes a terrible kind of sense. The way he's been following me. Memorizing my schedule.

"Evie, I'm scared for you." Leta drags her chair closer. She reaches out and gathers me in her arms. She smells like clean laundry as I press my face into the shoulder of her sweater. "We have to tell someone." Her voice is a low, trembling whisper.

"We don't have proof." I glance down at Mia's notebook, at the list of names. All we have is the scattered notes of a girl obsessed with true crime, and a bunch of yearbook pictures.

Even if my mother hadn't been a judge, it wouldn't have taken much to figure out it won't hold up in court.

Finally, after what seems like forever, I lift my face from her shoulder. Leta's eyes are dark and grave, and I look right into them and think about all those girls.

Slowly, I pull my camera up and place it on the table in front of Leta. "I'm going to do something about this. Whatever happens, don't follow me."

CHAPTER FORTY-SIX

Holland

I STAY IN THE WOODS for what feels like hours, curled on my side under the black walnut tree, bleeding freely onto the hemlock.

I'm losing my mind.

And worst of all, I hurt Evie. I scared her.

The Afterdark is taking me over, winding its roots through me so thoroughly I'm losing control. Being under the tree with her felt like a dream. Everything had been slow and hazy and unreal. Everything had been perfect.

All I'd been thinking was that she needed to stay with me forever.

That we needed to be here together . . . become part of the forest.

And then there'd been a blinding pain in my face, and I'd woken up on my back as Evie ran through the woods . . . away from me.

Guilt rips at my insides, making me feel sick.

I don't try to stop the pain or move from the fetal position, where roots dig into my side.

I deserve this.

I let myself give in, let myself touch her and kiss her, all the while knowing deep down that something like this could happen.

When the whispers start overhead, I hear her name. Over and over, until it fills every corner of my mind. When I shut my eyes, all I see is her face.

She can't stay. She'll never be safe here.

It's this resolve that forces me up, sends me staggering painfully back through the trees toward the school.

I need to get Evie off this island, and there's only one way I can think of to make that happen.

At the door to the principal's office, I pause, steeling myself. I haven't bothered to stanch the flow of blood. It fits with the story I'm about to tell him.

That Evie assaulted me.

He'll believe me. Who wouldn't? She's attacked Jack Aukley. And if famous Holland Morgan comes forward and says it happened, well, they're not going to argue.

I'll promise not to press charges, as long as she's expelled. As long as she's on a boat and away from this island before breakfast tomorrow.

Guilt is already weighing heavy in my stomach, but I shove it down. She won't listen to me. This is the only way to save her.

I'm so distracted that I don't notice anything until I reach for the doorknob and it rattles strangely in my hand. Then I step back, blinking down at it.

The door is splintering on its hinges, hanging crookedly.

What is this? My pulse picks up and I nudge it open a little at a time until I can step inside.

The office is in shambles.

The bookshelf lays on its side, books spilled out onto the floor, pages torn and crumpled. There are marks on the carpet, like it's been pushed over deliberately and dragged to barricade the door.

There's a faint, rotten scent inside the room. As I step in farther, it becomes apparent that the Rook was right. Principal Blackwood really has gone off the deep end.

There's a dark, oily substance smeared in spots across the carpet, and I move around it cautiously, pulse thundering in my ears. Closer to the desk, the wall behind the bookcase comes into view and I'm gaping all over again. It looks like he took a marker to the wall. The same message repeated over and over in slashing black letters.

Not Evie. Not Evie. Not Evie.

My heart crashes against my rib cage as I creep closer. The writing goes all the way down the wall, letters progressively spikier at the bottom, before veering sharply off into the carpet.

I pause and then wheel around, running full tilt down the hall, flying out the door into the daylight so fast it leaves me blind.

It doesn't take long to find Leta. She's standing on the front steps of Blackwood Hall, staring off into the forest with the kind of hundred-mile stare that makes my stomach plummet.

"Where's Evie?"

My voice is like the crack of a whip and she jerks. The look on her face is sheer dread.

"She's gone in," Leta whispers. "She's . . . . Holland, *wait—*"

I'm already running down the steps and across the lawn, hurtling through the gate.

Evie's gone into the woods and I think the principal has gone after her.

CHAPTER FORTY-SEVEN

Evie

IT'S EASY TO LURE Aukley into the forest.

I find him sitting on the front stairs and it only takes a few lingering steps, a meaningful look. When I head for the forest, he follows.

A few minutes in, I let myself melt into the trees, keeping my movements utterly silent. The forest helps, the thick mulch of leaves and rotting wood swallowing every sound.

The footfalls behind me pause. He's hesitating, has lost sight of me through the trees. But he must remember where I always go because, after a second, the footsteps start again. He's heading for the clearing.

Sliding behind the trunk of a towering oak, I let him pass, stooping to dig out a rock from the forest floor. I weigh it in my palm—it's about the size of a closed fist.

Aukley stops just under the walnut tree, turning slowly as he stares around the clearing.

I'm buzzing now. The darkness crashes through me like a wave breaking. I clench my fist around the rock and bare my teeth, stepping out from between the trees.

We stare at one another.

When his gaze drifts to the rock in my hand, I expect him to flinch or leap back. Instead, he narrows his eyes, waiting.

I circle him, dark energy sizzling. It wants me to lunge. Drive the rock into his temple. "I've wanted to do this since the day I first met you."

"I know."

"You killed Mia. And Beth's friend. And all those other girls."

"I didn't, technically," he says. "Your dad did most of the actual work."

A beat. A smile creeps over Aukley's face. He's enjoying the look on mine.

"What does that mean?"

"I don't know if he was supposed to give you to the Afterdark and she was a copy, or *she* was the one it wanted." He creeps closer, eyes fixed on my face. "I heard them fighting on the phone, you know. He didn't want her wearing makeup. He got mad when she bleached her hair . . . weird shit, until you realize . . . he wanted you identical."

Cold horror clutches at my chest.

"And then she died." Aukley snorts. "Just as he'd got up the steam to finally do it. And suddenly, it wanted his *other* daughter, and that was less okay. Just a little blatant favoritism, right? And he keeps trying to fool it with lesser copies, but it's not stupid."

My stomach drops, like missing the last step on the stairs. It leaves me reeling.

But it makes a sick kind of sense . . .

I thought it meant there was a "type," like a serial killer trying to recreate his first kill.

Only, there was no type. It was just me all along.

"He was trying to trick it." My voice is choked. "Make it think they were me."

"He's tried everything." Aukley's voice is scornful. "Using your clothes. Putting makeup on them. Calling them your name. It's pathetic . . ."

The awful picture of Mia sprawled beneath the tree comes back unprompted. The way her hair had been hacked off at her shoulders. "But Mia . . ."

"She wasn't planned. She just got too close to the truth with her true crime obsession. Started poking around." Aukley glares back over his shoulder, like he can see my dad from here. "He still tried to use her, even though you look nothing alike. He's getting sloppy."

"Why does it want us?" My voice shakes on the next question, the harder question. "*Which* one did it want?"

"If you're asking which one of you was the copy, I don't know." Aukley shrugs. "I doubt *he* knows, even if he acted like it had to be her. As for *why* . . . I thought that was obvious. It needs a new host. Your dad is falling apart."

My stomach twists and I clap my hand over my mouth, swallowing hard.

"You might survive." Aukley paces to one side and I go stiff. He's circling me. "You and Ada, you've been living with it all your lives. You're inoculated."

I back away. "So, what, you put me into the Afterdark the first time and it didn't work. This is round two?"

Aukley's mouth curls into an ugly smile. "Actually, I have something a little different in mind."

There's something in his hand now. Something that reflects the sun in a glittering arc. I go tense. *Aukley has a knife.*

"You don't even *want* what it's offering. You don't deserve it." His smile grows wider. "I keep telling you, we're the same. If you won't fall apart, I won't either."

I take a step back. "So go ahead. Accept the Afterdark and leave me alone."

He shakes his head. "It doesn't work like that. I'll need your blood."

I could argue, tell him to use his own blood, but something tells me Aukley is beyond reason as he circles me looking for all the world like a hunter advancing on his prey.

The Afterdark boils inside me and I charge. It's time to cave his head in, to spill his brains on the forest floor.

CHAPTER FORTY-EIGHT
Holland

I BOLT FORWARD, crashing through the forest, running until I get to the clearing . . . and I see them.

Aukley is half on top of Evie, his face stained with blood, expression ugly with rage. He has her by the wrist and she's got a knee in his guts, attempting to shove him off.

That's all I see, and then the Afterdark shoves violently at those small, remaining defenses. I let them fall.

A wave rolls through me, a surge of power so strong it knocks me back a step. My entire body buzzes and my eyes burn, vision coated in black.

I'm moving—or is the Afterdark moving me?—snatching the collar of Aukley's shirt, yanking him back so violently he falls halfway across the clearing. His face is a picture of shock as he scrambles to his feet.

The knife is on the ground between us, glittering against the forest floor. I dart forward and snatch it up, feeling the Afterdark pulse through me. I know what it's going to do—the same thing I want to do.

We want Aukley dead.

And then, there's the crack of breaking branches from the edge of the clearing.

Turning, I find myself rooted to the spot as a figure springs from the trees. The dark silhouette is on all fours, a twisted, hunched frame tearing toward Aukley.

I catch a glimpse of pale skin and contorted, spiderlike limbs, insect-black eyes in sunken sockets. Then the creature crashes into Aukley and they both go sprawling.

Aukley shouts, thrashing, but the creature pins him. It grabs him by the skull in an impossibly strong grip and *twists*. There's a sharp crack and Aukley twitches, mouth slack with shock, eyes wide and staring. Then his body slumps, sprawling onto the roots.

In my shock, the Afterdark recedes slightly and then flares again as the creature turns toward me.

At first, I'm sure it's another humanoid . . . that the monsters have finally broken through into the day.

But a second later, the clothing registers.

Its pale, skeletal frame is dressed in a dirty white-collared shirt and bow tie.

Principal Blackwood.

It's like the Afterdark has taken over completely. His face is gaunt and withered, stained with the inky black liquid streaming from his eyes. His expression is blank.

The bow tie is the only thing that makes him recognizable. It looks strangely bright against his pale, too-skinny throat.

He drops into a crouch, eyes fixed on me as he circles, and I pivot to face him, alarm making my chest tight.

From behind me, Evie gasps.

"Dad?"

CHAPTER FORTY-NINE
Evie

IT FEELS LIKE FOREVER that Holland and the creature face off. They're staring at one another, ready to spring.

And then my eyes slip down to the red bow tie and it feels like the ground tilts beneath me. "Dad?"

That black-eyed gaze flicks to me.

He's almost unrecognizable—the way he hunches over, the jerky movements.

Cold horror spreads through me, but it's accompanied by a sudden, fierce anger, as I remember the vision.

Mom and Dad under the black walnut tree; Mom spread out beneath the branches.

I take a step forward, fists clenched. "Did Mom even know what you were planning, or did you just drug her?"

He stops, black eyes flicking from Holland to me, head tilted. He seems to be listening, but I'm not sure how much he can be taking in. He looks like a wild animal, crouching low to the ground.

The back of my neck prickles but I'm too angry to heed the warning. "When you took Mom to the island . . . she came back different. What did you do?"

He blinks at me. One corner of his mouth draws down, brows creased. It looks almost like guilt.

The sight sends a stab of horror through me. I think about the copy of Beth. The story of the creature in the tide pool touching Henry Cooke . . .

"You *copied* her, didn't you? She was different when you came back because it wasn't *her* anymore."

That's why the fights had stopped. Why she'd withdrawn even more. Turned so cold. "She was going to ruin your plan. Was that it? So you got *rid* of her."

Dad flinches. Then his expression ripples and goes blank.

He tenses, like he's readying to lunge.

I'm frozen, too shocked to understand what's about to happen, until Holland reaches back to grab my hand. Her eyes are still black, but they're wide with alarm. "Run, Evie."

We run.

I sprint as fast as I can, breath tearing in and out of my lungs until my throat hurts and my chest is tight. Branches whip past, stinging my face. A few times I nearly trip over rocks and roots, but Holland catches me and hauls me up.

There's a crashing behind us, branches breaking as he gives chase.

I grip Holland's arm and we speed up.

Above us, a faint pattering begins, barely loud enough to hear over the sound of our ragged breaths. It's raining. The drops are coming down as big as pennies, splattering my bare arms and soaking my hair. I have to dash water out of my eyes to keep running.

And then we're passing through a familiar part of the forest—the huge shell of the lightning-struck tree, its hollowed insides big enough to hide us.

Holland lets out a muffled gasp as I grab her arm, yanking her through the tangle of brush. The blackened shell fits both of us, and we duck inside, sitting on the packed soil. We face one another, our knees touching, catching our breath.

We're flushed and shaking. Listening hard—for the snap of a twig or the sound of footsteps on the forest floor.

But there's nothing . . . just the rush and patter of the rain.

I press one hand to my chest, trying to steady my breathing, the muscles in my legs burning.

Holland does the same, leaning back against the tree. When she looks at me, the blackness drains from her eyes, trickling down her cheeks. She jerks in surprise and then blinks rapidly around at the insides of the tree, expression dazed.

"Holland?" I take her shoulders, searching her face. "Hey, still with me?"

"I'm . . . I think so." She looks shell-shocked. "Oh my god. That was the principal."

"I don't think so." I press my hand to my stomach, feeling sick. "Not anymore."

Holland's eyes are wide. "Evie, I . . ."

It's so strange. Even after everything . . . all I can think is that my name on her lips is the most beautiful thing I've ever heard.

"I thought he was going to kill you," she says, and then she seizes me in a hug, holding so tight I can hear her heart hammering in her chest. I let out a breath of pure relief, sliding my arms around her. For a few minutes, we just cling to one another there in the core of the hollow tree, and I swear, I'm never letting go.

The rain rushes down, but the insides of the tree stay surprisingly dry. There's a constant drumming of drops on the leaves over-head. It creates a soothing white noise and I can feel the tension leaking away.

My father is somewhere out there, but I don't think he chased us more than a few feet. He might look like a monster, but he must have gotten himself under control.

And he killed Aukley because he was trying to kill me.

There's still a piece of him in there. There has to be.

When I look up, I find Holland studying me. Her green eyes are dark, but her expression is soft.

"Evie, I'm so sorry. For everything." She shifts, knees pressing into mine. "I have to tell you something. I thought the Afterdark was reacting to how I felt about you."

I shift against the tree, startled to see a blush creeping over Holland's cheeks. My stomach flutters as she continues.

"But . . . it wants you."

"I know."

She looks surprised. "You do?"

"Aukley made it pretty clear back there." I let out a breath. "It's . . . because I'm next in line. Blackwood is my dad."

Holland sits up straighter, expression stunned. "I—I thought I heard that. Back in the clearing. But . . . you never said anything."

Even this close, with her hands on my knees and butterflies in my stomach, I can't help raising a critical brow. Holland's shoulders sag. "I know. I kept a lot from you too."

"No more secrets?"

"No more secrets." Holland curls her fingers around mine and they're surprisingly warm. I draw in a breath. "Then I think we still have a few to talk about. One is that Beth told me about Ada."

Holland's eyes narrow. "*What* did she tell you about Ada?"

I wish I could read her expression better. There's something guarded in her face and it makes my hands feel clammy. "That Ada outed you."

Holland's grip on my hand tightens. Then she lets out a sigh, and I see her throat flex. A rush of sadness goes through me, mixed with a kind of strange, aimless anger. It's anger toward a dead girl.

I shift, scooting around so I'm sitting beside her. "You don't have to tell me if it's too much."

"No," Holland says. "I want to."

CHAPTER FIFTY

Holland

IT ALL COMES SPILLING OUT: my whirlwind romance with Ada, six months of skipping classes and sneaking away at house parties.

I'd been so wrapped up in her, sure I was in love.

And then she'd been abruptly over me. And it hadn't been enough to break up. No, Ada had spun this strange, elaborate story: I was following her. I'd tried to force the friendship into something she wasn't comfortable with. I wouldn't leave her alone.

Of course, I was furious and hurt. I'd trailed after her, demanding an explanation. Showed up outside her classes, followed her at lunch.

I was so furious I hadn't realized I'd fallen straight into her trap.

And then her mother went to my father and everything went to shit.

Evie listens in silence, her grip on my hand tightening every now and again. When I finish, she lets out a breath. "Is that why they pulled you out for tenth grade? Everyone thought it was to film season two."

"It was, partly." I can hear the bitterness in my own voice. "But I was basically on house arrest. No phone. No laptop. No TV. I was allowed to film and that was it." I pause, feeling my face get hot, gaze dropping to Evie's arm. Even with the sleeve there, I can picture that scar. "I'm sorry, what she did to you was so much worse. I had no idea—"

"You didn't know." Evie shakes her head. "And what she did to you was bad. It was really bad."

My voice shakes, some of the old emotion returning. "I think the worst part is . . . I don't even know why she did it."

"Because that was Ada." Her voice is grim. "She liked to set things on fire just to watch them burn. When she died—" She pulls up short, looking at me with wide, tear-filled eyes. "No more secrets, right?"

I nod and she lets out a breath. "Okay, because I have to tell you something. And it's bad."

CHAPTER FIFTY-ONE
Evie

THE SPACE INSIDE THE HOLLOW TREE feels strangely warm. Or maybe it's my face burning as I shift against Holland, squeezing her hand tight. There's a second of silence in which the rain drums on the branches overhead.

I could tell her about all the things Ada did. Take her through the map of scars on my body. The mottled red patch on my palm, the slash of the scar on my arm. The spot where the needle she left in the carpet went through my foot, or the thin tracing of scars from the windowpane decorating my back.

But . . . that doesn't make it better.

"I was there when Ada drowned, and . . . I think I could have saved her."

I tell her everything. How cruel Ada was. How she took everything. Spread rumors all through middle school. Repeated the things she'd done and flipped the narrative, so I was the bully.

I tell her how I learned to hide from Ada and her friends at recess, or come home and try to explain the bruises.

How the physical beatings had stopped in middle school, changing to stranger, more vicious things. I show her the scar from the cross pendant, tell her about the needles in the carpet. The poisoned food. My cat, dead in the woods, and my "fall" from the cliff.

And finally, I tell her about the lake. About staring down at Ada while she choked on dirty lake water . . . until she stopped moving.

Holland stares, wide-eyed, when I fish the necklace from my pocket, letting it sit in my palm. Then she startles me by reaching out to take it. I watch as she tilts the pendant, pressing the point into her thumb. The cross sparkles in the sparse gray light.

"I'm just as much of a monster."

Holland shakes her head. "Evie, she tried to kill you. I mean, she *murdered your cat.*"

I wasn't expecting that, and it takes me a second to stammer out, "I know, but . . . it's different with people. It's worse. I mean, the whole reason I was in the forest was to kill Aukley."

She stares at me for a second, brows creased. I'm terrified she's going to pull away. Instead, she says, "You really would have?"

I flinch. We said no secrets, no lying. But I can't look at her when I say it. "He helped my father kill Mia. And Amanda. And probably a lot more. So, yes, I would have."

I can picture their faces—their wide, dark eyes staring at me off the page.

And it's slowly dawning on me now that only half the problem has been eliminated.

My dad was the one who did this.

"You aren't a monster, Evie."

Holland's expression is fierce, eyes glittering as she smooths a hand over my cheek. She grips my chin and forces me to look her in the eyes. "You *aren't*."

My lips part. I can't seem to get the words out. She kisses me, and when we finally break apart, my heart is beating hard against my rib cage.

It didn't end with Aukley.

I don't know if I believe in fate, but it seems clear now—there's a reason I'm here.

I finally know what I have to do.

"Holland?"

She looks at me, and she must see something in my expression. "What is it? What's wrong?"

I hesitate, then steel myself.

When I finally say it, my voice is cold and flat. "I think I have to kill my dad."

CHAPTER FIFTY-TWO

Holland

"WE'RE GETTING OUT, all of us."

Across the reading table, Leta and Stowe stare at me. Leta's dark hair is disheveled, like she's been raking her fingers through it.

"What happened? You guys were out there for ages." She looks from Evie to me, clearly concerned. "I was freaking out."

Evie winces. "Sorry. We ran into trouble."

"You could say that." I fold my arms over my chest. "Aukley nearly killed her, and then Blackwood killed Aukley."

"*What?*" Stowe says. At the same time, Leta says, "What *happened*?"

"Where is he right now?" Stowe sits ramrod straight in his chair, eyes on my face. "Holland? Is he . . . ?"

"He's . . . not an issue. His body was on the roots of the tree." My voice wobbles and Stowe's gaze combs over my face. It makes me aware of the sticky black film on my cheeks and I wipe at it hastily.

"The point is," I say, "we know what the Afterdark wants."

A beat, and then Stowe says slowly, "And it wants . . . what?"

"Me. I'm next in line to be host." Evie's expression is hard. Only the tension in her posture gives her away. "Blackwood is my dad."

She looks over her shoulder, in the direction of the forest. I know she's thinking of him out there in the woods. More animal than man.

I slide my hand into hers. The truth is, I have no idea if I can leave this island. My guts feel all tangled up with the Afterdark, like it's grown all through my intestines. Become part of my system.

But I'm getting Evie on that boat if it kills me.

Stowe stares at Evie, eyes wide. Finally, he slumps in his chair. "Hell, the resemblance is *right* there."

"Okay, back up," Leta says. "Why does it have to be *you*?"

Evie looks so weary that I take over. The horror on their faces when I tell them about either Evie or Ada having been created by the Afterdark makes Evie flinch, but thankfully neither of them asks the question. *Which twin is the doppelgänger?*

"So, we get off the island. I'm completely fucking down with that." Leta folds shaking hands on the tabletop. "How?"

Evie and I exchange a look. The study room door is shut and the library isn't busy right now. Still, it feels risky.

We talked for ages in the hollow tree. The space felt safe, secret. Here it feels dangerous to speak the plan out loud.

To say that it starts with Evie going into the forest to kill her dad . . . and ends with me taking kerosene to the oldest parts of the dorms. Hoping the fire will spread to the forest and burn it all down.

So, we tell them the bare bones. Just the escape.

"We're getting out," I finish. "I have to get Evie away from this place." I grip her hand tightly. I'll drag her body out of the Afterdark's grasp if I have to.

Tense silence drops between us, and I brace myself for questions. Or for one of them to scoff and say this is ridiculous.

Instead, Stowe leans back in his chair. "Alright. When are we leaving?"

"We need a couple days to prepare." And to work up our nerve. "Figure out timing."

A beat of silence, and then Stowe sits up straight. "What about Founders Day? During the luncheon?"

"It's two days away." Evie exchanges a nervous look with me.

She's the one who really has to steel herself. I just have to burn my school down—she's got the hard job.

"The Rook is expecting you to go out into the Afterdark," Stowe says. "He'll make sure the patrols are out of the way, that none of the teachers are around."

"He wants us to go out during the party." I frown, mind racing. "That means we'd have to catch the last ferry. It's cutting it close."

"Sure, but can you think of a more perfect setup? He's practically arranging our escape for us."

He's right. It's undeniably perfect timing. Again, Evie and I exchange a look. She finally nods, expression reluctant.

"Alright. Founders Day."

No one speaks for a moment, and then Stowe folds his arms over his chest, smirking. "Can we go over the plan again? I'd feel a lot better about this if you could put together a PowerPoint—"

A crash interrupts him and I whirl around, pulse skyrocketing. Beth stands in the doorway, her face a mottled red. She scans the table, gaze zeroing in on Evie's hand in mine.

"You just can't stay away from her, can you? You're like an addict, Holland."

"Everyone get out." My voice is sharp, and Stowe and Leta stand up, clearly relieved to duck past Beth and vanish down the hallway, though Leta shoots a wide-eyed look over her shoulder.

There are dozens of things I want to say . . . mostly that I'm finished with her. That we aren't friends anymore.

"Holland." Evie's voice is soft, and she shakes her head.

She's right, it's not worth it.

"Come on, let's go." I take her hand, turning to leave, when Beth steps in front of me. Her cheeks are flushed. She looks almost feverish, eyes glassy and wide as she stares at me.

"What aren't you telling me?"

I pause, trying to cram the anger down. I might hate her right now, but I also can't leave her behind. Not with that monstrous copy out there. "We're leaving. On Founders Day."

Beth's face goes slack with shock. "What? That's . . . that's in two days. You can't just *leave*."

"We have it planned." I struggle to keep my voice even. "Don't worry about it. You can follow me when I meet Evie at the gate."

It's like Evie's name triggers something. To my shock, she lunges forward and grips my wrists.

I dig my heels in. "Beth—"

"How do you not get this?" The words seem to explode out of her. "It isn't just this place that's dangerous. *She* is. You can't trust her!"

The fury comes crashing back all at once. I yank myself out of her grip, sending her staggering back. "You should talk!"

She gapes at me and the anger turns white-hot. The darkness inside is slowly unfurling. I'm too angry to be alarmed, too furious to push it down. "All this time I thought we were friends, and you were manipulating *everything*."

Beth only stares at me, and it all comes flooding out.

"I saw your box under the bed. The notes you stole. The list of contacts. Not only did you completely violate my privacy, you got a girl *expelled,* Beth. I can't even begin to convey how screwed up that is."

"I was trying to help!" Beth sounds almost hysterical now. "Those girls just liked you because you're famous."

It's not even close to a reason. I'm starting to realize how unstable Beth is.

"Please, you need to stay away from her." She says it like Evie isn't there.

"I'm over this conversation." I turn again, determined to leave before the anger comes bursting out.

"*Stop*, Holland." Beth lunges, snatching at my arms. Her voice is climbing to a frantic pitch. "Don't you understand? She's part of this place."

"*I'm* part of this place." It comes out in a snarl. Too late, I see the look of terror on Beth's face. I feel the stinging in my eyes and realize my vision has turned cloudy. I turn away, blinking rapidly, cool tracks trickling down my cheeks. *Shit.* "Let's go, Evie."

"No, *Holland*." Beth is almost hysterical, backing into the doorway, stretching her arms up to block the frame.

Outside the study room people have halted, staring at us, and I rub at my cheeks hastily, scrubbing away the black marks.

Beth's expression is twisted with rage, tears streaming down her face. "I kept them away. I made sure nothing like Ada would happen ever again."

I turn on her, angry all over again. "Who else are you responsible for? Did you put the pictures in Gianna's bag? Did Stephanie Boland even spread any rumors or was that you too?"

"Holland . . . please. We're going to graduate together. I've found an apartment for us in LA. You can go to auditions from there. It's going to be perfect."

I back away, throat tight. *She's delusional.*

I'm still holding Evie's hand as I move toward the door. Outside the window of the study room, I catch sight of the librarian making her way toward us, her face furious. Time to go.

Beth looks desperate. "I just want the best for you. You're my *best friend*, Holland."

I squeeze Evie's hand tight in mine, pushing past Beth in the doorway. "Not anymore."

CHAPTER FIFTY-THREE

Evie

BLACKWOOD HALL HAS BEEN extravagantly decorated for the Founders Day luncheon. The tables are decked out in white and blue roses, and elegant taper candles glitter all down the center.

The hall is packed with students. All of us dressed semiformal—the girls in dresses or blouses, the boys in fitted suit jackets and sweaters.

We should be a bunch of awkward teenagers, but we're too moneyed for that. Everyone is professionally tailored and polished, familiar with the rhythm of dinner parties and small talk.

There's a constant stream of talk and laughter, set to the background of jazz from the overhead speakers.

I blend in in my black dress, hair curled and glossy.

I try to relax, but my gaze keeps straying to the doors. The side doors are decorated with sweeping ribbons, and someone's opened one of the doors, revealing sheets of rain coming down. I almost expect to see the hunched, spindly figure of my father. Or . . . the thing he's become.

But there's nothing. The doorway stays empty.

Anxious, I tap my booted foot under the table.

Docs might not exactly scream *semiformal*, but they're going to be a lot better for running than high heels.

Across from me, Leta bites her lip and fidgets. She looks gorgeous in a short green dress. She'd changed a few times, trying to figure out something semiformal that would also allow for a flat-out sprint through the forest. It's a strange dilemma.

For me, it was picking a color meant to disguise my father's blood.

It's just good sense.

I start when Stowe sinks down across from me. He's wearing a suit jacket over a collared shirt, and he looks like he's just been out in the rain. I stare at him, baffled by the spreading bruise around his left eye.

"How did you manage to get punched since I saw you *this morning*?"

Stowe grins and shakes his wet hair at me like a dog, dotting my face with droplets of icy water. "Just a natural talent."

I'm about to whack him in the arm when Holland settles into the chair next to me. She nods and I know we're ready. She's left her supplies behind the dorms.

"Where's Beth?" I've already scanned the room a dozen times. There's no sign of her.

"She knows where to meet us."

Still, there's a deep crease between her brows, and I know what she's thinking. What if she's at the principal's office right now, ratting us out?

The first course is being served at the teachers' table. It's my cue, according to the timetable Stowe and I snagged from the office. Beside me, Leta clears her throat, pushes her chair back, and slips out of the hall.

Thirty minutes until the last boat leaves.

Fifteen to get to the boat dock (ten in a flat-out run). Another fifteen to get . . . the *other thing* done.

It's strange that something so life-altering can take so little time.

Watching Ada drown had taken minutes.

I get slowly to my feet and Holland gives me a grim look. Stowe leans back in his chair, playing with his napkin, purposely not looking at us.

We all know the plan. The Rook has cleared the hallways and unlocked the back door, paving the way for Holland, who's agreed to meet him just before sunset at the front gate.

Only, we'll be at the back gate instead.

I feel a pulse of guilt in my chest. Stowe and Leta don't know the full plan. They don't know I'll leave first and arrive at the dock last.

They don't know what Holland is about to do.

I weave my way through the tables and step outside, hurrying onto the split staircase. One hand is clutched to my face, like I'm upset about something.

A few people glance up, but no one knows me well enough to care, and I make it around the side of Blackwood Hall without being followed. I walk around Cooper House and the circular library building, heading for the side gate.

The woods are cool and shadowy, rain clinging to the boughs and drizzling down around me. I'm in the first layer of trees when I hear it—the distant, Klaxon blare of the fire alarms going off in Blackwood Hall.

CHAPTER FIFTY-FOUR

Holland

THE SOFT JAZZ FROM OVERHEAD is interrupted by the wail of the fire alarm. It drills into my ears, echoing around Blackwood Hall. A second later, chaos erupts.

Leta's pulled the fire alarm.

Nobody seems to know what to do . . . like we haven't had one hundred fire drills per year.

Everyone is up out of their seats, milling around, except the Gravesmen at their table, who sit there exchanging confused looks. It's almost amusing. They're clearly wondering if the fire alarm was one of them.

Gorski looms over me suddenly. She's in a long yellow dress, her glasses crooked on her nose. She directs everyone toward the exit and we spill out the side door and onto the steps.

Outside, it's not as cold as I thought it would be, though there's a steady drizzle of misty rain coming down.

I scan the forest beyond the wall. There's no sign of Evie, which means the plan is going like it should be. Everything is fine.

I check my watch. The countdown timer that will coordinate our plan. *Thirty minutes to curfew.*

Leta appears beside me, face flushed. "That was easier than I thought."

Snatching her sleeve, I shout over the noise, "Where's Stowe?"

"I thought he was with you."

"Okay, stick to the plan. I'll look for him. Meet you at the docks."

Leta looks like she wants to protest, but then she's borne forward by the crowd. I allow myself to be propelled forward until I reach the bottom step, and then I dart around the back of the building.

I know exactly where I'm heading: the greenhouse, just behind the girls' dorms. The door is still smashed from Evie's night in the Afterdark and I look over my shoulder before reaching in, careful of the jagged glass.

The lock clicks and I push my way inside.

It's cool and dark, the insides smelling of soil and grease from old tools.

Heading straight to the back, I find the stack of big ceramic pots. Earlier, I'd slipped a plastic grocery bag inside the one at the bottom. It's got everything I need to make sure this place is gone forever.

Breathing hard, I shift the first pot and then the next until I'm down to the second-last one. It's as heavy as it was the last time, and I strain something in my shoulder heaving it up and onto the ground. Then I lean in and grasp for the bag, fingers scraping the bottom. There's nothing there.

I frown, feeling around again.

Nothing.

I lean forward and squint into the pot. There's an old burlap sack I'd put on top of the plastic bag, and that's still there. But when I pluck it out and throw it aside, there's nothing at the bottom.

The bag is gone.

CHAPTER FIFTY-FIVE

Evie

MY INSIDES BUZZ as I move deeper into the woods.

Something about the way the late-afternoon shadows stretch out between the trunks, wavering as the branches dip in the wind, makes my stomach curl. It's a reminder that the Afterdark isn't far away.

While I advance through the trees, the branches block most of the rain coming down. The knife I've stolen moves against my hip and I keep my fingers wrapped around my camera strap to keep from touching it.

The knife scares me. It's a kindling knife—long and sharp, and far easier for Holland to steal from the lockbox beside the fire-place than it should have been.

That's the thing about this school . . . it's so busy keeping its unbelievable horror movie secret that it doesn't think about sim-ple things. Equally deadly things.

Stalkers. Psychopaths. Murderers . . . unhinged students with access to deadly knives and kerosene.

Several minutes in and I'm almost at the clearing, still sweeping the trees for some sign of his dark form. He's out here somewhere.

I'm not making any secret of the fact that I'm here, crashing through the woods as loudly as I can, the shrill of the fire alarm echoing behind me. He should have found me by now.

Unless he doesn't want to.

Shit. I don't have time for this.

Cold sweat sticks my dress to my back. I cup my hands around my mouth and call into the trees. "Dad?"

Another step, and another. I call out again and wait, but only silence answers. My heart thunders in my ears.

I'm not sure I can do this.

Behind me, a branch cracks and I spin around, heart jamming into my throat.

There's a slender figure in a black suit standing between the trees. His arms are folded over his chest, his white mask reflecting the orange of the setting sun.

"He won't come."

It's strange to see him here, in the middle of the forest. Sunlight filters through the trees, shining down on him like a spotlight. An eerie picture, the mask an unsettling pop of white against the green landscape. *The Rook.*

A chill drops down my spine. "Excuse me?"

"I tried to speak with him earlier, tell him what he needed to hear." His laugh is rueful. "He's got a powerful right hook for a man being eaten alive by the forest."

I stare at him, not knowing how to respond.

"He's out there right now, trying to placate it. But we all know how that will turn out." He steps closer. "You may think him an absent father, Evelyn. But he's struggled over the last year. He tried so hard to keep you safe."

My chest goes tight. He's talking about Mia and Amanda. Jessica Thorn. All those girls he tried to trick the Afterdark into taking.

The Rook continues. "I'm afraid his efforts have done more harm than good. The Afterdark is going to start taking us, one by one." He's closed the space between us, towering over me.

I'm frozen, unable to look away as he reaches out and cups my chin in warm hands, tilting my face up toward that cold, still mask.

There's something terribly sad in his eyes. "I'm afraid this plan is doomed. Holland can't leave the island anymore. I think she knows that, but she's willing to sacrifice herself for you. And I can't allow that."

I lock eyes with the Rook. Up close, the light reflects in their surface, showing intricate patterns of amber hidden inside. "Unless I miss my guess, you feel the same way."

My eyes widen. I'm momentarily distracted as the meaning behind his words hits me. "You're . . . ?"

"In love with her?" The Rook laughs. Then to my shock, he reaches up and tugs the mask off.

My head swims. Ewan Stowe sighs, raking his fingers through flattened curls. His newly bruised eye looks stark against his pale skin. "Since I was *eight.* I met her on set and fell hard. I never got over it." He shrugs. "And then, she showed up for eleventh grade last year. What are the odds of that? It felt like fate."

I'm still reeling. It doesn't make sense. "I've *seen* you and the Rook together."

"There are a few of us."

I remember it now, the offhand comment Leta made when I'd first asked about the Rook. How he has body doubles. *Like a medieval king.*

His gaze drifts back toward the forest. "There's only one way Holland gets off this island, and I think you know what it is. What you have to do."

I can only stare at him as dread settles in the pit of my stomach. Because I *do* know.

I give it what it wants, and it lets Holland go.

"This is what you were made for, Evie. It's your entire purpose."

I flinch, shaking my head. "Don't say that."

Ewan Stowe leans forward, voice dropping. "I knew as soon as I heard about your sister, how she died. I think you do too."

I continue to stare at him. Dread crawling up in my chest, tightening my throat. Cold shock goes through me, and Stowe's voice sounds suddenly distant.

"You've seen what the copies can do." His expression is sympathetic. "What they can survive."

There's a beat of silence between us, and I think about Not-Beth crashing through the window. Landing on the lawn hundreds of feet below before vanishing into the forest.

"You really think if you'd hit your head on the dock and fallen off, you'd have drowned like she did?"

He's right. I wouldn't have.

I wouldn't have fallen in the first place. Wouldn't have lost myself to the rage that always took her.

Ada had been bad-tempered. Savage. *Human.*

Some of the shock is receding now. It feels like I can breathe again.

"You should know how special you are." He steps closer, gaze combing over my face. "A copy born and raised human. A kind of hybrid. Strong enough to survive hosting."

I should be reeling. Instead, all I can feel are puzzle pieces clicking into place.

Stowe pauses, gaze drifting back to the forest. "Tell me, Evie. Do you know where your friend is?"

I jerk upright, blinking at him. "She's meeting me by the dock. You know that."

"Not Holland." He reaches out and I flinch, but he only takes a strand of my hair between his finger and thumb. "She's always been safe from him. Not the right color."

I'm still processing, and it takes longer than it should to sink in. And then Stowe's words come flooding back.

He's out there right now, trying to placate it.

Not the right color . . .

Leta.

He must see the realization on my face, because he smiles. "Better hurry. Sun's going down."

"*No.*" I whirl around, already in a flat-out sprint.

My father has Leta and he's going to sacrifice her to the Afterdark.

CHAPTER FIFTY-SIX

Holland

I'M OUT OF THE SIDE GATE on the dot, checking my stopwatch. Thankfully, everyone else is still crowded on the front steps. They haven't even begun to make their way to the muster point. Distantly, I hear Gorski's high, annoyed voice, trying to get everyone organized.

Nobody seems to notice when I slip around the side of the building, heading for the side gate behind the library.

I don't have time to second-guess myself, to agonize over who took my bag.

Maybe it was Beth.

She was supposed to join us . . . sit with us at the table and wait to go out last. Then meet me at the side gate. But I don't see her.

I slip out, closing the gate behind me.

All I can hear is the blood rushing in my ears as I make my way through the forest. It feels like it takes forever, especially since I keep glancing back over my shoulder, looking for Evie or her father.

Finally, I reach the hill and catch sight of the ocean stretching out before me.

The wooden boards of the dock come into view, with its single, small ferry. I pull up short, feet skidding on the sloping gravel driveway.

There's a solitary figure there, blond hair bright against her black jacket, hands in her pockets as she scans the forest. My heart sinks as Beth turns to wave. When I jog closer, she looks me over, face serious. "I told the captain to wait. You alright?"

I brush the question off. "What the hell, Beth? Where were you?"

She's saying sorry now, saying she was feeling sick and nervous. She couldn't make herself dress up and pretend to go to the luncheon.

I'm hardly listening, though, my pulse still racing even now that I've stopped running. I keep glancing back into the woods.

Our plan is coming unraveled. The sun is starting to sink behind the trees in the distance and Stowe, Evie, and Leta are all missing. "This isn't going well."

Beth shakes her head. "They're coming. Leta texted and said they found Evie after . . . well, you know. She needed a minute." She passes me her phone. Sure enough, there's a text from Leta that says that, almost word for word.

Still, anxiety clenches at my chest and I check my own phone. There's a text from Leta, I assume saying the same thing. Nothing from Evie.

And how does Beth know what Evie did?

I narrow my eyes at her. "My bag was gone when I got to the greenhouse, and now the plan is falling apart . . . I'm calling Evie."

Beth grabs my arm. "No. I . . . just leave it. You'll see her soon. We've got to get on the boat."

I've known her long enough to know she's lying. I jerk my arm back. "Beth, what's going on?" Nervous, I glance over my shoulder. There's no movement in the trees . . . no sign of anyone.

When I turn back, Beth has something in her hand—a flat, black box with a set of metal prongs on top.

"What is that?"

Her expression is pained and she clutches the box tightly, knuckles white. It sends a spark of warning through me.

"Beth . . . what is that?"

Her voice wobbles. "It's a stun gun. And I really don't want to use it, believe me."

I'm too shocked to be angry. This can't be real. "You're joking, right?"

Beth's expression turns grim. Her thumb twitches over the bottom of the box. There's a sharp crack of electricity and blue light forks between the prongs. My mouth drops open.

"Just . . . come with me." She steels herself. "This island is poisoning you and you can't see it. I'm saving you, Holland."

"By electrocuting me?" My voice comes out high and outraged, and Beth shakes her head vigorously.

"Not if you don't make me!"

"Where did you even get that?" It's so beside the point, but I can't seem to wrap my mind around that cruel black box in her hand.

"Crown and Grave." Beth's face goes dark. "From the Rook."

"You're working with him?" I stare at her blankly and she shakes her head. The look she gives me is almost scornful.

"He's the Rook, Holland. *Everyone* works for him. Even your precious Stowe. *Especially* him."

"What are you saying?" Now my head really is spinning.

"You think they're just sleeping together?" She sounds impatient, like she's talking to a stupid child. "Stowe is one of the body doubles, Holland. He's been reporting *everything* back to him."

Pieces are starting to click now. The way the Rook interacted with Stowe, at times teasing and then strangely backing off. The amount of stuff Stowe got away with. The way he acted so concerned, asking how I was, how the Afterdark was affecting me. If I knew what it wanted . . .

"Oh my god."

"We don't have time for this." Beth glances back at the forest, at the orange light piercing the trees. Then she turns and waves the stun gun at me. "Even if you don't care about your life, I'm going to save it. We're running out of time."

I glance down at my stopwatch and see she's right. There are only a few minutes left. It's just enough time to get on the boat and leave before the Afterdark rolls in.

I plant my feet in the sand. "Where are they? Where's Evie?"

Beth's face goes carefully blank. It sends a stab of alarm through me. "Beth, what is it?"

She hesitates. "Stowe said once it's over, you'll be yourself again."

"Once *what* is over?" Fear pitches my voice higher. I have a terrible suspicion I know what she's referring to. "Beth, what is he doing?"

Beth only shakes her head, backing up a step. When I start toward the forest, she lifts the box and electricity sparks again, making me freeze.

Her voice is strained. "Don't, Holland."

I lean sideways, body coiled and tense, thinking about darting around her and risking the shock. Beth seems to anticipate this because she steps sideways.

"I'll drag you to the ferry if I have to." Her voice firms up like she's finding her resolve. "If that's the only way to save you."

She's convinced she's doing the right thing. Sacrificing our friendship to save my life like some ridiculous martyr.

"You have a life waiting for you," Beth says. "An apartment in LA, a career. You have *me*. Don't sacrifice it all for a girl you just met, Holland."

I stare at her, shocked. Even after pointing a stun gun at me, she still thinks I'm going to sign a lease and move in with her. She's still planning some imaginary future with me.

Horror crawls over me. My gaze drifts to the black splotch above her cheek where the Afterdark marked her.

She's become more possessive over the past year. More demanding. But I'm starting to realize how detached from reality she is.

How much of this is because of the Afterdark? How much has it twisted her?

Beth is still pleading with me, but I'm only half listening now, gaze sliding past her.

There are shadows crawling over the distant treetops, sweeping toward us like an inky black tide. Beth's facing away from the forest, focused entirely on me.

Slowly, I slide my hand over my stopwatch and press the off button.

"You're seriously going to use that?" I keep my eyes wide like I'm still shocked and unable to do anything. "I thought we were friends."

"We are." Her voice turns pleading again. The tip of the stun gun angles upward.

The shadows are spreading faster now, barreling toward us.

The Afterdark swells inside me, a roar of satisfaction. It sends pins and needles down my arms and legs.

I've never felt it so strong before and I suck in a breath, shuddering.

Beth must take my expression for devastation because her eyes cloud with tears. "You don't know what it's been like, losing you to this place. Losing you to *her*."

That distracts me for a bare second. "You don't even *like* me that way."

"Not that way," Beth whispers. "But that doesn't mean she gets to."

"How do you not know how *selfish* that sounds?" I take another step closer and the stun gun levels off again.

"All I want is to start over." Her expression goes flinty. "We're going to go to the mainland, and then you're going to be yourself again, and we're going to move into an apartment in LA." Blue sparks jump between us. She's so wrapped up in this delusion that she doesn't hear the birds flocking over the forest, the distant beating of wings as they head for the school.

"I won't lose you, Holland."

I step back, suddenly incredibly sad. "You already have."

The wall of darkness crashes over us. Beneath our feet, the grass curls and dies, yellow spreading like a stain over the ground. Beth yelps and leaps back.

The trees have crumpled into skeletal silhouettes, branches stretching like fleshless fingers into an ash-gray sky.

Beth stumbles back, blood draining from her face. "No. *No*, we had time."

I lift my arm, showing her my watch. "I stopped it."

"Holland—"

The accusation on her face sends pain stabbing through my chest, but I don't get time to think about that. Something hurtles out of the woods with a bloodcurdling, many-voiced screech. It surges forward in a flash of bone-white skin and rotten, fang-like teeth and crashes into Beth with a scream of savage satisfaction.

I turn my back on the screams, sick with guilt, plunging straight back into the Afterdark.

CHAPTER FIFTY-SEVEN
Evie

THERE'S NO SHOCK LEFT NOW. No denial. Just a grim kind of determination settling over me.

Now, it's like the Afterdark welcomes me. I can see clearly by the light of the static sky.

A pathway opens, one I've never seen before. Narrow and twisting, full of roots and rocks, leading me through the towering trees with their too-dark, moss-coated trunks.

The path leads straight to the clearing. To the towering black walnut tree with its thick mass of gnarled roots grown through every square inch of soil, erupting from the surface.

There's a single, wasted figure sprawled at the base, and I recoil in horror.

Jack Aukley's corpse looks like it's been out in the elements for weeks instead of days, his skin withered, clothes tattered and rotting away.

The worst part is the roots.

They're wrapped tightly around his skeletal figure. One thick, knotted root has snaked up his torso, curling around his neck to pin him against the trunk. A second root, no bigger than my pinkie, plunges through one hollow eye socket, a slow trickle of black oozing down one cheek.

Even in death, the Afterdark won't let him go.

It makes me think about what Stowe said, that it won't let Holland go. That she'll die if we try to leave.

It's not hard to believe, seeing the way the roots wrap around Aukley's corpse, like the tree is desperate to hold on. It's like Mia all over again, and in my horror, it takes a moment to notice there's a second person there, and he's crouched over a motionless figure sprawled across the roots. My heart stops when I see her.

Leta's lashes shadow her cheeks. She looks like she could be sleeping, but her dark skin is tinted faintly gray. There's a familiar green cardigan draped over her shoulders and her hair has been hacked off, crooked and up to her shoulders.

The sight makes me edge closer, panic clawing at my chest.

If she's already dead . . .

Leta shifts and lets out a pained breath, and I feel my shoulders slump in relief.

The creature that was my father sways on his feet. His head snaps up and I freeze. His eyes are black pits, but they go wide when he sees me.

"Evie." His voice is barely a voice—just a tangle of overlapping noises. Veins trail through the skin across his forehead and cheeks like roots burrowing beneath soil.

"Aukley was right, you're getting sloppy." I take a step toward him and he jerks violently, face spasming as he edges toward Leta. "She doesn't even look like me."

He blinks at me. Can he even speak full sentences anymore?

"I came here to kill you." I reach into my bag to pull out the kindling knife, heavy in my hand. "But I think we need to talk."

At the sight of the knife, he goes still.

Cautiously, I bend down, placing the knife between us. "Talk to me, okay?"

He jerks again, his expression tormented. Like he's fighting some inner battle I can't see. Part of me wants to scream at him. Why did he do it? Why would he create something like me and then leave me to discover such a terrible thing on my own?

But Holland is what matters now.

"This place has its hooks in Holland. Almost as bad as you."

Saying it out loud makes me feel ill.

He continues to stare at me, his eyes insect-like. Soulless.

"Can she leave?" I ask. "Right now, can she get on a boat and go?"

Silence. For a second, I think he hasn't understood the question, that maybe he's too far gone.

And then, slowly, he shakes his head.

Icy fingers grab at my heart.

It's strange . . . I came out here prepared to kill him. To plunge the kindling knife into his chest.

But . . . maybe there's a different way.

I close the distance between us, eyes wide as I reach up and touch his face, fingers trembling.

"You thought keeping me away would save me." I blink tears back. "But I was literally made for this, and I won't let it take anyone else."

Stowe wasn't lying. This place is never going to let go of Holland . . . not until it has me. It's the reason I'm here.

I'm ready.

I've always known, I think. There are no happy endings for girls like me.

Letting out a breath, I fish around in my pocket, finding the necklace.

The cross glimmers under the strange, static sky as I let the chain swing for a bare, suspended second.

Then I open my fingers and release it, dropping it over the black roots of the tree. It lies there, glinting in the dirt.

I can't bring anyone back, but I can end this.

Turning to my father, I say firmly, "Show me."

He shudders, expression twisting in a quick, bright moment of agony. Then his face grows cold. It's like watching the shutters slam down over the windows, blocking out the light.

My heart kicks into a gallop when he reaches down and takes the kindling knife. But he only flips the handle around and draws the tip across his palm. He turns, pressing his hand onto the bark of the walnut tree.

His blood is a deep purple color, almost black as it crawls sluggishly down the rough bark and seeps into the crevices. The blood drains away, disappearing into the bark as the cracks gape wider with an awful splintering sound.

A portion of the great black tree splits away, a huge piece of trunk jutting out like a broken tooth. The edges of the crack aren't fresh, though—they're black and slimy, and I clap my hand over my face when the smell hits me.

It's foul and sweet at the same time. Flowers mixed with rotting meat.

The thing that is no longer my father steps back. His movements are different now. Skittish, like a feral animal.

There's a pounding in the back of my head, something I mistook for my own heartbeat. But it grows louder as I step forward, taking over the rush of blood in my ears. There's something jarring about it. It's terribly off-rhythm—too slow, too deep. The heartbeat of some ancient, sleeping monster.

The Afterdark inside me responds with a roar. Excitement that isn't my own courses through me, making my hands tremble, driving me forward.

I can't believe I ever thought I was human. I can't ignore this thing inside me.

When I'm close enough, I can see down into the cracked and rotting trunk. There's something moving in the tree, something pulsing with a slippery, wet *thump, thump, thump.* Trailing roots wrap around it, twitching and clenching around a solid fist of muscle and vein and putrid flesh.

A heart. There, at the center of the tree, is a horrible, black, beating heart.

When he takes my hand, I flinch, but this strange, black-eyed version of my father doesn't seem to notice. His grip is a vise around my wrist.

I suck in a breath as he presses the tip of the knife into my palm. It sends pain like a splinter through my skin and blood pools in the creases.

I don't know what I'm expecting, but when he draws my hand forward, I jerk back.

Bile rises in my throat, gaze fixed on that horrible mass of pulsing flesh . . . the thin, shivering surface, wrapped in roots that weep foul black liquid. My entire body recoils.

Wait.

The knife in his hand glitters and I think about snatching it. Driving it into the heart. But it's like the second I think it, the darkness inside me flares. It sends pain lancing through my arm, so white-hot I gasp.

It fades the moment I look away from the knife, but by then, my father is dragging me toward the tree. I dig my heels into the dirt, twisting in his grip. "Stop."

Not like this. This isn't right.

It's my choice. *My* purpose. When I glance up at him, my heart squeezes in my chest. He meets my gaze, eyes black and flat.

I let out a strangled cry as he seizes the back of my neck. There's nothing left of my father in that cruel, impassive face. He drives me forward, fingers biting cruelly into my skin. My foot snags on a root as he forces my hand down into the wooden shell.

It feels warm inside the ruin of the tree. Hot and damp.

"Stop." My voice is tight with panic as I thrash against him. My palm stings and I try to yank my hand away, fingers inches from brushing that rotten black surface.

I feel stupid and panicked. Tears burning my eyes.

There's no heroic self-sacrifice here. No dignity.

"*Dad*, stop. You can't—"

A dull thud from behind, and he jerks. I'm released so abruptly I stumble, my foot catching on a root, sending me sprawling on my ass.

Holland stands in the clearing across from my father. Her face is streaked with black and she's clutching a fist-size rock, expression wild with anger.

"Get away from her."

My father charges her with an animal snarl and my thoughts go blank in a burst of white panic. Holland dodges and he stumbles, crashing into a low, mossy rock with a howl of pain.

Holland whirls around and her face snaps up, pale in the static gloom of the sky. Her eyes mist over with black again, red hair a wild halo around her face. My father scrambles to his feet, black blood trickling from a gash near his eye. He readies himself to charge again.

"Dad, stop!" He doesn't notice me as he lunges toward her a second time, face twisted and savage.

This time, she swoops down and snatches something from the gap between two tangled clumps of root. They crash together, and I realize she's found the knife.

CHAPTER FIFTY-EIGHT

Holland

I KNEW I'D FIND HER in the clearing.

But I hadn't expected to see Leta sprawled on the roots of the great black tree, clearly unconscious. I hadn't expected Blackwood to be there, dragging Evie toward the tree as it split down the middle, forcing her hand inside, toward something that pulsed and twitched, wrapped in a nest of slick roots.

Snatching a rock off the ground had been a response of blind panic . . . hammering it into the side of his head, an act of pure terror.

I spot a metallic glitter in the crevice of roots at my feet. The knife.

It's in my hands as he smashes into me, knocking my head into the dirt, sending dull pain through the back of my skull. My eyes blur with tears and there's a crushing pressure wrapping around my neck. Someone's screaming as white spots jump in front of my eyes.

I remember the knife, swinging it up with all the force I can, burying it to the hilt in the spongy flesh above me. It sinks in with a squish and a pop, warmth gushing over my hand.

The black-eyed face above me barely twitches. He's still bearing down on my throat, cutting off my airway. I swing again, at his neck this time, blade sinking in with a crunch. Blood splatters across my face, viscous and dark. He goes stiff.

There's a scuff of footsteps. Evie is there, dragging her father off, letting him sag to the ground.

"Holland?" She leans over me, freckles standing out in stark contrast against her pale face. "You're bleeding."

I drop the knife, fingers aching, and touch my cheek, wincing when pain blazes through my temple.

When I struggle upright, I spot the body under the tree, blood pooling black underneath him.

There's a ringing in my ears. My heart slams hard in my throat, shock setting in.

Holy shit. I just stabbed Blackwood. "Evie, I'm sorry—"

"Don't." Evie's face is flushed and tear-stained. "Holland, look at me. That wasn't him."

It shouldn't be a comfort, but . . . she's right. I realize, now that he's gone, that I could *feel* him, the same way I feel the Afterdark.

The dark knot in his chest had been growing for years.

There wasn't anything human left.

More chillingly, I can feel the same darkness in myself. It's not as long-growing, not as all-consuming. But it's there.

It's only a matter of time.

As if in response, the thing inside me sparks to life. The pull is stronger now, coming from all directions. It makes me sit up, alarmed, scanning the forest.

"Holland?" Evie presses closer, her face anxious. "What is it?"

"They're coming." I can sense them. Every twisted, faceless creature in the Afterdark, all running for us at once. They reek of anger, of *want*, and their want is mine, pulling me toward Evie, toward her blood, screaming up from her skin like white-hot light.

The sound of the heart in the tree is overwhelming suddenly, the monstrous *thud, thud, thud* taking over everything else.

It's coming for her.

"It's sending everything." Despair rolls through me. I can't keep her safe. I can't keep the Afterdark away, not when I'm part of it. "Evie, go. Take Leta and run."

Any minute now, one of those monsters is going to burst into the clearing. It's going to seize Evie and force her to press her bloody hand into the heart, and then she'll be just as stuck as I am.

"Holland, it's okay." Evie reaches out and cups my cheek. "I want to do this. I'm *meant* to."

"No. We can figure something out." I scramble to my feet, blood rushing in my ears. "Run. Make for the boat dock."

"Holland." Evie pulls at me, fingers still locked with mine. "It's not going to stop until it has me. I think I've known for a while now."

"You can't do this." Desperate, I dart a look over my shoulder. "Please, you have to run."

For one mad second, I think about trying to throw her over my shoulder. Carrying her to the boat dock whether she likes it or not. But I won't make it. The Afterdark knows exactly where I am.

It's too late for me. I'm just as much a part of this place as Blackwood was. But Evie still has time. "I'll hold them off. Just go. *Please*, Evie."

"I'll be okay."

But it's so obvious she won't be. I can't help it . . . my gaze trails over to the still figure of her father lying under the tree. And the bloody knife at his feet.

The knife.

I turn back to Evie, drinking in her storm-gray eyes, the narrow, delicate features of her face. Closing the space between us, I reach for her, pulling her into my arms. She doesn't fight—she just wraps her arms around my waist, melting into me.

Her pulse flutters in her chest. I can feel its steady rhythm all through my body. She's not fully gone yet, not lost to the forest like I am.

And she doesn't have to be.

CHAPTER FIFTY-NINE

Evie

HOLLAND KISSES ME. Cupping my chin in her hands, pressing her mouth hard against mine. It's sweet and desperate, marking my face with her tears. It feels like goodbye.

She knows I have to do this.

Then she pulls away and looks down at me, her eyes a hard, glittering black. My stomach drops as I realize my mistake, but she's already moving. Darting across the clearing, snatching up the knife to drive the tip into her palm.

"No!" I start for her, but Holland shoves her arm straight down into the shattered trunk, pressing her bloody palm to the beating heart of the Afterdark.

Everything goes silent after that.

Neither of us moves, standing frozen, staring at one another. Nothing is happening, and hope blooms in my chest—it didn't work. The Afterdark is rejecting—

Holland jerks, her body spasming, eyes going wide. The beating heart grows louder as she shudders and twitches, and then black veins bloom under her skin, snaking up beneath the surface of her arms and legs before fading slowly, like her body is drinking them in.

She yanks her arm out of the trunk and the bark knits itself back together with a horrible splintering. Holland staggers sideways, shuddering, one hand held aloft. Her eyes screw shut and I'm reaching for her, desperate, but the earth heaves suddenly under my feet.

It goes on for one second, then two, the entire forest vibrating. It feels like the earth is going to split open and devour us whole.

And then it goes silent.

Only . . . it's not just the forest. For a moment, I'm not sure what's changed. And then I realize it's completely quiet inside my head. It's shocking, like the ringing silence that follows a persistent hum.

The only sound is my own ragged breathing.

"Holland?" I inch forward, fear clawing at my chest. "Holland . . . ?"

Her head snaps up.

When she meets my eyes, the panic in my chest expands into something verging on terror. Her eyes are a void, a starless night sky. They're so dark they seem to drink in the pale light around us.

When she rises, the movement is impossibly fluid. She stands in the middle of the clearing, and I think, for a second, I see the flash of black veins beneath her skin.

And then she's in front of me, so fast it hurts my eyes to follow. I want to reach out and take her face in my hands. But I am so afraid of what might happen.

"Holland?" My voice is a shaky whisper. She just stares, those alien eyes fixed on my face, expression flat and cold like her name hasn't registered.

My skin is crawling and there's a desperate ache in my chest. "Holland? Answer me."

Nothing.

Finally, I suck in a breath and reach out, trembling fingers brushing her cheek. Holland blinks and the ache in my chest blossoms into a burning sensation that reaches all the way up to the backs of my eyes. I blink back tears. "Still with me?"

When she opens her mouth, the voice that comes out is layered with that awful buzz. "Get as many as you can. Go to the boat."

"Holland—" She starts to turn, and I reach out and snag her sleeve. "But where are you—"

She whirls on me and I stumble back at her feral expression, the snarling red mouth and wide black eyes, the veins standing out on her throat. "Go," she bellows, and I stagger in shock.

Something is happening at the edges of the clearing; dark shapes appear. Shadows creep between the trunks.

Adrenaline surges through me and I rush to Leta's still form, hooking my arms under her armpits. She groans as I drag her out of the clearing and stumble toward the school.

I'm too slow, tripping over roots and rocks as I haul Leta's slumped body behind me. I keep glancing back, half expecting one of the shadowy figures to come after us, or even the black-eyed version of Holland.

I'm afraid she'll change her mind about letting us go. Her words ring in my ears.

Get as many as you can. Go to the boat.

Eventually, the peaks and towers of Northcroft rise above the trees in the distance. The sight gives me a boost of energy and I stumble forward, breathing hard. I weave around tree trunks and brambles even as tears blur the forest around me.

CHAPTER SIXTY

Stowe

WE STAND ALONG THE SHORE, fifteen Gravesmen with our backs to the black ocean. It's a relief to be rid of the Rook's mask, free from the oppressive white insides. There's power in the mask, but it cages you too. The Rook has always been a mystery. A reputation, handed down from one Gravesman to the next.

When Daniel Prince steps from the line along the shore, I hand it back willingly. We embrace with the gravity of ceremony, though when he pulls back, I can't help lingering for a moment, a hand on his arm.

He gives me his sharp smile, making my stomach flutter. "Congratulations, Stowe. A stirring performance, on so many counts."

He pats my shoulder before drawing away. That's Prince—always so careful. He can't show too much affection, never mind the times we've seen one another flushed and half-tangled in his bedsheets.

"You never lost sight of your loyalty," Prince says. "And I know how much she means to you."

I nod silently, throat tight.

"We can only hold the boat for so long." He smiles again, gaze drifting toward the forest. "We'd better hope Evie can get it done."

Silence, as we wait for some sign, all eyes fixed on the top of the enormous walnut tree. It's easy to make out, standing within a wide circle of its own making, wilting everything in its path.

After a moment, the branches shudder. It's only the slightest movement but we all see it. Under the steady wash of the sullen black waves, a strange, rhythmic sound builds.

The echoing pulse thunders in my ears and tightens my chest. With it comes the first low roar of the earth as it begins to shake, rattling my bones. It's so overpowering it feels as if the rhythm of my own heart skips and stutters, leaving me breathless. Behind me, the Gravesmen react, some bending over double, gasping for air, others stumbling back.

Then it cuts off abruptly. Over the tops of the trees, the black branches still.

The Afterdark seems different somehow . . . more alive. Even the sluggish rhythm of the waves seems to pick up, as if the very tides are stronger. The static sky brightens on the strand of rocky shore, creating a washed-out, white tapestry.

She did it. The tree opened for Evelyn Laurent.

Which makes the ceremony safe again.

As I move to stand next to the black waters, Prince intones the words. He projects his voice outward, and he's loud and clear.

But he speaks too carefully, as if he's written the ceremony down on a paper and memorized it.

Annoying. I always did like a good performance. I wish I could have done my own.

But then it's over. Prince speaks the last words and sweeps his arms wide. Excitement swells in my chest as I glance at him. He really is beautiful. But I'm ready.

I'm ready for rebirth. I've *been* ready, ever since I found out what it does. What it already did for Prince.

No more withdrawal. No more trembling nausea, or endless circle of recovery and relapse.

I'm going to take Holland and ascend with her. Together, we'll unlock new power.

And then, the thing I've been dreaming about for so long. I'm going home. I'm going to look my father straight in the eye and dare him to lay a hand on me.

I hope he does.

Sliding a hand into my pocket, I pull out the silver flask. It's something I'm never seen without, my initials carved into the center. I tip it over and clear liquid runs out onto the rocks. A smile tugs at my lips as Prince meets my eyes.

It's water. I haven't had an actual drink since the autumn dance, not since he pulled me aside after my last trip into the Afterdark and berated me. Told me to get my shit together. That it was my job to spy on Holland. He *needed* me.

I'll admit, his pitch might not have been nearly as effective if he hadn't kissed me.

I'm not an idiot. I know what he wants from me. Why he touched me. Kissed me the way he did. But I don't care.

It felt right.

I didn't touch a drop after that, but I kept the flask. It was Prince's idea. He said people underestimated me, and I should let them.

He's right. The last few weeks have been my greatest performance of all.

And now my prize is only a few minutes away. Once I'm reborn, I can save Holland Morgan. Show her she doesn't have to be afraid anymore.

Prince takes the flask and I turn back to the tide pools.

Drawing in a breath, I step closer until I'm directly over a pool, seeing my strange, warped reflection in the black water.

When a ripple breaks the surface, I steel myself, knowing what lies beneath. Knowing what wakes the second I brush my fingers over that oil-slick surface.

I sink down on the rocky edge, reaching out a hand.

There's a rising noise behind me, I realize. A hum of alarm from the Gravesmen gathered at my back. I jerk upright.

There's someone emerging from the trees, along the edge of the shore.

Flaming red hair. A black dress against pale skin. My heart jumps. *Holland.*

The closer she gets, the more alarm bells sound in the back of my mind. There's something different about the way she moves, the way she stalks across the distance between us: it's almost predatory. She stops a few yards away and I step back, alarm prickling my insides.

Holland's eyes glitter black. Her features are subtly different, face as pale and glinting as marble. Sharp. Hungry.

She moves closer. One step and then another, pacing slowly toward me. I almost expect her to circle me like a cat hunting a mouse. She seems to tower now in her midnight dress, red hair like fire against the washed-out background.

Realization is slow coming. It takes too long for everything to click, to look into those pitch-colored eyes and see the Afterdark.

Holland is the one who touched the heart. The tree took her, not Evie.

Dismay rocks me.

This isn't what I planned. I was supposed to take the gift and then show her how.

I was supposed to *save* her.

"Holland." My voice breaks on her name.

I go still as she moves closer, until her face is inches from mine and I'm looking into the void of her gaze. "What did you do?"

"What you were all too weak to." Her voice buzzes with layers of dark, crackling static. I flinch when she reaches out. Her fingers are cold but gentle, moving up to stroke along my jaw. "But it's done now. No one else needs to die. We fixed it."

"Not *we*." My voice is barely a whisper. "I didn't want this, Holland. Not for you."

"I didn't mean *you*," she says, and then she slides her hand around and grasps the back of my neck like a vise, yanking me backward. I hit the ground, breath leaving my lungs in a rush as my head strikes the rocky lip of the pool.

An ugly *thud* and a blaze of pain shudders through my skull. I'm flat on the ground, the stony shoreline pressing hard into my back, darkness swimming at the edges of my vision.

Holland looms over me, face haloed by her fiery hair, black eyes wide and shining.

Her smile is the last thing I see before I'm dragged into the darkness . . . and it's as beautiful as it ever was.

CHAPTER SIXTY-ONE

Evie

THE SPLIT STAIRCASE of Blackwood Hall is full of students.

Leta is stirring awake in my arms by the time we get there. A few people help me pull her upright, and we stumble to the top of the staircase. They ask questions, all of them ending with *what happened?*

I can't even begin to answer.

Talk of an earthquake fades as people step outside, spotting the alien landscape . . . the strange, static sky.

Northcroft's three-hundred-year-old secret is finally out.

At the entryway, one of the wide double doors hangs off its hinges, pushed back against the stone wall in a heap of shattered wood.

I help Leta stay upright, and she grips the railing with both hands as she stares out at the forest, expression shocked.

"I couldn't stop him. He kept saying it needed a replacement . . ."

She glances down, noticing the green cardigan for the first time. "Fuck, it all fell apart. Where's Holland?"

Tears sting the backs of my eyes and I shake my head, my gaze going back to the forest, to the shape of the hulking walnut tree.

Leta's gaze follows mine and she says softly, "Oh *fuck*."

And then we're both clutching one another, hanging on like we might be swept away, reeled into the heart of the forest, and eaten alive. There's movement around us, a low, panicked buzz as more students spill out onto the stairs. I don't look away from the forest, waiting for a flicker of movement, a flash of bright color through the trees.

It comes faster than I'd expected. Someone steps out from the tree line. Past the gate. Up the long path toward Blackwood Hall. Around us, the noise drops off as the figure draws closer, red hair brilliant against the gloom.

Holland. Or, some new version of Holland—a terrible, savage queen. She's white-faced and flint-eyed, tendrils of darkness blooming across her shoulders and up onto her throat. Black roots stretch and grow beneath translucent, moonlight skin.

Behind her, she drags a body. It's the slumped figure of a boy, his legs dragging along the grass. His head tipping drunkenly forward onto his chest.

The steps clear for her, students pressing back against the rails, pale and silent. As Holland climbs the steps, the midnight fabric trails over each one with an audible swish. Away from the forest and under the newly static sky, I can see every inch of her face, every subtle, horrible change the Afterdark has worked on her.

She stops at the top of the staircase, releasing her grip on the prone figure. He slumps to the ground with a moan and his head tips back. One side of Stowe's face is bruised, his curls matted with dirt and blood as he blinks blearily around.

Maybe I should feel bad for him, but I don't.

"Get to the dock." Holland speaks to me in those eerie, multi-voiced tones. She steps up onto the landing and seizes my jaw in cold fingers.

When she presses her mouth to mine, the urge to wrap my arms around her is almost physically painful. I cling to the stone rail, fighting it with all my strength.

Holland pulls away. Her hand drops from my face as she turns her attention to the entryway, stepping past the broken door and over the threshold.

As she does, the earth shakes again, a deep, primordial rumbling that sends terror shuddering through me. Leta shrieks and grabs my arm. I'm already moving, snatching her around the waist, dragging her down the steps.

"Go." I pitch my voice to be heard over the rumble as the ground sways beneath our feet. Something high overhead creaks ominously. "Run for the boat."

Leta and I launch off the crumbling steps and then we're sprinting. Hand in hand, straight across the front lawn as the earth trembles.

Something is happening across the lawn . . . that awful, trailing rot is *moving*, tendrils snaking down the stone walls, creeping over the grass. It heads toward Blackwood Hall—a monstrous creature answering the call of its master.

I watch the black trails as we run, heart crowding into my throat, but none of it heads toward us. And then we're out, past the gate, flinging ourselves headlong into the dark and twisted forest.

Leta is panting, gripping my hand painfully tight as we run through the towering trees. I keep expecting to see movement between the hulking trunks—shadows peeling themselves from their hiding places, creatures with blank, featureless faces. But there's nothing. In fact, there's a narrow dirt path running along our route, and we make our way onto it, picking up speed.

Even through the panic, I suspect it's Holland's doing.

We're flying past the trees now, running so fast I'm nearly at my limit. Leta almost falls, foot snagging a root, and I haul her up, driving us onward until a thin, blue strip appears through the trees.

The ocean. *We're almost there.*

And then abruptly, there are no more trees . . . only a sloping gravel driveway. Our shoes fling rocks up, and I nearly slide down all the way into the water before Leta catches me. There's a single white ferry moored at the edge of the dock, bobbing gently on the waves.

I've never seen anything so beautiful.

Leta must feel the same way because we stumble to a halt, and she laughs, a high-pitched, almost hysterical sound.

There's thrashing in the woods behind us—high, terrified voices and pounding footfalls. It's more Northers, pouring out of the woods.

Our feet make such a racket on the dock that it rouses the captain. He appears over the edge of the boat just as Leta leans out cautiously to touch it, like she isn't sure it's real. That we're really saved.

"What's going on?" The man is rumpled-looking, gray hair standing on end, his shirt half-buttoned as he squints around at us. "Was that an earthquake?"

"Let us on board." I try to keep my voice firm, blinking away the burning in my eyes. "We need to get out of here."

CHAPTER SIXTY-TWO

Evie

NORTHCROFT FALLS AWAY a piece at a time. We watch from the deck of the ferry, Leta and I clinging to one another, breeze whipping our hair across our faces. The deck is full of students, all doing the same.

The Afterdark crawls up the towers, rusting the shiny metal flagpoles, eating holes in the limp flags. It collapses the roofs of buildings and crumbles the brickwork away. Rot spreads up the sides of the library, paint peeling and flaking, the dome of the roof slowly caving in. It splits the front of Blackwood Hall and trails grasping black ivy up the sides.

It's like watching a time lapse of corruption. One by one, the buildings collapse into mold-covered heaps, vines and weeds sprouting through cracks in the crumbling sidewalks and pathways.

At last, the rot reaches the gate, rusting away the sign, metal flaking down onto the shattered stones below. I can't see it from this distance anymore, but I can picture it—the Afterdark crawling over Northcroft's proud crest, spreading its putrid black mold across the open book with its delicately painted tree. All of it rotting away until the golden words *Veritas Ante Omnia* crumble and disappear, and the sign, just like the school, collapses in on itself.

Three Months Later

LETA LIKES TO FALL ASLEEP to the TV—local news channels, mostly. I think she finds it comforting. The constant background noise of dull, everyday reports: a freeway shut down for construction, university students protesting parking fees, a reporter warning of the early rain season.

It's a comfortingly beige reflection of the world.

I often find myself awake in the early hours, watching the gentle blue flicker of the screen.

I don't sleep much. I don't trust it.

I'm not supposed to be here. I wasn't meant to *continue*. If I let myself slip into the grasp of sleep, the universe might course correct, the darkness finally swallowing me.

So I lie awake, half listening to the quiet murmur of Channel Four News while I stare at the picture on my camera.

It's the one of Holland by the walnut tree, hands in the air, hair stirring around her face in some invisible breeze. She's caught forever laughing, green eyes fixed on me behind the camera.

"... at three. Recent developments in the investigation into a gas leak at a remote boarding school off the coast—"

The TV clicks off. I let the remote drop onto the bed, shivering as I slide my legs out from under the covers and pad over to the window. I don't remember leaving it open, but the curtains Leta's mom put up are rippling in the breeze. Reaching out to grasp the window latch, I pull up short.

There's a small white square of paper on the ledge, folded in a perfectly compact rectangle.

My chest flutters as I scoop it up, glancing back at the bed. Leta is a soft-breathing lump beneath the comforter, her face pressed into the inside of one brown arm, her black hair spread out on the pillow. She doesn't stir as I slide the window shut and sink down on the sagging mattress.

Fingers trembling, I unfold the paper.

The writing is black and stark, written in a way that dents the paper.

Still with you.

ACKNOWLEDGMENTS

Thank you to my family. As always, to Shaun, for dealing with the chaos. To Charlie, who is six, and therefore did not help with the actual book-writing process, but deserves a mention anyway. To Karen and Rick, as always, who provide endless support in so many ways.

To Kayla and Rebecca, who helped with brainstorming on more than one occasion. And the Word Nerds who also did. And to literally every friend and family member who had to hear me natter on about spooky forests and monstrous girls, thanks for listening.